THE BRIDAL PARTY

by Anna Holmes

©Anna Holmes, 2021

For the one who married me

1
Summons

Cassandra Friend wasn't much of one, unless you needed a bridesmaid. It wasn't that she was shy, or that she didn't like people. It was more that she never stopped being a bridesmaid.

When the words *three months' exclusive contract* caught her eye, she almost didn't know how to feel. No jumping from consult to consult, no trying to remember which bride was which, no triple-booked weekends. The letter assured her that the pay would more than make up for the inability to book and promised a wide degree of latitude. It seemed good. Big break good.

Too good.

Cassandra's other problem with friendship was that she was terribly suspicious of everyone at all times. A good quality in a mercenary. Less so in a person, let alone someone trying to run a business.

She carefully folded the letter and shoved it into the pocket of her worn blue leather coat and resolved to run it past people with more reasonable brains.

The problem with that was that the only other brains she had access to belonged to the party.

Jules jumped up from her precarious spot on the back of the broken-down blue sofa in the office. "*Shit*, yes. What are you asking *us* for?"

Gideon observed his perfectly sculpted nails for imperfections, predictably found none, and folded his hands behind his head. "Because she's not sure she wants to commit. *Obviously.*"

Bjorn brushed wood shavings from his beard. "It is not our wedding, Cassie-duck. No need to get cold feet."

Cassandra slammed her hands on the desk only she ever used. This was only an office in that it's where they talked business. In reality, it was where Gideon…crashed, since devils didn't really sleep. It doubled as Bjorn's carving studio, Jules' hangout spot, and probably home to some of Thalia's creepy shit under the floorboards. The pale slip of a girl didn't even bother looking up from her straw doll making when the dust went flying from the desk.

"Hey," Cass barked. "You are not taking this seriously. And we have talked about the duck thing."

Bjorn spread his hands wide. "You walk like duck."

Gideon uncrossed his long legs and stretched his hooves out away from himself. "Ohhhh, Bjorn, it's not nice to make fun of people's walks. Okay, Cassie-not-a-duck. You have reservations. Let's talk it out."

"What's not to like?" Jules demanded. "Three months on contract. That's probably some nights or weekends free. From some lord, right?"

Cassandra unfolded the letter again in the dim light past the patched curtains. "Alexander Fremont. Upper Echelon. Keeps to himself. Runs the schools. Don't know much else."

"Upper Echelon! We've never had an Upper Echelon job. That means three things. He's loaded. The food will be great. And if we pull it off, we're set on jobs. Possibly for life!"

Thalia shifted her wispy black hair from her weird light eyes, setting her husk doll into her lap. "But it could mean fey curses. Or demons."

Cass held out her hand. "Thank you. Yes. That's what I mean. There are no details. This could be a seventh son of a seventh son. A fated couple. The powers that be love to fixate on those noble kids, and the nobles love to keep vital details secret. Three months? I think we're looking at something big here. Star-crossed, or worse."

Gideon shifted his weight to lean back on his hooves. "True. But that's the job, isn't it? Unless you only want to take spurned lovers and disgruntled uninvited family weddings till we're sick to death of it."

Cass tucked a short black curl behind her ear and huffed out a breath. "I just—after Johann got eaten, I've been a bit…wary of the demon cases, all right?"

Jules tapped her chin. "Oh, yeah. Any luck on getting a third bloke?"

"Ha ha, no. Between that and what happened with Rocco and the pixies, and the thing with the fairy queen and Geoff—"

"And Duncan fell into the hellmouth," Thalia added helpfully.

"We have a bit of a reputation," Cass snapped. "We'll have to keep making do with five. That's the other thing. They may not want an imbalanced party."

"Well, that's just it, isn't it, love," Gideon commented. "We don't know. And we won't know unless we talk to His Lordship, so, really, all the angst is premature."

Jules perked up. "Yeah. We should just talk to him."

"Ah, no." Gideon waggled a finger. "*Cass* should talk to him. No offense, doll, but last time you and Bjorn talked to a client you started a brawl with the bride's father."

Bjorn rolled out his neck. "He was asking for it."

Cass prodded at her forehead. "Bjorn."

He blinked. "No, I mean literally, he was asking for me to start fight to give excuse to stop wedding."

"And that is what we *don't* do when the bride hires us to make sure the wedding goes on."

Jules sighed. "That…was my fault, yeah. I thought the dad hired us. But yeah, talk to him. See if he's on the up and up. And if he is…." She grinned at Cass. "Money? Weekends off? That sounds pretty nice in exchange for maybe punching some demons, yeah?"

"Maybe," Cass sighed back.

Gideon frowned. "Okay, okay. Beard, Barmaid, Witchie-Poo, out. Cass, you stay. We're talking strategy."

A general grumble filled the room, but dutifully, Bjorn gathered his carving, Jules righted her chair, and Thalia collected her…supplies. Gideon was persuasive by nature—devil—but he was also fully aware that appearing as he did in his shirtsleeves and sometimes even his bathrobe gave the appearance that the office was his living room and everyone was imposing. As long as he used it for good, Cass didn't mind.

Today, he ducked back into his little room off the main space and returned with a rarely seen bottle of whiskey and a pair of glasses. "You look like you need this."

"Are you buttering your boss up?" Cass snorted, taking a glass and watching him pour. "Because if so, it's working."

"I'm prying," he answered bluntly, as was his way. He stoppered the bottle and set it on the scarred table next to the sofa.

"Funny, coming from you."

"Yeah, yeah." He glanced at the contents of his glass, then at the window. "Come on."

"Come on—where?"

"How long have you had this office?"

"Three years," Cass answered slowly, watching him shove the window open and swing his long legs up and over the sill.

"And you never bothered to look up? Cassie." He pulled a face, his angular features mocking and gentle both. Then he disappeared to the accompaniment of hooves clanging against metal.

She supposed there were ladder rungs in the side of the building. She hadn't thought much of them. Carefully, she gripped her glass in one hand and swung out to follow him up with the other.

She emerged onto a roof—certainly not the tallest in Amaranth, but one tall enough to look across the brass, glass, and brick skyline in the dying sunset. Purples and oranges above, glints of white light in the street lamps below. At the crest of it all, the Wyvern's Rest, grand castle, home to the ruler of the city-state, lit with the greenish pallor of mage-light. It was a mess, this cluster of buildings never meant to hold so many people, but from this vantage…the fondness welled up in her chest.

"All right," she conceded. "I should have looked up."

Gideon stepped to the edge of the roof, rested his forearms on the stone finial in front of him, his whiskey still untouched. "It's so…big," he murmured.

"We're running out of space," she said, confused.

He laughed, swirling the contents of his glass around. "You say that being able to extend your hands above your head and not touch rock. You could keep going up…and up…for how long, I wonder? It must be horrifying. And thrilling."

Gideon didn't talk much about the hells. Cass knew about as much as any mortal did about the underworld. Subterranean caverns featured prominently in the stories. She just nodded for fear that prodding for further information would shut him up like a bear trap. He looked over at her sideways and sighed heavily. "Listen, darling, if we're going to do this, we're going to do this."

"I don't know what that means."

"I know you don't." He downed the entirety of his glass and coughed slightly. "Ugh. All right. What's going on with you? You're burning out. Don't try to deny it. I know it when I see it. Extremely well."

"See that a lot in hell, do you?"

"I went through it a lot in hell," he answered plainly. "It's why I left."

He hadn't talked about it much, but from everything he had said, Cass gathered that being a fiend, or for that matter, a celestial, was like being born into accounting. They weren't necessarily creatures of sublime evil or good as some stories told, or noble custodians of the solemn duty of ushering souls of varying moralities to the Beyond. They were people, doing a job. A necessary one. A strange one that she didn't quite comprehend.

"What did you do?"

Gideon didn't look at her. He kept his pupilless red eyes trained on the sky and the stars beginning to peek out. "Cass, you know this."

"I know what I've been told. I want to know the truth."

The corner of his mouth quirks up. "All humans say that. I don't think you do. But I'll tell you this. I reformed souls. That was my mission. I prepared them for neutrality so they could move on to the Beyond."

"Neutrality? I thought you made them good?"

"Oh, that's the goal, of course. But realistically? No. If you're bad enough to get sent my way, no, there's not much likelihood of getting them good. And the methodologies…hmm. They vary. I'll leave those to your imagination. Whatever you think of…it's probably true or worse."

Her stomach curdled. "And you…enjoyed that?"

His eyes traveled to his empty glass. "I was supposed to. And for a while, I did. But the work became wrong, fit wrong, rubbed wrong." Now he looked her way. "I'd like to save you the trouble of that if I can. Is this wrong?"

"Well, you said it yourself. How can I know if I don't talk to him?"

"Not this job." His pale white spaded tail jabbed her softly in the ribs. "Where's your confidence? Is it really losing the party symmetry? Or is it fitting wrong?"

Cass downed the rest of her drink. "Gods. You're really going to make me talk."

"Yes. I know. It's probably been three years since you've cleaned out the office—or your brain. Give it a try."

"You're such an ass."

"Am I? Or am I just not letting you wriggle out of talking?"

"I don't know! I don't know." She raked her hand through her curls. "It's just…weddings. Supposed to be happy, right? And here they are, prime targets for demons and fey curses and spirits. Shitty people I can handle. But even the supernatural forces of the world say fuck your happiness. Your happy times are our targets."

"So are funerals," he commented.

"Well, that's shit too. A different kind of shit. Just…makes you feel helpless, you know?"

For a moment, his eyes locked onto hers. "Yeah. I do. But we're not. I think that's the illusion."

"One more question," she said quietly, "and then I'll stop. Is that why you wanted the job bad enough to put up with people?"

He looked away again, this time taking in the skyline. Gideon laughed a little, rolling the glass between his long fingers. "You know, probably. Hadn't thought about it until now. I also needed to eat and exist somewhere and shit and things."

"Yeah, that is why most of us work."

He stepped back from the finial and took her glass. "Just…it's not hopeless. Don't let yourself get where I did, all tired and angry and the next thing you know you don't care who you piss off, and oh look, you've managed to get thrown out of hell and you have to go live among the humans in a foreign city where there's actual *currency*, barbaric as that is, and you wind up living in a tiny box with a squirrel in your wall."

Cass straightened. "There's a squirrel in the wall?"

"I've named him Wallace. Don't you dare remove him."

"That's…probably not good for the…."

"I have grown very attached."

"It's…probably fine."

He beamed, which was a sight with his pointed incisors and blood red eyes. "That's the spirit. Now. See what the morning brings us. If it's an exclusive contract with a possibility of demons, but one that might alleviate the heartache of taking on forty times as many spurned lovers…do consider it fully. We're not as helpless as we feel."

"You're sure of that."

He extended his hand. "I'd even shake on it. Yes, the stories are true."

Cass regarded the hand for a moment, then looked at him. "I wouldn't…feel right taking advantage of you like that."

Gideon's white eyebrows rose high into his equally colorless, artfully messily coiffed hair. "That is very decent of you."

"I try to be decent." She took in a breath. "All right. We'll see what this is about, then."

2
The Job

When the morning came, she tried not to regret her decision too much. Her nerves made it difficult to stomach more than toast before she put on the fancy client-meeting outfit. It cost more than she cared to remember, but Mum had said it was worth it when they'd pooled their money for it. It would make a good impression, she'd said, and the fitted coat's peacock blue brocade brought out the warmth of Cass' brown skin and the depth of her dark eyes. Mum, of course, had followed it up with 'maybe it'll snag you a special someone and I'll finally be a mother-in-law', but the initial compliment was nice enough that Cass remembered it when she put it on.

It carried her with confidence across the bustling streets of the housing quarter, to the office in the Market District to draw up the standard contract, to the wide brick staircases joining the Lower Ring of the city to the raised hexagon of the Upper Echelon. Here brick and dust and iron gave way to stone and porcelain and carefully tended greenery.

Cass never quite knew how to feel about the Upper Echelon. She could see that it was beautiful; she enjoyed lingering in the public gardens, which were in fact open to everyone.

But she knew how many people lived crammed in her apartment building while these enormous estates she passed housed single families and a small cadre of servants. It didn't seem quite right that the Lower Ring kept having to build up and up and up while it felt like very little changed here.

The rationale was simple enough. The noble families were charged with running a difficult portion of the city-state's welfare. This particular lord oversaw education. Education for thousands upon thousands of children, a number growing by the day. That must be hard, she had to admit. But did he even have time to enjoy this massive sprawling green she crossed? Would he really miss a corner of it to give some regular folk a little more breathing room?

There was little point in wondering. He would likely have some justification or another or refuse to answer outright. And it would be his right. It would be terrifically rude to ask.

But she wanted to.

She paused on the cobbled path up to Lord Fremont's house to indulge herself in a breath. The space was nice, and while it was available to her, she didn't mind taking advantage of it. The edge of winter wasn't fully gone from the air yet, but it did smell like spring. The whole of the property — at least, as much of it as she could see — was ringed by tall trees bursting into bloom in bright colors and thorny baneroses, whose sweet fragrance and enormous blossoms effectively hid their wicked stingers. An apt metaphor for the nobility.

She reached for the large bronze door knocker and rapped.

A moment, five, ten. Cass glanced up at the brick and plaster manor, crawling with vines. The dusky purple baneroses crept up trellises along the sides. Burglar deterrent, or perhaps even assassins, if Fremont was paranoid enough. Many of the windows were covered. Secretive household. It was odd; nobles loved to shit-talk each other and their servants loved to shit-talk their bosses, but there was not much to be had on him. Either he lived a very unremarkable life, he was a complete hermit, or he diligently quashed rumors. Given that he was hiring a wedding party, Cass leaned toward the latter.

The wide mahogany doors creaked open, and Cass was startled out of her contemplation by a clearing of a throat. "May I help you?"

She found herself face-to-several-inches-from-the-top-of-head with a squat man with pristinely combed gray hair, a large pair of silver spectacles, an impressive bristly mustache, and a bemused expression.

"Oh! Yes. Sorry. Just admiring the building. I'm Cassandra Friend. I think Lord Fremont is expecting me?"

He reached into his red plaid waistcoat for a little notebook and peered through his glasses. "Ah, yes! Very punctual, Miss Friend. I thank you for your diligence. May I take your overcoat?"

"Thank you."

An awkward dance ensued, her bending backwards at the knees and him standing on his toes to help her off with the coat. Cass was perhaps a little taller than most, but not gigantic. Rarely did she feel this graceless. At last, she freed herself from the shoulders and handed it off with a little smile of appreciation by way of apology.

He busied himself immediately with a coat hanger and a perfectly placed stool to put the coat away. "If you would be so kind as to follow me to the study, Miss?"

"Oh, right. Sure."

He led her through the expansive foyer across blue and black and white marble tiled floors patterned like stars and clouds in a night sky. Pretty and almost dizzying in a way.

"My name is Humphrey. I am Lord Fremont's butler and personal assistant. If there is anything you require during your visit, please do not hesitate to ask."

"Thank you," she said. Everything out of his mouth was both efficient and polite, but something about the combination made her feel like she was about to run a foot race and the stakes were high. She wished she'd thought to bring Gideon to distract one or both of them. The halls were long, and she couldn't shake the feeling that Humphrey was waiting for her to say something. Was she failing some sort of test?

At last, he paused in front of a stately set of double doors, knocked, and called, "My lord?"

From inside, a baritone rumbled, "Enter."

Humphrey opened the door and held it for Cass. "Presenting Miss Cassandra Friend of the Friend Event Company, here on prearranged business."

In the center of the large room lined with over-full bookshelves, a finely dressed young man sat hunched over piles of papers. "Ah, yes. I will be with you momentarily. Please have a seat."

Humphrey turned to Cassandra. "If I may present his Lordship Alexander Trevelyan Fremont, Steward of Knowledge and Letters, fourth in line for the Amaranthine Throne, Knight Attendant to the Crown—"

Vaguely irritated, the lord in question stirred. "Thank you, Humphrey, that will…." He finally lifted his head and his long silver hair shifted away from his face as he stood. His light eyes caught on Cass', startled. A rabbit in the lantern light. "…do," he managed to finish, as though the air had been compressed from his lungs.

Cass swore a flicker of a smirk crossed Humphrey's features. He inclined his head. "As always, sir, ring if you require me." With a sweep, he disappeared quickly enough that Cass had to question if he'd been there at all.

Lord Fremont rounded the desk and extended a hand. "A pleasure, Miss Friend. I apologize for Humphrey. He is strangely fixated on keeping me gentlemanly in the face of my workload, even if he has to be a little rude himself to do it."

Cass took up his hand. It was warm—really warm. Instead of the limp noodle handshakes she was used to from his type, he turned her hand palm down, as though he were greeting a lady of status, and elevated it firmly and politely. The gesture of respect was a bit of a genuine surprise, but she did her best to keep it from her face.

She smiled in a bland mannerly sort of way. "I understand. My desk has looked something like this."

He turned his angular face back toward the papers strewn about, a mild hint of despair setting into his features. "Your contract is exclusive. Mine, I'm afraid, is no such thing. But that's what you're here to discuss, unless Humphrey's conduct has eclipsed that matter."

She couldn't help a little laugh, though she stifled it quickly. Cass was fairly certain that was meant to be a joke, but a laugh at the wrong time had ruined people in this city. "No, definitely the former."

"In that case, please, have that seat." He indicated a plump leather chair in front of the desk and returned to his side of it. He observed the wreckage of his work and started shifting piles of papers. "Perhaps I can clear some semblance of a space here. Humphrey may be right. I should be better prepared."

Cass perched on the edge of the chair despite the upholstery beckoning her backward. She wanted to sink in, but she was staying professional. "It's really all right. You should see my office."

Fremont finally retook his chair and looked at her in a way she couldn't quite read. There was a bit of shrewdness there, but something else—a touch of anxiety, or shyness, or embarrassment. At length, in a practiced, even voice, he said, "I've heard a great deal about your company, Miss Friend. You come highly recommended."

By whom? she wanted to blurt. They'd done a few minor lords here and there, but certainly nothing that a man *fourth in line for the throne* would have heard about. "That's good to hear," she answered, hopefully casually. "We…give a referral discount, if your friend wouldn't mind you mentioning their name."

He folded his slender hands on top of his desk and observed them for a moment, then looked at her. It was her turn for the breath to get knocked out of her lungs. Cass saw a lot of people, read a lot of people, suspected a lot of people, but Alexander Fremont was possibly one of the oddest. Earnest and evasive in the same moment. "I would like to propose we drop the pretenses. I think it would be more comfortable for both of us. Does that suit?"

"Yes, please," she said, deflating.

"Thank you." He shifted a sheet of paper from the bottom of one of the stacks to the top. "I trust you made some cursory inquiries about me. What did you find?"

"Not much," she answered. "Humphrey told me more about you in the doorway, actually."

He chuckled. "I do enjoy my privacy. By necessity. I am very close to the Crown Prince, who is about to announce his engagement."

Cass felt momentarily as though her mind flew from her body and floated there as all the pieces fell into place. All the vagueness, the mysterious knowledge. "We didn't come recommended," she realized aloud. "There were spies."

"I apologize," he said, and again, he looked so genuine and yet so slippery at the same time. "I'm sure you can understand that the Crown Prince's safety is taken extremely seriously."

Crown Prince Ruhan, two years older than Cass, had weathered four assassination attempts, one of which had claimed the life of his father. Weakly, she asked, "All due respect…why us?"

Fremont's lips, pretty, just the palest blush of pink, twitched. "Are you not up for it?"

"That's not it. I just…he's a prince, with the finest guards and mages. We're nobody."

His smile dropped almost immediately. "There's no such thing as nobody, first and foremost. Second, you're possibly the most qualified people in this city for the job." He lifted the paper, read from it. "Bjorn Torrenson. A melee brawler who knows no fear. Is said to have taken on a demon with six snake heads and tied them together."

"Two of the heads," Cass corrected. "They…made a bit of a mess."

"He also has the distinction of being from the same nation as the bride-to-be—Princess Ifalna of Joranhelm. This will be a great boon. Thalia de Monde. Graduate of the Amaranthine School of Sorcery with honors, daughter of two very infamous witches."

Cass sat up a little straighter. She wasn't going to tell him to his face, but she was fairly certain he knew more about Thalia's background than she did. "She has a good deal of experience with wards against spirits, demons, and curses. That's all the qualifications she's needed with us."

"I should say so." He squinted at the paper. "Banished a warlock attempting to send a groom to a shadow dimension. Serious business, and not something your cottage variety witch can boast. Jules Evards-Milner, formerly Lady Julia Evards. I am…quite familiar with her work from childhood."

Interesting. Jules hadn't seemed to remember him. Some follow-up questions were in order. Fremont wasn't done. "Any inquiry into your group immediately turns up gossip about a demon."

"Devil," she corrected. "A distinct difference. The name he's chosen is Gideon."

"My apologies. Gideon is what I will use. I understand his past life has given him intimate knowledge of demonic intervention in mundane affairs and how to disrupt them. Particularly how to handle rogue demonic entities working outside the fiendish order."

"That's correct." Gideon's demon-spiting abilities were the few things she knew about him in exacting detail. Some of them were learned, some of them were inborn, all of them made him extremely effective against certain types of incursions. The fact that Fremont was bringing this up seemed significant. "Is his expertise needed?"

"There's a strong possibility. The difficult thing about planning a royal wedding, I'm finding out, is that the list of threats is longer than the list of guests." Fremont lifted his silver eyes to Cass. "And then there's you."

She swallowed around a dry mouth. This power play had gone on long enough. "I understand. You've done your research."

"Are you uncomfortable with praise, Miss Friend?"

More like uncomfortable knowing the good parts were the only ones he'd vocalize while remaining fully apprised of the bad ones. "I know who we are. I'd prefer to know more about the situation."

He set his paper down. "Fair enough. They did say you were direct, and the slightest bit paranoid."

Once more, a small laugh escaped her chest. Before she could catch it, the backtalk came out, too. "I *am* uncomfortable with praise, Lord Fremont, but that doesn't mean you have to insult me."

He smiled back, for once all genuine. After a moment, he cleared his throat. "The point of that particular bit of theater is that I take Prince Ruhan's safety extremely seriously. Having reviewed the…exhausting list of known entities who would like to see this wedding end poorly, I believe the guard can handle the political threats. If they can find information on a devil who has only been in Amaranth for a year and a woman who stays about as quiet as I do…they'll do fine. And what they turned up about you in the meantime makes me feel confident your group can handle the more disturbing threats."

Cass wanted to feel irritated, but on a professional level, she respected the cleverness, and to his credit, he wasn't overly smug about it. "Have you received any direct threats?"

"Not yet. However. When asked to bless the engagement, the elders reported a disturbance in the portents. Some put stock in that. Some do not."

Cass nodded. That was the sort of thing Thalia and Gideon both would want to have a look at. "You've been thorough. I presume you have a list of guests for me to look through?"

He moved the surveillance paper and extended a packet already carefully bundled together, but paused just before handing it to her. "This is, of course, assuming you're taking the job?"

She hesitated. Demons. Exclusively demons, by the sound of it. A small possibility of other malefactors, but probably demons. She folded her hands in her lap again. "Three months exclusive?"

Fremont nodded. "Knowing now who the groom is, I'm sure you can appreciate the necessity of focus and limiting other appearances."

"Three months exactly?"

"Ah…no. He hasn't set a date yet. It will be within that time frame."

"I assume we won't be working with His Highness or Princess Ifalna directly."

"Most often, no. I will be your primary contact. I will introduce you well before the day and you may of course ask him questions, but his schedule is demanding. If you think my desk is frightening…." He shuddered. "As for the Princess, she remains in her homeland until next month."

"Are there other restrictions or demands on our behavior or time?"

Fremont sat back in his chair and thought, his eyes tracing the molding around the edge of the ceiling. "Obviously don't run about telling everyone what you're working on. Other than that…don't be dismayed if you hear of others being hired to do your job. It doesn't mean anything."

Cass lifted an eyebrow. "Really."

He raised his hands, dossier still clutched in one. "Some disinformation is to be expected. You know how these things work."

"Right." She narrowed her eyes. "You work in education?"

Fremont smiled, a bit sheepish. "That is an attitude that does not bleed into that work, I promise."

"All right." She leaned forward again in her chair. "I would like to take this job. For my team's sake, if nothing else. They're tired. They want stimulating work. And since we're being honest, the recognition from working an event like this…."

He nodded knowingly. "You'd have your pick of jobs from then on."

"Yes." She fixed him with a look. "But your spies are right. I *am* paranoid. So my stipulation is this. You keep me in the dark and we're done. You can work with one of your other teams. Understood?"

"Perfectly," he answered, still direct and dodging.

Fremont extended the dossier. She eyed him a moment longer, waiting for something. She wasn't sure what. The mask to slip, a facial tic, a mustache twirl. But he was perfectly clean-shaven. At length, she took the dossier and began looking through. He sat back in his chair again. "You haven't even asked me about payment."

She stopped. "That…would be important, yes. I have people who like to eat and pay rent. Well, nobody likes rent. Except lords."

The corner of his mouth quirked up again. "My spies were right. You are both extremely focused and slightly impertinent."

The part of her that had barely stomached the toast screamed at the rest of her. Most of the time she managed to keep the impertinence to a minimum, but he had been so impertinent first! More of his tests, and she had failed. Or maybe she hadn't. She tried, "It can't be too much of a problem if you invited me here despite that."

"Not at all," he answered with a broader smile. "Name your number. It's yours."

Cass blinked. "I…can name some pretty large numbers."

"So can the prince." He pulled open a drawer on his desk and withdrew a black velvet bag that clanked heavy with coin. "This deposit to hold your services is from me. The final payment on services rendered will come from him, and he has instructed me to tell you to charge whatever you believe is fair."

Unusually generous for the Upper Echelon. She managed to remember her manners enough to take up the purse with a gracious bow of the head and put it into her pocket without looking like a squirrel stuffing nuts into a tree. "Kind of him."

"It is genuinely a pleasure to be his best man," Fremont says. "Despite the danger. Ah, yes. I'd nearly forgotten. Your group is uneven. Will it suffice to have me stand in?"

Humphrey had said the word *knight*. "If that's your wish, then yes, although it can be…."

"I heard about the last fellow."

She winced. "I did tell him to back up."

"I shall endeavor to listen to instruction, then. I'd prefer not to tour any esophaguses."

Cass reached to her side and produced the contract. "Well, if that's the case, then it's doubly important we do this." She slid the contract to him. "Standard limit of liability, we're bound to bride and groom, not to the hiring party, bridal party not responsible for loss of wedding gifts or cards, rider with reception needs, and a few things to note about reception duties versus ceremony duties."

Fremont pulled the contract closer and began reviewing. "Reception duties versus ceremony duties?"

"It's a boilerplate we don't usually need to go over with most contractors and I don't suspect will be a problem here, but we don't do toasts, we don't get anyone's drunk uncles off tables, and I absolutely do not dance. Some of the others do, but that's on them."

He chuckled. "I see. No, that would be my job." He pauses. "Has—has a hellmouth really…?"

"Yes."

"You must have some stories."

"Many."

"I look forward to haranguing you into telling them. Perhaps tomorrow afternoon? Around three?"

She stood. "Of course. I'll look over this brief tonight and compose some thoughts. Perhaps I'll bring along Gideon to talk demons, if that suits."

Fremont stood as well. "I'd be delighted. As delighted as anyone ever can be to talk about demons. May I escort you to your coat so as not to alert Humphrey?"

"Please," she said, trying not to sound overly grateful.

He smiled and held the door open for her. As they walked, she tried to guess his fighting style. He was long and lean, only the faintest bit muscular. Probably not hefting around any broadswords or axes or throwing people like Jules and Bjorn. Neither did he seem to have the quick eye or spark that Thalia or Gideon wielded. It could be that his title was for show and that his training had come to nothing while he fought only mounds of paper. She would have to find out if he was going to be standing with them.

But there would be three months for that.

In the foyer this time, she felt a little more at ease looking around. Two massive portraits flanked the room, draped in thick red velvet curtains. One was of a woman in a white lace gown, her hair pulled into a curling knot, a little smile on her lips and a small book in hand. The other was a stern man whose eyes seemed to bore into Cass' soul.

Fremont caught her gaze. "Father had a way of doing that," he said with a short laugh.

Because she felt uncomfortable in the painting's eyeshot and it seemed he did too, she turned toward the other. "Your mother, then?"

"Yes," he said, softening. "It was her study we sat in. Most of those books belonged to her first."

"An appetite for reading. Lucky, being in education."

"Voracious, unmatched, and unyielding." He smiled a little fondly. "A good job she got born here and not, say, to the sewer family."

"That might be rough."

"I wonder if the Fulbrights ever had a plumbing design prodigy the way Mother went after learning. I should ask sometime. As if my reputation needs that."

Cass found herself grinning. "You haven't got a reputation at all. I checked."

He grinned back. "If only. But no. She cared very much for learning and for helping others learn. Carrying on her work is…at times my only direction." He trailed off briefly, then interrupted himself with a laugh and headed to the closet. "Oh, but listen to me go on. You have plenty of better things to do."

She felt the strangest urge to turn and tell him *actually, not really*. It wasn't at all true. There was a weighty stack of papers in her hand waiting for attention and a quartet of specialists and weirdos, depending on who one asked, who needed to be briefed.

At last, as he helped her on with her coat, she settled on, "I'm unsure about better, but additional, yes. I thank you for your surveillance, your patronage, and your generous tolerance of my impertinence, my lord."

"It has been my genuine pleasure and no hardship whatsoever, Miss Friend," he answered with a slight bow. "I do enjoy trading impertinence. It's why they only let me out for special occasions."

"Same," she laughed en route to the door. "Which is why you hired me. Until tomorrow, then."

"I'm looking forward to it."

Cass was somewhat dismayed to realize she was, too.

3

His Lordship

Five *thousand* for each of us," Jules confirmed in disbelief, pushing the last stack of vaguely purplish scale coin away from herself. "And we get to ask for more?"

"Yeah," Cass answered, discarding her scarf and coat on the arm of the couch.

"Holy shit," she said reverently.

"What you're conveniently skipping over is that they're paying so much because the work is basically starting from scratch and probably very dangerous."

"And *terrible*," Bjorn interjected. "This is terrible news."

Thalia frowned. "Did you know this Ifalna or something?"

"Did I—? There is not a man, woman, or child of my homeland who does not know of the Princess Ifalna's beauty, courage, and strength." He pounded a fist on the table, his face mottling red. "We *mourn.* Mourn the loss of our chances."

"Riiight," Cass said slowly. "This isn't going to a problem for you, is it?"

"In accordance with tradition, as all warriors of Joranhelm must, I weep for seven nights," Bjorn declared. "And then life proceeds."

"Okay. And you're not going to fistfight the prince or anything?"

"Why would I do that?" he asked, puzzled.

"This is some weird straight-people shit, isn't it," Jules commented.

Gideon leaned over. "I think this is how they celebrate engagements. Much wailing and gnashing of teeth."

Thalia did one of the most unsettling things Thalia could do, which

was to pull her pale fist up to her mouth and giggle. "Blood rituals to follow."

"Can we focus?" Cass interjected. "We have a lot to do ahead of us.
Thalia, I'm going to need some standard wards and protection charms,
plus maybe a little something for demonic presence detection. Think you
can get to work?"

Her smile curled from anticipation into an unsettling eagerness.
"Hmm. I don't have everything I need here. But my stores in the wood
should have just what I'm after. I'll go tonight."

"Good. Bjorn. Between…weeping, I'd like you to think a bit about the
spiritual forces of your homeland. What might tag along with the princess
when she comes next month, any maleficarum that may wish her harm
there. If you don't know, try thinking of who might and get writing. We
have some time, but I don't want it getting away from us."

Somberly, he nodded. "This I will do. Come, little witch. I will walk
you to the wood."

Thalia rolled her eyes. "I told you. I can look after myself."

"I know you can. But it is more pleasant to go with company. I can tell
you more of Joran herbs."

Her petulance dropped off quickly. "Ooh. Okay. Bye."

"Be back tomorrow night," Cass yelled as the door swung shut.

"They'll show up at lunchtime," Gideon laughed. "They get hungry."

Jules stretched out her muscled biceps. "I should get going too. Ellie's
been stressed lately with work, so I want to surprise her with a nice dinner."

"So domestic," Gideon remarked.

"She is my wife and we do live together, so…yeah."

"Hang on a minute," Cass said. "I'm not done with you yet."

Jules clucked through her teeth and sat back down on the sofa.
"Should have known I wasn't getting out without homework."

"Yeah, I see you trying to skip out on it being all lovey-dovey and cute.
Won't work." Cass folded her arms and rested her elbows on her knees.
"Lord Fremont sends his regards. Apparently he thought very highly of

your work in childhood. Any idea what he meant by that?"

Jules worked her brunette eyebrows, thinking hard and worrying her hand in and out of her short-cropped hair. "Honestly? Not at all. I don't think I ever met the guy."

"What did you do when you were a kid?"

"Come on, Cassie. You know all about that."

"He said *work*."

"Seriously! I didn't do much except disappoint my parents every chance I got and get into it with the other noble brats. Sure he wasn't just being clever?"

Cass shifted her weight on the ratty stool she perched on when she got tired of pacing the room. "Oh, he was plenty clever. I think we're going to have to watch out for him."

Gideon tilted his head. "You think the milkmaid is shifty if she starts with a different cow on Tuesday two weeks running."

"There was a lot of…dancing around the point with him. Distractions, jokes. Flirting."

Gideon and Jules swapped looks. Jules cleared her throat. "Cass, he might have just been flirting with you."

"What? No."

"What's your explanation, then?"

"Well—he mentioned hiring other parties."

"Okay."

"So he was probably just trying to keep me complacent."

"To what end?" Gideon asked.

"So we don't quit and continue playing whatever our part is."

"And what could that *possibly* be?"

"Best case? We're a diversion for a better equipped party. Worst case? He has us working on demons because he's actually working with human assassins from an enemy nation to finish off the Amaranthine throne."

Jules buried her face in her hand. "Do you *really* believe that?"

"No," she said, hugging her arms to herself defensively. "It's really un-likely. It's even *less* likely that he's the demon himself trying to throw suspicion away from himself. But these are possibilities, and we consider possibilities."

"What's likelier? That he's just trying to keep you sedate, or that he thinks you're fun?"

"I don't—" Cass looked at Gideon.

He shrugged. "The simplest explanation is often the likeliest."

"I just don't think that's the case this time."

Jules spread her hands. "What's not to like? You're fun. You're cute. You're dangerous."

"He seems about as paranoid as I am."

"Then you'll have plenty to talk about."

Cass lifted an eyebrow. "You don't think that's weird?"

"Oh, we think it's incredibly weird," Gideon put in. "But there are plenty of reasons that might be true. Nobles are weird."

Jules snorted. "Ohh, if that's not the truth. You wouldn't believe some of the shit I saw before I got…before I left. Lots of secret kids. Love children, stepkids, kids like me." She paused. "Come to think of it, that's probably why I don't know this guy. What's his first name again?"

"Alexander," Cass supplied through gritted teeth.

"And he's a Fremont. I didn't think they had any…wait. That's right. Skinny little thing, like a ghost, silver hair, used to run around with the prince." Her face relaxed into a grin. "That's where he knows me from. Heh. Work."

"Want to let the rest of us in on this?"

"So used to be, and I'm betting there still are, these horrible parties you had to go to when your parents are nobility. All the adults would go stand around in the big room and talk about all the same shit they talked about during the day, and they would plunk the kids into another room. But they didn't bother differentiating between like…a five year old kid and a fourteen year old. So there'd be thirty or forty of us of varying ages all running around. The older ones would have been told by their parents to start making alliances. The younger ones would still be…kids, but any normal little kid fights that started could wind up derailing business for a whole generation."

"That sounds like, and I am speaking from experience, hell," Gideon commented.

"And some of the little shits knew it, too. The politics were brutal. So the reason I didn't really recognize Alexander Fremont is...well, it's kind of shitty." She shifted her weight on the couch. "He's adopted."

"Is this the part where I'm supposed to gasp?" Cass asked.

"Yeah, see, you say that, but there's context. I don't recognize him because I wasn't allowed to talk to him. My shithead parents—and others—don't believe that adopted children are eligible nobility and therefore, if not rendering services, don't need to be spoken to."

"Okay, yeah, that is pretty shitty."

"And they'll have appointments with my former colleagues for it later," Gideon muttered, mostly to himself, but purposely loud enough for them to hear.

Jules pushed at her forehead. "The extra shitty thing is—so lords and ladies each have a thing they're in charge of, right? My dad's in charge of the city orphanage. Yeah. Let that rattle around in there for a bit. Okay. Context. So. We're all at this party. Little kids are playing. Big kids are politicking. I'm like...twelve. This band of Upper Echelon snots are going around taking it upon themselves to ask everyone what their work was going to be one day and like...sorting kids."

"I don't like where this is going."

"You shouldn't. They've all of a sudden got groups going and 'you can't be in this one, you're going to be in agriculture' and 'go stand over there with the other social services'. And they keep marching in and out, and this little spindly kid on the bench kept trying to tell them he was going to oversee education and they just walked past him and said things like 'do you hear something? No, must be a draft.' So when they got around to me and they asked me what my work was going to be, I said I was going to be nice to orphans. And then I punched the worst one in the face."

Cass laughed. "That sounds like you. Did that cause problems?"

"Oh, yes. It was the beginning of the end with my old man. But it was worth it." She grinned. "And he remembered that? Huh. Sorry, Cass, but that puts a damper on your 'he's a demon' theory."

"I don't *want* him to be a demon. I'm just prepared for the eventuality."

Gideon shook his head. "Let's settle this. Did his home smell of sulfur?"

"No."

"Did his form ever seem to discorporate?"

"No—"

"And I'm assuming he didn't ask you for your soul, eat you, or imprison you in a magical circle of indefinite torment, so I'm going to go out on a limb and say that he is a human man who has the tingly feelings and you should stop overthinking it."

Cass sighed deeply. "It's…a possibility."

Jules nodded approvingly. "Closer! Anyway. That's most of what I know about him. But if you're going to ask me to lean on Lissa, I can do that."

"Yes, do that. I want to know what she has on him. And Gideon…."

He leaned back in his chair. "I'll go with you tomorrow and put your mind at ease. We'll settle this once and for all. Is Lord Fremont a flirt or a demon? Though I'm fairly certain you know the answer."

Cass was pretty sure she did, too, but she wasn't sure she was ready to say so yet.

The sky decided to open up and bombard Amaranth with almost every form of precipitation it had to offer. It wasn't quite cold enough for snow, but pellets of hail battered at the grand windows of the sitting room and collected in the planters of baneroses outside. Fremont shivered and stood to prod at the fire in the large hearth. "Forgive the draft," he said. "Believe it or not, this is the warmest room in the house."

Gideon glanced out the window from his tense spot on a plush armchair. "So I'm completely clear: this is unusual, but not concerning?"

"Pretty much," Cass answered from a sofa across from him.

"You're not at all worried that the air is coming down in bits of ice."

"It's…uh—just chunkier rain."

Fremont burst out with a laugh that he failed to repress well enough, so it came out in a sort of *snrk* noise. He cleared his throat. "Excuse me. I just—find the concision both technically correct and charming at the same time."

Cass shot him a frown. "Well, how would you explain it, Lord Educator?"

"Ah, I'm afraid I'm merely an administrator. I'll leave the teaching to the ones who actually know what they're talking about."

"So we're not going to die," Gideon interjected.

"No, we're not going to die," Cass returned.

"Good. Good. Okay."

"You lived in the literal hells and weather is what makes you nervous?"

"How can you predict it?" he demanded, frowning. "It just—started doing this."

"You don't, I'm afraid," Fremont answered. "We guess at it, but that's the best we can do."

Gideon shook his head. "Mayhem. Give me demons. Speaking of, Cassie gave me the basics. Portent bells specifically."

"I understand it's a controversial method of detection," he said, coming around to sit on another sofa.

"Among humans, perhaps," Gideon answered, folding his hands beneath his chin. "It's perfectly legitimate as long as your clerics are accurately keyed into the spiritual flow of things. I don't suppose anyone recorded the ringing of them?"

"Not in written form. But the priest who observed should be along shortly to share his observations."

Gideon's expression, up until now mostly pensive, turned cautious. "I should take my leave. Priests tend not to take kindly to my type."

Cass tilted her head. "Gideon—you're the expert."

"And that won't matter if he tries to banish me, will it?"

Fremont shook his head. "The Amaranthine Church, in theory, takes a neutral stance on devils. Neither revered nor feared. You are safe."

"Safe, yes. He wouldn't *succeed* at banishing me, but I fear this will become quickly unproductive if there's an argument over my presence."

"I don't believe it will come to that. But if it does, you have my word, I will deal with it expediently."

Gideon surreptitiously glanced in Cass' direction and waggled his eyebrows suggestively when Fremont busied himself with a teacup. He mouthed, *he'll deal with it.* Cass rolled her eyes at him. He shrugged back at her and grinned.

She pushed at her forehead. "So that might give us some direction," she said. "Then we tailor the investigation. In the meantime, I'd like to hear more of the basics."

"Of course," Fremont answered. "What would you like to know?"

"Don't take this the wrong way," she said, flipping a page in her notepad, "but is this an arranged marriage or not? It makes a difference in demonic circles."

"Ah." He looked down into his lap. "Believe it or not, both. Ruhan and Ifalna met in diplomatic conversation and happened to quite like one another. Their families had been in conversation for years, but it worked out they met first, so they just…went with it."

Cass glanced up at Gideon. "What does that mean for us?"

Gideon frowned pensively. "I'm…not sure," he admitted. "That's a loophole."

"They love loopholes."

"They do love loopholes."

Fremont leaned forward. "Does this endanger them?"

"It may, and it may not," Gideon admitted. "The reason Cass is concerned, and rightfully, is that certain demons make use of contracts. An arranged marriage is a contract, and the wedding itself is the fulfillment, which is the culmination of the spiritual power of said contract, which the demon is interested in harvesting for itself. So if it's an arranged marriage, they're vulnerable to that sort. There is a separate sort of demon that feeds off of emotion. Those are the ones you find preying on births, weddings for love, funerals, et cetera. This wedding could very well be uniquely vulnerable to both. And the fact that they are both heirs to entire nations is…."

"Bad," Fremont supplied, even more colorless than usual.

"Probably," Cass answered, watching him carefully. He seemed appropriately concerned, at least, though traitors likely don't usually pause to do secret jigs when talking about their treasons. "Because it's not just the bride and groom they're feeding off, right? It's the guests. Big wedding, lots of guests. State wedding, lots of guests and people having feelings about it at home. Lots of little moving pieces to that contract. There's a dowry. There's alliances. Money changing hands. Which is why you hired us, of course, but the scope just doubled."

Fremont nodded a little blearily, like he'd taken a few hits to the head. "Is this going to be too much for you alone? Will you need reinforcements?"

"Unlikely," Gideon said. "Demons do not like to work in large groups. If it is two opposing forces, the numbers should still be small enough for us."

"Lucky for us," Cass laughed a bit weakly.

"Luck has nothing to do with it." Gideon leaned forward, his hooves bobbling on the floor, elbows resting on his knobby knees. "We are most likely looking at two factions. One strong and clever, another more reliant on brute force. They will both have underlings, but not terribly many. Under fifteen."

Cass nodded. "Our goal will be to draw them out and reduce them before the wedding without leaving enough time for new factions to plan assaults. That will move in waves that will overlap each other, beginning with investigation, moving into wedding planning and warding, then reconnaissance, then a hopeful operation, final wedding preparation, and the ceremony itself."

Fremont listened intently and remained frozen in place for a solid moment. Cass was beginning to wonder about the pause, when he lifted his eyes to her in genuine puzzlement. "You…do this for every wedding?"

"With a demonic threat? More or less."

He shook his head. "I…I'm sorry, I had no idea. I've been invited to more than a few and I was of course aware there *was* a wedding party. I've heard of some scuffles at some of them, but I hadn't realized how much goes into…well. You'll have my support, whatever you need. Ruhan is my oldest friend, and obviously demons are…bad."

Gideon chuckled. "Eloquently put, my lord."

Cass shot him a look. "Hey."

"Oh, so only *you* can sass our employer?"

"I, at least, am trying to stop."

Fremont laughed and smoothed a piece of his long silver hair back. "Please don't. I am still trying to wrap my head around it all and I do believe the sass is an essential learning tool."

"I can put it in the contract if you like."

"That reminds me." He rose and moved to a table near the entrance and withdrew the contract. "Feel free to review it and ensure it's in order. Especially the portion about dancing."

She took it from him. "It's important. If you ask me you're just as in breach as if you neglected to hand over the final payment."

Fremont smiled. "A shame." From the foyer, a bell rang. "I…should preempt Humphrey. Excuse me." He exited quickly.

Gideon leaned over the arm of his chair. "Cassie, my dear, my sweet, my darling, you are *blushing*."

She finished signing her portion of the contract and threw her pen at him. "Shut up."

"He's definitely flirting."

"No shit."

"And by my expert estimation, I have seen no signs of demonic interference."

"Okay."

"And he is *really* pretty."

She swatted her hair from her eyes and grumbled. "So what do I do about it?"

Gideon batted his ridiculously long eyelashes. "What was that?"

She threw a frantic glance at the still open door to confirm the hallway remained empty. It was, for now. "Stop wasting time and tell me. Is it inappropriate? Unprofessional? Should I shut it down till the job's over? Is he just doing it for fun? Should I stop?"

"You're clearly both enjoying it."

"I think so?"

He waved a parchment-white hand. "Then do you, dearest. Just don't get us fired."

She clenched the arm of the sofa so hard her knuckles threatened to pop. "What does that *mean* — ?"

Footsteps from behind, and Fremont returned accompanying a slight man in deep lilac robes trimmed in silver. A priest of the Amaranthine Church, a young man with tanned skin and close cropped black hair. Unusual. Typically the bell minders were codgers.

"Friends," Fremont said, "this is Brother Hubert of the Order of the Harmonious Bells. These are Mistress Cassandra Friend and Master Gideon of the Friend Event Company. They are assisting His Royal Majesty and therefore me on business related to the wedding."

The young priest bobbed his head twice. His eyes did linger on Gideon for a moment longer, but he made no motion to hold the meeting up. "Glad tidings." He glanced to the window and brushed his shoulders clear of still-melting hailstones. "Er…mostly."

Fremont gestured to the room. "Please, make yourself comfortable and warm…er. There's tea."

"Thank you, Lord Fremont." He took up the other armchair next to Gideon, fumbling with a long scroll. "I have been musing on the portent bells since the ringing. Ah." He looked up between Cass and Gideon. "Are you both familiar with the ceremony of the portents?"

"Gideon is," Cassandra said. "I've got a rough idea."

"Right. Well. Good. On the day His Royal Majesty came seeking the blessing of the elders, I'm afraid that of our order, only two of us were there. We performed the ceremony on his request. Ah — Lord Fremont was present."

Fremont nodded. "I have to confess I know very little about what happened, but I trust Hubert's extensive study."

Fremont was a little less formal than most nobles to start, but he was casual with Hubert. She wondered how they knew each other. "It seems unusual," she said, leaning forward, "that the Crown Prince arriving and asking a blessing would not be better attended."

"Ruhan is…." Fremont sighed, a small smile in place. "A romantic. It was less a planned thing and more of a gesture to Ifalna. I told him it was a bad idea."

Cass bit her tongue. She personally couldn't see a world in which *hey, let's go find out which supernatural threats want to ass up our wedding* seemed like a cute date idea, but to each their own, she guessed. "Is he an optimist, perhaps?"

"Terminally."

She made a note. Hubert unrolled his scroll. "Since there were only the two of us, there was no one on hand to solely make note of the tones played, but I have since recreated what I believe I heard. There is…some disagreement between myself and the other listener now."

Fremont sat up. "That differs from when we were there."

He nodded. "Brother Armen has since said that he believes that the resonance was higher than we thought, indicating a more general threat. I cannot agree. There was some higher resonance, resulting in confusion, but I remember. I remember a lower diatonic, a repeating tone. A knell."

Gideon leaned forward. "May I?"

Hubert held out the long roll of paper. Cass too leaned forward to get a look at his notations. All she saw were what looked like very long ovals of various lengths, set apart from each other at intervals. She glanced over at Fremont. He too looked like he was trying to comprehend a foreign language. But Gideon and Hubert both seemed like they were solving some sort of equation.

Gideon pointed. "That doesn't make sense."

"I thought so too," Hubert said. "But that's the one thing I really recall strongly. It kept repeating, again and again, this pattern." He hummed a low note that hung there for a moment, then fell away and came back shorter four more times.

Cass didn't know why, but the close-shaved hair on the back of her neck felt like it was moving independently. Fremont sat up abruptly and rubbed at his upper arm, shoulder. An old wound acting up. Cass felt it too, in her knee.

Gideon frowned deeply. "Wait," he said. "Turn the paper over."

Hubert complied. Gideon took the scroll and held it high so that the firelight shone through, the ink reflected like a shadow.

Hubert's eyes flashed with awareness. "I see it," he murmured, grabbing Cass' discarded pen and quickly, frenetically filling in more ovals.

The prickling in her knee escalated past pinpricks into full blown pain. Fremont jumped from his chair. "What is this?" he asked, gripping the back of it.

Gideon barely acknowledged the question. His eyes seemed locked on Hubert's pen, and the more it moved, the wider they seemed to grow. Panic burgeoned in them. Mostly Gideon pretended distaste or amusement. Cass leaned forward. "Gideon?"

Hubert, too, seemed gripped with a horror as he worked, like he didn't exactly want to believe what he was writing. But write he did, until his arm fell slack.

Gideon's voice creaked out of him in a whisper. "No."

"Azorael," Hubert breathed.

The fire in the hearth roared outward in a blast so hot it felt as though it consumed the room. On instinct alone, Cass dropped to the floor. The fire didn't reach her skin, but the heat itself was immense and the light was blinding. She couldn't make out any other figures in the room.

"Gideon!" she yelled, and her voice cracked and died in her throat.

A silhouette moved somewhere in front of her—she couldn't judge the distance—and she heard a voice, deep, resonant, familiar, but greater somehow. "Dmitri Irividius, your presence is cast from this place. In the name of sacred balance, I *rebuke you.*"

The fire roared once more before it collapsed on itself, leaving a dark, cold room. Gideon stood directly in front of Cass, his hand still held out. Hubert was sprawled on the ground, his hands full of ash.

Fremont sat hunched on the ground, shaking. Cass managed to pull herself toward him, reached out. "Are you all right—?"

"Stay back," he snapped, breathing hard, pulling his arm to himself. Cass retracted her hand, and his silver eyes made contact and softened. "Please," he added.

She sat on her heels and looked over at Gideon, whose gaze was still locked on the now empty hearth. "Was that him?"

"No," he answered. "Just an extension of his will. He himself is much more powerful."

"You know his true name," Hubert stammered.

Gideon's head swiveled toward the priest, pointed teeth bared, and for the first time in her entire working relationship with him, Cass saw why people might be afraid of him. "Do *not* mistake that for affinity, priest, and were I you, I would never speak either of those names aloud again. They carry power."

"I—I know that. I felt—I felt compelled."

Gideon's rigid posture went slack, and he raked his hand through his hair. "Of course you did. What else should we expect from the Lord of Demons himself?"

4
Demonic Dealings

The only good news was that there would be only one faction of demons. Everything else was a shitshow.

They moved from the sitting room, because it was hard to feel cozy in a room that had just been invaded by something called Azorael, Lord of Demons. Humphrey insisted on forcing food on them, partially because they moved to the dining room, partially because it was around dinner time, partially because it was something to do. Cass appreciated having a fork to stab things with.

"So are we going to talk about it, or…?"

Gideon blotted politely at his mouth with his napkin. "People process things different ways, Cassandra. I know you like to charge ahead, but others may still be turning things over."

"Okay, but aren't we in danger now?"

"Yes and no. It's in the Lord of Demons' best interests to allow the wedding to continue."

"*We* don't need to be around for that."

He nodded somberly. "He controls a cabal of assassins, above and below. An attack is extremely likely."

Fremont put his forehead in his hand. "Perfect."

Hubert looked between them cautiously. "It's worse than that."

He dropped his hand and looked shrewdly at the priest. "Oh. Really. I hadn't guessed."

Humphrey entered from the kitchen door and refilled Fremont's glass. "*Eat,* Lord Alexander."

Fremont shot him a murderous sort of look, which the tiny man stared down with equal ferocity. With a small amount of petulance, Fremont at last gave in and managed to cut into the meat. Humphrey patted his arm and set about checking on the other glasses before bustling out again.

"Go on, Hubert," Fremont said.

"The Lord of Demons is a recent conqueror of the underworld," Hubert supplied. "Usually a figure of his magnitude would be centuries old. He has gained all of his power very, very quickly. So much so that some of my brethren believe he is a myth. Which may be why Brother Armen changed his story. He may have figured it out before we did."

"So you believe his influence is pervasive," Cass said.

"We know it is," Gideon returned, looking away. "I have encountered him myself. The last soul I attempted to work on."

"Wait—"

"Light conversation for dinner," he sighed. "A demon is a last resort. Bet you didn't know we make them on purpose."

Fremont nearly dropped his fork. "You *make* demons?"

"Right, right, here's the deal. You're a bad person, or at least a person who has done very bad things. You die on this mortal plane, your soul gets sent to hell, it's assigned to a devil. They work their specialty. Best case scenario, your soul is reformed, gets to move on, all is well. In most cases, it takes some elbow grease, but we at least get a soul to reconcile what they did, achieve neutrality, move on, things are acceptable. But when someone cannot, will not see the depths of their evil, will never repent, will never be safe to return to the spiritual flow of things, it's our responsibility to keep them out of it. That's what the underworld was supposed to be for. And then it went wrong."

Hubert tilted on his chair, his face ashen, as though he wasn't entirely sure he should be listening to this. "Are you suggesting…?"

"Yes, Hubert, demons were people, keep up. They were meant to serve their time in the underworld, supporting the operation of the hells. A productive outlet for them, a peaceful solution to the 'what do we do with the bad energy' problem…except some of the demons developed powers, broke away from their wardens, and began terrorizing the mortal plane.

And instead of solving the problems they caused, my superiors instead decided to ignore them for a thousand years and pretend they had been separate entities all along until you accidentally rebelliously discover the truth and get kicked out like me." Gideon folded his hands primly. "So."

All three of the humans around the table stared. Cass sputtered slightly. "I—I don't understand. You told me you were the persuasion guy. Whatever the hells *that* was didn't feel like it could have been talked into being good."

"No, you're right," he said, smiling tightly. "And if we don't get him now, we will all pay for it. He spoke almost exclusively of how he wanted to become a demon, and then the higher ups ignored my recommendations and made him one anyway."

Fremont looked nervously in Cass' direction. "You're sure you don't need backup?"

"No," she said honestly.

Gideon sighed. "While he is abnormally powerful, given the time he's had, he's still a criminal and not some mastermind. Keeping our number small and obfuscated is our best bet for now."

Cass nodded slowly. "All right. I'll keep options open as we work." She turned to Fremont. "You know the political situation far better than we do. Should we apprise the prince?"

He hesitated. "He is aware there is a threat to his life, though if I am being entirely honest, that has always been true. It seems this is growing, but I'm uncertain what this entity wants. Is it the power from the union or to meddle in the affairs of the nation?"

"Primarily the power, I would expect," Gideon answered. "In life, he was from Port Oranos. I can't imagine he'd have much bad blood with Amaranth or Joranhelm."

"But if he has designs, it would probably become obvious through investigation," Cass mused.

Fremont nodded. "All right," he said, subdued. "Let's keep it between us for now."

Gideon pushed his chair back and stood. "I'm going to check the sitting room for traces, just to be safe. Hubert, why don't you join me?"

"I think you thoroughly banished him," he said, confused.

He looped his arm through the priest's and hauled him up. "Can't be too sure. Come on." He caught Cass' eye and winked before pushing Hubert from the room.

Cass wasn't too sure she *wanted* alone time, but here she was. She put her napkin in her lap again and made sure she seemed appropriately busy. But not *too* busy; that would be weird, too.

Fremont cleared his throat and leaned forward. "I—should apologize for my behavior earlier. I—"

She shook her head quickly. "I understand. When battle wounds hurt, they tend to make you think you're in battle."

He stopped. "You…how did you know?"

Cass laughed a little. "The other side of the paranoia coin is just called being perceptive. Maybe even empathetic sometimes."

"You astound me sometimes."

"Sometimes?"

"Frighten me at others." He smiled down at nothing in particular. "I still—it may not have been my chosen reaction, but I regret it. Please, allow me to ask your forgiveness, Cassandra." He stopped and turned a vibrant shade of red. "And—twice, now, for helping myself to your name. Good gods, what's gotten into me."

She laughed and shook her head. "Where'd all your impertinence go? Cassandra, Cass, Cassie, anything. And it's forgiven."

"Anything but Alex," he said in return. "I abhor Alex. Don't ask me why, because I don't know."

"Anything?"

"I should have known you'd take that literally." He paused. "Can I ask you something?"

"You are literally paying me to consult, so yes."

"It's a bit outside of the professional scope. You've been at this a while. How do you just—go about your normal life knowing there are demons running about, doing…this?"

She laughed a little. "I will tell you when I figure it out."

"I see."

"Sorry to disappoint."

He smiled again. "Not disappoint. Never disappoint."

Cass felt her face heat up again. She fussed with the length of hair in front of her right ear and cleared her throat. "It helps me, somewhat, that my normal life is trying to stop them. It won't be forever, but for the time being, at least peripherally, yours is too. Perhaps that can be a little comfort."

"It is," he said. "Thank you. As much help as I can be, anything you need, you have it."

Cass smiled a bit. "Jules says hi."

"Hello back. How has she been since, er, leaving the Upper Ring?"

"Mostly good. She came and worked for my mum pretty shortly thereafter, which is how we became close."

"That's good to hear. I'd always hoped she'd done well for herself making her own way."

Cass' smile picked up of its own accord. "It's really her fault I'm here. In several different ways, but it really just used to be her and me and whichever two fellows we could hire for a night. It was for fun, once."

"And now?"

What a question. She mused over a sip of wine. "Do you want the cynical answer, the polite one, or a real one?"

He chuckled. "All three sound like fun in proximity."

"Politely, I like safeguarding people's events. Cynically, I like surviving and that costs money, unfortunately. Realistically, it's what I can do. It's what I'm capable at, it's the best way I can help. They're all true."

Alexander nodded thoughtfully. "You do like it?"

"Mostly. But that's a level of honesty for another day."

"You're not a wedding person, are you."

Her lips twitched. "What gave it away?"

He laughed. "Perhaps the dripping cynicism."

"Poor you. An utter romantic on the throne and the precise opposite at your dinner table and demons coming out of your fireplace."

"It is perhaps a bit more than I bargained for, but apart from the demons? Not disagreeable."

Her face warmed again, but this time, she didn't feel in such a hurry to damper it.

On their way out, Cass and Gideon had a look about the wider grounds. It was cursory—the place was enormous—and Gideon wasn't sensing any more magic or demonic energy with the runes he spun from his hands as they walked, but it was worth a look as they walked to the gate. He nudged her. "So. Have a nice talk?"

She rolled her eyes. "Yeah. Thanks for that."

"My pleasure. You were overdue for a good flirt."

"What I'm overdue for is information about the godsdamned Demon Lord that popped out of his fireplace."

Gideon's face fell. "Yeah, about that. I think I have a lead."

"Usually that's a good thing."

"Yes, however, it involves some…rekindling of contacts I'd rather not touch," he muttered. "Think you'll still be flirting with the lord tomorrow night?"

"The flirting isn't on a schedule. What do you need from me?"

"You plus someone else. Maybe Thalia. Yeah, let's go with Thalia. Could use the magic. Dress nicely."

"How nicely are we talking?" she asked, gesturing to her fancy lord-meeting outfit.

"Oh, no, I mean like grab an old client dress."

She arched her eyebrows. "Oh. Where are we going?"

His face darkened. "You'll see. Meet you at the office."

Cass grasped his elbow gently and stopped him. "Look. I don't ask a whole lot of questions, but I need to know. How did this lead come up so fast?"

He sighed deeply, looked to the shadows on the ground. "Let's just say there was a personal matter I was pursuing that just unexpectedly became professional."

Gideon was nervous. She didn't like it when Gideon was nervous. He was usually so hard to flap, and he usually hid it very well when something did get him. She never knew what the right amount of prying was. Did he need her to pry?

Maybe she'd pry tomorrow.

5
Devil in the City

Cass picked the least bridesmaid-like of the dresses she still had taking up space in her pathetic closet. It was a bluish-purple number with small silver spangles like stars around the hem. She'd liked those grooms.

Gideon caught her hand and gave her a twirl as she entered the office. "Ooh, Cassie, you clean up good. Sure you don't want to stop by the lord's place?"

"Would you stop it?" she grumbled.

"I will *not*. It's fun to see you blush. It's almost like you're a human being. Thalia, come look at our boss."

Thalia stepped out from behind the supply cabinet in a gauzy red dress that Cass did not remember wearing. She folded her hands behind her back and pulled her equally red lips into a smile. "I remember that one. It was fun."

Gideon sighed. "We're going to need to get you something you *haven't* worn for work one of these days."

Cass cocked her head. "And you? Why aren't you dressed up?"

In fact, he was the opposite of dressed up. Cass didn't know Gideon owned clothes in this state of disrepair. He preferred to be meticulous in all things, but here he was, in a threadbare shirt and a pair of trousers with, of all things, a hole in the knee.

"I have my part to play," he said. "As do you."

She frowned. "Gideon, are we bait?"

"Yes," Thalia whispered, excitement building in her face.

Gideon gestured broadly, fishing for his keys. "Think of it less as bait and more of…set dressing. Our fellow isn't going to just talk to somebody in any circumstance. We've got to make him feel comfortable."

"Yeah, we're bait," Cass grumbled, folding her arms.

"What did you expect, kitten?" He ushered them from the office and locked the door. "I'm the devil. What you see is what you get."

"So basically," Gideon finished as they ascended the last stair to the Market District, "Helshefzor is a prick who makes a point of taking a little vacation to the surface each of your months."

"Hold on," Cass said, listing a little more than she'd like to admit. There was a reason the contract said no heels these days. "You guys pick the names you use, right?"

"Yes."

"He *picked* Helshefzor."

"Listen, things are a little different back home. Which leads me to my point. I always thought it was a little weird he'd take his R&R up here. Most devils strictly do not care what happens on your level. No offense to you, but…like I said, things are different."

"How so?" Thalia asked curiously.

"Sure you want to know? Might offend the sensibilities."

"I have performed blood rituals."

Gideon, unflapped, sighed. "When you're dealing with…the kind of shit we see, and oh, your gods, do we see some shit, pretty much everything one might do to relax is fair game. There is no such thing as overindulgence, so long as you're not being a dick about it. Down there, specifically. If you choose to come up here, the rules are different. We're supposed to follow *your* rules. Morality, mortality, all that. So why, when given the rare chance to kick back, would a devil choose to come here where alcohol poisoning, fidelity, and a strange unyielding commitment to heteronormativity are things? No offense. I know some of you aren't all that into it."

"None taken, I guess," Cass said. "So you think he's involved in something."

"I suspected as much, but I couldn't quite figure it out. Then all this Lord of Demons stuff started coming together, and…poof. Unfortunately. I did some digging with someone I know who supplies taverns down below. We catch up every now and again. I buy his terrible whiskey. Turns out it's really hard to distill stuff in hell, something about pressure. I know nothing about it, but basically devils need humans to get drunk. Go figure. He told me Helshefzor asked him for some recommendations. Classy places, but not like…." He gestured to the direction of the Upper Ring. "No offense."

"None taken?" Cass said with a nose wrinkle.

"So the fellow tells him about a place here that does a shrimp…thing once a month. Next time he sees him, Helshefzor tells him he loves it, hasn't missed a month since. It's tonight. You're going."

"I see," Cass said. "What's the angle?"

"It's simple," Gideon answered, his shoulders slouching, tail drooping like a cat's. "Obnoxiously so."

Cass and Thalia stood in the alley in front of the Crystal Corridors Restaurant and Bar, which shed its eerie pale green light over the puddles on the cobblestones while she superfluously fiddled with her purse. Thalia tapped her foot impatiently. "The reservations," she said, looking back anxiously.

"I know," she said. "I know they're here somewhere."

A reddish hooved man in a black velvet coat started his way past them. Thalia politely attempted not to stare, but failed—after all, there weren't many devils in the city—and failed to notice the other one coming up behind and wrapping his arm around Cassandra.

She shrieked.

"Your money or your wife," Gideon snarled, a knife dangled precipitously at Cassandra's chest.

Thalia made panicked eye contact with the devilish man passing by, a flash of connection, a plea. In that instant, Helshefzor declined. He kept walking. Gideon yelled, "Well?"

And then he stopped short, turned. His face split in a grin. "Belfar?" He snorted. "Is that you?"

Cass felt Gideon shake at her back. How much of that was performance and how much of that was real, she wasn't sure.

"That's not my name anymore," he spat.

Helshefzor stepped closer. He reeked of cologne. Expensive cologne. "Too right," he said. "Look what's become of you."

Thalia sputtered wordlessly. Gideon tossed his head in her direction. "Shut up. Shut up! I will kill her."

"Oh," the interloper laughed, stepping forward. "You could never. That would mean seeing *me* at the end of this measly little lifespan you've bought yourself. You don't have the guts. I mean it. I'd run out of guts to strew about the depths far before I was done with you. And you know it."

Gideon's fingers moved over the hilt of the blade. "Yeah. You always were a dick."

Thalia stepped back—far back, as instructed—just as Gideon let go of both a warbling sort of energy that surrounded Helshefzor and the knife. Cass caught the knife, pivoted, and held it to his neck.

"Thanks for stepping in," she told him. "Here's what's going to happen. We're going to go further down the alley. You're going to remember that you're playing by *my* rules here. Morality, mortality, all that. You're going to tell me what I need to know. Are we clear?"

He nodded once, stiffly. Gideon's spell kept shifting over him in a way that made his muscles twitch. Not painful-looking, per se, but not comfortable, either. Thalia's head tilted curiously as she took in the effects of the spell. Gideon's magic wasn't usually this aggressive.

"Good," Cass said, tapping at a hoof with the toe of a shoe. "Lead on."

Gideon slipped in front, keeping a close eye on his handiwork. Thalia hung back, keeping an eye out. Once well out of sight, Cass regarded Helshefzor. "So. Lord of Demons. What does he have you doing up here?"

He looked balefully at Gideon. "That's your game, is it?"

"You're talking to me right now," she reminded him, pushing the blade closer.

"You're mad if you think that little thing scares me more than His Eminence."

"And you're bluffing, because this little thing'll send you straight *to* His Eminence, and no. I won't have a qualm about it."

He glanced down at the knife again, then back to Gideon. "So this is what you're doing now? Telling the divine secrets to the mortals for scraps?"

"The broken secrets," he said with a shrug. "Come on. If *His Eminence* can play the system, the system is broke, and you helped break it. Let's not feign outrage about it now."

Helshefzor let out a little heh. "Fine. You want to know? I'll tell you. But you're not going to be happy."

"That sounds like a me problem," Cass said.

"There's a guy up here. Fourth in a long line of shitstains. I know. I processed the last three. I got instructions from His Eminence to meet him for dinner once a month and chat. A social call. Strictly that. No business. Somewhere nice." He nodded toward the restaurant. "So I do. That's it."

"That's it."

"That's it." He smirked. "Told you you weren't going to be happy. But hey. That's a you problem."

Gideon stepped forward. "There's more he's not saying."

"I'm not lying! Do your thing, Belfar. Make me tell the truth. It'll be exactly the same." He tilted his head. "Why won't you do it?"

Gideon ignored him, stepped up next to Cass and started checking pockets. He sent a huge coin purse plopping to the ground, what looked like a half-eaten jerky stick, a few scraps of paper. At last, he came away with a brass sphere with a ruby set in the top and a dark mist swirling inside it. Gideon's head snapped up, and his face darkened.

"You son of a bitch."

"Ever a tender heart, weren't you," Helshefzor sniffed. "If only—"

Gideon reached out and the shadows seemed to rip away from the corners and rise up as tentacles, clawing, coiling. Even Thalia squirmed uncomfortably as they shot past her. They snatched Helshefzor's arms and legs and tail and neck and yanked him from Cass' grasp, pinning him to the brick side of the building next to the restaurant. They tightened until his ruddy skin bulged.

"Set it free," Gideon demanded.

Helshefzor coughed. "Do it yourself."

Cass whirled to Gideon, eyes wide. "Gideon."

He looked at her, his own eyes wild and wet. "Don't you see, Cassie? It's a soul. He's trading souls." He turned back to the devil. "Open it!"

"You bound me!" he wheezed. "You should be able to do it. Unless you're too human now."

"Stop it," he hissed, his whole body shaking, his hands held out in front of him.

"You are, aren't you? Are you sleeping yet?" He shook his head in wonderment, even as his face turned more purple than red. "It's no wonder I barely recognized you. I don't even think Laufit would." He paused, choked, and still managed to sneer. "Well. Not that you'd recognize *him* much these days, either."

Gideon let go of a strangled yell and reeled back and punched him square in the face. He staggered back, stared at him, stricken, and then hit him again. The tentacles vanished, and Helshefzor's body slid down the wall. Gideon punched him again and again, blood flying from his hand and the devil's increasingly swollen face.

Thalia caught Gideon's arm and pulled him back. "Enough," she told him gently.

Gideon breathed hard, tears streaming down his face. Cass checked Helshefzor. On his way out. She took up her dagger and helped him along. The second she pulled back, his body was consumed completely by fire, leaving only a cologne-scented scorch mark to indicate he'd been there at all.

She stood and sheathed the knife under her skirt, then came to Gideon and put her arms around him. He held on and shook. "Let's get you a drink," she said at last.

*   *   *

It took three, but it gave him something to do while Thalia used the ice from the wine bucket and yet more alcohol plus a little bit of magic, done subtly, to do something about the wreckage of his hand. Cass talked a waiter into giving up a napkin.

"You are very lucky," she told Gideon, "that you didn't break your thumb. Don't tuck it in."

He wiped at his face. "I…really didn't intend to do that."

"Yeah, we can tell." She knotted the makeshift bandage and sighed sympathetically. "Listen. I don't ask you much very often."

"And I appreciate it." He slammed the last of the remaining whiskey in his glass. "But I owe you something after all that. I know. I've been trying to figure out how to say it a while anyway."

"Did you figure it out?"

"No," he laughed. He held his empty glass and observed it in the low mage light for something to do. "I told you the Lord of Demons was the last soul I worked on. That was true. He passed unsuccessfully through every other devil in hell. Every single devil. Including…." He took a breath. "My husband. Laufit."

"Your husband," Cass said quietly.

"I know. I don't seem the type, do I." He smiled a little into the glass. "Like I said, things are different. But he is my whole heart. Until…when he started working with the Lord of Demons, things began to change. Laufit became…attached to the rules. I couldn't quite understand why, especially when he knew I had begun to question them, and previously he had been supportive."

"Tell me about these rules," Thalia said.

"There are a host of them, of course. Procedures. Some of them for good reason. Some of them," he sighed, "I struggled with. It seems simple. A murderer dies, he should go to hell and face repercussions, shouldn't he?"

"Sure," Cass said slowly.

"And if this murderer killed someone in desperation? Should he face the same torment as the murderer who killed for fun? It was still wrong, yes. Driven by rage, not righteousness, which is the distinction between an honorable killing and a murder as far as the balance is concerned."

"I—"

Bitterly, he shook his head. "If you're having a hard time with that, you'll love questions about war and abuse. Pain begets pain. The longer I worked, the more I saw it, the less I could ignore it. My charges were often the injured souls. I could talk to them, reach them, set them straight. Too late, but better than never. Laufit's were a different sort. He was there to induce remorse. His tools were words, too, but used in a different way than mine. I reasoned, cajoled. He reopened wounds, tore out cancers. And he spent…a very long time on this one."

Cass folded her hands on the table. "No one saw that it wasn't working?"

"I believe someone must have. And I think they turned the other way. Laufit was growing more and more agitated as time dragged on, obsessed. I…." He turned his face away. "I reported him. I took charge of the soul, tried to understand what he'd done. It was too late. This one was determined to become a demon, and shortly after he did…he took Laufit with him."

Cass reached out and set her hand on his arm. He shut his eyes, his cheeks growing wet again. He tried to compose himself, failed, tried again. "For all intents and purposes, my husband is dead," he croaked. "And at some point, so will be the devil I was. The longer I'm here, the more…. He was right."

"It's not so bad," Cass said with an attempt at a smile. "I think you'll like not getting horns stuck in things. Does it hurt?"

"No, thankfully. Not yet."

Thalia rested her chin on her hands. "Gideon…are you sure he's really gone?"

He slid his glass along the smooth tabletop. "I've never heard of anyone turning back from a demon into anything else. Even if he did…." Gideon trailed off, looking up at the glass walls to the nighttime streets of Amaranth. "What I *can* do is stop the Lord of Demons. Whatever his ultimate aim is—it's bad. He's already corrupted half of hell to do it. Laufit and that piece of shit in the alley aren't the only ones he got to."

Cass shifted uneasily. "And they're…smuggling souls."

Gideon swore under his breath. "There's a lot a warlock could do with a soul."

Thalia wrinkled her nose. "Could, but that's disgusting."

Cass looked her way. "You talk about blood rituals."

She bobbed her head, frowning as this were the most basic of basics. "Uh, yeah. You can always get more blood. You got an extra soul stashed somewhere I don't know about?"

Gideon waved her off. "*Regardless* of value judgments. I think that's probably how the human assassins are taking their payment."

"Four generations of shitstains. He's not talking about the River Rats?"

"The sewer gang?" Thalia asked.

"They're certainly well connected enough to get to both the Upper Ring and our more humble abodes."

Gideon mumbled, "I wonder if we messed up the deal, or just delayed it."

"Let's hope for the former. I'll ask Jules to look into that more specifically."

"I can do it tonight," he said listlessly.

"You need to rest. That hand is going to swell, and she is going to give you a lot more shit for your punching technique than I am. Also, if you've been avoiding alcohol for the reason I think, you have an unpleasant surprise coming in the morning."

He smiled grimly. "Sometimes I think you'd make a good devil, Cassie."

"I'll try to take that as a compliment."

Thalia giggled. "He just means you see through people. The way he can see through anybody. Even you."

He lurched a little. "You try so hard to hide things. Like your lord. You liiiike him."

"I think you've established that," Cass sighed.

"Good for you," he pronounced. "I mean it. Good for you. I can tell there's some noise in there about that. You're letting yourself be open again."

"Can we not?" she said sharply, finishing off her drink.

"Sorry," he said. "Old habits."

"No, I'm sorry," she corrected herself with a sigh. "I want you to talk to me. I want you to feel like you can tell me these things. Just because I'm emotionally constipated doesn't mean you should be."

"Oh, darling. Don't think you invented that."

"I wasn't…always."

He patted her hand. "I know. Really. Too well." He sighed, looked around the restaurant. "Everyone in this room is, though. They just learn to stop up different tubes."

"Ugh."

"You made the metaphor, sweet pea. I'm just following it to its logical evacuation."

"Please stop."

"I haven't even found a good sphincter joke."

"Is this what you did in hell?"

He grinned. "Just with the special cases."

Thalia mused, "There's some kind of joke to be had about rectums, but I haven't got there yet, either. Rect…ifying…."

Cass paused a moment for Thalia's joke to die. "Are you okay?" she asked Gideon.

His breath leaked out in a hiss. "No," he admitted. "And yes. Maybe more than I have been in a year. The telling felt awful, but it's good to have it out."

"He won't get at this wedding."

"It's more than that," he said, shaking his head. "The wedding…it's just a step for him, Cassie. A means to an end. A way to accumulate power. If we don't end him here…."

Her guts went cold. "What are you saying?"

"This isn't a one-and-done banish job."

"We're not—we aren't heroes. We're mercenaries. We have a job to do and we do it."

"It is greater than that," Thalia said even more ominously than usual.

"Do you like having a world to live in?" he said seriously. "Do you like your soul?"

Cass' breath caught. "Gideon."

"That's what's at stake here, Cassie. This man died on purpose, put himself through every conceivable torture hell could contrive, and when he arrived at my doorstep and I asked why, he looked me in the eye and told me. Power. That's all. And we gave it to him. I will not repeat that mistake." He looked at her, pained. "I asked you why you do this job. You dodged. You say you're not a hero, but look at you. Look at you."

She folded her arms uncomfortably. "I don't know what you mean."

"Your friends, Cassie. Bjorn is in self-exile. Thalia is…weird."

"I accept the compliment," Thalia said wryly.

"Jules was disowned," Gideon continued. "I was cast out. You gave us a place. You keep taking these jobs, not just because of the money, but because they *help*. They help us. *You* help."

She just kind of stared, a little slack-jawed.

He shook his head and smiled. "There's your blockage," he went on. "You're trying to stop up that help pipe, because that lets people in to hurt. You thought if you charged money for it, you could pad it a bit. Gruff it up. Call it mercenary work. Can I pay you, then? Please, Cassie. Help me. Help us all."

She shook herself. "*Gideon*."

He squeezed her hand. "Think it over. I'll ask again when we're less drunk and shook up."

Thalia looked around uneasily as though someone were watching. As far as Cass knew, someone was. Thalia spoke in a near-whisper. "I'm not the demon expert—your demon expert is understandably wasted right now—but wouldn't sending Hell-shelf-orb or whatever back to his master ring some alarm bells? We should probably begin warding His Lordship's home tomorrow."

Gideon pointed to her. "You are *right*. He'll probably try to look at him again."

"Shit," Cass muttered. "That means you probably need to get to work making stuff."

Thalia nodded seriously. "Like…yesterday."

"And you—" She looked at Gideon. "Can you sober up enough to do some preliminary work?"

He leaned his head back and sighed dramatically. "Ughhh. If I have to."

"You can drink more later. I'm going to have to talk to our employer about demon safety." She tugged at the ugly necklace a bride three years ago insisted she wear to match her mother's heirloom jewelry. It felt like a weight around her neck. Fremont liked his privacy. He wasn't going to enjoy this.

6
Demons and Doilies

Humphrey was irritated. "It is very unusual for Lord Fremont to entertain guests this late."

"I understand that," Cass said placatingly as he walked them through the hall. Thalia had gone back to the office, feverishly stringing twigs and crystals and straw together like her life depended on it. It very well might. Cass and Gideon were here apparently being very rude. "Unfortunately, there is a very serious problem he needs to be apprised of. Urgently." One they might have caused. She left that out.

This softened his rigid shoulders. "I see. In that case, I think he will brook the interruption."

Cass suspected the *he* in the sentence might be Humphrey.

Gideon looked up at the ceiling as they went. "Are these the original moldings?"

"Why, yes," Humphrey said, sounding pleased. "So few notice the finer details of the house. I can give you a tour if you like."

"Yes, actually," Gideon said, still looking upward. "I would like that very much."

"Splendid." He knocked at the study door. "Begging your pardon, my Lord, but Miss Friend and Master Gideon—"

The door opened suddenly, and Alexander appeared in the doorway. "Cassandra," he said, surprised. "You—you look lovely." Humphrey cleared his throat, and Alexander shook himself. "Please, come in. Excuse the state of me."

To say she hadn't noticed that he was more on the disheveled side would be a lie. The vest was cast aside, and his sleeves were shoddily rolled up. His usually smooth hair was mussed on one side, like he'd been worrying his hand in and out of it.

Gideon said quickly, "Well, I think I'll take Humphrey up on that tour now. See if I can't get started on some recommendations."

"Recommendations—?" Humphrey started.

"You're going to want to protect the house. But I do appreciate the moldings."

The door shut, and Cass folded her arms and pushed out a quick breath, then attempted a smile. "I see we're not the only ones working late."

"Scrambling to get some things done before tomorrow," he said ruefully. "It's always this way. Leave plenty of time and yet they still seem to catch up with me."

"I'll try to be brief."

"I welcome the distraction." He went to his desk and sat on the edge, his fingers drumming on the wood. "Something's wrong, isn't it."

"I'm afraid so."

"Leave it to Ruhan to somehow have a more complex wedding than international politics allow for. What is it?"

Cass had of course thought about how to explain this on the way over. She'd had it down word for word. But looking at him now, all concern and attention despite obvious weariness, it was all…off. Was anybody this earnest? Was he just listening this closely to get her to leave? Did that matter?

"We looked into the matter of a devil accomplice of the Lord of Demons this evening. Not only is the affair much more complicated than we thought, we…were left with no choice but to kill him."

His face went a little gray, but he nodded. "Unfortunate, but I imagine that is part of your line of work at times."

"It is. And ordinarily, I wouldn't even report it to you, but here's the thing." She shifted her weight off her left leg and set her hands to her hips. "When a creature whose soul is bound to a demon dies, that demon gains possession of it. The Lord of Demons is now aware that we are aware of this aspect of his operation. Not only might he look in, he may retaliate. Most likely by attempting to sever our contract."

Alexander pushed his face into his hand and breathed. "By killing me, I presume."

"Yes. Or me. Likely both to be safe."

"May I—may I ask…why the dickens would you let him know?"

Cass wanted to grit her teeth and argue back, but it was a thoroughly fair question. "That is a more complicated question than you know."

"Try me," he said flatly.

"For one thing, he was stealing people's souls," she said, maybe a little hotly. "Trading them to magicians as currency. So there's that."

Instantly, Alexander's irritation faded into nausea. "That's…that's a *thing* that can happen?"

"Yes, and apparently, it's going to happen to a lot more people unless we take *every* advantage from this Lord of Demons," she told him shortly. "That means making the choice between tipping him off and removing a tool from his belt. I am sorry. Really."

He shook his head. "I'd…have done the same," he admitted.

He did have *knight* in his litany of titles. Cass looked at him. "That doesn't mean we're leaving you on your own. Gideon's looking at how to magically fortify the house right now, and I can come by often."

For the first time since the news broke, a smile cracked his exterior. "Well, then I will welcome that distraction often."

And again! What did that *mean?* She pushed her hair away from her face and avoided his eyes. "I can move my operations here if that suits you. That way we can respond quicker, and you can be on top of what we're up to."

"Yes, please do." He looked at the ground. "Cassandra…danger is not new to me. It traveling down *this* avenue is."

"We'll apprise you of about major movements more promptly."

"Thank you. It's a relief." He glanced at her, indicating her dress. "May I ask what the occasion was?"

She laughed a little. "Work. Not much call for dressing up otherwise."

"That is a shame," Alexander said. "Perhaps…if you're amenable to the idea, of course…there might be call for something like a restaurant?"

Cass blinked a few times. "I…I'm sorry. Did you just…?"

"I…did," he said, sounding surprised about it. "I apologize, that was forward."

"I would like that," she said. "If there were a call for such a thing."

He flushed brightly. "Ah. Good. Well. Perhaps sometime in the coming days if you're not terribly busy and I'm not terribly busy…."

A riddle cloaked in a mystery, this one. One moment an absolute flirt, the next stumbling over himself as though shocked words could come from his mouth.

Cass reached for his shoulder to stop him. "Yes," she said simply.

Gideon had to return sometime, and pleasant distractions had to give way. Alexander escorted them to their coats in the foyer as Gideon recounted his recommendations. "I didn't find any lingering hints of His Lordship, but that doesn't mean this place is invulnerable. His name was spoken here."

Alexander shifted uneasily. "What consequences does that carry?"

"Immediately, very few, but the longer it goes unaddressed the more power it gives him. He may be able to look upon the sitting room as early as moonrise tomorrow. Thalia is already at work on wards. I will join her immediately. If we work quickly, we may be able to beat him to it."

"What…would a ward entail?"

Gideon unstuck the collar of his coat from the point of his horn and finished getting himself together. "Nothing intrusive. Some sticks, some herbs, a faintly glowing rock here and there. We do have to get up into your rafters, though. All of them."

"All."

"If we protect just the one room, there's a chance he might be able to start corrupting wards from the outside," Cass explained. You want a complete seal." She leaned her weight away from her still vaguely complaining knee. Alexander seemed peaky, nervous. Demons again. She understood. They made her nervous enough she almost didn't take this job. "They're the best at this in Amaranth. They'll have you covered."

"I don't doubt it, it's just—it seems a time-consuming process."

Gideon nodded. "A house this size…we're probably looking at a hundred individual charms, plus the warding spell itself, which takes a few hours. We'll definitely be working through the night."

Alexander shook his head. "I'm sorry—tomorrow won't work."

"I…really can't recommend leaving your home unprotected, Lord Fremont. Not even a day."

"I understand, but unfortunately there are complicating factors out of my control." He looked up at the ceiling. "It had to be now."

Cass tilted her head. "Alexander. Listen." His eyes came back down to meet hers instantly. "Whatever it is—we're not prying—it will have to wait, or move, or something. You can't reschedule the Lord of Demons."

"No, I can't," he said with a tense laugh. A bit of an edge returned to his words along with it. "But neither can I change this particular, *classified* appointment, much as I wish I could."

She knew she shouldn't, but she frowned at him. If she was allowed to be impertinent for flirting purposes, she'd take her license for offense, too. "I said we weren't prying."

He blinked, like he'd been startled out of a reverie. "You're—you're right. I misplaced my frustration and it was indecent. Once again. I apologize. I swear I am not always an ass."

Cass cocked an eyebrow and a corner of her mouth. "I think I'm going to need you to prove that."

"And I will, with a clean slate of good behavior. Unfortunately, the fact remains that it will have to be the day after tomorrow," he answered with a rueful smile. "I truly wish it weren't the case, but I'm obligated by my duty to the throne to keep this place locked down tomorrow. I'm sorry, that must be as frustrating to hear as it is to say."

Gideon looked between Cass and Alexander for a good few moments, then cut in, "All right. In the meantime, instruct your man and any others you may have working for you to stay out of the sitting room entirely.

Perhaps even the adjoining hallway. If there are sounds, cover your ears immediately. With luck, he may peek in once or twice and decide nothing interesting is going on and leave it be."

The doubt in his voice well filled the gaps in his words and the air in the foyer, but there was nothing for it but to nod.

Cass added, "Oh, and keep the windows shuttered in there."

Alexander paused. "We usually do if we're not using it, but what…?"

"Light does funny things to demons," Gideon said. "Might be good, might be bad, best not to find out which by accident."

He looked a bit queasy again. Cass stepped hesitantly up to him and placed a hand tentatively to his forearm. "Day after tomorrow. We'll take care of it."

Alexander covered her hand with his briefly and managed a bit of a smile. "Thank you. I'll be better behaved."

She smiled back. "But not too much. I enjoy trading impertinence."

His smile widened. "Good night, Cassandra."

Gideon was strangely quiet. Cass expected substantial ribbing. On the long steps down from the Upper Ring, she nudged him with an elbow. "Where's your head?"

"Hell," he answered with a sigh. He tilted his face up to the clouds, which had since filled in the sky. "This feels a little more familiar, actually. Like a ceiling."

"The demon lord got to you."

"Yes," he said bluntly. "And I'm worried he may be getting to you."

She paused on the step. "What?"

Heavily, he said, "I'm sorry, Cassie. I didn't see it until Fremont told us we couldn't come tomorrow. He wavered."

"You mean…?"

"He's shifty. Some sort of shapechanger."

Her stomach dropped. "Gods *damn* it — !"

"I know. I'm sorry."

"I hate being right," she muttered darkly, stalking past him.

He trotted a bit to catch up. "There's—a chance you're not. There are some benign shapeshifters."

"Like what?" she demanded. "They're fey if they're not demons."

"And you think fey are all what you've been told they are? Cass. Look at me. Has devilry turned out to be anything like you thought?"

"Sort of? Like, thirty percent?"

"Yeah. Exactly."

She folded her arms in a tight X across her chest. "Come on, Gideon. You know that this is shady."

"Yeah, it probably is," he sighed. "But it might not be. We'll have to see."

Starting with learning what was so secret about tomorrow.

"You look like shit," Jules whispered over the lip of her comically small and frilly teacup. "Did you sleep?"

Cass tried not to look too openly petulant. The tearoom was full of Upper Echelon assholes, which was exactly the reason they were there, but between that and the sheer number of tassels and doilies and linens you weren't actually supposed to use, it wasn't a terribly comfortable place to be petulant. "Yeah. Not well. But yeah."

Jules clucked sympathetically. "Gideon told me. We'll figure it out! Every relationship has a weird miscommunication or two when they're just starting out."

Cass leaned stiffly over the table, trying not to knock into the china. "Most *miscommunications* don't involve fundamental facts like *are you a demon actually.*"

"Yeah," she admitted, downtrodden. The bell at the front door rang, and her dark eyes lit up. "Oh, it's Lissa!"

The slight blonde girl looked to Cass like she'd dressed in tearoom camouflage. Lace dress, lace gloves, lace hat. She was basically a porcelain doll draped in doilies. She caught sight of Jules and waved cheerfully. Not petulant, Cass tried to remind herself. Hard when she was wearing daggers and everyone else was wearing doilies.

Lissa Ironwelt was the firstborn daughter of a lord whose position was mostly ceremonial. This meant that the time most noble kids spent learning how to take over governance of trades and civic duties, she spent picking out yet more doilies and collecting gossip. Most disparaged her for it, but Cass recognized that in reality, Lissa traded in information, and that probably made her the most formidable and untouchable noble in the Upper Ring. It gave her the relative infallibility to still associate with a disowned friend.

Up on her toes, she placed a delighted kiss on both of Jules' cheeks and settled into a chair. "Ladies, always a pleasure. Has my payment been procured?"

"Petit fours en route," Jules confirmed.

Her sharp blue eyes shone. "Excellent. Let's begin, shall we? I do have a salon to attend this afternoon, but I could *not* pass up the opportunity to see my Julia and her droll friend Cass. Say something droll!"

Cass leaned back in her chair and gestured to the next table. "Um… sorry, if you're looking for a poodle to do tricks, you'll have to borrow that lady's."

Lissa clapped her hands together and let out a little squeal. "Oh, there it is! I've missed you both so. How *are* you? How is business? It seems a lifetime since your work has brought you here."

"Yeah, mostly been taking Market level stuff," Jules put in. "But not right now! We've got a big one we can't talk too much about. Exclusive contract."

"Oooh! Catnip! But I'll weasel it out of you later when the boss isn't watching."

Cass poked at the sugar cube dissolving in her teacup. "I can hear you."

"Of course you can, darling. That's why you're here. Let's see, let's see. Alexander Fremont. If you've already talked to the usual biddies, you know the basics. Best friends with the Crown Prince from childhood. Reclusive yet well-mannered, not antisocial in the slightest. Handsome, well dressed, but not over-concerned with appearances. Attends gatherings neither rarely nor frequently, but never throws them. Watches over the teachers and their pupils. That's about it, right?"

Cass nodded, trying not to grit her teeth too hard as she realized that that, more or less, was still about all *she* knew about him, too. "I hope you have more for us."

"Bits and pieces, dear, bits and pieces. Ohh, cakes!" Lissa clapped as the waiter placed a tray full of delicately iced sweets on the table in front of her, as though knowing that that was where most of them would disappear. She scooped some of each onto plates for Jules and Cass both and busied herself with the remainder.

Jules chuckled. "Lissa, I still don't know where you put those."

"I have a separate stomach for desserts," she said, wiping at her mouth primly. "Is there something in specific you were hoping to know?"

Is he a demon? Cass wanted to shriek. She'd buy Lissa all the cakes in Amaranth if she could answer that question. "He was adopted."

"Mm. Sad bit of business. The Fremonts were an older couple. They had been unable to produce an heir. Julia's father—" She quickly turned her eyes down. "Lord Evards…suggested they take in a foundling. By all accounts, they quite took to young Alexander immediately."

"How old was he?"

"Very small. Two, I believe. Julia and I were only a mite older so I cannot say for sure."

There went her Fremonts accidentally took in a demon theory. Demons were tricky, but she didn't think even they would embed themselves in a human household for decades for a scheme like this. "And his parents were also private?"

"Not at first, but they became more so as Alexander and Lady Fremont took ill."

Cass tried not to sit up too far. "Took ill."

"Mmm. Yes. We were…twelve, so he must have been about eight or nine, wouldn't you say, Julia?"

She flushed slightly. "Oh. Oh, yeah. I remember that."

"Poor thing. He wasted away in the span of a month. All the color drained from him. Even his hair!"

Cass tried not to frown too intently. That sounded more curse than illness. Curses could come from anywhere, manifest lots of ways. They could corrupt or not. "And his mother?"

"She'd always been frail. It wasn't much of a surprise when her health took a downturn after his did. She finally passed when he was…thirteen, I believe. From then on the elder Lord Fremont took up Alexander's education and duties until such time as he was old enough to discharge them. He was…"

"An asshole," Jules mumbled into her teacup.

"Strict," Lissa corrected.

"If that's what you want to call that."

"He never did anything improper."

"And that's the measure of a good man?"

"Are we waxing philosophical?" Cass interrupted.

"Apologies," Lissa answered. "Either way, he was severe in the public eye. One can reasonably assume he was severe at home."

Cass tried not to let the bouncing of her leg joggle the entire table. They were getting further from what she needed. "Any talk of what they caught?"

"Mm. No." She hesitated. "Though…it did coincide, strangely, with — but I'm sure that's nothing."

"What?"

She shook her head. "Forgive me, my mind is wandering. There was an excursion the young prince and lord undertook with some minders and other young lads for training out of the city-state. I can't quite remember where. In the wilds somewhere. I suppose it may have been something exotic he brought home."

That was more relevant. "I don't suppose you could find out where?"

"I could ask, but will it really help?"

Jules put her cup down. "Cass likes to have all her flanks covered."

"Surely you don't suspect…?"

"No, no. It's more of a preliminary…without saying too much, we're just checking on historical connections outside Amaranth. Even an illness might count."

"All right," she said slowly. "There were a few excursions like that. Some for a length of time. Fairly normal for a knight attendant, although his young age at his appointment was very unusual."

"I meant to ask about that," Cass added, trying to sound casual. "His service record must be impressive."

She laughed. "Oh, goodness no. He's never seen combat."

"What? You're sure."

"Absolutely. His father passed four years ago and he took charge of the education system the moment he graduated university. He'd never have had time."

Cass stood abruptly. Jules swallowed awkwardly around a mouthful of cake. "Cassie? What's wrong?"

"I just—I should get going. Sorry. Jules—you have it from here."

"Sure, but—"

Cass felt herself start wandering away as though she was sleepwalking. Angrily, but the parlor still passed in a haze. She made it to the street before she felt her arm catch. She whipped around to find Jules there, face creased.

"*Hey.* What is going on with you?"

Cass clenched her jaw hard a moment, then pushed out a breath. "That bastard lied."

"We…knew that, though, didn't we?"

"Well— yeah," she fumed. "But it's…it worked. Like, really worked. That shit doesn't usually work on me. Anymore."

Jules sighed, reached out for Cass' arms and took up her hands. "Oh, Cassie. I'm sorry. You let your guard down."

"And it was a bad idea, so I'm going to go deal with it."

"How?"

"Poorly, probably."

"Cass."

"I just want some answers," she said. "And I'm not finding them here.

I'm going to hunt down some records or something. That's all."

Jules tilted her head. "Not going to go do something dangerous?"

"Not planning to."

She let go of Cass' hands and nodded. "Okay. You…coming back to the office today, or you done?"

"Don't know yet. Depends on what I find. Thalia and Gideon are working on crafting wards and probably will be till late. Bjorn's doing supply runs. You're in charge."

"You'll come get backup, right?"

Cass started walking backwards, spreading her hands. "I told you I'm not planning on doing anything dangerous."

"Okay, because it looks like you're going to go yell at the guy."

"Nah. Won't help. Just want to."

She managed a smile. "Okay. Let me know what you find out. And then I'll help you punch if punching is warranted."

Cass gave her an appreciative little smile and walked away from the tea parlor and directly toward everything she just promised her best friend she was not going to do.

7

Moonrise

The gate to the Fremont estate was locked tight. Cass was neither surprised nor put off. She kept her hands in the pockets of her leather coat and walked around the tall hedge and rows of conical trees that blocked the rolling grounds from the streets at large. She knew from her past visits that there was also a low stone wall tucked between those and the ubiquitous baneroses.

She still hadn't figured those out. They weren't terrifically pretty. Not ugly, but not the lavish blooms in most gardens of the Upper Ring. They were used to ward off certain pests, but usually on farms, not in the yards of lords. Either way, they carried prickles, and if she dropped straight into them, she wouldn't get back out cleanly.

As she continued her casual stroll, she kept an eye on the inhabitants of the streets. The paradox of the Upper Ring was that it was built for the few, but the people moving through were often not the nobles or wealthy merchants themselves, but those who served them. There were the live-in staff, like Humphrey. Career staff who were part of households for all intents and purposes, a sort of middle-class. But the bulk were servants and skilled workers who commuted from below. Most of them didn't even see Cass, so absorbed in their own lives, talking to each other on their way home, escorting cadres of rich kids, running out for one last ingredient, taking a walk in the fading afternoon light. Strangely, she didn't feel as out of place as she thought she might. It made the work easier.

Whoever kept the grounds did a very, very good job. The hedges were nearly immaculately uniform all the way around except a spot on the north side where the sun didn't quite reach. A bare spot in the hedge very near a corner, tucked far away from the main street. A good place to start. She waited for the stablehand carrying an armful of tack to the dirt path down the way to disappear completely, then wedged herself into the bald patch between the hedge and the wall and observed her cover.

The hedges came up two or three feet over the top of the wall. If she kept herself low at the apex, that would keep her hidden from the street side. The trees on the other side varied in height, probably on purpose. She gritted her teeth and turned to face the wall.

Damn him and his carefully considered cleverness. She'd have to do this the hard way.

She clambered up, finding purchase on the oddly-sized edges of the stones. If he'd been really smart, he'd have gone with bricks. Bricks were smooth. He thought the hedges and the brambles were enough, but you don't cut corners if you're going to commit to this much secrecy.

Cass crested the top of the wall and peeked over. The rolling green of the lawn spread ahead of her, punctuated by trees and a stream. A ways to the southwest, the manse, mostly closed up save for a few lit windows. The property carried on a good distance to the southeast, mostly woods, it seemed.

She wasn't sure what she thought she was going to see—armed mercenaries everywhere, or the prince's guards, or a bunch of demons—but it was so quiet. Not a soul in the garden as there had been on her first visit, no movement from the house. Tentatively, she edged to her right where the cypress trees were a little taller on the garden side and carefully rolled herself up and over the wall.

It was a better idea in theory than in practice. It felt like she was going to roll off the other side and drop the full ten feet to the ground, alert anybody who might be here, and that would be the end of it. She managed to throw out a hand and snag the edge of the wall to dangle precipitously for a moment. After the panic passed, she took a breath and controlled the descent. Not silent, but quiet enough. Good.

Whatever was happening here would be at the house, and probably at night. He had been particularly distressed about the amount of time that it would take to do the warding.

She glanced up. By the looks of it, she had maybe an hour more of sun. She put her back firmly to the wall and used it to edge her way bit by bit toward the house the way her mother had shown her how to thread a cord through a channel to gather fabric.

It gave her plenty of time to stew. It was one thing for her to be toyed with. The last two before Alexander had done plenty of that, and she'd learned from it, kept on. That was fine. But she wasn't about to let her people be dragged into some supernatural double-cross involving the godsdamned Lord of Demons—which he had seemed genuinely surprised about. She didn't doubt *that* was genuine.

A sharp bramble caught on her thigh, and she bit back a curse word and paused for a moment to let the sting pass.

It was not unheard of for the fey to have turf wars with demons. There was a possibility he was some sort of changeling entity embedded with a noble family. Potentially dangerous, but possible to strike a bargain with and then hopefully exile to the wilds where he belonged.

Or he could be a rival demon now in way over his head, which felt somehow much more likely. All the deflections about being afraid of demons would be *precisely* the sort of thing a demon pretending to be a human would do.

There were fringe possibilities, she guessed. A warlock, or some sort of charmed one, or possibly even a demigod from one of the further flung countries. The mythology was expansive, and it felt like every day the arcanists claimed new discoveries from some corner or another of the world.

She knew for sure that fey and demons were real, and he lied with the ease of both. Ugh, she had been so sure he was genuine. Foolish.

With the house in sight between the trees, waiting for the cover of night, she paused to reflect on the sightlines. The lawn dipped in a little valley that she could use to move laterally parallel to the house if she wanted to, keeping her reasonable protected from the windows. The difficulty was moving in any pattern other than a straight line. If circumstances led her to the wood, she'd have plenty of cover, but the lawn was such an open expanse.

In the end, she decided on a small copse of trees just atop the upward slope. It put her within sight of the front and side doors with a decent view of the path from the back door, which led around to the wood. It was just a matter of getting there.

Cass kept low and her eyes locked on the house as she emerged from the cypresses. There were two spots where she was unavoidably exposed. So far, she'd seen and heard no one, but she still meant to move as quickly as she could through those spaces.

The baneroses grabbed for her, but she detangled herself quickly and rushed across one of those vulnerable spots into the valley and waited, listened. She heard no shouting, scrambling, any indication that she'd been spotted. Okay, she told herself, giving her heart a moment to slow down and the rest of her a moment to catch up. Not bad.

From there, it was simple enough. Inch along the valley, keeping her crunching footsteps to a minimum.

Last moment of exposure. Cass gathered herself and bolted from her safe spot toward the trees.

A few steps shy of the copse, the front door opened.

Of course. Of bloody course.

She suspended her breathing and burst into a full sprint toward cover just as Alexander and Humphrey emerged. Thank gods, they seemed too absorbed in their own conversation—a weary one, by the look of it—to notice her last flailing footsteps. She was still a little far to hear, but they were walking along the path toward her. If she kept to the shadows, stayed still….

He looked different. Every time she'd seen him, he'd projected a sense of carefully cultivated ruffled-ness—a deliberate *oh, you've caught me in the middle of my work with my vest open, but I am still in fact wearing a coordinating perfectly tailored three piece suit* air. Today, he was just rumpled in his shirt-sleeves and breeches, maybe even yesterday's shirt, his long hair hastily tied back. He seemed peaky, slouched.

Humphrey was Humphrey, hustling alongside. "…take advantage of your absence this evening."

"I'm substantially less concerned about my social standing right now," Alexander answered wearily.

"You should be more," Humphrey tutted. "If you miss another of these, questions will be asked."

"All right, all right, put me down for the next one. Or just put me down. Might be kinder."

"My *Lord*."

Alexander threw his hands up, stopping short on the path. "Does *any* of this matter, Humphrey? You know what's about to happen tonight. What sort of thing's made me hire mercenaries in the first place. You expect me to frolic and exchange niceties with these spoiled barely functional overgrown children with…*that* happening in the background?"

Humphrey fixed him with an impressive glare. It must have been hard to stare down someone with two feet on him, but somehow, he managed. "It will keep them from questioning you while you accomplish what you must. So yes, Lord Alexander. It matters."

Alexander's jaw set like he was about to fire back something, but he stopped, his posture going stock straight. Humphrey opened his mouth, but Alexander held out a hand to quiet him and looked around.

Cassandra held her breath and remained motionless.

"What is it?" Humphrey asked.

Alexander scanned a moment more, then looked back, disoriented. "I thought…never mind it. Rattled nerves, I suppose."

"I'll have the house prepared for the warding by the time you've risen tomorrow. That should help."

He nodded, casting one more uneasy glance toward the darkening lawn before turning back toward the wood and moving along. "Best get moving. He's not going to wait for us to settle my affairs."

Cass swallowed her hammering heart and watched them get a ways ahead of them. Once they got into the wood, she might be able to follow unseen, but she had to let them get that far first. She counted paces in her head, let them get a good lead, then darted forward into the trees.

She could hear them, see Humphrey consult a notepad by the light of his lantern a few times, but couldn't quite make out the words until they stopped again, this time by some sort of stone building built into a natural ridge. Alexander held his hand out for the lantern and hung it on an iron hook while Humphrey fell to handling a large ring of keys.

"Is the offering ready?" Alexander asked somewhat grimly.

Humphrey stopped. "Lord Alexander, please, call it something else."

"Something other than what it is?"

"Thinking of it is going to make me old," he mumbled queasily, resuming his search. "Yes, and it came in this morning. Hopefully that should be sufficiently…fresh."

"I still don't know why he rejected the last one," he muttered, looking around and rubbing at the back of his neck.

"No use fretting about it," Humphrey answered. "Aha."

He fit a key into a large lock on the front of a massive steel grate. The whole thing swung open with a shriek. Cass couldn't see what was beyond, but it seemed dark and cavernous. Alexander glanced in and sighed. "Remember. Plug your ears tonight, all right?"

"What if you should need me? I won't be able to hear the bell."

Alexander placed his hands on Humphrey's shoulders. "That's not important. Lord of Demons. We talked about this."

"Yes, yes." He reached up and patted Alexander's arm in a foreign, fatherly sort of way, like it didn't happen very often. "Be…be safe, my lord."

"Good night, Humphrey."

Alexander squared his shoulders and walked into the dark. Humphrey swung the grate shut behind him with a clang that Cass could feel reverberate through the trunk of the tree she crouched behind. Humphrey snapped the lock shut and paused for a second as though he wanted to say something else, but thought better of it, collected the lantern, and walked back toward the house.

Cass waited. Her mouth felt like the dirt during long stretches of drought, but she didn't even dare wet her lips. Offering? That sounded like demons. She wasn't in a good spot to do much about that on her own, but she did want a glimpse of exactly what they were dealing with.

A scream split the stillness of the forest. The kind that unfurled out of a person when the agony was too much to hold in.

Cass sprang forward to the balls of her feet and tried to listen. A man's voice. Alexander's? Or…?

He'd mentioned an offering.

She bolted toward the cavern and pulled the daggers from the sheaths at her thighs.

The screaming grew louder, the sound distorted as she ran. It played in weird ways off of the trees, the back of whatever hole in the hill they were using like a cell. The voice grew hoarse, cracked, croaked. She made it up to the bars, tried to see in. The dark was too complete.

"What are you doing to him?" she shouted.

No answer but low moans of pain. She could smell blood.

"Hold on." She dropped a dagger back into a sheath and fumbled for the lockpick she kept tucked in the hidden pouch on the underside of her pocket's flap. "I'm coming for you. I won't let them do this."

It was just as well she could barely see the lock. Most of picking a lock was the feeling, the way the springs gave when she manipulated the pins inside. This was harder with her hands shaking. The groans were getting quieter. She felt time slipping from her as his strength seemed to be fading from him.

When the shaft finally clicked loose, he was reduced to whimpers. Cass threw all of her weight into pulling the grate open. Even still, she only managed to drag it enough to squeeze through. It would have to do.

She struck a match at the mouth and pushed her way into the cavern. At last, she could see that there were in fact, two collapsed figures inside. One was a deer carcass—the source of the blood smell, an arrow still stuck in it. The live, trembling body was eerily reminiscent of a man in some ways, but not enough. It was covered in silver fur and sinew, and Alexander's clothes lay folded next to it.

Cass started to back up. Shit. She'd been wrong. Extremely wrong.

The figure stirred. A pair of eyes gleamed in the match light. Cass scrambled to the outside of the grate. "I'm sorry," she called in. "Really. I thought—something else. Are you…?"

Alexander unfolded a bit at a time without a sound. Cass swallowed hard and shoved at the grate again, fumbling with the lock at the same time. The match had burnt out, but even without she could see the shape of him, hulking, hackles up. He wasn't conversational.

With a snarl that sounded horribly too much like his human voice tortured into a lupine growl, Alexander lunged for the grate. The force of the impact flung Cass back to the dirt, knocked the air from her lungs.

The good news was that the grate was still between them. The bad news was that she had a few seconds before he figured out how to circumvent that. She grabbed a handful of dirt and slung it into his eyes. He turned his face away and snarled.

"Sorry," she shouted as she scurried to her feet and started climbing the grate like a ladder.

He recovered himself by the time she hefted herself to the top of the mound, but to catch up to her he would need to go around. This gave her a bit of a head start, at least.

All right, she thought to herself. He and Humphrey had clearly thought this through quite a bit, down to a meal in the bunker. If she ran to the house, maybe he had some sort of protocol for dealing with an escaped…transformed…? That hadn't quite sunk in yet, but she was sure it would when he started crashing through the underbrush behind her. She made a sharp turn around a tree and made for the direction of the manse.

Except Alexander seemed to have given up on running up the slope and jumped straight up the embankment, which dwindled her head start some. Shit. He loped along easily on all fours, unnaturally elongated angular legs flying. He was going to outrun her.

So what was left? Was she just dead?

He hadn't climbed the grate. She leapt and seized a tree branch and started climbing again.

Alexander skidded to a stop at the base of the tree, rearing and swiping up at her. She swung her legs out of the way of his claws and hurriedly grabbed hold of the next set of branches. "Can you…tell who I am?" she gasped.

She wasn't expecting him to sit down and have a chat, but she did watch for any hint of comprehension, a flare of recognition. He dug his claws into the bark and tried to haul himself up after her, slid back down. Cass hauled herself up a few more layers and sat for a moment.

"Are you chasing me because you're angry or because you're not yourself?"

Alexander crouched low and prowled in circles around the trunk of the tree, evaluating. His face was all but unrecognizable, pulled into a long snout. The eyes were…uncanny. His, but not his. She was going to guess he wasn't himself. If the offering was the deer, then the "he" rejecting it was likely this creature. Him, but not him.

The offering. If she waited him out, perhaps he would move on to easier prey. She leaned her head against the trunk of the tree and breathed for a moment.

"I probably taste bitter anyway. Shit." She dislodged a pine cone from next to her and tried tossing it behind him to see if it would catch his attention. No such luck. "Still too smart for that. Should have guessed."

He huffed and circled the tree a few more times, growling low in his throat. He reared again and slammed into the trunk with his…hands? Front paws? The tree shook, but held firm. He tried again and again, snarling his frustration in hot clouds of steam in the rapidly cooling night air. Cass wrapped her arms around the tree and held on. The roots weren't giving way. As long as she didn't, she'd be all right.

Sitting still gave her a chance to breathe, but it also gave her a chance to process. What the hells. She wasn't an expert by any means, but she knew a curse when she saw one, and this one was distinctly fey in flavor. They came in two varieties: vindictive and chaotic. Either somebody wanted to pay him or his family or the country or humanity in general back for some perceived slight, or somebody got bored. Either way, it was cruel, and now she felt like an asshole who probably deserved to be chased up a tree.

She'd done her due diligence, she tried to tell herself. It was sketchy as hells.

Nah, she was an asshole. The tree swayed under repeated assault, and she clutched harder. Jules had tried to stop her. Good old Jules. Usually had her back.

"You're just going to hurt yourself," she told him. "I don't want that. You don't want that. Come on."

He slammed at the trunk once more and stalked a little ways away, pacing, his body rigid. His eyes, formerly fixated on her, scanned between the horizon and the dirt as he grunted his dissatisfaction. Could he be reasoned with? Maybe not completely, but something seemed to shift. She watched, waited, tried to make herself uninteresting. Alexander's pacing began to range wider and wider, and after a time he disappeared into the trees. A howl too much like the tenor of his voice uncurled in the darkness a ways off.

Cass shivered. Okay, she told herself. He'd left. Possibly not forever, and he could certainly change course at any moment. She shifted around the tree so that when she climbed down, she'd already be on the side closer to the house. And then she started down as quickly as she could.

When her boots hit the forest floor, she paused and listened. There was no immediate spring or growl or scatter of leaves. A good sign. She let out a hopefully quiet breath. Being quick was good, but what she really needed to be was quiet. His hearing was likely very good. She stepped as lightly as she could and edged her way from the wood.

Cass wasn't sure how long it took her, but the lawn came into view at last. That in and of itself was a long walk to the house, but closer. She was getting closer, and she could probably afford to move a little less cautiously. She picked up her pace once she hit grass and moved down into that valley, hoping it would keep her blocked from sight if Alexander emerged from the wood at its height, about where she estimated she heard him. From there, she'd hop up to the bridge and take the path all the way back to the house. She could do this.

The surroundings cooperated, stayed quiet save for the pad of her footsteps and the occasional whistle of the wind through the collection of baneroses growing along the underside of the bridge in the ravine. These looked less deliberately planted and more like they'd spread from the cultivated ones on the property and no one had bothered to remove them. Cass reached around a tendril to find a handhold on the old wooden bridge and started her climb upward.

Behind her, thundering footfalls. Her stomach lurched. She scrambled to try to throw her leg up and over the side of the bridge's platform, but the sheer adrenaline of hearing something barreling straight for her made finding the dexterity for that unfortunately a bit difficult. Instead, she swung back into the ravine below. Alexander was charging from above. Perhaps—

He was careful, and the baneroses were odd. There was a reason they were here. She swallowed hard and forced her way through an opening just a little too small for her between bushes. The thorns scraped at her skin, stung, grabbed for her clothes, but she didn't care. She wedged herself in and prayed.

The massive wolfish shape landed in the ravine with a slam that dislodged some rocks and sent them clattering across her. His jowls were matted with blood—either he'd found the deer or something else—and his eyes locked onto her hers as he prowled forward.

"You want me to be afraid of you?" she asked shakily. "Well. It's working. I'm hiding in a rose bush. Come get me if you want me."

He huffed. The warmth of his breath hit her from there, the overwhelming stench of the blood causing bile to rise in her throat. Alexander took one more step closer, then jerked back as though something had whipped him. He snarled in the direction of the plant.

Cass closed her eyes unbidden. "Thank you, you brilliant, paranoid lord," she whispered. "You're pissed at yourself now but you'll be much happier in the morning."

The wolf-version kept snarling, snapping, trying to circumvent the bush. He approached from all angles and every single time yelped and turned back. What was it? It produced some sort of oil that made pests hate it. Maybe it was the same. Unlike the tree, however, the frustration didn't seem to bore him. It enraged him. He tore at the bridge, tried to dig at the rocks, howled his anger into the air.

"I'm not leaving," she told him. "Sorry."

His eyes snapped to her again, fury boiling over. And then he turned and thundered away.

She sat and shook in the baneroses until she was certain she couldn't hear him any longer. Could she stay here all night? Baneroses weren't poisonous, but the stings were starting to burn. No, this was a temporary respite. She needed to get somewhere meant to be a more permanent shelter.

The thorns dragged across her thigh as she stood and emerged from the bridge. She braced herself and looked around. No sign of Alexander. She gritted her teeth against the burn starting along the slash and started to try to clamber out of the ravine.

Too slowly she realized that the burn quickly faded into utter numbness. The leg went out from under her, her head hit something hard, and that was that.

8

Daylight

"Cassandra!"

There was nothing but a dull throb where her mind should have been and an irritating brightness. She blinked. Something was moving her, shaking her by the shoulder. "Cassandra. *Cassandra.* Don't do this."

She managed to force her eyes open and met blue sky, dust, and just a bit of a very worn out, very dirty, and very undressed Alexander. "I'm—up. I'm awake."

"Are you hurt?"

"Sort of."

He looked her over. His eyes seized on her leg. "Did I do this?"

Her head still felt sluggish. "What?"

"Did *I do* this?" he demanded.

"No—got caught in the roses."

He collapsed backwards out of her range of sight, his hoarse voice cracking. "Good. Good. Shit."

"That's…about right, yeah." She took stock. Her head hurt and the gash across her leg stung like a bitch, but other than that, she thought she might be okay. She reached up to her neck and unwound her scarf, unfolded it into a large rectangle of cloth, and held it out to him. "I…am really sorry."

He took it from her and hastily fastened it around his midsection so he could sit up. "I should hope so! Why the *hells* would you let me out?"

She sat up too, rubbed at her head. "I thought you were being attacked."

"Why did you come here in the first place? I *told* you it was out of bounds."

"Yes, well." Cass winced. "I also thought you might be a demon."

He frowned deeply. "So you thought I was a demon who was getting attacked."

"I don't know—it was all pretty confusing, all right? You were evasive and hiring other people and then all of a sudden it's *the Lord of Demons* and after that Gideon tells me you're—surprise—also a shapechanger and you're taking risks about not protecting your house from the godsdamned *Lord of Demons,* so yeah, I'm going to check that out!"

Alexander's frowned intensified. "Why?"

"Because you bloody hired me to!"

"Yes, *I* hired you to!"

"I am bound to the couple, not the contractor. That means you're a suspect, same as everyone. Did you read the damn contract or didn't you?"

He stared into the dirt for a long moment, and then he started to laugh, the sort of laugh that came out completely unbridled and unbidden. He covered his face with his hand and laughed into it until it passed. "Ruhan, we're both fools. Again."

Cass leaned forward. "You…er…all right?"

"Oh, you know, just having my worst fear realized," he groaned. "The one I've worked to avoid my *entire godsdamned life.*"

"I—am really sorry about that."

He laughed again, let his hand drop. Perhaps he didn't. The closer she looked, the more she realized that his entire body seemed to be trembling. "I suppose it just means you're very good."

Carefully, she got to her knees, tested her own strength. Aside from the stinging, her leg seemed all right. She got to her feet and collected herself, then held out her hands to him. "Humphrey will be worried."

He looked at her hesitantly a moment. Now that she was more alert, she saw that the arm he'd cradled when the Lord of Demons had come calling had been torn open at some point long ago several times. Angry red and white layered scars snarled from his shoulder all the way to his wrist, spread onto his chest. Yeah, she was an asshole.

Alexander took her hands at last and allowed her to help haul him unsteadily upward. He *was* shaky, and far colder than she remembered his skin being. She took his arm and slung it over her shoulder so she could help him along. It seemed to take most of his strength, so she let him carry on in quiet.

He broke it himself as the house came into view. "I can't help but notice you're handling this surprisingly calmly."

"You've seen the company I keep," she answered. "I'm overly suspicious, not judgmental."

He managed a brief laugh. "I see. You don't find anything about this odd."

"Oh, I find it extremely odd. But plenty of things are, including each of the people I work with, and I've already pried enough. I am sorry, by the way."

He nodded limply. "I did rather…knock you around for the trouble. You're sure you're not hurt."

"Not by you."

Ahead, the front door flew open and Humphrey shot out across the lawn. "Lord Alexander! Dear gods above, where have you *been*—? Miss Friend?" His eyes narrowed as the pieces must have started fitting together in his head, and he clearly did not like the picture they made.

Alexander lifted his head. "Humphrey. It's fine. We'll call it a misunderstanding until we're rested enough to argue about it properly."

Well, that boded poorly. Cass supposed she was glad she wasn't just fired or disposed of on the spot. Humphrey took up Alexander's other side, glowering at Cass on the way. "Yes, of course, we must get you to bed. You must not have eaten much."

"Doesn't seem that way, does it."

"I will make the broth extra strong. Rest first." He paused to shut the door behind them.

"Show Cassandra to a guest room, please."

Humphrey and Cass both looked around Alexander's chest at each other as though this was the worst idea they'd ever heard. "That's really kind," she started, "but I can…."

"It really isn't," he answered. "We still have much to discuss, and you're covered in banerose rashes. Neither of those can be addressed too terribly much later."

Ah. She was being held. She supposed that made sense. She breathed out. "I understand."

He looked her way briefly, a hint of contrition passing across his features. "I hope we can come to an understanding."

"The word *please* might help."

Humphrey glowered. "You are not in much of a position to—"

Alexander stopped him with a look, then separated from them and braced himself along the wall. "Thank you both for your kindness. I can see myself to bed. Humphrey, please make Cassandra comfortable, and I mean that."

"As you wish it," Humphrey said, clearly wishing he'd said something else. "Follow me, please."

Cass fell in behind him without complaint, mostly because she was tired herself, and if she was going to be detained, it might as well be in a lord's guest bedroom. He led her down a long hallway of more paintings, some of people, others of places. Humphrey opened the last door at the end of the hallway and gestured for her to step inside. She did, pausing in the entryway.

"I didn't mean him harm," she said. "I still don't."

"I am not at liberty to comment," he returned tightly.

"No, I guess not. I hope it's a little comfort, though."

"Hmm." He stalked past her into the second door, which led to the guest suite itself. A bigger bed than Cass had ever seen in her life sat in the center of the floor. Humphrey drew back the dark blue silk curtains and tied them to the bedposts, then went back toward the door. "There is a bath in the door to your right. In the armoire, a robe. If you deposit your clothing on the chair in the vestibule, I will have it cleaned or replaced."

"Oh. That's really nice, but—"

"Do you want to keep having a rash?"

"I…suppose not," she answered.

He nodded curtly, then looked back at her. "You did return him. For that, you have my thanks."

What would I have done with him? she wanted to snap, but she stopped herself. There were plenty of legitimate, unsavory answers to that that other mercenaries may well have considered. She just nodded.

Humphrey peered at her over his glasses a moment longer. "There is a powder in a green glass jar on the vanity," he said, a bit of the edge to his voice gone. "It should help with the banerose sting. Put it on before you bathe."

"Thank you," she said.

The surliness returned. "It is my duty, madam. Leave your clothes and shut the door to the suite. I will fetch you when Lord Alexander has risen."

He turned and stalked from the room. The door locked behind him with a heavy click.

Cass felt like she should enjoy the sudden luxury with which she found herself surrounded. The bathtub was larger than her entire kitchen, and the bed! She could compose love poetry for that mattress. She hadn't known furniture could *be* this comfortable. The exhaustion numbed her to the novelty far too quickly, and she washed and shambled her way to that miraculous bed only to fall asleep within moments.

If she dreamt, she didn't remember it.

This time, consciousness came at the hands of a knock, accompanied by Humphrey's voice. "Miss Friend. Are you well?"

She sat up abruptly, making absolutely sure her robe was secure around her front. "Yes—yes. Sorry. I must have been tired."

Humphrey opened the door a little ways, politely not looking quite at her. "Lord Alexander informed me you took a blow to the head and instructed me to let you rest. However, the lateness began to concern us."

Cass touched her forehead carefully. There was a nice swollen lump precariously close to her right temple. "Sorry about that. Again. I'm usually such a light sleeper."

"Do you require a physician?"

"No—no, I think I'm fine."

He eyed her skeptically, but in the end, straightened. "Good. Lord Alexander requests your presence. If you are able, you will dress. I regret that I was unable to suitably clean your shirt and breeches. I hope you will find the replacements acceptable."

"I'm sure it will be fine," she answered, slowly swinging her legs out of bed. The slash stung, but with the oil gone it seemed mostly irritated. "Thanks, Humphrey."

He nodded once and retreated. She put herself together and wondered how she could find the violet-blue silk blouse and well-made linen breeches unacceptable, especially given that she was still not in good standing. Maybe this boded better. Maybe she needed to stop trying to figure out how things were before she knew *what* they were, since that seemed to be the initial problem. She knocked on the outer door for Humphrey.

This time, he led her past the sitting areas, the formal dining room, everything that was meant to make an impression. They passed through the kitchen—light, tiled, surprisingly cozy, arranged for utility, and currently in use. It smelled of something savory baking away. Humphrey gestured to a nook off to the side and pulled an apron off a hook. "You're needed in there. I'm needed in here."

"All right," she answered slowly. "Thank you."

He waved her off and immediately fell to making quite a bit of noise with pots and pans. Cass edged around the corner and found Alexander at a table in the nook, papers and an open ledger spread out in front of him. He was still in a robe and sleep clothes, his hair tied back, eyes sunken.

"Do you ever take breaks?" she asked.

He glanced up, set his pen down. "Do you?"

A fair point. He'd tried to force her to take the night off and she wound up wrestling him in the rosebushes. She folded her hands in front of herself. "I'd…like to extend my apologies again."

"Come have a seat," he said wearily. "Let's block out the Humphrey sounds. At least for you."

Cass gingerly edged into the wooden bench on the opposite side of his, and he reached out to swing the little breakfast nook door shut. They looked out onto the same rolling lawn she'd snuck around. In the noon sun mottled by some fresh clouds, it was fresh and emerald and…truly embarrassing to look at. She set her hands on top of the table and waited.

Alexander looked at her frankly. "You likely have questions."

"You owe me nothing."

He observed her keenly. "Are you expecting castigation?"

"A hell of a word."

"I am in charge of education."

She sat back, looked at her hands. "I don't think I've fully figured out what's going on here," she admitted. "There's a piece I'm missing. You're not conspiring against the prince as I feared. But there's an element moving that I wasn't aware of that I bumbled against last night."

"Correct."

"If you tell me, will I be in danger?"

"You're already in danger, Cassandra," he answered, a silver eyebrow arced. "Triply, now. I tried to keep you out of the last two pieces of it."

"And I ran straight into it."

He nodded. She set her hands in her lap and sighed, watching the shadows of the clouds move over the grass.

"And still, I'm surprised," he said, following her gaze. "You just let me shut you into a very small room with one of the dangers."

She shrugged a shoulder. "Whatever Humphrey's making will taste better than me."

Alexander laughed in spite of himself, then looked down into the steaming mug next to him. "You're half right. This broth is…wretched."

"It must be good for something. You've drunk half of it."

"How do…?" he stopped. "You're clearly a fine investigator. And you were right to suspect me."

Cass shifted her weight. "Are…you admitting to…?"

"You are already guilty of treason by the letter of the law, Cassandra. I'm explicating a little more." He sighed. "I don't wish Ruhan harm. I love him as my own brother. To my own detriment. Repeatedly. But I must work against his law to survive."

"Wait," she said. "Did you hire us to—?"

"To protect the wedding. Nothing more. My treason happens in the margins, and ideally, you were supposed to know nothing of it."

"All right, so maybe you do owe me some explanation," Cass said, frowning.

Alexander leaned back against the window and closed his eyes. "I have spent the last twenty years ensuring this story was never told," he said at last. "I have buried the words under lie upon lie. I'm not convinced people weren't killed to cover them."

"You don't know?"

"I was a child."

"The trip out of Amaranth."

He glanced up. "Ah. You did some additional digging. Yes. I was eight. Do you know much of how the social circles of the Upper Echelon move, Cassandra?"

"Not much," she admitted. "Jules mostly frames them in profanities."

"She's correct. Everything is fair game." He picked up his mug and glared into it. "The friendships children form. With whom your elderly uncle likes to play checkers. It's fucking awful." Cass lifted an eyebrow, and he drank heavily from the mug and made a face. "Speaking of fucking awful. Yes, I swear. Nobles are people. I'm mostly people."

"I'm mostly relieved we're dropping all the pretenses."

"Well, I literally bared everything to you this morning and I'm metaphorically doing it now. May as well." He pushed at his forehead. "My father was…ambitious. He saw that Ruhan and I got on well and he encouraged it. We were happy enough with it, since it meant we got to play together, but that is…well, it's a bit strange, when one of you is a prince. Unless we slipped the minders, which we certainly did plenty of, there was a certain amount of…."

"He always won the games, didn't he."

"And decided what they were. And when they were done." He grimaced. "Ruhan didn't care for it either. We managed to be friends despite all that forced time, not because of it. This excursion to the wilds…I hadn't wanted to go. Father insisted. All of the children seen as Ruhan's closest compatriots would be going. It was every bit as ridiculous as I'd feared. These children, given spears, jockeying to be closest to a young boy who is uncomfortable but feels like he has to allow it, in the middle of fey territory with a handful of guards for protection. Whatever could have gone wrong?"

Cass leaned forward. "You don't need to tell me."

He shook his head, smiling crookedly into the depths of his mug. "Oh, let's dig it all the way up. Why not? I didn't throw elbows like the other children. There wasn't a point. Even if you did win the spot next to Ruhan, you'd lose it two minutes after. I think he noticed me keeping to the outside. He came to me, told me the whole thing was stupid and that if he could really pick it would be him and me in the back like this and the others could smack each other around in the front."

"That's…a lot to put on kids."

"It was," he said heavily. "It was also the best two minutes of my childhood, because it was possibly the only time I felt like someone saw the same nonsense I did. It ended. Something charged out of the brush straight for Ruhan. I saw it coming, so I pushed him out of the way and took the attack in his place."

Cass bit her lip, leaned her arms on the table in front of her. "Why?" she asked quietly.

Alexander laughed. "That's what I was supposed to do, Cassandra. What do you think they were training us for?"

"Where were the adults? The guards? That was their *job*."

He seemed slightly taken aback. "I…well. Even if they reacted late, they did fend it off before it could drag me away."

Cass felt herself about two inches from yelling. They didn't even *kill it?*

She refrained, because he seemed a touch fragile in this moment, but everything about this felt wrong. "Did they know what it was?"

"No," he answered heavily. "And I'm grateful. It permitted me to get home, at least."

"What does that mean?"

"There are no curses in Amaranth. Had they discovered I was carrying one, I would have been left behind."

Her hand balled up in her lap. "You were a *child*. You wouldn't have survived."

"The intended effect, yes." Alexander gripped his mug tightly, his knuckles whitening.

Cass sat there for a moment, trying to sort through fury and confusion and the feeling like she wanted to take that mug and just hold onto his hands until he felt like he didn't have to clench anymore.

"I don't understand," she said, trying to make her voice gentle even though she felt like shouting. "You saved the prince's life. You took the curse *for* him. And still they would…?"

"Ruhan doesn't know. Well, he does. To a point. Ugh. Context."

He looked around the nook as though for something to illustrate his thoughts. In absence of a chalkboard or a textbook or something to fiddle with, he went back to holding onto the mug of broth concoction.

"So," he resumed, "I came back, chewed up, sick, and starting to do some strange things. My mother wanted to go to the King and Queen and ask for protection for me in light of what I'd done. My father, on the other hand, thought he could fix me if he just brought in the right witch or doctor or…." He shook his head, words apparently failing.

The door to the nook opened, and Humphrey slid two plates onto the table. An enormous golden brown flaky biscuit housing bacon and cheese and spinach and egg and yet more layers of more things that smelled delicious sat in the center of each one. He also bore a fresh mug, which he swapped for Alexander's old one. *"Drink it,"* he commanded with a hand to his shoulder, then disappeared and shut the door again.

"Who's the lord?" Cass asked.

Alexander laughed weakly, staring down the new serving of broth. "In terms of commanding this home, it's certainly Humphrey. He's the one holding this place together since the first full moon."

"Is that the trigger?"

"The unavoidable one. The others I've learned I can resist." He glanced distastefully at the mug. "I'm going to get it over with. Forgive the unseemliness."

Cass hadn't seen someone throw a drink back like that since she and Jules were younger and more interesting. She got the distinct impression that Alexander wished the drink was less interesting. The second he was done, he grabbed a napkin and coughed to disguise a gag.

"What's in it?" she asked.

"Do you really want to know?" he wheezed.

"Curiosity, cats, all that."

"Rabbit bullion, beef broth, a collection of herbs, some chicken feet, I believe, and whatever was left of the poor creature I didn't utterly destroy last night left to boil."

"Oh," she said.

"I lose a lot of strength between shapes," he said, a bit defensively.

"I'm not judging, I'm just…that's a lot."

"Why do you think I've kept it buried?" he asked, gesturing with his fork and knife. "It's not how most people prefer to have breakfast. Hells, it's not how I prefer to have breakfast."

"This does smell good, at least," she said.

"Humphrey has perfected this aspect of the morning consolation."

"So he's been with you the whole time."

Alexander nodded. "He and my mother were close confidants and equally cunning. It was their intervention that secured the tenuous but decently secure arrangement I have now."

"The knighthood?"

He balanced his fork on the edge of his plate and looked at her. "Has he told you?"

She shook her head. "A guess."

"How could you *possibly*—?"

"I had been trying to understand how that piece fit," she answered quietly. "I don't know many knights who gained their titles at ten years old. And then I remembered that knights of Amaranth carry certain protections from prosecution so long as they remain in good standing and fight for the crown. Humphrey is concerned with your standing."

"You…are absolutely the most dangerous person I could have hired for this job," he said with a little laugh. "Yes. By the time I was ten, my father had run out of reputable people to try cures on me. Around the same time, the King passed away. Ruhan's father was…well, I'm sure you remember some things."

The state funeral passed through the town and turned into a festival. "My mother's tavern was busy that day."

"Yours was probably not the only one. Mother and Humphrey saw an opening to speak to the Queen, who had been somewhat silenced by her husband those years. It was a gamble, but so was leaving me to my father's devices."

"They told her?"

He nodded. "They confessed what had happened. What I had become, what I had endured. The Queen was grateful I had saved her son, so she showed mercy. I received a knighthood in exchange for two conditions. No one could ever know about my affliction, and I would take a binding to render me unable to transform. Mother eagerly agreed, for which I can't blame her. If such a thing existed, I'd probably take it voluntarily."

"Did she…ask you?"

Alexander smiled down into his lap. "No."

Cass leaned her forearm on the table. Hesitantly, she reached across and found his hand. He tensed, and she pulled back, about to apologize. He shook his head and softened his posture again, extended his hand to meet hers.

"I…. Did you speak to me last night?" he asked.

She nodded. "Hopefully nothing offensive."

"I can't recall with any clarity. I just—why?"

"Why wouldn't I?"

"Why—? I could have killed you."

"You didn't."

"Not through any action of mine. You survived, and I am so…." He trailed off. "I'm thankful you're talented enough to handle me, but I need to be clear. That can never happen again."

She nodded, putting her hand back in her lap. "I understand the situation now. It won't."

"As far as the crown goes," he sighed.

"You don't think the prince would understand?"

"I don't know," he answered, and the honesty sounded so wretched that she understood why the half-truths came so much easier. "I know what he's been told about the law. I know what he's been told about me. The Queen, rest her soul, told him I controlled it years ago and lock myself up out of an abundance of caution. That would be why the grounds are off-limits once a month by order of the prince."

"I see," Cass said. "So we're both in violation."

"Correct." He pushed his hands together and rested the fingertips against his chin. "If things were to proceed the way they usually would up here, this is where we would use our mutually assured destruction against each other. If you're truly the investigator you seem to be, you've realized that I disdain this sort of maneuvering. I also don't think you're that sort of person."

Her mouth twitched up in a bit of a smile. "We could try trust."

"I would prefer that."

"The mutually assured destruction is still there as an option, though."

Alexander winced. "I was trying not to pull attention to that."

"Where's the fun in that?"

"You're…really not going to ask any questions."

"I could, if you want me to."

"I suppose I'm just astounded at how calmly you're taking this."

Cass hesitated. "Just one," she said softly. "Has no one ever talked to you before?"

He looked up, off guard. "It wouldn't make any difference," he answered. "That other me is not—not the best listener."

"It seemed to make a difference to you this morning."

Alexander fumbled with his words, looked away again. "It did," he said at last. "Thank you." His fingers found hers under the table, then pulled back. "May I…?"

She reached for his hand and held on in quiet for a while. "There's still been a demon in your house," she said at last.

"I'd been trying not to think about that."

"I know. I can send Gideon and Thalia. Um…."

"You said he caught me."

She nodded. "Devils can spot shapeshifters if their forms are unstable. I guess yours is."

He pinched the bridge of his nose. "It can be threatened by a good startle. Like a demon showing up in my house."

"He can be discreet." Cass paused. "Although I suppose he did tell Jules when we thought you might be a demon."

The color drained from Alexander's face. "People are *not* supposed to know, Cassandra."

"I know, I know. They were just very worried about me. They talk about me behind my back. It's irritating—in an endearing, nosy sort of way."

He looked at the table, his face troubled. "And can you ensure that it's just behind *your* back?"

"Yes." She leaned forward, searching for his eyes again. "Hey. Yours is not the first secret uncovered in the course of duty. Not even close. It's safe with us."

He glanced up. "All right," he said.

"Okay," she replied, disconcerted.

Cass retrieved her coat and limped her way to the door, juggling her right dagger sheath under her arm since wearing it across the thorn cut didn't feel wonderful. She needed to get Gideon and Thalia here right away. She hadn't heard anything from the hall, but that didn't mean any-thing, and demons loved the hell out of secrets. Lots of them got spilled this morning. Maybe she'd send Bjorn and Jules just for the extra sets of hands.

"Miss Cassandra," a voice behind her called. She turned. Humphrey, his apron discarded. He looked her up and down, his voice low. "Lord Alexander trusts you a great deal. Please. See that that trust is not mis-placed."

She watched him carefully. His posture was as stiff as ever. Nothing about the way the words came out was any different than he might have delivered them any other day. But she saw the fold to his eyes behind those glasses that he just couldn't help. The fear. She smiled just a little.

"How lucky he is to have you," she said, glancing to the portrait of the late Lord Fremont glowering over the foyer. There was no fear in those eyes. Conviction.

Humphrey looked to the floor. "I suspect I shall see you shortly."

"I hope someday you'll look forward to it."

Just the tiniest hint of a smile. "Someday, perhaps."

9
Before the Crown

Gideon spent a lot of time in the rafters over the next week. Alexander had gotten used to watching for dangling hooves and tails before entering rooms, and Bjorn walked around with his arms instinctively outstretched in case a devil or a tiny witch wanted to plop into them. There had been no repeat appearances of a supernatural nature.

Not unexpectedly, Humphrey had retrieved handwritten threats for Alexander and Cass both from the post. With the manor already warded and the targets of said threats gathered in one spot, the work moved from the tired office to the Fremont estate.

Jules and Cass passed a few hours each day on the floor of the parlor Cass had absorbed as a base of operations, dissecting handwriting and syntax, trying to match assassins to gangs preemptively.

On this particular evening, Jules hauled in a box. "Found the threat box."

Cass put down her notebook. "Oh. Good."

Alexander poked his head in from the study adjacent. "You found the what?"

"My catalogued box of ransom notes and threats," Cass answered, opening the lid and paging through the tabs. "Sometimes they're useful to cross-reference."

"And this is a thing you've used…more than once."

"Oh, yeah," Jules answered. "You hire us, there are people other people hire to try to stop us. Sometimes we get lucky and it's somebody we've dealt with before."

Cass bit her lip as she compared an old note. "Sometimes. I'm going to guess not this time, but I'm not going to *not* check and let this be the one time I'm wrong."

His chair creaked as he stood and came into the parlor. "I suppose I'm still hung up on the fact that you've kept the threatening messages you've received. And they're numerous enough that there's a box."

"My clients, mostly," she corrected. "A few of them were for me."

"Cass is the kind of person who keeps jam jars because they might be useful someday," Jules informed him.

"Hey. Take it easy, rich kids. It's different on my side of town."

"See, I get that, but opening your cabinets is a legitimate avalanche danger."

"You're embarrassing me in front of the client."

"I think he still thinks your death threat box is cute if not a little intense."

Alexander laughed and disguised it with a cough. "I believe it's a good time for some tea. Would anyone else care for some?"

"Please," Cass answered.

"Thanks, but no," said Jules. "I think Cassie's going to send me on errands to punish me in a minute."

"Keep digging and I will."

He touched Cass' shoulder and excused himself.

Jules waited until he left, then looked at Cassandra. "So."

"Nothing new. Drop it," she answered, without looking up from her files.

"Okay, okay." She stretched out her arms. "It's nice to see you happy."

Cass smiled a little in spite of herself and kept paging through for a while. "Jules, can I ask you to look into something for me? I'd do it myself, but I think I'm going to be needed here thanks to the contract severing issue. He's demon skittish."

"Sure, what's up?"

"We found a connection to the River Rats."

She made a face. "Ugh, the sewer gang? Why is it always the sewer gang?"

"Because the world loves making you smell like shit. Can you and maybe Bjorn go under and find out who the human connection between the demons and the Rats is? Faster than going through the threat box."

Jules rubbed at the back of her neck. "Yeah…I can do that. Does it have to be right this second?"

"I mean…sooner rather than later would be good," Cass said, lifting an eyebrow. "It's a matter of time before somebody makes a swing at us or the client."

"Yeah. I just—Ellorin is having a rough go right now at work, and I need to be there for her."

"You're so *domestic*," Cass remarked.

"And you? You're cozy enough here."

"Oh, come on. You know embedding with a client isn't the same thing."

"Even if you're dating him." She snorted. "Em*bedding*."

"I don't know what we're doing," she mumbled, handily ignoring her. Years of practice. "But yeah, I mean, I guess do it when you can. But soon."

"Yeah. Soon."

Abruptly, Alexander appeared again. "Cassandra," he said, the color gone from his face. "May I see you in the kitchen a moment?"

She rose and followed after him. Cass was about to make a joke about the tea giving him that much trouble, but when she looked up, she noticed bits of silver fur poking out from the back of his shirt. "Alexander," she said, catching his arm.

He looked down. There was a patch of it on his arm, too. "I—may be panicking," he said.

"What do you need?"

He took a breath, smoothed his long hair back over his ears and shoulders. "I'll be all right. Let's discuss."

He pushed open the kitchen door, revealing an equally nervous

Humphrey, pacing the length and breadth of the kitchen with a gold-capped scroll in his hand. "Miss Cassandra," he said. "Good. You're here. This afternoon in town, I was approached by the prince's Knight Captain. He came with this."

He handed over the scroll, which she unrolled.

His Majesty Crown Prince Ruhan Wilhelm Carian Amaranth requires the presence of Lord Alexander Trevelyan Fremont and his retained expert Cassandra Marina Friend for consultation and review of current circumstances. You will present yourselves at the throne room at nine tomorrow morning.

Cass lowered the scroll. "This isn't exactly unexpected, is it?"

Alexander shook his head. "The formality is."

Humphrey took the scroll back. "And someone is watching."

"What do you mean?" Cass asked.

"The Knight Captain asked me if all was well on the grounds. He said a woman of your description was spotted repeatedly walking the outer boundaries last week, and that something was heard howling."

That would be why he was panicking. Cass managed a breath. "What did you say?"

"I confirmed that you were retained and that it would not surprise me if you checked on the property. As far as the howling, I said I personally had not heard any, but Lady Trusca does have those hounds."

Cass looked to Alexander. "Was there anyone other than me here that night?"

He pressed at his forehead. "I…don't believe so."

"Any previous association with the Knight Captain?"

"Oh, plenty. He despises me, since my title is unearned at first glance." He paused. "You think he's making problems?"

"I think it's a possibility. I also think we don't know what the prince wants for certain."

Alexander put his hands to his hips and breathed out. "I…you're right. It's just unusual for him to pull the throne room on me unless there is something serious to attend to. Either way—I had expected a bit more notice to prepare you."

"Me?"

"There are so many irritating etiquette demands. Ruhan could not possibly care less about them. His court, on the other hand, cares immensely. I had anticipated introducing you privately so that you met the man before the crown prince, but apparently he had other ideas."

"Oh," she said a little numbly.

Humphrey looked skyward. "There are *reasons* for these things, Lord Alexander. They aren't arbitrarily designed to annoy people."

"No, they're designed to make people feel small so that one person can feel large, and that is worse," he countered. "We'd also need to find you something to wear if you wish to present well."

"Can't I just wear my nice clothes?" Cass asked weakly.

"Not to court," Humphrey said. "There are rules. I can handle that if you'll allow me to take measurements."

"I…guess I don't really have a choice, do I?"

"You do," Alexander said. "You could make whichever impression you choose."

But it would reflect on him. Doubly, if anyone realized they were… doing whatever they were doing. Humphrey seemed impetuous, frustrated that they might even consider anything other than the optimal choice. She glanced over at Alexander again. Between strands of silver, his ear stood out, a bit pointed. At length, she nodded.

While Humphrey measured and lectured and made her practice as though Gideon were royalty, she sent Bjorn to make a few conspicuous loops of the grounds. Thalia promised to climb trees noticeably every now and again. She might have just done that anyway. Alexander made himself scarce.

Once she no longer needed to be physically present, she ventured back into the parlor. The study door was shut. She knocked. "My turn," she said softly. "May I see you?"

A space of silence. After a moment, he called, "Come in."

Cass edged in and closed the door behind her. Alexander stood in front of the huge window looking out on the wood, his arms folded to himself. When she entered, he turned toward her with an apologetic smile. "Sorry to disappear. I am…unused to bustle, it turns out, after all this solitude."

"Was that purposeful?" she asked. "The solitude."

He nodded, looked back out the window. "Humphrey was the only one they kept on. Everyone else either became occasional visitors or stopped coming."

"Is it too much? I can move my people."

"No," he answered. "On the contrary, it's been wonderful in a way I can't articulate. I want to become used to it."

"But…."

He turned to face her, a strained smile on his face. "It's too lovely, this charade."

"What charade?" she asked, searching his expression. Cass reached out for his cheek, brushed his hair back from his ear. "This is the most honest you've been."

Alexander took hold of her hand where it still lay close to his cheek. "The very attractive farce that I'm a person."

"What sort of—? Of course you're a person."

"I wonder if you'd still say that if you knew the extent." He let out an anxious breath. "We hint at it, don't we. You ask if I saw anyone else that night. I tell you I can't recall. You nod and let it be. Why don't I recall, Cassandra?"

"Because there was something else clouding your mind, yeah."

"Does it count as clouding when it's always there at some level?" He shivered, looking away. "That's what I'm trying to tell you. Do you understand? I am not worth—any of your trouble."

Cass looked up at him skeptically. "Right now? The same way you did then, you want to attack me?"

"Not—no. It's…ngh."

"Tell me, Alexander. You wanted me to ask questions. Why are you so afraid?"

"Because I still am very aware that you have a cut that hasn't healed just by the smell," he burst out. "Because I can hear your heartbeat and mine *rises* to meet yours when I manage to make you smile. Because if gods forbid I skip a meal, I cannot think about anything else until I eat, and the longer I go the more likely it is I get desperate. There is a reason they want me controlled or destroyed. They are not wrong."

Cass had stood there at arm's distance for all of this, but now despite herself she stepped up toe-to-toe. "They *are* wrong. And so are you. I decide who is or is not worth my trouble. I was with you that night. I spoke to you. I *do* recall. You were there. You weren't in control, but you heard me. Maybe the wolf thoughts are always with you, but the opposite is true, too."

Alexander blinked down at her as though she'd suddenly broken a pane of glass between them and the sharpness of her image startled him.

She grasped his hands, held them close to her chest. "You're a person," she said. "You're…." She pulled him in and pressed her lips to his.

Alexander's hand found her cheek, moved into her hair. It shook a little, but he held on. When they parted, he placed his forehead to hers and held her hand to his chest. She couldn't hear his heartbeat, but she could certainly feel it racing away.

"You are…remarkably intimidating," he said with a laugh.

"Did it work?"

"Consider me suitably tamed."

She rested her cheek against his chest. "Good. Don't speak of yourself that way again."

He pulled back so he could look at her. "I may have to tomorrow."

"Is he your friend or isn't he?"

Alexander went quiet, tucked Cass' hair out of her face. "Half of me."

"You don't think he could understand?"

"I think he could. I don't know if that's enough. Power makes it complicated."

"Yeah, I understand that," she said. "I just kissed my boss." She realized for the first time what she'd done. Heat sank into her ears, her face. "Ohh, no, I just kissed my boss."

"Is…that a problem?"

"It's unprofessional as hell. I think. Nobody in the Company's done this, kissing our boss. Maybe this is a bad idea."

He lifted his eyebrows. "Being fair, I always thought of the arrangement as the other way around."

She stepped back. "I'm being serious. This is my livelihood."

"So am I," he answered. "I'm in your world right now. Your livelihood. If all I am to you is your employer, so be it, but in the space I inhabit… personal and professional are intermingled constantly. There's very little escaping it."

Cass looked at him. "If…that's the case, perhaps inhabiting your world a little wouldn't hurt. How would that work, exactly?" She cleared her throat and smiled weakly, putting on an officious voice. It sounded like Humphrey. "Lord Alexander Trevelyan Fremont, Cassandra Marina Friend of the Friend Event Company renders unto your household the application of the beginning stages of a casual romantic entanglement pursuant to the—"

He stepped up to meet her and laughed, stopping her with a brief, shy kiss. "Have I mentioned that the trappings of my surroundings frustrate me somewhat?"

"Right. Go out with me sometime?"

"Yes," he said.

"Do you want to stay quiet? Bjorn will probably have found some rocks he'll want to show off."

"Do I look presentable?"

She looked him over. Honestly, there were some noticeable points here and there, but her people weren't going to say anything. She smoothed his hair back down over his ears and the fur protruding from his shoulders. A useful reason to keep it long.

"There. No one's the wiser."

He smiled a little nervously. "I think I like bustle," he said, holding the door for her. "In moderation."

"Moderate bustle," she agreed.

As she emerged, the parlor door opened, and in came Bjorn from his rounds. This precipitated a Gideon drop from the ceiling.

"Surprise prince sighting!" he cried dramatically, dismounting from Bjorn's well-muscled forearms. "Quick! Make a formal show of obeisance, Cassandra Marina Friend, or I shall *have your head*."

Alexander lifted an eyebrow. "Ruhan isn't—"

"Silence! The crown has spoken! Now. Avert the gaze. Right hand on heart, left arm out gracefully. And bend the knee. And hold. Two. Three. Four. And rise. Two. Three. Four."

Cass attempted to oblige as she had through every increasingly demanding prince ambush so far, but on the upward movement her knee creaked, locked into place, and she stumbled. Alexander lunged and caught her by the outstretched arm. "All right?"

"I would be," she said through a grimace as he eased her back up, "if *someone* would stop putting me through my paces like a show pony."

Humphrey prodded Bjorn further into the room and retrieved a footstool, which he nudged in Alexander's direction. Humphrey declared, "These things do take practice."

"I get that, but I do think there's such a thing as over-practice." She sat on the offered stool and unkinked her knee with an audible crack. "I'm a big girl, Humphrey. I can run a business, I can tie my shoes, I can greet a prince."

Bjorn chuckled. "Ask her how she hurt the knee."

"Oh, please don't."

Gideon looked up at the rafters as though wondering if he should disappear into them again. "Here we go."

Jules looked up at him. "Five?"

"Ten," Gideon said.

"You're on."

Bjorn gestured to the group. "You are wondering why we are five and not six, yes? We were six once. Three boys, three girls, makes sense. We had Duncan." He rolled his eyes. "Duncan was pretty."

"Yeah, he was," Gideon muttered.

"Duncan spent most of the time making himself pretty. Very concerned with 'peak fitness', less with being fast. So we are doing wedding for big toy making family. Cassie is fighting maybe…ten demons on her own."

"Ha," Gideon said.

"Damn it," Jules muttered, tossing him a gold.

"It was three," Cass interjected. "Why do you always have to exaggerate that?"

Undeterred, Bjorn carried on, his eyes wide. "Jules and I are busy, eh? Thalia and Gideon don't touch the demons. So Cassie tells Duncan to help, and he holds out his finger shushing-like and he says, *I am stretching.*" Bjorn mimed grasping his ankle and making a scene of pulling out his hamstring. "So the demons go to attack Duncan instead because he is an idiot, and Cassie is too kind to let him get eaten, so she lunges quick to attack them all at once. One two three, all on same blade. Too much weight for the knee, but saved Duncan's life. He had nerve to tell Cassie about stretching."

"I presume he is no longer with you, then, because he was fired?" Humphrey inquired, trying to mask his curiosity.

"No, he fell in a hellmouth," Thalia said from behind him.

Humphrey jumped, his hand to his heart. "Miss—Thalia, I wish you would not *do* that."

She blinked. "He was a bad listener," she said, confused.

Cass saw the twitch to Humphrey's eye. "All right, I think that's enough reminiscing. Perhaps we should be going."

The twitch somehow intensified. "I wondered if perhaps you might wish to stay the night in our guest chambers, Miss Cassandra. After all, you will be departing from here in the morning."

This must have been wounding him inside, which meant there was something else at work. She knew by now that it was benign enough— he wasn't going to poison her or anything—but he definitely wanted to keep an eye on her. She glanced at Alexander. "What do you think?"

His face went a little pink. "I—er, of course would welcome the extra time…but if you have other matters to attend…. Then again, it would save you time, and perhaps we might have lunch after if all goes well— and here I am angling for more time. Excuse my avarice."

Humphrey's eye twitched harder, Jules smirked in Gideon's direction, and Cass smiled. All right, that made it worth it. "In that case, I'll gladly accept your generous offer, Humphrey. Thank you." She rose stiffly from the footstool and touched Alexander's arm. "I'm going to walk them to the gate and debrief. Should I say goodnight now?"

He shook his head. "No—no, I'll say it properly when you return."

"All right." She took a step—or tried to; her knee went wooden again. He caught her again. "Thanks."

"Any time. You're sure you're all right?"

Bjorn laughed and clapped Alexander on the shoulder. "That is not a good question to ask Cassie. You will learn. Pleasant dreams."

Once outside, Cass glanced back. In the parlor, Humphrey gestured. A lot. Alexander sighed, made placating motions.

Jules hooked Cass' arm on one side and Gideon grabbed the other. "I do believe an 'I told you' so is in order," Gideon said.

"What?" Cass sputtered. "No."

"I did mention the possibility the shapeshifting was benign."

"All right," Jules said. "We're just happy she's happy. You are happy, right? If you're not happy I'll break his shifty little—"

"I'm probably happy," Cass said quickly. "Good gods, the pair of you. What I am is nervous. We're not making much progress on the demon lord."

Gideon stroked his chin. "I think I got a guy I can ask about that. Cassie, come with me day after tomorrow. Jules, you in?"

"I…can't," she said with a wince. "Ellie's got a work thing. I told her I'd go."

Gideon threw his head back. "You're killing me."

"But you would let Cass flirt?"

"Cass' flirting is 1. Flexible, 2. Rare and something we are trying to *encourage,* and 3. Fun to observe. You're all…married."

"Sorry to disappoint," she said. "But you two can handle it."

"On our own and broken-hearted."

Cass glanced her way. "Well, since you're going to owe us one—and speaking of Ellorin's work—can you do me a favor?"

"What obscure law do you want me to look up?" Jules asked.

"The justification on banning cursed people from Amaranth. I hope it's not, but I'm starting to wonder if it's going to be a factor in the case."

"Because the demon lord on top of international politics isn't complicated enough?"

"You're telling me."

Jules nodded. "I'll see what I can find."

"Keep it quiet."

"I'll wait until three in the morning to open the books really quietly."

"Smart ass." Cass held the gate open. "Bjorn and Thalia are going to make some more perimeter check-ins."

Gideon shrugged. "I'll make my way over if I get bored in the middle of the night. Cassie, dear…." He hesitated. "Be careful. There's nothing like mortals vying for power. Tyrants are well and bad, but watch for those who wish they were."

"Like my frigging dad," Jules mumbled.

Cass nodded. Gideon patted her cheeks. "Well, you're nervous enough. Get your beauty sleep. Don't just cavort with your pretty lord all night."

"Excuse you," she said, her words muffled with her face smushed between his hands.

"I'm teasing. You haven't even had the *what are we doing what are we* talk, have you." He looked at her and shook her head for her. "I thought not. That's all right. In your own time, love." He let her go and sighed at the ground with a little smile. "Everything in its time."

10
Court of Vipers

The carriage awaited outside in the morning mist. "I'm confused," Cass told Humphrey as he finished checking her teal and gold beaded gown for, gods forbid, stray strings. "The Wyvern's Rest isn't far from here. Why wouldn't we just walk?"

Humphrey sighed. "It's about presentation, Miss Cassandra."

She knew it was useless arguing with him, and yet she couldn't help but go over the costs in her head. She'd worked with vendors before. She knew how much it cost to hire a driver and horses, and it seemed a terrible waste just to keep up appearances.

Cass shook herself internally. It wasn't 'just' right now. Appearances were actually important today, which is why Alexander was taking his time getting ready, trying deliberately to maintain an air of calm. He came at last into the foyer in a nicely fitted blue suit trimmed in gold, pulling nervously at the cuffs. He stopped short and smiled at the sight of Cassandra.

"Good morning. You look very nice."

She fluffed her skirt in a self-conscious little mock curtesy. "Thanks. I clean up okay."

"More than. I wish the occasion were different, but truly, lovely."

She smiled, trying not to look too giddy about the compliment. He smiled back, apparently trying just as hard not to look too giddy about giving it.

Humphrey cleared his throat. "We should be off."

"Right," Alexander said, his smile diminishing. "The vipers await."

"Lord Alexander."

"I'm just getting it out of my system," he said. He guided them out of the manse and locked the door behind them. "I am capable of behaving myself, if you can believe that."

"I can," Humphrey said. He walked to the carriage at Alexander's side. "I raised you, if we're to be blunt about things. I am concerned, however, about your uncouthness today of all days."

"I'll be perfectly…couth." He made a measured bow to Cassandra and held out a hand to help her up into the carriage.

She took it and settled to the overstuffed green velvet cushion. Cass wasn't trying to overhear, per se, but bits of conversation wafted in from outside. "I know you're nervous. I'm nervous. I need you to trust me."

Humphrey sighed. "I do. I do. Just…please. Remember. Consider your standing. Nothing unseemly."

"I understand." The carriage gave a bit of a lurch as Alexander joined her inside and shut the door. "Forgive him. He clucks like a hen when he's worried."

She laughed a bit nervously. "He…doesn't like me much. I don't think that's helping."

"Humphrey?" He blinked in surprise. "No, he's just…how do I explain?" The carriage began moving as Humphrey got onto the front, and he shifted his weight on the seat. "He has a knack for this game we're about to walk into. Much more than my mother had, and I dislike playing, so I abstain as much as possible. He mistakes my disdain for failure to take it seriously, and with you, I do tend to openly mock it, because frankly, you sense it's mostly pretentious bullshit too. It's my doing. Please don't take it personally."

"He likes the pretentious bullshit?"

"Oh, no. Not at all. He learned to wield it as a weapon. Many successful heads of households need to." Alexander rubbed at the back of his neck and sighed regretfully. "It's…I'm afraid you'll see it firsthand in short order. It's deeply unpleasant."

"Any worse than fighting vampires?"

"I can't say for certain," he said with a bit of a smile. "You'll have to tell me when we're finished."

"Vipers?"

"That's always rather how I've seen them," he said quietly. "They tend to coil around each other to strike when it's opportune."

"Who are they? Separate from the nobility?"

"Ah. No. The selfsame. Members of the Upper Echelon." He leaned back and watched the Upper Ring pass by the window. "They come to court to advise the crown prince on matters of governance, should he ask for their input. It's largely ceremonial. He has the elected officials from the districts to consult. But still they come, hoping to bend his ear, to be seen, to make connections with some of those officials."

"Have you gone?"

"Occasionally, when I must." Alexander touched his ear nervously. Still rounded. "I have chosen to do much of my work myself, whereas many of my peers rely on hiring battalions of clerks, which frees their time up for court. Neither is an inherently superior approach, but one certainly keeps me safer."

"What is it they want?" she asked quietly.

He seemed hollowed out, the way he had the morning after the full moon. He considered his words as if selecting the right ones might winnow the cost a bit more acceptably. "A variety of things. Some want security for their own families, to ensure they stay right where they are. Others are more cruel and really just want to see others embarrassed for their own satisfaction. Still others are obsessed with some perceived hierarchy. If my house were embroiled in scandal and the prince were to cast me from my place, another family could be elevated to my work. Education is seen as a more noble pursuit than others, and therefore would carry more social capital."

Cass frowned. "And how many untitled people would get hurt for this maneuvering?"

"More than I can bear to think about. It's why I keep my head down."

"Do you think that's enough?"

"I'm—sorry?"

"You know about the consequences of these ploys. Is simply surviving them enough for you? You don't feel any responsibility to end them?"

Alexander looked back at her in a mixture of panic and curiosity. "I… suppose I hadn't quite considered that until now. I have been focused on maintaining my post—not for myself, mind, but because I…I mentioned my mother, yes? She felt strongly—as do I, having benefitted from her guidance—that education is the surest way to better a person, a people, and a society."

A bit of her irritation melted. "The public schools. That was her."

He nodded. "It was not well-received. The idea that all children should be taught past what would be needed to produce monetary gain. She pushed at her father for *years,* and when she came to inherit his seat she risked every bit of social cache that she had. Quite dangerously."

"My mum said that was when things really changed."

He nodded, a bit of pride pulling at his lips. "There are still those who would prefer to teach only basic sums and reading and then send children straight to work. I don't want to see that happen. I don't wish to risk that."

"I understand that," she said begrudgingly.

"And I understand what you mean. If I could change it all, I would."

"Your friend could."

Alexander laughed quietly. "Not entirely untrue, but not as simple as it sounds, either. I hope that someday he can. I hope to be part of it."

The carriage moved over a different sort of cobblestone, and Cass glanced out the window. They were crossing over a long, high, thin white bridge she'd only ever seen at a distance. The mist started to burn off, leaving the beginnings of an endless blue sky.

He forced a deep breath that by now she recognized as an attempt to stave off the other Alexander trying to make an appearance. She leaned forward and took up his hands. His long sleeves covered the scars—all except one that peeked from under the edge of a cuff. Cass touched it gently with the edge of her thumb. "You'll be all right," she promised.

He tendered her hands within his. "Whatever happens in there—I am happier for having had the chance to be honest with you. Truly."

"I still wish I'd used my words."

Alexander shook his head. "I wouldn't have...I don't think I would have had the courage to admit it. This is how it had to be."

The carriage rolled to a stop. They held on a moment longer, looked at each other, leaned forward for a kiss. The door opened, and they had to pull apart instead. Alexander gave her an apologetic glance and got out to extend the little stairs so that she could follow.

She emerged to the spires of the Wyvern's Rest rising in front of her, bright white and gold in the daylight. They stood in the cobbled forecourt, lined with topiaries trimmed into curving wisps. A few steps toward the edge of the platform, and she could see the whole towering bowl of Amaranth spreading below, the mountains to the south and east, the sea to the west, the wild wood to the north. It knocked the breath back into her, the vastness of the world. Sometimes she felt the city-state might be all of it. Not even close. Alexander came up close behind.

"Tell me this is still amazing to you," she said, barely louder than a whisper.

"It is," he confirmed.

"We *have* to show Gideon. He's fascinated with heights. This will break his—" Humphrey cleared his throat behind them. She nodded and turned to follow him.

They crossed the forecourt through the wide maw of the gateway. On the other side, white stone planters full of flowers and trailing vines overflowed over canals of still water. Across the open space, Cass could see terraces leading down to streets.

"Are people living here? Like...part of the city?"

Alexander nodded. "A part of the Upper Ring called the Corona. Is it not widely known?"

"Not at all," she answered. "Everyone thinks this is all castle."

"Oh," he said, eyes widening. "No. Goodness, no. This is all allocated. Really? That isn't being mentioned in school? It's about an eighth of our population." She shook her head, and he frowned deeply. "That's perturbing. I'll be making a note of that." He held up a hand to placate Humphrey. "We are still walking. Don't worry."

The guards, dressed in lilac silks and silver armor, began to cluster more thickly together along the colonnaded walkway. A pair stood in front of a set of large doors, and at the sight of Alexander, stepped aside and held them open. A large, airy hall stood waiting, equally pristine marble floors, columns. Huge windows mirrored the view from the forecourt, exposing Amaranth to the room. Hints of vines trailed in from outside through gaps near the ceiling. Purple banners draped from the high ceilings, and over one of the two thrones toward the front of the room. Symbolic, Cass, supposed, since the passing of the late Queen. A long purple carpet cut down the center to the dais, and to either side stood groups of people in fine clothing, waiting around, chatting, discussing, arguing. No hissing, yet.

Alexander led Cass and Humphrey near the top rear of one of these clumps of people, far enough away that they were not inserted into anyone else's conversation, but near enough that it didn't look like they were actively attempting to avoid any one. Cass made use of her well-practiced peripheral vision. Mostly older people, by the looks, though some of them had relatives Alexander's age or younger in attendance. They *definitely* noticed his presence, by the uptick of whispers and glances in his direction. Humphrey made a point of showing Alexander something in his notes. Maybe it was something they genuinely needed to discuss. Maybe it wasn't. Either way, they appeared too busy to care about the others caring about them.

Just in time for a fanfare to sound, source unseen. The horns reverberated off the marble in an imposing way as the doors opened and in clomped a bunch of metal-clad knights. In the center of them, a man Cass had only seen at a distance. Crown Prince Ruhan himself, average height, athletic, his dark brown face set in a practiced subdued smile. He looked more like he'd be at home in that armor than in the regal purple tunic and fine fawn breeches. His hand instinctively found the sword at his belt, decidedly *not* a ceremonial one. The whole room as if on cue made the informal bow of the head, and he paused at the base of the dais. "Rise, my friends. It is good to see you. Knights, to your posts."

The knights clanked their way to the outer perimeter of the room and took up spots facing in, all except one. His armor featured hints of gold, and he carried his helmet under his arm. He also looked directly at Alexander, his keen brown eyes narrowed. The Knight Captain, then. He stayed at the right hand of the throne as Ruhan took his seat.

The crown prince leaned forward and observed the congregated court. "Today is a special day indeed. To have the honor of my dear friend Alexander Fremont's company in this court?"

Alexander stepped forward and executed a perfect bow, as if he could have done it in his sleep. "You did call for me, Your Majesty."

Ruhan stood again and stepped down from his throne to shake Alexander's hand. "Have I not made it clear that you need never bow to me, my friend?"

"And have I not made it clear it's no hardship to do so?" he said with a smile. Cass had to give him credit. Anyone else watching would probably never know he spent part of the last evening pacing holes in his floor. She saw the stiffness to his back and the way his smile never quite extended all the way to those dimples in his chin.

Ruhan clasped Alexander's shoulder, and for a moment, Cass saw the smile grow a little more real, a little less nervous. The prince grinned, too, and he turned to everyone else. "Alexander has been by my side since we were too young to see over this dais. He has done me a greater service than I could ever ask. And I have asked him here today to burden him further for it, I am afraid."

Ruhan's hand slipped from Alexander's shoulder, and he stepped back up to the dais to regard the crowd. Alexander stayed still, his expression unshifting, but his eye caught Cass'. She tried to look encouraging, but she could only imagine what this had to feel like. Exposed, while the vipers waited.

At length, Ruhan looked up. "He has saved my life when we were only children, seen me through the death of both of my parents, my ascension to the throne. He has rightfully been knighted for his bravery, worked hard to provide a good start in life to all of Amaranth's children, and serves honorably in every way he is asked to. And so I hope that he can forgive me for what I'm about to do." He looked apologetically over at his friend, and then back to the nobles. "I must charge ahead and announce my engagement to Princess Ifalna of Joranhelm."

He held out his hand, and a door opened to the left. A young woman stepped in, pale, slender, her golden hair in two long plaits to either side. She looked tentatively out at the gathered people as she came toward the room, her diaphanous purple skirts flowing behind her like smoke. All right, Cass admitted to herself, it was still overkill, but she could sort of see why Bjorn might want to weep for a bit. The princess was beautiful.

She curtsied deeply before Ruhan, who held his hands out to her. "Please, my love, don't," he said. "Come, face our people."

She took the steps up the dais and looked out to the court. "I am blessed to feel the welcome of your country and the kindness of your prince," Ifalna said demurely, her voice soft.

The nobles clapped politely. Ruhan looked over apologetically at Alexander again. "My friend. I'm sorry. I know that my haste has made your life difficult, and that you had not anticipated this announcement for some time. Friends of the court—Lord Fremont has of course been asked to serve as the best man, and I am certain he is cursing his decision to say yes."

Alexander looked absolutely wan, relief and anxiety chasing each other around his features openly now. It wasn't for him. None of this was for him. It still complicated things for him immensely, and by proxy, Cass. Her mind raced to list all of the things she'd need to start doing immediately.

"Of course not, Your Majesty," Alexander said. "It is my highest honor, although the bulk of the work is not mine. If I may introduce the court to the woman who already has begun safeguarding your union?"

Cass' stomach dropped. Right, that was still happening.

Ifalna smiled and said softly, "Please."

Humphrey stepped forward to hand Alexander some notes. Alexander didn't unfold them, but looked to Cass with a brief smile, and then back to Ruhan.

"Her company has banished several major demons, successfully married off no fewer than thirteen fey-cursed brides and grooms, seen to the blessing of five prophesied children, and handled the wedding of two seventh sons of seventh sons to each other. It is my pleasure to introduce Miss Cassandra Friend of the Friend Event Company."

She walked forward and counted off the steps to the formal curtsey in her head, just as she had when Gideon ambushed her from the rafters. Avert the gaze. Right hand on heart, left arm out gracefully. And bend the knee. And hold. Two. Three. Four. And rise. Two. Three. Four—

And just as it had the last time Gideon ambushed her from the rafters, her knee locked up.

Just out of eyeshot of most of the attendants, Humphrey put out his notepad to block Alexander from moving to her and shook his head just barely. Alexander looked at the floor, mortified. Cass wobbled her way back up and felt her face, her ears, the whole of her burn in embarrassment with the most important eyes in the country on her as she struggled to just get back up.

Ruhan spoke up. "An impressive resume, Miss Friend. Alexander does not speak praise lightly, if ever."

She had to find her voice. She had to say something. "Thank you, Your Majesty," she managed. "Any praise he might have belongs to the members of my company. They have worked hard to become experts."

Ifalna took up Ruhan's arm. "Modesty does you credit, too," she said. "I am eager to know of your plans."

"Yes," Ruhan said. "We must all talk—we have many things to discuss, I am sure. But for now…." He turned to the court at large. "The news has been shared. Let it be known. In three months' time, we wed."

More polite clapping, some cheering. More time. Cass caught her breath. At least the timeline of the wedding itself hadn't changed. This would normally be the part where she would have a stern talk with the client, but…future King and all. Alexander caught her eye, similarly winded-looking.

The Knight Captain leaned over to the Prince, who nodded. "Now then," Ruhan said. "Ladies, gentlemen, good persons all, please, excuse us and Lord Fremont and Miss Friend while we fall to discussion. Good day."

The court filed out with relative haste, leaving them alone in the throne room with the knights. Once the door shut, Alexander turned. "Ruhan."

"I know, I know. I'm sorry," the prince said. "Things…happened."

"Things keep happening!"

"That is called life, my friend."

Alexander looked to the ceiling as though there might be guidance written there. "Angels above and devils below, you're going to make me old."

The Knight Captain cleared his throat. "A familiar mode of address to His Majesty."

Ruhan waved him off. "We are familiar. That's all right. You had a concern, Knight Captain Gerund?"

The man clanked forward. He was neither young nor old, streaks of gray just beginning in his close-cropped brown hair. "On the matter of the Queen's Edict of eighteen years ago. It seems there may have been some violations. A woman of this description was seen prowling the outside of Lord Fremont's home at a time it should have been off-limits. At the same time, a disturbance was reported on or near the property."

The prince rubbed at his short beard. "Hmm. Miss Friend, were you aware that there are periods that the Fremont estate becomes a restricted area by royal decree?"

Wonderful. Pretty much the second thing she ever said to the prince and she was in trouble. "I had been instructed as such by Lord Fremont, yes."

"What brought you there at that time, then?"

This was easy enough. It wasn't a lie. "I had been in the Upper Ring on other business and I recalled that something hadn't struck me quite right in a conversation we'd had previously. A vulnerability—" she glanced at Alexander, then at the Knight Captain. "I'm not at liberty to say in specific by the rules of my own contract. But suffice to say it was on the outer wall, so I thought that I would check it on my way home."

"I see." He walked on from in front of Cass, then stepped down from the dais altogether and stood at Alexander's side. "How are you feeling lately? No changes?"

Alexander laughed wryly. "Ah. No."

"That's all I needed to hear. Thank you, Knight Captain. Consider the matter at rest."

It was clear from the Knight Captain's face that he *did not* consider the matter at rest, but he didn't argue. Humphrey's posture eased ever so slightly. Good, Cass supposed. Alexander glanced back at her and then at the Knight Captain again, a questioning eyebrow in the air. She wasn't exactly sure what that was supposed to mean. She could probably have figured it out, but the embarrassment was still lingering warm from earlier.

"All of this aside, Ruhan," Alexander said, shifting his approach, "why rush this?"

He glanced back to his bride, who folded her hands and stepped down from the dais. "It is my fault, I am afraid," she said quietly.

"Ifalna—" the prince started.

She held up a delicate hand, then bowed her head toward Alexander. "A hundred and one apologies borne by the ravens," she said. "There is attempt to marry me to another King if Ruhan does not declare his intent quickly. My ship turned back for Amaranth at once when we heard this."

"I see," Alexander said, deflating. He looked to his friend. "Why didn't you just *tell* me?"

He winced. "Things moved quickly, and you were indisposed."

"A note would have done fine. Ruhan. I don't just say this for my own sake. There are pieces in motion here, and we need to remain informed."

The Knight Captain's mouth moved just an iota. Cass kept her face pointed toward the prince, but she watched Gerund while Ruhan spoke.

"Do you know of a specific threat?"

The Knight Captain leaned forward ever so slightly. Cass spoke up. "We do. At this point, it's not safe to say much more than that in a public space."

Ruhan seemed taken aback. "The Wyvern Guard are sworn to secrecy. If you can say it to me, you can say it to them."

Alexander stepped forward. "It's not about the Guard, Ru. It's about the building."

"Oh—oh," he said, as two and two fit together in his head.

Ifalna's eyes widened. "Demons. I was warned of them on this continent. I did not expect them so soon."

And this one was a doozy, Cass wanted to tell her. "Unfortunately," she said carefully, diplomatically, "where demons are concerned, Your Highnesses are vulnerable as public figures in a public space with a wide array of people around you at any given time. However, there is some good news."

Ifalna looked hopeful. Ruhan looked nauseous. "By all means," he prompted. "I could use some of that."

"They won't want to attack you," she said. "They will do everything they can to ensure the wedding proceeds."

"That is good," Ifalna said with a sigh of relief.

Ruhan looked over at Alexander. "Why do you look worried?"

"The bad news," he answered.

Cass translated, "They *will* attack *him* to leave the wedding vulnerable. They already have. And they will use any method at their disposal. Including social threats."

Ruhan turned and looked at the Knight Captain briefly. Good, Cass thought. He understood. "I won't have that. I'll assign guards—"

Alexander shook his head. "No, please, don't."

"Xander, please. I know you value your privacy, but this…I put this on you!"

"That's not what I—" He sighed and started again. "I am following expert advice on this one."

Cass said, "An understated response is the safest way to start out. Keeping the cards close to the vest."

Ruhan's face fell even further. "And I just made a public announcement."

"Precisely," Alexander said, folding his arms and observing the marble. "You've asked me to handle this, Ruhan. Let me handle it, please. And by that, I mean let the extremely competent professionals who know what they're doing handle it and let me translate between you, since that is really what I'm here to do."

The prince looked into space for a moment, obviously pained. He nodded at last. "I am…sorry. I had not anticipated so much…danger to you. I thought you'd hire consultants and make embarrassing speeches, not…."

Live my daily life, Cass thought, trying not to sound bitter even in her own head.

Alexander shook his head. "You're the one who made the embarrassing speech today. Oldest friend, all that. I do it gladly."

"Who knows?" Ruhan said, an eyebrow cocked. "Someday perhaps I can return the favor?"

Alexander just laughed slightly, like he had something lodged in his windpipe that he needed to clear. "Perhaps."

Ifalna pulled Cass aside. She was lovely, if not extremely quiet, and extremely…bland. Like one of those pretty cookies they served at tea, the kind Lissa always ate last. Much more about presentation than taste. She peppered Cass with questions about her work, about what the next three months would look like, about what Cass needed to do her job, which she appreciated. Most brides saw her as a box to tick so they could get on to the interesting stuff.

Across the room, Ruhan and Alexander talked, sometimes about the wedding, sometimes about other things. She heard them laugh occasionally. Humphrey hovered, the Knight Captain hovered. She felt watched. To Ifalna, she asked, "Do you feel at home yet?"

"No," she whispered. "Too many eyes in the dark. Ruhan is not like them, but he must live around them."

"I know the feeling," she said uneasily.

Cass waited in the garden with Humphrey, silent. *With* was not exactly the right word. They were in the same garden within eyeshot, waiting for the same person, but roundly ignoring each other's existence. She was definitely doing it pointedly. She didn't think he was.

Cass wandered the garden, reading the little brass placards. Some of the plants came from very far away, labeled with far-off kingdoms as well as the occasion of their gifting. Some of them were older than she was. Some of them were older than her whole family line.

This was nice, at least. She still felt the tension of the throne room, the shame, the feeling like she kind of wanted to shake Humphrey by the shoulders of his coat a bit, but the plants were soothing.

She came to the garden's edge where she could see the very beginning of the Corona. It was strange. She expected it to be the upper-est of Upper Ring, but really it was a microcosm. Like if the Market District and the Lower Ring and the Upper Ring all were organically one. She guessed that's how most cities were. She'd just been so used to the divisions that had been imposed all her life.

Alexander came up behind her. "I'm sorry, he wanted to talk a bit about her father. *That* is a bit of a mess. I'll spare you the details." He paused. "Are you all right?"

"Me?" she asked tersely. "Why bother with that?"

He reached out for her shoulder and stopped midway, his expression falling. "Cass."

"I'm going to say something we'll both regret if I keep going," she muttered, turning back toward the garden. "This is probably not the time and definitely not the place."

He looked down at his feet, then back at her, pained. "Wait for me one more moment?"

Cass took in the earnestness on that angular face of his, still boyish despite the stress that took away any chance of holding onto any pudge, and damned her lack of resolve. She nodded once. He crossed the garden and said something to Humphrey in a hushed voice that didn't make its way over to her. She told herself she didn't care, anyway.

Humphrey didn't seem angry or particularly displeased, but he also wasn't happy. He gestured a few times, and Alexander shook his head. At length, he nodded, wrote a few things down, and left through the large gateway. Alexander made his way back over to her.

"What was that?" she asked.

"I asked him to go on ahead," he said.

"And he actually agreed?" Her incredulity carried a bit across the marble floor.

"He isn't…." He sighed. "I understand what it must seem like."

"I'm unseemly."

He cringed. "Cass—"

She glanced behind her. There were still guards around. "Sure you want to do this here? Might get spotted getting familiar with a peasant."

He turned toward her, taking her hands. "Cassie, *please*. Try to understand the position I was in."

She let her hands slip out of his. "I have been doing nothing but. And I *know* you understood mine. Because I saw you. I saw you try to help. You know I'm a mercenary. You know my reputation is my job security." She started to pace. "I was in front of my client, in a room full of potential clients, or people who could prevent me from ever getting clients again, and I stumbled. I showed weakness. Weakness I wouldn't have shown if I hadn't been trying to understand your position. And in that moment, you decided your position was more important than mine. And you did nothing."

Alexander stood there, quiet, horrified. "I want so badly to say you're wrong," he said softly. "But that's what I did, didn't I."

She shrugged. "Why wouldn't you? That's what you were taught. So I'm here, trying to convince myself it's not a big deal. Because I do get it, yeah? That's why I'm here. Well, no. I'm here because I don't get a choice, realistically. But if I did, I'd be here, because I understand your position."

He let go of a long breath. "I am…Cassandra, I am sorry. I said I wouldn't act like that and I went and did exactly that."

She grasped his forearms and looked him in the eyes. "I don't…I don't want the apology, Alexander. I want you to choose. What am I to you? Do I keep your secrets or *am I* the secret? One of those I do gladly. The other hurts."

Alexander pushed the curls starting to loose from her careful arrangement out of the way and shook his head. "Cassie. That's not how I see you."

"I know. But you also know, don't you? You've been the secret. It doesn't matter how much kindness it's born from, does it?"

He looked at her, stricken with the realization. "I just…. You saw what Ifalna has to do. Paraded like a dog at show just to marry whom she chooses. None of this is fair. None of it is right. I wanted to outwit it somehow."

"Not on your own," she breathed. "You have to *talk* to me. I have to *talk* to you. What are we? What are we doing?"

Quiet fell over the garden. They'd moved closer together, as though pulled by a magnet. He looked down at her. "I'm afraid to be wrong," he said quietly.

"That's the thing I'm most afraid of in my life," she laughed mirthlessly, leaning in.

Hesitantly, he took up her arms. "I…am extraordinarily fond of you, Cassandra," he said at last."This last fortnight…I can hardly fathom it. Without much reason — I've not even been able to give you a night alone — you still see it fit to grace me with your courage and your insight, and I find myself wanting to spend every moment possible with you." He swayed nervously. "I hope that's the right answer."

Cass' hand settled to his chest. "Well, if it's anything like how I can't even resent that we've had to steal every moment we've had from the Company and Humphrey, because I can't get enough of you and your mind, then yes. It is."

His chest rose. "That does seem similar."

"Also you used the word fortnight."

He paused, ran his hand down her arm. "I have never once been ashamed of you. I need you to know that. They are their standards. Not mine."

She nodded, catching his hand and holding it. "I…know. Even when I was angry, I knew."

"But you will face those standards. More than I will, even, and they will be brutal. Are you sure?"

Cass nodded. "I don't want to hide. Whatever that may mean."

Alexander reached for her and kissed her, openly, defiantly, without an ounce of hesitation or concern for standing. *Her* standing bowed a bit, her knee angry about the shoes and the marble. He caught her. "Feel like causing a scene?" he inquired.

"Hmm. A good one or a bad one?"

"You tell me. There's a restaurant in the Corona that the vipers like to go to after court." He tilted his head and put out his arm. "We could go, too."

She took it. "To ruin and/or make their lunch with our scandalous fling? Lead on." Her reputation could take it.

"You're dangerous for me, Cassandra."

"You could use a little safe danger."

He waited until they were in full view of the street and kissed her again.

11

Home

Cass stood in front of the doors and steeled herself. It didn't matter how many times she put herself through this trial, it was still grueling in ways she was never ready for. She checked her knives in their sheathes, straightened her clothes and the dress she'd worn the day prior in its garment bag, rolled out her neck, and pushed her way into the tavern.

The woman behind the bar half-turned the second the bell on the door jangled. "Be with you in a minute. Bit early for—" She finished her whole circle and tossed the mug she was drying and her dishrag to the counter. "My *baby!*"

Cass stopped in the doorway. "Hey, Mum. What have I told you about shaming the morning drunks?"

Lyriana Friend raced out from behind the bar and caught Cass up, immediately smothering her in kisses. "Bad for business, I know, I know. What brings my *firstborn daughter* to my establishment, her *childhood home,* for such a rare visit?"

"Mother. I came by last week. You're being dramatic."

"It's never enough, baby, never enough." She smoothed her apron over her rumpled red dress and tilted her head. Her curls, much like Cass', though longer, a full head of them, graying, spilled leftward. "Are you eating? You look like you haven't been feeding yourself."

"I've been eating! More than usual, actually."

"Aha. I knew it. Sit down. I'll make you eggs."

"Mum," she groaned. "I'm here to say hi, ask a question, maybe take *you* to lunch, and then get going. I've got a lot going on."

"Jules did say you have a job," she said, picking the mug back up and getting back to wiping. "*She* visits."

"She lives next door."

"So tell me about it. What are you up to?"

"Okay, but you can't say much about it."

Lyriana leaned against the bar. "Cross my heart, hope to die."

Cass laid the garment bag she'd been carrying the dress in over a table and sighed. "I'm working the crown prince's wedding."

Her mother all but dropped the mug, catching it at the last second. "You *what*?"

Cass walked through the empty tavern and started pulling chairs down from tables, stuffing the usual empty matchbooks under the uneven table legs and glancing up at the carved wooden rafters to ensure there weren't *too* many visible cobwebs. "Yup."

"Cassie, that's…you're going to be rich. Or dead! Oh, honey, that's a lot."

She shook her head. "Mum. I'm not going to be dead." Her stomach lurched as she remembered Gideon in the restaurant, and she redoubled her speed taking down chairs. "It's a good thing. It's the kind of job that can get us any other job we want."

Her mother nodded slowly. "Right, right…and you'll have help, right? Lots of help from all the knights?"

The Knight Captain who wanted to kill her sweetheart for getting cursed as a child. Sure. "Yeah," she said cheerfully. "That's right. Plenty of support from the prince. It's a ways out yet, and it's the only thing we're working on, but we've got our hands plenty full with it."

"What's the castle like?" she asked. "Always wanted to know."

"Oh, it's pretty," Cass answered. "Lots of shiny white marble and silver and gold trim. A pretty garden out in the front with all sorts of plants from all over. Did you know there's a whole part of the city up there?"

"No!"

"It's called the Corona. It's all done up the same way. I walked around it yesterday. Maybe I'll take you sometime if you can get away."

Lyriana grinned. "Look at you, getting to go to fancy occasions. What did you wear?"

"That's what I'm here about. Can you show me where the cleaner you use is?"

"Of course, dear, if you show me the dress."

Cass sighed and went to the garment bag and unbuttoned it. She held it open and her mother gasped. "Cassandra! You *wore* that?"

"Yes, Mother."

She reached out and touched the beads as though she could scarcely believe they were real. "But where…where did it come from?"

Cass looked at the floor. "I need you to be calm about this."

Lyriana's eyes turned on her, wide. "No."

"Mother. You need to promise me that you are going to be silent. Do not react."

"I don't know if I can do that if you're going to say what I think you're going to say."

"I am a little afraid of what you think I'm going to say, so I'm just going to get this over with. I am…seeing the best man."

"Does that mean he's…?"

She flinched. "A lord."

Lyriana clapped her hands over her mouth and remained motionless for a solid minute. At length, she removed them and said, "A fancy one?"

"Upper Echelon," she answered tiredly. "It's—not a big *thing*. Please don't make it a thing."

"How long?" she squeaked.

"Two-ish weeks…?"

"That's—"

"Not a whole lot of time, so please, do *not* make it weird," she said, lifting her eyebrows and tilting her head forward. "Okay? Got it? Not. Weird."

Lyriana nodded silently, slowly. She walked around the bar, put the dry mug away, started to pick up another one to start drying, then put it down immediately. "So are you going to marry him, or…?"

"*Mother.*"

"Things move fast up there!"

"*I* don't."

She put her hands up. "All right, all right." She paused. "But if you wanted to, you could have my wedding ring."

Cass swallowed really hard so she didn't laugh out loud. For one thing, she didn't want to hurt her feelings—she knew the offer was meant to be kind—and for another, she didn't want anything that man had touched. It was probably cursed. At last, she said, "Thanks, Mum. But that's…that's a ways off. If ever."

"He's good to you, right?" She picked up a kitchen knife from the suds. "He'd better be good to you."

"Don't worry. Jules has intimidation covered. And yes. He's very, very good. Too good for his own good."

"Which one is he?"

"Which one? Gods, Mum. Just ask me what his name is."

"All right, then tell me."

"Alexander Fremont."

"Oh," she said, pleasantly surprised. "The school man. I like him."

Cass finished buttoning up the dress bag. "You've…met?"

"No. But I saw him speak when the school down the way was fixed up. It was quite the struggle, finding the money for the building. He had to push pretty hard. He was down here a lot, talking with folks, trying to get them to lean on certain lords, promising he would, too. He seems like he works hard."

Cass smiled. "That sounds like him."

Lyriana wiped her hands off and came around the bar again to chuck her daughter's chin. "Ah," she said softly. "I like him even more now. Come on, then. I'll take you to get your dress cleaned, and then we'll get Jules and Ellorin so I can have all my girls, and we will have lunch."

"Will you stop teasing me?"

She hung up her apron and considered. "Less," she conceded.

She supposed that was as good as she was going to get from the woman who raised her to be her.

*   *   *

Jules' apartment looked very little like what one might assume Jules' apartment might look like, upon first seeing Jules. There were shockingly few punching bags and many more cushions embroidered to look like cats. Part of that was Ellorin's influence. The wisp of a woman with huge silver spectacles and white blonde hair in a curling bob absolutely seemed like the kind of person who might have a dozen cats if she weren't deathly allergic, but the pillows had actually been Jules' hobby first.

Every inch of bare wall was covered in bookcases and shelves. The pillows and plethora of candles were Jules, but the entire wall of law books were Ellorin. She was an up and coming barrister, and the fact that she was home in the middle of the day surprised Cass immensely. Jules made sure Ellorin was entirely absorbed in conversation with Lyriana and whispered, "She, uh…lost a case."

"Oh," Cass said. "Bad luck."

"She's never lost a case before."

"I mean, bound to happen at some time, right?"

"You think so, I think so, but…." She shrugged. "She's taking it hard. She took the day off. I've never seen her like this."

Her normally paper-pale face was red and blotchy, and when she laughed at something Cass' mother said, it sounded just a bit strained.

"Hopefully lunch will take her mind off it," Cass said uneasily.

"Oh, hey. Speaking of law. I didn't get too far because, oh, boy, turns out, there is *a lot* on curses." She turned and pointed. "That whole shelf? All curse law."

Cass stared. "What?"

"I know. It's a whole lot of writing. What I *did* get through? Seems like people went back and forth a lot. It is their fault. It isn't their fault. That's why it's so convoluted."

"What's convoluted about it? He was literally attacked."

She shrugged a shoulder, wincing. "And I *chose* not to marry the guy my dad picked out, and you *chose* to hurt your knee, and your mom *chose* your shit dad. That's how these people think. Anything to push the difficult to think about stuff further away, right?"

Cass gripped the edge of the strap that ran from her belt to the sheath at her leg. "I hate people sometimes."

"No, you don't. But there's some good news. When you get more than thirty arguments layered on top of each other like that, you have what's called dueling precedents. Ellie's used that a couple of times. You can argue that it's so fuckin' complicated to comb through that much backlog and cancel out the cancellations that you can basically force a brand new law."

Cass frowned. "What if the new law sucks?"

"I mean, that's the risk. But the prince is his buddy, right? He saved his life. And you can appeal the new law back and forth."

"Thirty more times?" Cass asked dully.

"Or more," she said brightly.

Cass sighed. "Well, thanks for looking."

"I'll keep reading."

"I never heard—did you and Bjorn poke around the River Rats?"

"Right, that."

Cass bit down on a sigh. "Can that jump priority? I think that's our assassin connection."

"Hmm," she said. "Does it have to be today?"

Cass tried not to sound frustrated. "It would be good."

Jules gestured to Ellorin. "It's just…."

"Yeah, all right."

"Cass."

"I get it," she said.

"I'm not looking to duck out on you," Jules told her, grabbing her upper arms a little pleadingly.

Cass pushed out a breath and tried to push the annoyance down with it. "You are my person for underworld connections. Gideon can pull double duty some of the time, but that time is not now. I can do that some of the time, but that time is really not now. I have been way too visible to walk into—"

"I know."

"You can do it tomorrow. That's fine. I don't know that they're going to want to move on us at all. But I need you to be on top of this. I don't have anyone else right now."

Jules nodded and let her hands drop. "I…I'll do better."

Cass swallowed a lump in her throat. "It's not just the client," she managed. She looked over at Ellorin, at her mother, talking and laughing obliviously in front of a sun-soaked window. "Gideon says that the Lord of Demons…if we don't stop him now, that there won't be any stopping him ever."

Jules looked too, her face falling even further. "You're sure?"

"I…I don't know. But *he* knows what he's talking about. I know he believes what he's talking about. I know he tried to *pay me*…." She shook her head. "Damn it. He says nothing's changed. The job is still the job, we do it the same way. We just need to make sure it's done. Like…done, done. We do a good job. We always do a good job."

Jules nodded again, her resolve stiffening. "Yeah. We do. We got it. Lord of Demons? More like Lord of…Dumb…Shit. Uh. That sounded better in my head."

Cass smiled and punched Jules in the arm.

Mid-afternoon when Cass returned to the estate, and a little earlier than she had planned, Thalia waved to her from a tree. She waved back and headed inside.

She heard voices coming from the sitting room. That's right. Alexander had a meeting today. Humphrey came hustling toward her. She said quietly, "Don't worry. I'll wait somewhere unobtrusive."

He sighed. "I'm not—I simply fear it may be a while. This is not terribly productive."

The voices carried. "I simply don't see how pouring thousands of gold into districts where little will be required of these children is worth the investment," a man's voice harrumphed.

"Well, when you put it that bald-facedly," a woman replied in distaste.

"I don't see your rebuttal, Lady Corrin."

"I too am against spending quite so much, but you can at the very least pretend to have an interest in the people."

"Ladies, gentlemen," Alexander's voice cut in. It sounded tired, but remarkably patient given the circumstances. "If investment is all you're worried about, let's put it this way. One day, gods willing, you and I will be old. When that day comes, the children that we have educated today will be running Amaranth. Would you rather be at the mercy of people who have learned our history, learned from our mistakes, learned more of the world around us than we know, explored more of the way things work, and could perhaps give us a more comfortable way out than we gave them a way in, or would you rather only teach them what some narrow minded person thinks they ought to know?"

Silence. Cass grinned at Humphrey, who shook his head with a small smile of his own.

Alexander continued. "I would rather teach for the goodness of teaching, but if you can't find that in yourselves, at least think of your returns. Then negotiate a number."

Humphrey gestured at Cassandra to follow him away.

She whistled low. "You taught him well."

"That was his father's doing."

"I doubt that."

"Well, the brutality at the end, anyway," he said with a small chuckle. "To what do I owe the pleasure?"

"Oh, don't put on the show for me, Humphrey. I'm just here to return the dress and thank you for its use and check in on Alexander. It was lovely."

He looked a little baffled. "Miss Cassandra, it's yours."

"What? Really?"

"Of course. What—did you think I would expect you to perform for Lord Alexander's benefit and then return the costume?"

"Honestly? Yes," she answered.

"I see," he said. "I do believe we have started out on the wrong foot."

She managed to restrain herself, but she did allow, "I think it's a little more than that, Humphrey. It's all right. I can deal with not being approved of. Just…for his sake, try to accept it."

"Miss Cassandra, are you quite finished?"

"Excuse me?"

He set his fists to his hips and looked her squarely in the eyes. "You are a bright young woman, and quite often you are right about things, but not every time, and you are not right about this. I do not disapprove. I have not disapproved. You have decided I disapprove."

She cocked her head. "Come on. I saw that move in the throne room."

"It wasn't a personal referendum."

"I'm a commoner. Alexander is a lord. Him touching me is unseemly. Right?"

Humphrey set his jaw. "I have one charge in this household, Miss Cassandra. One that was left to me on the death of Lord Alexander's mother. I keep Lord Alexander alive. Much as I wish this were not the case, some of that charge hinges on keeping him looking good by their horrid standards."

She lifted an eyebrow. "Horrid."

"You think I like these people? You think I don't understand why Alexander pushes back at them every chance he gets, even though it might be his own downfall?" His face got ruddier with irritation the longer this went on, and he looked like he might burst. After a moment, however, he took a breath. "Of course you do. I've spent long enough here I no longer know how to take the mask off."

"Would you?" she asked. "If you could."

"I'm not sure," he confessed. "I am not sure what's left underneath." He took in a breath. "I regret that my actions have caused you distress. Unfortunately, I cannot regret them. I know what these people are. I can't let them destroy him."

Cass shifted her weight off her knee, starting to ache after too long, too much. "I understand. But you know he doesn't want to play the game. Will you act against his wishes?"

"No," he said quietly. "I can only try to convince him. And I'll confess he has been harder to convince lately, and it *has* occurred to me that perhaps your arrival may have had something to do with it. But his mind is his own. Neither of us can change it for him."

"If it were that easy, he would hate himself a hundred percent less by now."

Humphrey's mouth twitched up—not quite a smile, but acknowledgment. "He is happier. Undeniably. I cannot disapprove, even if I wanted to."

"Do you want to?"

"No."

"I want him safe, too," she said. "That's why I'm here. That's why I went. But I also want him happy. I think he can have both, and I think he can choose that for himself."

Humphrey thought quietly to himself for a moment. "How strange, the way the gods recycle words in the mouths of others," he murmured. "Alice used to wish for something like that for him. His mother."

"He told me you were close."

He nodded. "In a way, we were brought up together. She'd have liked you. Whether or not society at large approved." He turned. "If you wish, I can place your dress in the room you have been using when you stay here."

"Thank you," she said with a little smile. "That would be nice."

"And, if you like, you may wait for Lord Alexander. I suggest the patio. The breeze is nice and you won't have to overhear the miscreants in the sitting room."

"Humphrey," she laughed in disbelief.

"They give me heartburn," he muttered, taking the dress.

Cass watched him disappear, then wandered down the hall to the side door. The patio was a pleasant little area off the lawn, paved with bricks, ringed around with those ubiquitous baneroses. She stooped to examine them more closely. The flowers themselves were a dusky bluish purple, not quite as delicate as regular roses, but still roughly the same in how the petals were arranged on the stem. They clumped thicker together, grew like wild brambles. What made them different? She stood and carried her wonderment back to the iron swing tucked up next to the house and nestled into the cushions to watch the clouds pass overhead and dangle idly.

Most of the sunlight had faded by the time the door opened again and Alexander joined her with his vest unbuttoned and a glass of wine in each hand. He slumped to the swing next to her and handed her one. She leaned over and kissed him. "That good, huh."

"If I never see any of those people again, it will be too soon. Alas, my luck is not that good."

"Did you win?"

"In the end," he said with a sigh of relief. "Less than what I'd have liked, but more than I expected."

She patted his leg and left her hand there. "Well done."

Alexander wound his arm around her shoulder and leaned her to him. "You're thinking. Shall I come back later?"

She shook her head. "The thoughts aren't going anywhere anytime soon."

"Ah. I know that feeling." He rested his chin on her head. "Can I be of help?"

Cass hesitated. He probably could, if she could get herself together enough to ask. He listened well and talked well and really had very little room to judge and knew it. Instead, she blurted, "What makes the baneroses work?"

"Oh," he said in surprise. "They're alchemically created. That's what I went to school for."

She sat up. "Shut up. You *made* these?"

"Made is a…well, I guess it's an accurate enough term. They're a hybrid."

"You're an alchemist."

"Is that so surprising?" he asked with a bit of a laugh.

"I mean…no," she answered. "But yes. Humphrey lets you play with that stuff?"

"Oh, he objects strenuously, but I did make him a self-heating tea kettle, so he's mostly on board."

"That is *amazing*," she sputtered. "Tell me about the roses."

"It's a different varietal than you'd find on a farm, but the same idea. The reason the farm roses work is that they're seeded around a bit of diatomaceous earth, which repels the pests. Mine are seeded around a silver alloy." He sighed and pointed up at the rising moon. "Werewolves and silver don't get on."

"Is that the term?"

"I've been called such. It's aggravating at best. Poisonous at worst."

She turned her sights on the flowers around the patio, around the house, the whole of the property. "You made these…and planted them. To protect against yourself."

Alexander leaned his head back against the cushion, looking at nothing in particular. "Nobody really likes themselves as a teenager. Let's be honest."

"You've kept them up."

"Seems to have worked out for us recently."

She couldn't argue with that, much as she wanted to on principle. He'd had a long enough day. She left it. "What else do you make?"

"It's been a long time since I've had much time to have at it with any sincerity." He thought. "There are some lights that come on by themselves in the larger rooms. A few more things to help Humphrey. A few gifts for Ruhan—weapons modified for a bit of flash, mostly."

"That's wonderful. I've always admired people who make things."

He laughed a little. "And I've always admired people who can think on their feet."

"Takes all sorts, my mum would say." Her stomach turned over. "I visited her today. She's, um…she's a character. She's extremely excited and somewhat surprised you exist."

"I'm flattered," he said with a laugh.

"Says more about me than you." She studied her glass of wine.

"Are you all right?"

"I'm trying to find a delicate way to put this."

"Be indelicate. I can take it."

"She has…expectations, based on your nobility. Expectations that I realized I never really asked about."

He paused. "Expectations…oh. Oh. Goodness."

"Yeah, so when we did that whole *what are we doing* thing I thought we were done, but…." She cringed. "Are you, like…courting me, or is that a thing you even are allowed to do, or *want* to do, or…?"

Alexander laughed nervously. "Shit."

"I thought you said you could take it!"

"I thought I could! Um. First of all, if we're being indelicate, fuck what we're 'allowed' to do."

She nodded sagely. "That makes sense."

"Second of all, do you even *want* to be formally courted?"

"No," Cass snorted, "but if you wanted to…."

"There's no but at the end of that sentence, Cassandra."

She paused. *"Do* you want to?"

"Oh, good gods." He availed himself of his wine glass and looked at the scenery for answers for a while, then to her. "This…is one expectation of noble life that was lifted from my shoulders."

"You weren't pressured to marry?"

"No." He pressed his lips together. "In fact, I was forbidden."

Cass stopped. "You…what?"

He couldn't hold her gaze any longer. He turned to the gathering shadows over the lawn. "It is…unknown what effect my affliction might have on any descendants. My father made himself very clear. My family line dies with me."

She sat up abruptly. "Who is he to decide that for you?"

He sat up a little, too, not angry, but a bit startled. "He did keep me safe all these years, Cassandra."

"He kept you isolated. Your mother is the one who made the deal that gave you a life, and you know what—?" She shook her head, blinking. "Fuck that. These fucking hypocrites. He adopted you, didn't he? You could do the same if you wanted to. You could marry and have no kids, if you wanted, or stay single and adopt a dozen. But he just wanted you to keep being alone because he said so. Fuck that, fuck him, and you know what, fuck my shitty controlling dad, too, while we're at it."

Alexander reached out slowly and took her hand, pulled her back toward him. She sat there, raw, like an exposed nerve. This was not how this was supposed to go. She wasn't sure how this was supposed to go, but this definitely was not it. Thank the gods his colleagues were gone and the house quiet in the night.

"Is he still around?" he asked softly.

"No, he fucked off a long time ago," she said bitterly. "I still haven't decided if I hate him for it or thank the gods for it. Maybe both." She shook her head. "Sorry."

"What for?"

"I'm supposed to have it together."

"Says who?"

"Adulthood, probably."

"Mm. Fuck that too." He set her head back against his collarbone. "How long ago?"

"A long time. I barely remember much of him. He was mean and blonde and smelled like gin. That's about it."

"Funny. My father's drink of choice. No accounting for taste."

"Oh. Good."

"The body remembers," he said a little distantly. "Even before this curse, smells and tastes and sounds of those unpleasant memories stuck. They stick with you, and they build, and they make little root balls, just like those poison roses. And sometimes, you go to pick a flower, and you get stuck unexpectedly. It's the most human thing in the world." He set his glass aside on a small table beside the swing, and took her hand. "Don't be sorry."

She held his hand close and leaned forward to kiss him. When they parted, a bit breathless, she said, "What I should have said is that you deserve to have the happiness you want, when you want, with whom you want. Forget—"

He smiled. "I did say fuck what we're allowed."

"Yes. Yes, you did."

He smoothed back her hair. "Can I tell you what I want?"

"Please."

"Your company. In whatever capacity you see fit to bestow it."

"That, I can do," she answered, grasping him by the shirt and pulling him into another kiss.

He reciprocated in kind, one hand shifting down her back, another into her hair. Cass traced her fingers down his chest. He shuddered, pulled back, breathed out. "Cassandra, before we continue."

"Mm?"

"It's been…an *extremely* long time since I've tried to do anything like this."

She propped herself up on an elbow. "Are you all right?"

He nodded, flustered. "I'm fine, I'm…gods, you're pretty. I mean—there's something you should know."

"I'm listening."

He looked upward, trying to focus, his face turning extremely red. "The last time, there were some, er…instinctual…physical…."

"Oh," she said, sitting up higher.

"Is that…?"

"Oh, no, that's okay," she said, taking his hand.

"That really doesn't bother you," he returned, perplexed.

"I mean, it's…new, but I'm not shy. Are you?"

"Yes, extremely," he answered, eyes widening.

"Okay, all right," she looked around. "Would going inside help? We also don't have to…."

"Dear gods, I want to," he answered, his hand tightening a little around hers like he was afraid she might vanish.

"Okay, inside it is," she said.

Humphrey was thankfully absent from this part of the house, and they made it to Alexander's bedroom and closed the door with no interruption.

After a quick rush to get all the curtains closed and the locks locked, they barely even paused to pick up where they left off.

Cass pressed him up against the wall and ran her hands along his hip bones. He shivered into her shoulder and kissed her neck voraciously. For a long time since the last time, he wasn't missing any steps. She reached for the lacings of his pants and paused. "Is this okay?" she whispered.

"Yes," he breathed.

She took his hand and guided it to the buttons at the front of her shirt while she got to work herself. Once she had the waistband loose she hooked her thumbs on gently and pressed against him in another kiss. He groaned, shivered, a whole body thing that seemed to rollick outward from his core. She pressed in again harder. This time, her lip met a pointed tooth, and when he shuddered, the groan was more of a grunt, deep, animal, frantic.

All at once, Alexander pulled himself away, breathing hard. "I'm sorry," he gasped, curling in on himself, collapsing to a knee. "I'm sorry, I —I can't."

Cass pulled herself together in an instant, dropping down next to him. "Alexander. Hey. Are you all right?"

His shoulders hunched, clenched, slackened. He covered his face with a hand and breathed out hard. "Aside from wanting to perhaps drop dead of mortification, I…think so."

She settled in front of him, took his hand from his face, found his other one. His voice still didn't sound quite normal, and his teeth were definitely…. He looked away in embarrassment.

"No," she said, tilting her head. "It's okay."

"If I had just…." He shook his head. "You were all right with it. If I could have just controlled myself like a man…."

"What happened?" she asked softly.

Alexander deflated, settled to the ground, rested an elbow on his knee. "I am terrified," he said at last, "of any bit of instinct that isn't mine. I thought I was ready for it this time. I prepared you. I prepared me. And at the first sign, I panicked. Me, Alexander. Not the beast."

"It's not like you were exactly raised to understand it."

"Oh, absolutely not," he laughed. "And rightly."

"You think?"

He turned his head to look at her questioningly. "What on earth could possibly come of studying the whims of something that wants only to devour, defend, or duplicate that's *nested* in my head?"

She shook her head. "I think it's more complex than that, and I think that's why no one's been able to touch it. Not even you." He stiffened. "That's why you became an alchemist, right? Your father wanted you to?"

"How do you bloody *do* that?"

She shrugged a shoulder. "My mum runs a tavern and my dad was a raging narcissist bastard. You get good at reading between lines. Listen. Did the beast want me or did you want me? Answer me honestly. It's all right. I won't be upset."

Alexander looked somewhat repulsed as he searched himself. "Both."

"That's the thing. That's the thing you're missing. He's you." She reached out and touched his hair, tucked it behind his pointed ear. "He's a distorted version of you, yeah, who does things beyond what you would ever, but you get scared when he *does* line up with Alexander."

He stared into space, his eyes horrified. At length, he trained them on her. "And you still…?"

"Of course I do," she said, taking his hand and holding it to her chest. "Because you and the rest of these nobles need to get it through your heads that it's not your fault that he's here in the first place. It was never your fault."

He wiped at his face. "I don't know what to do. That separation…that was all that made it feel bearable."

"It wasn't real." She kissed his knuckles. "Nothing has changed, except now…now you might have a way to expose yourself to him carefully."

"What…what do you mean?"

"Think about it. If you shut down in fear every time you feel a bit of instinct, you never learn to tolerate it. Now if you know what it is, you may be able to learn to endure it. A bit at a time. You've been white-knuckling every time you feel a bit of panic, and that's gotten you to stop transforming, yeah? Theoretically, if you greet it more calmly upfront, then maybe…."

He nodded slowly. "That…makes sense. The one healer who ever seemed to help said something like that. I kept trying to stave it off, but it only ever made it worse. Father, of course, fired him because he was more interested in managing the condition than eradicating it." He nodded again.

"Can I ask…?" She hesitated.

"Ask," he said with a tired laugh.

"What is it you fear?"

"Killing you," he said plainly. "Consigning you to my fate. Two of the three things the beast wants fairly strongly. Maybe now that the third is in play it will…*I* will…." he seemed unable to finish.

"Have you ever done either of those?"

"No. Thank gods. I have injured people. Humphrey. My father. Doctors. I'm more sorry about some than others."

"Do you feel…can you feel anything when you…?"

Alexander took a breath, steeled himself for the answer. "It's like… have you ever had a dream where you are watching, and you know that you are the key player, but only rarely can you affect the direction of the dream? You can react, you can…want things all you want, but only sometimes will it change, and not always the way you thought."

Cass' throat developed a lump that she almost felt she couldn't breathe past. "Yeah," she said. "I know those. They're shit."

"At the end of mine, I might have hurt someone."

The lump closed off, and she leaned forward and kissed his forehead once, twice. She tried not to do the pity thing, but it hurt her not to do something to acknowledge it. "I'm going to help you," she said at last.

"Cassie. There's nothing—"

"You said it yourself," she told him. "All anybody cared about was getting rid of it. Not me." She held his face, kept her forehead to his. "You deserve to be happy."

He held onto her hand. "You do, too," he managed at last.

"I'm the happiest I've ever been," she told him. "And there is literally a Lord of Demons who wants to kill us and then take over the world after your friend's wedding."

He pulled back. "Wait, what?"

She shut her eyes. "Shit, yeah, I forgot to tell you about that last part. Gideon let it slip in a drunken stupor one night."

"Oh. Right. So. No pressure."

"You're telling me. I've been practically wanting to retch about it for weeks."

"And you've been letting me go on about my shit?"

"Everybody has stuff."

"*Demon Lord,*" he pronounced.

"And yet, life goes on."

"I will never understand this," he said weakly.

"It's okay. The hope is most folks won't have to." She wobbled up and held out her hands to help him up. He took them hesitantly. When she was sure he was steady, she put her hand to his chest. "All right?"

"Yeah," he said. "I'm sorry."

"Alexander."

"I was hoping I'd outgrown this impulse a little since scaring that poor boy when we were seventeen."

"Aw."

"We did *not* get this far." He cringed. "I am…sorry for the panic."

"What for?" she asked. "It's the same kneejerk fear that happened with me. Still the most human thing in the world."

He laughed. "Have you looked at me lately?"

"Still human. Sorry."

"I get the worst of both," he sighed. "Though I guess…my mother did find one amusing bit. May as well tell you."

"What?"

He took her hand and extended the pointer finger, crooked it, and set it behind his ear. "Go on," he sighed again, heavily.

She scratched, and despite his best efforts to keep a straight face, he laughed, and his leg twitched. Cass' eyes widened. "You should *not* have shown me that."

He grasped her hand again to keep her from going too mad with power. "I'm trusting you to use it responsibly."

"That is a grievous mistake."

Alexander pulled a face, and she smiled and he failed to maintain it. He glanced down a little regretfully at their proximity. "Even if I'm not supposed to be sorry, I am. It was…a very nice time, for as long as it lasted."

She tugged him toward the bed. "There will be other nights, and there are other nice ways to be close in a bed."

"Those…I admittedly have never tried."

"I've been told I snore."

"I've been told I turn into a snarling wolf monster if I'm startled awake, so. You know. Fair."

"I'll take my chances."

He ran his hands down her arms. "Are you sure?"

She kissed him. "I can take you."

12

Blue Night

He woke up quite a few times, which woke her, but she didn't mind. Alexander wasn't used to the shift of another body in bed next to him, the sound of someone else's heartbeat in the room. She picked up her head from his bare chest. "Hey. Just me," she reminded him blearily.

His breathing slowed again, and his hand found her head. "Hello, you," he said.

"Are you getting enough rest? I can go to the other room."

He pulled her back to him gently, nestled closer. "Stay. Please."

"Okay." She reached out and stroked his ear, his hair until she felt him lull against her again. Her eyelids drooped heavy in the dim blue light of the moon peeking in past the gap in the partially open curtains.

They had closed those curtains.

She reached for the daggers she left at the side of the bed a few seconds too late. The movement did wake Alexander in time for him to see the figure standing at his side of the bed coming.

He had warned her. He had just enough time to push the attacker out of the way before his body writhed, shifted. This time, there was no prolonged painful thing. He barely yelled before it turned into a snarl, and he was on his feet and ready in seconds. Metal flashed in the dark, glanced across his shoulder. He yelped, reeled back, slashed with a claw.

Cass vaulted across the bed and felt warmth spray across her. A voice cried out—feminine, young-sounding. Cass reached out, found an arm, yanked her back from Alexander, threw her back, and interposed herself.

"Leave her," she told him firmly, casting about in the darkness for the girl's weapon.

It was clutched in her fist. She struggled to hang onto it, kicked out at Cass. Alexander advanced slowly, growling low in his throat.

"I swear to gods, if *any* of what I said earlier stuck, now's a great time to start thinking about it," she snapped.

He snapped back, licking at his jowls. Cass huffed out a breath. "You're right, I apologize," she said, trying to keep her voice calmer and keep the panic out of it. "I have it…under control…if she would just give me…the godsdamned…knife."

"What the *hells* are you doing?" the girl screeched.

Alexander's ears flattened against his head, and he crouched low. Cass kneed the girl in the gut and managed to pin one arm against her back. "Trying to save your damned life," she muttered. "Gods know why. Alexander. There might be others."

His focus wavered. He turned from Cass and her target, and Cass finally wrested the knife from the girl. She tossed it away and pinned the attacker's arms down. "Don't move," she instructed.

"What are you going to do?"

Cass dug around in the nightstand one-handed. There was a robe folded in the top drawer. She pulled the waist tie loose and used it to lash the girl's hands together, pulling tight, knotting more than once. "Making sure I can ask you questions later. Stay put." She finished tying off the binding and scrambled to her feet, recovering both her knives and the one she tossed from the attacker. "Alexander—"

Something hit her in the side of the head, knocked her to the ground. At first she thought it might be him, but shortly after she heard the sound of his loping gait thundering toward her from the other direction. With a snarl, he jumped over her and leapt at her attacker, who hit the floor with a heavy thud. This one was a fully grown man by the sound of it.

No matter what, she didn't want Alexander's teeth in him. She blinked the stars from her vision and struggled back up again.

Their outlines seemed to be wrestling in the dark. The man had his hands clamped around Alexander's jaws while Alexander stood over him attempting to get free. Cass pushed her shoulder against Alexander's to try to shove him off. He stumbled back a bit, and she struck at the man's nose with the butt of a dagger. He yelled. Alexander tried to come back, but the man threw Cass into him, which knocked them both back. He got up, threw open the bedroom door, and staggered away down the hall.

Alexander wasn't far behind. She called after him as she watched his tail disappear around the doorframe. "Fuck," she muttered, grabbing hold of the dresser to pull herself up to run after.

Humphrey habitually left some of the hall lights lit—possibly some of Alexander's alchemical design. They burned low, which let her avoid some of the things that the intruder and his pursuer had already crashed into and sent scattering across the tile.

The saved seconds were just barely enough. She made it into the sitting room as the man—a portly bald man with grayish skin, flaps of gills at his chin, and the characteristic metallic blue scale tattoos on his face marking him as a River Rat—threw the fireplace screen at Alexander. The heavy steel and brass crashed into him, pinned his body down. Panting, the intruder drew closer, pulled a knife, held it over Alexander's throat.

As panic gripped her, Cass shouted something unintelligible even to her and flung her own dagger end over end. It stuck in the man's chest, and he dropped.

She breathed hard in the doorway, her palms damp, her small clothes sticking to her with sweat. The second she got feeling in her limbs again, she moved to Alexander, straining against the screen. "I've got you," she breathed out.

Someone else came into view in the doorway, and she froze, holding out the girl's knife. Instead of a new attacker, she found Humphrey, his face paler than her bed sheet. "Miss Cassandra!"

"Humphrey. You're all right."

"You too, thank gods—Lord Alexander."

He hurried over and helped her heave the screen up and off, then backed away quickly. Alexander straggled up, his shoulder badly bloodied, clearly in some significant pain by the shake to his posture. He turned his eyes on Cass and Humphrey, his lip curling up in a snarl.

And then something she'd yet to see happened. His eyes shifted. They were his, completely, and they were frightened, the same fear she'd seen earlier this evening.

Cass reached out. "Alexander—"

He turned and ran, straight for the large windows lining the wall. He rammed his upper body against one hard until a latch clicked, opened, and he fled into the night.

Cass started forward, but Humphrey grabbed her wrist. "Let him go," he said, pained.

She shook her head. "That was him. We need to get him back inside."

"The situation can turn fast, Miss Cassandra."

"You don't understand," she said, holding up the knife. In the light, the blade glinted brightly except the places where his blood had dried. Those had stained a strange tarnished color, not unlike the petals of the baneroses outside when they dried. "They knew. They were ready for him. There could be more out there. This could all have been to draw him out, and he is alone and already hurt."

Humphrey's eyes widened, and he grabbed a set of keys from the drawer and beckoned her to the side door. She ran out into the grass, searching the shadows. "He can hear well, can't he?" she asked quietly.

Humphrey nodded, hoisting a lantern. "Very."

"I'm going to walk out there and call for him. Stay here and do the same. Quietly. Shout for me if you need help."

"For gods' sake, be careful."

She nodded and took off, trying to keep low. Out here it was freezing, and the wet grass felt like razors on her bare feet. What she wouldn't give to push all of that from her mind. Finally, she stood out in the open on the lawn, feeling exposed in her undershirt and shorts and the moonlight.

"Alexander," she said, as though talking to herself. "It's all right. None of this was your fault. But you have to come back. Please."

All she got in response were some unseasonably early crickets or frogs or something from the wetlands down the way.

"The weapon was silvered," she said, holding her arms to herself. "We need to take a look at the wound, and there might be more in hiding, and…." She laughed slightly. "I'm frightened too. I admit it. It's easier to be frightened together."

She stayed quiet, watched the edge of the woods. "I need you to come back," she said. "Please, Alexander."

A silver shape darted out from the treeline, and Cass about swallowed her heart. She started to back toward the house, still watching. "Thank you, thank you, thank you. Okay. Come on. Quick."

It went against every sense she had to just walk backwards slowly while he barreled toward her, but she held firm. She wasn't sure which Alexander she was getting yet, and there really wasn't any knowing until he was here. His gait was ragged, his breaths coming out in uneven clouds. Pain was probably not good. Her pace quickened, and she turned and sprinted back to Humphrey.

"Hold the door," she called to him, maybe a little more panicked than she'd like with Alexander on her heels.

He bolted to get back to the side door and held it open for her. She still wasn't sure if Alexander was following because she asked or if she was baiting him, but either way, she ran damn fast and slid under the dining room table, putting table and chair legs between her and him. He skidded, hit the wall, panted hard.

"Hey, you," she called. "You there?"

A small growl in return.

"What's that supposed to mean?" she asked, cautiously pushing a chair out to get a better look.

Humphrey's short gait sounded in the hallway. "Miss Cassandra—oh, dear."

"Keep a bit back, will you?" she said, easing out a little from under the table. Alexander stayed collapsed against the china hutch, still only vaguely growling. She inched out further until she could bend forward and reach him if she chose, which she didn't. He looked up at her with glassy eyes she couldn't quite read, but made no movement. She kept her eyes on him but called back to Humphrey, "I assume he figured out something to put on silver wounds."

"Yes. I'll fetch it."

"And a belt, please," she said uneasily. "A clean cloth. Some alcohol, some water. Be careful. We still don't know who's here."

"Right away."

Cass lowered her head, let herself breathe. That was a mistake. That was when all of the adrenaline came rushing in. She balled her fists at her knees, squeezed. "I should have told her to do it today," she muttered. "I'm sorry. I let it go. I didn't think they would have it together…they're not this organized. Who's this organized?"

It was a stupid question and a stupid time to ask it, but it felt better than staring him down in silence, and it felt better than assessing his wound with nothing to do about it yet.

A crash sounded somewhere behind them. Alexander sat bolt upright. Cass grasped onto his ruff. "Please don't."

He pulled away roughly and was gone immediately. She groaned and got to her feet again and shoved the chair out of her way. "Humphrey!"

He was in the front hallway, and a wiry man was sprawled out at his feet. Alexander pounced on the man's chest, distinct claw marks in blood across it. Humphrey held the shattered remains of a vase over his head, his eyes wide. The man was definitively unconscious. Cass wrested Alexander off.

"Good job," she breathed out. "You okay?"

"I think so," Humphrey eked out.

She let Alexander roll off her forearms, fully expecting a return volley. Instead, he slumped back to the floor, breathing hard again. She flinched and turned to Humphrey. "Is there a panic room—an Alexander-proof room somewhere? Where did you put him in the house when he was little?"

Humphrey cringed. "We, ah…just used the outside cell even then."

"Oh, for gods' sake."

"Take it up with the late lord."

She'd frigging love to. There were a lot of things she'd love to say to that man. "A basement. An interior room with one door and no windows. Something."

Humphrey paused. "Lord Alexander's workshop."

"Perfect. Take us there."

"Come."

She approached Alexander again and showed him her hands. "I'm going to help you up so we can get you somewhere safe. No more running. Yeah? But we're keeping our teeth to ourselves."

Humphrey looked down. "Miss Cassandra…he can't hear."

"No, he can't quite *remember* in the morning," she answered tightly as she edged her hands underneath Alexander's body. "There's a difference."

"It doesn't…."

"It makes a difference," she told him coldly. "And perhaps if the late lord had spent more time figuring that out than—we don't have time for this."

She eased Alexander up to his paws, steadied him, ran a hand softly over his fur once. His body tightened, but in the end, he glanced up at her and followed after Humphrey.

The workshop had probably once been a panic room, actually. The heavy door swung shut and latched in place with a lever. It smelled of minerals and soil—most of the benches were given over to baneroses seeding under mage-lights, though there were some cabinets with some more interesting things of dubious origin along the far walls. Cass watched Alexander lurch to the floor again, then glanced to Humphrey.

"Can you see to him? I need to get my people to clear the house."

Humphrey looked uncertainly at the door. "I'll go."

"There could be any number of them on the property."

"Which is why you should be here. If they breach the door, you can protect Lord Alexander."

"And if they find you?"

He shut his eyes briefly, then turned to her. "Then I've done my best to fulfill my promise," he said. "I'm not going to be foolhardy about it. I'll use the passage out of the estate."

"There's a passage."

He smiled weakly. "Miss Cassandra. It's a noble house. Of course there's a passage."

"There's a *passage.* And I'm just *now*—?" She nodded vaguely. "Okay, okay…take this." She handed him one of her knives. "Do you know what to do with one?"

"I can dice, mince, filet, and spatchcock," he said, confused.

"Uh…spatchcock, I guess." He offloaded the supplies she requested, and she juggled them under her arm. "Gideon lives in our office in the Market District. Central Street, in the building with the statues of the women holding up the pillars. Third floor. He'll know how to get the others very quickly. Tell him to clear the house first and then the grounds. He knows what that means."

He nodded and lifted the latch again to let himself out. "Lock it behind me."

"Be careful."

He glanced back at the silver heap on the floor. "Take care of him."

"I will."

Humphrey nodded once more, gave her a brief smile, and disappeared around the corner. She shut the latch, took a breath, and returned to Alexander.

He lifted his head listlessly and looked her way as though trying to decide whether she was worth expending energy. Cass knelt and set down her supplies. "You're hurting. I'm going to try to help stop it."

He whuffed.

She tilted her head. "That an okay?"

Cautiously, she reached out to stroke the top of his head. Alexander didn't seem to know what to do with it, but he didn't try to take her arm off. After a moment, he relaxed, his eyes sinking halfway shut.

"It's going to get a little worse before it gets better," she guessed, still moving her right hand softly.

With her left hand, she found the belt. She slipped it up higher toward his head. He made no movement, didn't even look at it. Did he know what she was doing? She paused, switched over to watering down some alcohol on a cloth and readying it. Still nothing. Cautiously, she pulled the edge of the belt around his snout. Now his eyes flicked to her. "I know," she said apologetically. "But I think you'll be happier about it tomorrow."

His eyes drifted upward again. She looped the strap through the buckle and gouged a new hole in the leather, and before he had a chance to change his mind, strapped his muzzle shut. He huffed through his nose, his ears flattening. Cass knew she was losing her goodwill. "I'll be quick," she promised.

Alexander settled. She leaned over and carefully parted the blood-matted fur. She wasn't sure what she expected to see, but it was still unnerving to see his pale skin at the base of all the fur, scarred just the same as she'd known it to be when she'd rested on it that evening; distorted, but still…his. A deep, angry slash ran across the shoulder blade, the congealed blood the same tarnished color that she'd seen on the knife earlier. Everything else was just red, raw, hot.

She tried to clean as quickly as she could. He snarled, his body jerking. "I know, unpleasant," she said, dodging a claw as she inspected. It looked clean enough. He growled, pawed at the belt. It would have to be clean enough. She reached up higher into his ruff, smoothed down the hackles, stroked his head until the sting seemed to calm a little by his posture. He seemed confused and vaguely annoyed, like he wasn't exactly sure why it was working. Cass set her hand to the top of his head and smiled her own bemusement to herself. As irritated as Alexander might have been by the imposition of the beast's instinct on his human will, it seemed to work both ways. Nobody had gotten close enough to find out before.

Cass picked up the jar Humphrey left. It smelled very much like the powder he'd given her for the baneroses. She supposed that made sense in a way. She dug out a bit with the cloth. The second it came out of the jar, Alexander picked his head up, his lip curling underneath the belt. "Hey," she said. "Do you want the poison gone or not?"

Another quiet growl, but he laid back down. Cass ran her hand over his head a little bit more, mostly for an excuse to get her hand closer to the belt. "Almost there. Just going to get this ready. Keep breathing."

She gave one more stroke down the side of his head and in the same motion grabbed the strap and pressed the salve into the wound. Alexander thrashed, struggled against her grip, flailed out. She felt a sharp sting, warmth as a set of claws made contact with her chest and dragged down. She leaned forward for leverage and kept the strap taut, his mouth closed, and that cloth pressed to the wound the way it had been to the cut on her leg. "Almost there," she told him. "Just hang on."

Alexander howled his rage and discomfort and tried to throw her off. His body shook, and the howl turned quickly into a whine, more of a plea. Cass bit her lip, her eyes dampening. "I know. I'm sorry."

What little upward motion he'd gained, he lost again, collapsing into a heap. He gasped, whined, and still she held him down. Cass pulled the cloth away. Still a little of that tarnished color. She braced herself and reapplied the cloth. He cried out, and she leaned her forehead forward into his fur. "A little more," she said around the burn in her throat. "Just a little more."

He tried to jerk away, but there just wasn't enough fight left to him. He trembled and whimpered in place. She tentatively let go of the belt and hugged him to her, tracing a pattern in the fur around his ear. "I love you," she told him.

He fell mostly still. Cass picked up her head. He still breathed—in fact, a little better than the last few times she'd noticed—but other than that, he didn't move. She pulled her cloth away and inspected the wound. No more tarnish. Still bleeding, still inflamed, but at least relatively what a clean wound should look like. Her chest burned. She half-crawled her way to his head. He seemed dazed, tired. Carefully, she picked up his head and set it in her lap. Foolish? Probably. But she just couldn't bear to leave him lying on the floor in a converted panic room surrounded by flowers designed to mildly poison him. She let her head thump against the leg of a workbench and rested her eyes for a bit with her hand on his head.

Her eyes shot open again when his body lurched. Alexander cried out, curled in on himself, clenched. The fur started to retreat, his bulk shrank, every muscle contracted, shook. His voice went hoarse. Cass kept running her hand over his head until she felt his hand grip the bottom of her undershirt. His shoulders shook, and she felt the cloth grow wet.

She bent and kissed the top of his head. "I have you."

His hand found hers shakily. "Did I…?"

"No bites."

He tried to sit up. "But I did—"

She repositioned him so he was no longer facedown, but still kept him down. "You kept yourself and Humphrey safe," she said firmly.

He closed his eyes. "You're bleeding."

"Yeah, they knocked me around a bit, but I'm okay." She pushed his hair from his face. "We're okay."

From outside, the sounds of something shuffling, thudding came. Alexander tried to sit up again. Cass grasped her dagger and propped him up against the workbench, putting her finger to her lips.

"Cassie-duck?" a voice boomed.

"Bjorn," she breathed in relief. "Is it done?"

"None remain aside from the one you subdued. There were twelve."

She let her shoulders go slack. Twelve. "How many did you down?"

"Eight. They fought to the end." He paused. "Will you not let me in?"

She glanced back at Alexander, who had once again wound up without clothes. "Give me a minute. We'll be right there."

Alexander, still looking drawn, looked up at her, troubled. "Twelve. That's…."

"A small army. I know." Not at all characteristic of a bunch of street criminals. It was immensely bothersome. She stooped, got under his arm. "Do you think you can stand?"

He tried, wobbling dangerously. "There's…some planting cloth in that cabinet, if you don't mind."

"Ah. Yeah." She helped him arrange it as best they could across his waist so most everything was hidden. Cass surreptitiously pulled her undershirt higher to cover the scratches across her chest and pulled open the door.

Bjorn stood in front, still holding his very large axe. He looked them over. "Lord and Cassie are both—" She frowned deeply, and he finished, "wounded. In time they will make nice scars."

"Thanks, friend. Please move."

"Want me to carry Lord?"

"No, I got it," she said, pulling Alexander past Bjorn toward the lit hallway. Humphrey appeared in the doorway, and she relaxed. "You made it."

"Yes, thanks to your friends." He rushed forward to grasp Alexander's other arm. "My Lord, you're…! I expected at least till morning."

Alexander grimaced. "One surprise after another tonight. I'm so glad you're safe."

Humphrey patted his chest. "Not as glad as I am to see you are. Miss Cassandra did a good job."

She looked away. No, she hadn't. Twelve people had gotten here and wreaked this havoc. Eight were dead, there was a ninth still held here, and three had gotten away.

As they passed through the foyer, Jules caught up, still in her sleep clothes. "Cassie—"

"We'll talk about it later," she returned tightly.

Bjorn called, "Oh, Cassie-duck. The small one from the bedroom. We move to the sitting room for questions."

Good. Something to do. She looked to Humphrey. "Get him resting. Thalia can help check him out on the mundane level."

Alexander caught Cass' hand. "And you? What are you planning to do?"

"My job," she said, patting his cheek. "Yours is to rest off what's left of that poison."

"You were hurt too, Cassandra. There's—a lot of blood, I can tell—"

"I've had worse." She bowed his head cautiously to kiss his forehead and slipped her arm free. "Go. Humphrey...."

He nodded knowingly. Alexander cast a look back, and she turned quickly for the sitting room, pulling her undershirt up again.

Before she even opened the door, she heard a loud voice, yelling, she thought at first. When she opened the door, she saw the kid she tied up with the robe sash leaned back in a chair singing loudly.

Gideon sat on a footstool, prodding at his forehead. He glanced up at Cass. "You're alive," he said. "Good."

"Thanks for bringing the cavalry."

"You did pretty good holding off twelve on your own, although this one is...." He shook his head. "Good luck. I tried."

Cass moved forward and stepped hard on the front leg of the chair. It rocked forward precipitously, rollicking its occupant with it.

"Hey!" she shrieked.

"You done?" Cass asked, glaring. "This isn't a game."

The kid pushed a wild mess of red curls from her face, and Cass' heart sank. She *was* a kid. Probably no older than twelve. The River Rat tattoo was all but shredded by Alexander's claw marks, her face was absolutely smeared with blood where she'd wiped at it, and the eye was a half an inch from ruin, saved only by the fact that the brow took the brunt. That was going to do a number on him.

The kid glowered back. "Nothing's a game anymore. There should be more games."

"All right, fine. We'll play one. It's called 'answer all my questions without being a shit about it and maybe I won't give you to the guards'."

She made a loud *pshh* noise. "Yeah. Right."

"Yeah. Right." She folded her arms. "So?"

13

Society Brats

The kid took her time thinking about it. Cass let her. She went, put on some clothes, told Bjorn and Jules to keep making perimeters even though she was relatively sure nothing else was coming. By the time she made it back to the sitting room, there wasn't any more singing, and Gideon….

He'd sort of dozed off in his chair. She stopped short. Devils didn't sleep—Gideon didn't even have a bed. The asshat they'd finished at the restaurant had taunted him about it, but she hadn't thought he was serious. Gently, she reached out and jostled his shoulder. He sat up abruptly. "What? Where—? Oh. Sorry."

"It's okay. Do you want to take off?"

"No, I'm good." He cleared his throat. "I got this."

The kid looked at them strangely. "You guys are weird. And I grew these like…last year." She blew air into her cheeks and her gills fanned out like frills at her neck.

"Very nice," Cass said dryly, dropping to the sofa. "Probably comes in handy in the sewers."

"Yep," she said brightly. "Helps me breathe your shit."

"If you're waiting for me to snap at you, it's not going to happen. I perfected this game, kid."

She wrinkled her nose. "What?"

"I was a brat, too. Nobody paid attention to me. Hated school, hated being told what to do, hated following the rules, hated the stupid adults yelling at me or trying to control me, so I said whatever I thought would piss them off the most. And I got really, *really* good at figuring out what that was really fast." Cass tried to cross her arms, but the slashes across her chest stung, so she leaned back instead. "You can do your worst. It's not going to get me."

"Where's your dog?" the kid asked.

There was the attempt. She had to hand it to her, it almost worked. Gideon was sitting next to her, after all, and he still didn't know the specifics of the curse, though knowing him she guessed he had it narrowed, at least. Cass kept her face neutral. "Sleeping, no thanks to you. Where'd you get the knife?"

The kid sat silently.

Cass stood up again and grabbed the dagger. "It's nicely made. Not the stuff you guys usually work with. And silver is *expensive.* Did you know that's what you were holding? That if you sold it instead of trying to use it you probably could have paid your way out of the sewers?"

She snorted. "No point. I'm already a Rat."

"You think nobody's ever stopped?" She observed the knife a second longer. "Did they even tell you who you'd be up against?"

The kid kicked her leg. "They said if I got him in his sleep it wouldn't matter."

"They didn't tell you it's damn near impossible to sneak up on him, did they. How many times did he wake up?"

She bit her lip and stayed quiet. Cass watched her. Her plain clothes were worn, maybe two sizes too small length-ways, but not yet squeezing her, so she was still wearing them. The Rats didn't take care of her.

Cass asked, "What's your name?"

"Kaye."

"Cass. This is Gideon." She glanced over to find him dozing. She sighed. "He's learning how to sleep for the first time."

"No shit?" she said, sitting up.

"Yeah, and he's sensitive about it, so if I catch you giving him a hard time I'm going to make sure *you* don't sleep for a while."

Kaye paused. "Why...why did you stop him from killing me?"

"You mean the lord you tried to kill? The man I care very much for?"

She looked down. "He's…a monster, right?"

"Is that what they told you?" Kaye nodded. Cass sighed heavily, pushing her fingertips into her forehead, and tried hard not to scream at the kid who'd clearly been through some shit if this was where she wound up. "You want to know why I didn't let him kill you? Because he is terrified that he might. Monsters don't do that. They just kill people without feeling anything about it."

"So…he's like…a person."

"Not 'like' one. Is one."

There came a frantic knock at the door, and Gideon sat up with a startled snort. Jules poked her head in. "Cassie. There's a bunch of knights marching in."

She stood up. "What?"

"They're at the gate. Bjorn's talking to them, but you know how well that goes."

"What are they doing here?"

"They said they heard there was a disturbance and they've come to take command of the scene."

"Oh, fuck that," she snapped. "Couldn't get here in time to handle the assassins, but now they want control of my scene?"

Gideon rubbed at his eyes. "Why is it knights and not guards?"

"Because Upper Echelon," Jules answered anxiously. "There are an *awful* lot of dead guys around."

"They attacked us and wouldn't quit," Gideon said. "The butler saw it."

Clanking started to sound throughout the house. The door opened, and Bjorn and Thalia were marched in. Behind them was an unfortunately familiar face—the Knight Captain, as unpleasant as before.

"Miss Friend," he said. "Knight Captain Gerund."

"Yes, I believe we've met. Is there something you need? This is not the best time."

"I can see that," he said dryly. "My men were alerted to a struggle here, and we've arrived to find several dead and your people on the lookout. Why don't you tell *me* what you need?"

"At this point, sleep," she answered frankly. "My people handled twelve assassins tonight after Lord Fremont and I were awoken quite unpleasantly at knifepoint."

"I see," he said, peering around Cass to Kaye. "And who is this?"

"I captured one of them and have been questioning her, as is my prerogative. I think you'll find my contract in order, as well as my credentials."

He strode forward. "A River Rat. Unusual this high up."

Unusual that he'd know what one looked like. Kaye watched him, for once keeping her mouth shut. Maybe she felt intimidated by the armor, or the fact that there were now sixteen heavily armed knights surrounding her and she was tied to a chair. Either way, it was smart.

Cass didn't like this. Perhaps it was that she knew he didn't like Alexander, or perhaps it was the way he was evaluating this kid, or maybe she was really just pissed that he walked in like he owned the place after helping not at all.

"Yep," she said. "And I'd really like to get back to it so we can wrap this up. If there's paperwork you need to see, I can go get it."

He glanced briefly to Cass like she was a fly buzzing around his head. "We are His Highness' royal guard. If you truly believe that five untrained commonborn individuals can safeguard his wedding, it's small wonder this altercation happened the way it did."

The door opened again, and Alexander pushed his way past the formation of knights, this time in nightclothes and a robe, Humphrey not far behind. "What on earth is going on here?"

"Lord Fremont," the Knight Captain said, stepping back and regarding him with a certain amount of surprise and disappointment. "You seem unwell."

"I did just get stabbed," he said, leaning against the sideboard. "And I would love to rest, but there is an entire regiment marching through my house. The company has handled this to my satisfaction, Gerund."

"Really."

"Quite. The timing and severity would have been unanticipated by anyone."

Cass' hand curled around her sheath. "If the Knight Captain has questions of efficacy, I will answer to them."

"I won't hear of it." Alexander said.

Gerund watched Alexander a little too long for Cass' liking. "Well," he said. "Since I am here, I will need to bring a report back to His Majesty and tie up the loose ends for policy's sake. We can remove the corpses."

Alexander made a stiff bow of his head. "I thank you for that, and so, I assume, will Humphrey."

Humphrey did look a touch floury at the mentions. Bjorn clapped a large hand to his shoulder.

Gerund looked at Kaye. "You. You came with the intent to kill Lord Fremont. Yes?"

She stayed silent, her lips pinched together. Cass' gut churned. This was not going to end well for the kid. "Tell him."

She glared up at Gerund. "Yes, sir."

"And you were paid to do so by an outside client?"

"No. It was a Rat job."

"So your leaders asked you to do it."

"Ain't nothing *asked* about it," she muttered.

"Speak. Up."

"Yes. Sir."

Gerund walked in front of her. "Curious. How did you get that wound on your face?"

Alexander tried to keep his face expressionless or at least annoyed, but Cass watched the horror sink in as he pieced it together. She put in, "That was me."

Gerund turned, looked at her as though she might have attempted to tell a knock knock joke. "What sort of weapon did you *use*?"

"I had to hold her knife and mine in the dark. It got unwieldy, all right?"

He looked at Kaye. "Is this true?"

She looked him dead in the face in that practiced way that all brats know how to do. "Yes, sir."

"Huh. And Miss Friend, you feel as though this little Rat has been forthcoming?"

"Very. I don't think they told her much on account of her age."

"I see. Well." He drew his sword and put it to Kaye's neck. She shrank, her brown eyes staring at Cass, pleading. "Nothing left but the sentence, then."

Alexander shot forward. "What the hells are you doing?"

"She confessed to attempted murder of a Lord of Amaranth. The sentence is death."

"She is a *child*," he sputtered, pulling Gerund's arm back. "Have you completely lost your mind?"

"If she's old enough to intend to kill, she's old enough to face the consequences."

Cass interposed herself between Kaye and Gerund and steadied Alexander, who was doing a wonderful job of pretending to be all right, if not weak. In actuality, she could feel him shaking just by proximity.

He lifted his chin and fixed Gerund with as steady a look as he could manage. "I am the aggrieved party," he said. "As such I claim my right to restorative compensation, and further, as nobility acting under the authority of the prince, I can take prisoners. I assume custody of this girl and will carry out her rehabilitation."

Gerund blinked. "That…."

Jules piped up, "The combination of two laws set down by the crown supersedes the application of a law set down by the nobility." She paused. "My wife is a lawyer."

The Knight Captain frowned. "Is there a reason you're so hellbent on protecting the wretch who tried to take your life?"

Alexander looked a little incredulous. "Is there a reason you're so hellbent on beheading a child? Then again, it isn't the first time, is it."

Cass' hand found the crook of Alexander's arm, and under her breath, she said, "Careful." Gerund watched intently. Aloud, she said, "Knight

Captain, I believe that concludes your business with our prisoner. Company, if you want to show the Knights to the bodies for disposal, that would be helpful."

Gideon brushed his hands together. "Right. Lots to clean up. Come on, let's let his Lordship get back to sleep."

Gerund stared at the ground for a minute while his knights dispersed.

Cass asked, "Do you need something else, or can we call it a night?"

His eyes flicked up to her and he glared in a way that curdled her stomach. It took a lot to outright scare Cass—her job was to fight intimidating things—but the Knight Captain was on his way. Without another word, he stalked away.

Humphrey shut the door behind him, his face ashen. "What was he *doing—?*"

Cass held up a finger and mouthed, *Wait until he's gone.* Alexander sagged slightly, and she caught him. The rest had all gone, leaving the four of them.

"Holy shit," Kaye squeaked.

All three turned. She slumped in her chair, her knees knocked, her body trembling. Cass sighed and looked at Alexander, who seemed to be sliding back and forth between that same horror looking at her face and grappling with the realization that he'd gained a ward over the course of two minutes.

Kaye squinted back. "Um…thanks for saving my life. I'm, uh…sorry I stabbed you."

Alexander nodded stiffly. "I'm sorry about your face."

"Oh. You know. That's fair."

"I should be the one apologizing," Cass said firmly, very aware of the armor sounds still echoing off the tile. "I'm the one who did it."

"Nah," said Kaye with a little grin. "You're not bad."

"You're a brat. But so am I."

Alexander sighed. "We will need to have a talk about expectations. But frankly, you stabbed me."

Kaye nodded. "You probably want to go to bed."

"Very badly. It will have to be tomorrow."

"Okay." She looked a little nervous. "Uh…sorry. Again."

Alexander nodded tiredly. After a moment, he stood a little straighter. "Gerund is gone. The other knights are mostly outside."

Kaye tilted her head. "You can tell all that?"

"And you can breathe underwater. We can compare notes another time."

Cass looked to Humphrey. "Did you call for the knights?"

He shook his head emphatically. "I would never, not with Lord Alexander's condition."

She looked back to Alexander. "How much do you remember?"

He sighed. "More than full moon nights, less than an average day. Why?"

"Would you call any of that a terribly loud scuffle?"

He considered. "I…don't think so, no. Granted, I don't know anymore how you hear things."

"And they showed up thirty minutes after the whole thing, forty minutes after it began? Something isn't right. I think he's how the Rats knew."

Alexander stopped. "You think he came by to clean up after the fact?"

"I think he was a bit surprised to see you up and about, yeah." She picked up the knife again and handed it to him, careful to give him the wrapped part of the hilt. "Twelve of these aren't cheap."

He shook his head. "This coating is about four thousand gold pieces a blade. Gods, no wonder I feel this bad. What is the…point, though? Why go through all this for me? The contract?"

"They said…bad things," Kaye said quietly. "About you."

"You keep saying they," Cass interjected. "Who's they?"

"I don't know. It was a Rats job. It…." She sighed. "Look, if I tell you, they're going to kill me."

Cass shook her head. "That big guy I have out there, Bjorn? He can tear a tree in half. The spindly guy with the horns is a mage. The scary looking girl is a witch. And the lawyer's wife used to clear barroom brawls by herself."

Alexander sighed. "And unfortunately, you've seen what we can do."

Kaye looked into her lap. "So the Rats, we have dens. We're all in a bunch of different dens. The dens have leaders. All the dens work for the Boss." The fourth generation shitstain Helshefzor mentioned. Cass nodded. Kaye said, "So yesterday all the den leaders got told to pick a person from their den. I got picked. We went and saw the Boss, and he and the leaders said that there was this guy who...." She glanced guiltily at Alexander.

He smiled wearily. "Whatever it is, I can take it. I've probably said worse about myself."

Cass sighed. "If only that weren't completely accurate."

Kaye steeled herself. "They said he was a monster hiding among the lords and grifting the humans. Getting away with everything we can't. They said he was going to spread his curse and then we would have to go to war, and that there was a guy who offered to pay, but it was a matter of honor, so we were going to do it."

Alexander laughed. "All right, I wasn't quite prepared for that one. Dear, did you know I'm building a werewolf army for a turf war?"

"Where have you been keeping them?" Cass asked, bemused.

Humphrey exploded, "This is hardly funny! This is the sort of rumor that will get you killed or exposed or both! It almost did tonight!"

"I am fully aware," Alexander sighed.

"The good news is, the Boss is also absolutely aware that it's bullshit," Cass said.

"How do you know?"

"The tactic." She glanced regretfully at Kaye. "If this was a firmly held belief he was going to circulate to his people, he would have done it widely to the dens. Instead, he had his people pick...sacrificial lambs. Either we would have finished them here—"

"Or the Knight Captain would have to cover his tracks," he realized.

Kaye stared into space. "That's not...they wouldn't...."

Cass kept quiet. They absolutely would. The River Rats were not known for being the most loyal of communities, and she was pretty sure

Kaye knew that.

Humphrey said, "This can't stand. If he is orchestrating attacks, we must tell the crown prince."

"We don't have evidence," Alexander said heavily. "If I were to go to him now and say *he showed up late when people tried to kill me,* I will look absolutely batty and more than a little petty."

"So—what? We just wait for the next attack, the next assault on your legal standing, the next…?"

"We have no choice. We can attempt to observe him and outplay him. Potentially catch him in the next attempt. But this may be nothing but a distraction."

Humphrey opened and shut his mouth. "Miss Cassandra, help me talk some sense into him!"

Cass shook her head apologetically. "If we're too rash, we risk everything. Trust me, I want to rush out there and kick him in the head and force him to talk, but that's not…. We're playing your game, Humphrey."

He looked seasick. Alexander patted his shoulder. "Now you know how we feel."

Sometime in the late morning, Humphrey woke Cass with a polite *ahem* and asked for her help in bringing Kaye around. It made sense. She'd be better at getting through than Humphrey. She peeled herself off the sofa and gamely joined him in unlocking Kaye's door. He waited in the entry and she proceeded in.

"Hey. Breakfast."

No answer. Cass approached the bed. The covers were tossed aside, but there was no one in it. She turned. The bathroom door was open. "Godsdamn it," she muttered.

Humphrey said, "Didn't you secure the windows from the outside?"

"I did!" Cass went to them, yanked the curtains aside, tested them. Still shut tight. There was one in the bathroom. She went to tug on that one too. It didn't budge. "What the hells," she said.

From behind her, a fully clothed Kaye sat up abruptly from the bath, sending water splashing over the sides. "What? What? Gods!"

Cass jumped. "What the hells are you doing?"

"Sleeping," she said, as though the answer was the most obvious thing in the world.

"There's a perfectly good bed!"

Kaye shifted uncomfortably, water streaming out of the slits under her chin, from the coils of her hair. "It's…too soft."

Cass looked incredulously at the porcelain tub and weighed the virtues of arguing about it. Her mouth and head both felt fuzzy and she didn't really feel like it, so instead, she just said, "You are called to breakfast. Get dried off and changed."

"I don't have any other clothes."

"Humphrey got you new ones." Cass pulled a towel off the rack and plopped it on top of Kaye's head. "Come on. Unless you don't want breakfast."

Kaye's stomach growled audibly. Cass smiled and left the bathroom to rejoin Humphrey. The water sloshed around and Kaye's bare feet padded around the floor as she muttered to herself. When she emerged, she tugged uncomfortably at the lacy cuff of the fresh white blouse, her knees bowed strangely under the hem of the blue skirt. Humphrey nodded approvingly. Kaye grumbled. "I don't wear shoes," she said.

Cass got the feeling it was a miracle she was in her new clothes at all, so she would have opted not to fuss, but Humphrey's body mass was fifty percent fuss. She cut ahead of Humphrey and he said, "Well, for today it won't matter, but that may have to change."

"Nrgh," she said eloquently.

Cass said, "If you like this, you would have loved prison."

Dryly, Humphrey remarked, "I'll take that as a complement."

Alexander was already working, his left arm propped awkwardly on the table to keep the pressure off his shoulder. Cass went to him and kissed his cheek. "Please let Thalia look at that today."

"Good morning to you too," he said, attempting to kiss her back and finish reading something and missing both. "And we'll talk about it."

She glowered and seated herself next to him. "That's Lord Fremont for no, isn't it."

"And that's Miss Friend for 'you'd better rethink that'." He set his pen aside and gathered his papers. "Good morning, Kaye."

"Morning," she mumbled, not quite making eye contact.

He looked away a little guiltily, too. In the light of day, the gashes across her face were stark. There were also freckles on her pale skin, not yet quite the gray of the long-term Rats', and a few scars.

The two of them awkwardly avoiding engaging with one another all morning was not going to let her get on with the rest of her day. She took Alexander's hand, then looked over at Kaye. "So. Let's have breakfast and a nice talk. Emphasis on nice, Kaye. What do we say to that?"

Alexander squeezed her hand in appreciation. "Yes."

Kaye shifted on her chair, looking around the room. "Okay. Are you going to make me work here?"

Alexander looked up. "What do you mean?"

"You know." She squirmed again. "If you don't do what the Boss says, he makes you work for free and you don't get to leave, and if he's really mad, he makes you do it somewhere my sister wouldn't let me go—"

"Oh," he said, his face softening. "No, Kaye. That's not at all what I have in mind."

She looked relieved, although still wary, as though waiting for the other shoe. Cass tilted her head. "Has he threatened you with…working for him before?"

She bit her lip. "Not me. What's rester—restorative condensation?"

"Compensation."

Alexander explained, "In Amaranth, when a judgment is made, instead of a punishment, a victim of a crime can instead request that the perpetrator be given a chance to make the situation better, if possible, and take steps to become a more whole person. To compensate the victim and restore themselves."

Kaye turned the answer over. "But why…why would you do that?"

"Why wouldn't I?"

"Because if somebody does something to you, don't you want to do something back?"

"But then they do something back, and then you do something back and it just keeps going, doesn't it."

Kaye still looked like she was still trying to puzzle out some sort of riddle coming out of his mouth. Until Humphrey came in. He deposited plates of griddle cakes and eggs and bacon in front of them then bustled back out, and Kaye's eyes widened. "This is *all* for me?"

Alexander nodded, setting his napkin in his lap. Cass told her, "Small bites if you're not used to eating this much, okay."

Kaye stood up, her face distressed. "I don't get it!" she cried. "Why are you being nice to me? I stabbed you! I can't make that right. I can't un-stab you!"

Alexander looked a little surprised. "Please, sit." She did, still flustered, still staring in disbelief at the food on her plate and then back at him every so often. He sighed. "If it helps you, I'll tell you the whole truth. I did it because the other option was to let him kill you, and I couldn't let him do that."

"You could have, though."

"No." He made a face and took a drink of the mug of broth Humphrey had brought for him. "I was several years younger than you when I was bitten by the creature that gave me my curse. Knight Captain Gerund was present the day my curse came to light, and his first response was to stand over me with his sword. He only stopped because he was ordered to. I know very well how that felt. Would you stop him from doing that to someone else, if you could? Someone smaller than you?"

She nodded, her eyes cast down. "Yeah. I would."

"You can't unstab me. But no one can be unkilled, and that is much worse." He offered a smile. "Besides. I owe you some restorative compensation myself. We can start with breakfast if you like."

She smiled a little back and picked up her fork and started to eat. Cass lifted an eyebrow.

"As I'm in charge of security around here for the time being, I need to lay out some rules." Alexander gave her a cautious look. "For security," she assured him. "All members of the household must comply, it's in the contract. You make the rules about other stuff."

"Fair. I'm thinking I should reread that contract."

Cass counted her first finger. "No more stabbing. In fact, how about no knives."

"*You* have knives," she said.

"For my job. Your job is to make up for the stabbing. That means no knives."

Kaye looked to Alexander for help, or maybe a verdict, and Cass did as well. Was she overruling him? That wasn't what she'd meant, though she would, if it meant his safety. He looked like he wasn't sure what he was meant to do then finally said, "I agree."

"Fine," she sighed.

"Rule two," Cass said. "There are scarier things than you, me, and Lord Alexander running around. That means no wandering alone, especially at night."

She wrinkled her nose. "Scarier things than…?" Alexander nodded slowly. She pointed with her fork. "What are *you* scared of?"

He chuckled. "Plenty of things. In this case, demons."

"Which leads me to rule three," Cass said. "If any one of the three of us or any of my people asks you to do something, you do it, immediately, without asking questions, no sass, no talking back. Sometimes it might be because something is happening, and sometimes we literally cannot tell you anything."

Kaye's shoulders tucked up around her ears. "I can fight."

"Not demons, you can't. I don't even let Lord Alexander touch demons." He lifted his eyebrow, so she gave him a warning look. It didn't matter that they'd only really run across the partial manifestation of one. She needed Kaye to take this seriously. He acquiesced.

"It's true," he said. "It must be in that contract somewhere."

Cass looked back at Kaye. "Rule four. Do not touch anybody's weapons. Ever. Rule five. When we leave the house, and we will leave the house, we don't talk about certain things that happen in this house. Those things include curses and demons and tricking people like the Knight Captain. Rule six. We're done with the Rats. That's for *your* safety. The Knight Captain is not happy you're still around and will tell the Boss that. Stay out of the sewers."

She seemed the most hesitant about the last item, but in the end she nodded. "Are you done yet?"

Cass thought a second, then nodded as well. "That should cover everything."

Alexander said, "There are a few more things. I expect that you treat Humphrey with respect. If he asks you to help out, do so. And in some form or another, I expect you to attend to your schooling."

"School?" Kaye asked uneasily.

"Yes," he said firmly. "We can talk about options, whether that is a tutor or a school or something in between. But that is my condition for restoration. Anything else we can address as it arises."

At last, Kaye nodded, her expression still absolutely reluctant. "Yes, sir."

A bell rang from the direction of the foyer. Cass stood. "Those must be mine."

Alexander caught her hand. "You've barely eaten."

"It's going to be a busy day. Probably the next few, to be honest. At the very least I need rotations established, preferably two hours ago."

"That doesn't mean skipping things like eating and sleeping," he said, curling her fingers up and pressing the knuckles to his lips. "Don't think I didn't notice you didn't come back to bed."

"You shouldn't have noticed, because you should have been sleeping."

"I was nagging you first, dearest."

"I'll trade you," she said. "I'll come back and finish this after briefing if you let Thalia look at the shoulder."

"Yes," Kaye blurted. "That's—restorative—we can call my face even."

Alexander laughed liked he'd been hit in the windpipe and looked at the ceiling. "What have I done? I've outnumbered myself."

Too kind for his own good at all times.

Cass settled back against the table. "Questions? Now's the time."

The party looked back at her, also tired, maybe a little less than she was. Bjorn scratched at the rusty blonde stubble on his jaw. "Should we not strike back?"

"Fool's errand," Thalia answered. "There are too many. We'd be overrun."

"I don't want a constant payback war," Cass said. "As it is, I don't think the Rats will be sending anyone else. They expected to lose people. If we start striking at people they didn't want to lose, we'd be starting shit."

Gideon shook his head, fiddling with the flap on the pocket of his vest. "No. We should focus. Keep our heads low, stay defensive, gather information. We know the Rats connect to the devils who connect to the Demon Lord. The Rats also connect to the Knight Captain. I'm going to guess there are a few links we're missing."

Cass nodded. "I want to know what they are. If there's going to be another strike, I don't think it'll be Rats again. I'd like to be actually ahead of it this time."

Thalia leaned forward. "I can look in on our Knight Captain. With the aura he exudes, it should be simple."

"Will he know?"

"There's always a possibility. But then, were I him, I'd expect it."

Cass thought, then nodded. "Yes. Let's do that while we work mundane angles. Who do we know among the knights? Jules?"

Jules sat up a little. "Um…Ellie has some contacts. I'm nervous about using them. It could reflect on her."

"I'm nervous she's going to get stabbed along with the rest of us," Cass said bluntly. "We're in a vulnerable spot. We dithered yesterday and it hurt. Let's not do it again."

Jules nodded and blew out a breath. "Okay. I'll see what I can do."

"Take Gideon with you. I'd like to know what the Knight Captain's subordinates think about him and what he's been up to lately. See if he has any particularly close allies or strange habits. Be discreet and take the contract."

Gideon nodded. "We can do that."

"I want watches here consistently at night at least until we have more information. We'll all take rotations."

Uneasily, Jules asked, "Can't Gideon take them?"

He coughed slightly. Cass said, "Even if he could, I wouldn't ask that of one person. We'll split them evenly." Cass sighed. "Apparently I need to go finish breakfast. Bjorn, please go check that the wall wasn't breached anywhere. Thalia, I have a reluctant patient for you when you're done peeking at the Knight Captain."

"Ooh." She sat up. "Is he afraid of spiders? Bring him to me."

"'Ooh' is usually not the response, but okay. I'll…ask." She stood up. "You lot draw straws for first watch. I'll take second."

Cass started back for the dining room. Jules caught up to her. "Hey. You okay?"

"Not really," she answered without turning around. "Long night."

"Yeah, I bet. Um…."

"Let me guess," she said darkly.

"Cassie, please don't do this."

"Oh, me?" She turned sharply to face Jules. "Telling *me* not to do this? After what just happened?"

Jules looked at the ground. "It's only easy for you to do both because for now he *is* the job. Sooner or later you'll get where I'm coming from."

Cass set her jaw. "Nah. I don't let everyone else slide when I fall in love."

She stalked off.

Kaye had apparently been excused and Alexander had returned to his work. He glanced up when she walked back in. He smiled a little. "You came back."

She forced a smile. "We did trade for it."

"I...well, I suppose."

She reseated herself even though her guts felt very little like breakfast at the moment. "Thalia says to ask you how you feel about spiders."

Uneasily, he asked, "On me?"

"I have to assume so."

"Oh, dear."

"She is some sort of *magical genius*."

"I know," he sighed. "Gods. Well. You did come eat breakfast."

She nudged him gently and fell back to eating. He fell back to his work in reasonably companionable silence that for her was born out of trying not to stew in her alternating fury and sadness, but occasionally she felt his eyes wander over to her. At length, she put down her fork. "All right. That's all you get from me. With apologies to Humphrey and my mother both for not clearing my plate."

He put down his pen again and turned to her. "Cassandra—have I done something?"

"What?" She asked.

"I...you're...." He fidgeted with his right hand on his knee. "You're distant."

Cass tented her fingers and hid under them, pushing her breath out. "No, it's not you, it's not...." She shook her head.

"Were you injured? I don't recall everything."

"No, no." She took another breath. "I just...I can't shake it. I got complacent, and then...."

Alexander's anxious posture melted. He took her hand. "Oh, Cassie. It's not your fault."

"It *is*, though," she said, probably a little too tersely. "I had the information. I had the opportunity to insist we act on it, and I let my guard down because I thought *of course* they wouldn't act that quickly."

"Which was perfectly reasonable to assume. Twelve men mobilizing in one day at the behest of the Knight Captain is..."

"Not outside the realm of the impossible. That's my job here. That's what I'm supposed to do." She stared at the table. "I'm supposed to be paranoid."

"You think you're losing it?"

"I don't know. Maybe? I got taken in by you, and then…."

Alexander laughed a little—quietly, mirthlessly. "I have been trained for two things my entire life: to take over my mother's work and to lie about my curse, and like you, I am a perfectionist. I have practiced endlessly—and in the end, you found me out anyhow, so was it even truly a failure?"

Her lips twitched. "This is an incredibly strange thing to comfort me about."

He smoothed down her hair. "We are strange people."

Cass closed her eyes and nodded. "There is one more thing," she said quietly.

"What is it?"

She unbuttoned the top two buttons of her blouse, higher than she'd usually fasten it, and took another good breath before opening it to show him. Two of the claw marks were deep set. The third was lighter, a scratch, and the fourth was all but gone now. His eyes closed.

Quickly, she said, "It was an accident. The salve for the silver hurt a lot, it seems, and you jerked back. I was not as careful as I could have been. I'm not upset, but I—I knew it would hurt you, and I couldn't do that. Not last night."

His hand shook as it found hers. "Cassandra, I am…so sorry. I…"

She shook her head and gripped his hand tightly. "Listen to me. It wasn't even an attack, it was…I was literally in the way when you moved. You did *so* well last night. You heard me. You listened."

Alexander's eyes, watery and tired, opened again. "I remember bits and pieces. It was as you said. I fought him less, he fought me less, and it—worked. I was…in the same room. With you and Humphrey both, unrestrained, and I didn't…."

"Not once. Not even this wound."

"That has never happened before."

Cass squeezed his hand. "You weren't given many chances."

"No, you're right."

She reached out and wiped at the dampness escaping at the corners of his eyes with her thumb. "Be as understanding to you as you just were to me. Please."

"Hmm. I'll trade you."

She laughed. "Damn. Should have seen that coming."

Alexander reached out with his good arm and pulled her close—carefully avoiding his shoulder, but a good, firm hug all the same, the kind that filled holes worn in one's soul. "I love you too," he told her softly.

14
Fairy Tale

Thalia sat on the floor in front of the low table normally set between the sofas, her legs folded under her. She had a piece of leather branded with a set of complex circles and symbols spread out across the table, and between her outstretched hands she dangled a pointed crystal on a chain so close that the tip very nearly grazed the leather as it swung. Her eyes had gone the same lavender as the quartz she dangled, and she muttered to herself. "What are you going to do with that? You dog, you actually know what you're doing, don't you."

Alexander looked over at Cass, disquieted. She held up a hand and moved to Thalia and tapped her twice on the lace-clad shoulder, their signal to let her know someone was there when her senses were elsewhere. She said, "Just a minute. He's being weird. You're going to want to know what he does."

Cass perched on the edge of the sofa behind Thalia and waited. It was never easy, being patient watching Thalia watch someone else. Every reaction, she just wanted to grab her shoulders and demand *what do you see?* Thalia felt it necessary to narrate it to herself—made it feel more real, she said. "Good luck chasing me out," she muttered. "You'd need a—" The chain went perfectly taut, as though it melted and solidified again into a long straight pin with a rock on the end of it.

"Fuck me sideways." Thalia's eyes came back into focus, and she dropped the chain in disgust. "He shut me out. Oh. Hi, Lord Fremont. Sorry about the fuck."

"It seemed appropriate," he answered, coming to sit on one of the chairs.

"It is," Cass said, her stomach sinking. "It's only happened twice."

"It happens all the time to people who aren't me," Thalia put in, tapping at her red lips in irritation. "But most people don't even notice I'm looking, and if they do, there's not much they can do about it. But this creep has a lot of really fun toys. Including, it looks like, a fey charm of warding."

Alexander's eyebrows lowered. "A lot? What do you mean a lot?"

"I mean that I started looking in on him as he was talking about normal boring stuff with his people. Nothing to do with last night, nothing to do with the wedding. Then the charm lit up, and he rushed back to his room and opened up a locked cabinet full of very rare, very expensive magical items."

"Like that fey catching bottle?" Cass asked.

"No, much more expensive."

"Shit."

Thalia folded her arms. "He then used one of those items—another fey implement, something I haven't seen before—to force me out, the cad. It's like hospitality doesn't mean anything anymore."

"That…. A knight's salary is not lavish."

She shrugged. "The rest of the room looked terrible. Maybe he spends all his money on this stuff. Either way, he's ready for me."

Cass rubbed at her forehead. "Charm of warding. Those don't just get handed out."

"Nope. Closely guarded secrets among the seelie. Stolen by the unseelie. Sometimes sold to mortals, but never for less than your firstborn. This bloke's up to something."

"Far be it from me to defend him," Alexander cut in, "but mightn't there be a possibility he wishes to be protected from intrusion because of his proximity to the throne?"

Thalia shrugged. "Sure. But the Wyvern's Rest is really particular about only utilizing celestial or arcane magic because of their hangups, and both of those have methods of protection against little bothers like me."

Cass rested her forearms on her knees and tried to ignore the still raw feeling of the gashes across her chest. "Are we out of luck on the magical front?"

A somewhat unsettling smile curled across Thalia's face. "Oh, no, my dear Cassie. I have my own toy box at home."

Alexander asked, "Is this going to be a war of attrition?"

"It sounds more like escalation," Cass said nervously.

"I'll be careful," Thalia answered, rolling her eyes. "It's like I have *three* moms now."

"You did notice he's the captain of the Wyvern Knights and has the power to just execute people on sight, yeah?"

"Has to figure out who I am first." She folded up her mat and crystal and stuffed it into her bag, then pulled out a few smaller pouches, some of which clanked. She tied back her long black hair and eyed Alexander. "Cassie says you're reluctant. Why's that?"

Cass sighed. "Most people say hi before asking why they don't want spiders on them."

"Most people are inefficient. So what is it?"

He made a face. "Oh, well…."

"Is it the spiders?"

"Not until right now, honestly."

She set her bags on the sofa beside them and sat on the footstool in front of him, her hands in her wine-red skirt in her lap. "I'm not going to do anything until and unless you're comfortable."

Cass felt her eyebrows lift. This was so different from the usual Thalia, who seemed to relish discomfort. She was even…smiling, and not in an off-putting sort of way. Cass had assumed she must have some sort of a bedside manner underneath all that, but she'd never actually seen it at work.

Alexander looked at her hesitantly. "I…don't know that I can be completely, if I'm honest. There have been many doctors in my life, and most of them have been…."

"Pompous. Thoughtless. Strangely unconcerned with your physical well-being."

"Yes."

Thalia tilted her head and looked to the ceiling. "Yeah, I went to school with those. I don't suppose assuring you I'm not them will help."

"It's really nothing you've done."

She nodded and glanced back to her skirt. "So now the question is—are you too uncomfortable to proceed?"

"No. Go…go ahead."

She patted his uninjured shoulder and stood. "Good man. Shirt off, if you please. Cassie, come give me a hand."

She obliged, coming to stand behind Alexander. When the fabric pulled away from his wound, she flinched. It was still irritated, still a little tarnished. Not nearly as bad as it had been last night, but not as normal as she'd hoped.

She looked at Thalia. "What do you need?"

"Here." She grabbed Cass' arm and positioned it so she held it out, palm up. Then she took Alexander's hand and stuck it in hers. "That'll do for now while I get cleaning."

Alexander laughed. "I believe you were just prescribed."

"Yeah, I'm not sure how to feel about that," Cass answered.

"Feel how you like," Thalia said, readying a jar of something clear. "Don't mind me. Do get ready to squeeze, though."

"What?"

She set a cloth soaked with the stuff to Alexander's wound, and involuntarily the muscles in his arm tensed, as though reflexively catching her hand to keep her from falling. "Squeeze back," Thalia told her. "Makes the feeling come back faster."

"Is it supposed to go numb all at once?" Alexander asked, eyes widening.

"Not really, but you really should have let me look at this last night. You'll be okay." She lifted the cloth and peeked under it and set to work cleaning it. She worked carefully, quietly. Occasionally, she drew something else out of her bag and applied it to the area around the wound—the tarnished looking area. Cass caught her eye. She pretended not to notice and kept bustling around the table.

Alexander's arm was starting to relax. Cass caught his elbow and supported it while wrestling with herself. Thalia was trying to give him deniability, which was decent of her, but she felt *he* should know that she knew. How the hells did she know? "Thalia," she said at last. "Tell him, please."

"Tell me what?" he asked, nerves coming back.

Thalia shot Cass a look. Cass shrugged a shoulder. "Shouldn't he know what you're doing?"

"That's generally true, but under the law…," Thalia said.

"We've already shot the law to hells and back," Cass muttered.

Alexander blanched. "You figured it out."

Thalia came back around the chair. "I figured it out."

"I knew this was a bad idea—"

She tipped him back into his chair. "It absolutely was *not* a bad idea. You've still got silver in your bloodstream. If you didn't see me you'd be in a world of trouble later tonight."

He set his face in his non-numb hand. "The list of people who are aware has quadrupled in size in the last month and it is *extremely* uncomfortable."

Thalia tilted her head. "Yeah. I get it. Which is why I was going to just treat it without saying anything. But Cassie's also sort of right. I'm not really supposed to treat things without saying anything. And it also wouldn't change the fact that I know. So."

"Yes, there's that," he said curtly.

"Want some leverage?" she said, lifting her eyebrows.

"Are you offering me blackmail material?"

"Sure. If it means I get to make you not die." She stood up and stretched her arms out. "Keeping secrets pickles your insides, anyway."

"What on earth—?" Cass started.

Thalia took hold of her own nose and blew outward, like she was attempting to rid it of extra water after swimming. Instead, her whole image shimmered. When it subsided, what was left was Thalia, but more angular, ethereal, hollow. Her long hair was instead cropped close, and nestled in the top like a crown were a set of low-lying black antlers jutting just above elfin pointed ears. A pair of small, delicate lacy-looking translucent wings folded behind her back. "Tada," she said, waving her hands.

"You're fey," Alexander said, unbidden.

"No kidding. Well, you're half right. One mom is fey, the other's human. What came out is me."

Cass involuntarily took a step back. "When were you going to mention this?"

"When it came up." Thalia folded her arms insecurely. "It just came up. Look, don't be weird about it."

"That's—fine, but it's—I've known you three years," she said, fumbling with her words.

"And in those three years I helped you beat the everloving hells out of a bunch of fey assholes, so you can see why I might not have been in a rush to put myself in the same boat." She looked down at Alexander. "But it's for a good cause. I haven't lost a patient and I'm not about to start. I know about you. You know about me. As my snobby relatives would say, our fates are equally weighted. Please. Let me help."

Alexander looked to Cass, more than a little flabbergasted. She still stood there propping up his elbow, trying to sort through her thoughts. At length, she said, "Is there a cost?"

Thalia's lips pursed. "Was there a cost when you thought I was all human?"

"I…no. I suppose not."

She sighed. "I can't blame you, exactly. It's not like the courts have sent their best examples of behavior in the last few centuries. And it's their fault that this curse exists in the first place."

Alexander swallowed. "It is?"

"Yes." She paused. "No one's ever told you?"

"No. Most said there wasn't much to know."

Thalia grumbled something under her breath. "I have never met a greater clot of incurious intellectual refuse than the arcanists in this city. If it's not already in a book, it's not worth knowing. I'm hardly an expert, but I'll tell you what I know. May I please treat the silver poisoning as I do?"

Alexander pushed out a breath and nodded. Cass moved a little warily out of the way as Thalia passed her and picked up her tools again.

He glanced back. "May I ask how you came to Amaranth? This is, as you know, not a hospitable place for those outside the usual paradigm."

"Mmhmm. Well, the good thing about the city is people leave you alone if you're weird when you're poor. I'm already a bit weird. If I play it up, they never expect anything at all from me." She glanced up at Cassandra and winked. Cass looked down, shame tinging her cheeks with warmth. "Truth is my mothers are both famous witches in their own right. Well, one is, and the other is a fairy pretending, but same deal. I went to school to follow in their footsteps. It was a breeze, I could easily go join their practice, but living in the shadow of a practically immortal fey being and the human she loves is not the easiest thing in the world. And the courts aren't pleased I exist, either. I have to exist *somewhere,* so here's fine for now."

Cass lifted her eyes again. "Does Gideon know?"

"Oh, yes, definitely. We had a very tense staredown on his first day with the company. But once he figured out that I actually quite like healing rather than, I don't know, swapping babies out and turning lost travelers into satyrs, things were fine. As with all things, simplifications complicate." She tilted her head and prodded gently at the wound. "It's a reduction to say all devils love to torture, that all fey live to trick, and that werewolves are mindless tragic beasts. That's what you've been told while they tried to stamp it out of you, isn't it."

"It…is rather what I've lived as well," he said, leaning away from the cloth by reflex.

She pulled him back to sit upward. "You've been done a disservice."

"I'm not sure that's entirely true."

"You'd eradicate it now if given the chance?"

"Obviously," he said with an incredulous laugh. "Do you know a way?"

"No," she said. "In fact, I know there is no way."

Cass felt his frame weaken, like the support structure of his bones gave way. She held fast, squeezed his hand. He barely seemed to register. She glanced to Thalia. "Is *this* helping?"

"It's like what I'm doing now. Not comfortable. But necessary." She set aside her cloth and reached instead for a glass pipette. She started to fill it with a mixture that seemed to radiate a soft light, but when Cass tried to look at it directly, just looked like water. "There are two kinds of fey curses. Chaos for chaos' sake and vindictive lessons. One they're willing to let go of when it stops being fun. The other echoes down generations until the stories are oversimplified and nuance lost. And that is where you are."

"Was there a story?" he asked apprehensively, unsure if he wanted to know.

"There's a story for everything. This is going to hurt like the dickens for a solid three seconds, but once it's done, you're going to feel much better. Here we go—"

"Wait—"

Thalia didn't wait. She emptied the contents of the pipette directly into the wound. Alexander gritted his teeth and rocked forward, barely suppressing a growl. Cass kept bracing his arm with one hand, and with the other, ran her hand over his hair. When he got his breathing under control, he straightened and managed, "That could have been incredibly dangerous."

Thalia answered, "I think letting you anticipate it would have been worse, no?"

"Perhaps." He grimaced. "What was that?"

"Water from the Spring of Light. It attacks toxins. Unfortunately, the venom that is now inextricably part of your body is resistant, which is why it hurt, but the silver is completely gone." She patted his other shoulder and turned back to the table. "If you can tolerate it, I'll let my eight legged assistant close the wound and you'll be good as new."

"A spider can do that?" Cass asked.

"With some magical guidance," she said. "I've enchanted its silk to produce a fiber that helps the skin to heal quickly. No need for stitches. But I can do those if you prefer."

Alexander sat there a little limply, still struggling to catch up with the therapy getting thrown at him. At length, he said, "The spider, I suppose? Gods."

"Good," she said cheerfully. "And with her working on it it, that frees me up to tell you the story. What I remember of it, anyway. Like I said. Lots of stories. Cassie, you're going to want to prop up his arm like so."

Cass wobbled, her own arms starting to tingle with the strain of holding the position. Thalia uncorked a jar and tapped gently at the bottom of it. A violet spider which for all the world looked like glass crawled out and played over her hands. She smiled. "Hello, darling."

"That's strangely pretty," Cass commented.

"Isn't she? Found her in the corner of the office. Saved her from Bjorn. She enchanted up nicely." She carefully guided the spider to Alexander's shoulder and directed it to the wound. He twitched slightly. Thalia murmured something under her breath and drew a shape in the air with her hand.

The spider began to spin back and forth across the chasm of the open gash, weaving a thin gossamer film over it. Thalia watched for a bit, and once something about it was to her liking, she leaned back against the table. "So. Once upon a time and all that in the woods, there ventured a human knight whose liege thought to conquer the seelie court. She was a scout, sent to report on the doings of the fey folk and return to her queen. She caught sight of what was forbidden for mortals to see and was caught."

"What was it?" Cass asked.

"I'm not allowed to know," Thalia snorted. "The antlers and the fluttery bits are really about all I got. So the Fairy Queen bestows upon this knight a curse and sends her back to the human queen just as the moon turns full. The queen and most of the other knights get bitten, and are compelled to run to the wood. The Fairy Queen makes a deal: serve her as the wolven protectors of the seelie court and she will release them from the bloodlust. They accept their role and live chastened but purposeful fey-extended lives. The human queen in her pride refuses and flees into the woods, becoming lost and attacking travelers for generations."

Alexander sat quietly, clearly trying to ignore the tapping of spider legs on his skin, mulling over her words. "Do you believe it's true?"

Thalia checked the wound. "I've seen stranger."

Cass said, "It sounds like a children's story."

"There's a reason they're called fairy tales." She collected her spider and set it back in its jar. Alexander sagged in visible relief. Thalia retrieved a roll of bandages and set to work wrapping his shoulder back up. "Cassie, I'm leaving you with a few of these. You should change them at bedtime tonight, then in the morning tomorrow, and so on. You also should keep the arm bound up for a few days. Yes, I know, it's annoying, but it's less annoying than a repeat spider sitting and then a few more days of wearing your arm in a sling."

Alexander conceded with a chagrined nod which turned pensive. "May I ask…you said the venom is *now* inextricable. Does that mean that when I was bitten, if someone had used what you just used, it might have…?"

Thalia tucked in the end of the bandage. "Clever lord. No wonder Cassie likes you. I wonder, though, if knowing the answer so long after the fact would help."

He looked at Cass briefly, guiltily. "It wouldn't help me, but someone else…in the future, if it becomes necessary."

"I see," Thalia said softly. "Yes. It would have, within the first few hours."

Cass shoved a lump from her throat. It wasn't a bite, she wanted to shout at them both. It wasn't even an attack. Alexander deftly avoided her eyes for a few moments more, but she put her hand to the side of his face and brought his gaze to meet hers. "I'm all right," she promised.

He nodded. The belief wasn't fully there, but he tried. Like the spider, it would do.

Thalia put all her tools away and her human disguise back on and shouldered up her bag. "Well. I have an espionage war to wage."

Cass nodded, trying to avoid looking at either the blood stain on the foyer floor or the painting of the late Lord Fremont lording over the place. "Thank you. Really."

"Yeah. Seriously, though. You did the right thing, both last night and today. It would have been much worse if you let the wound go and probably too late to do anything about it by tonight."

She shifted uncomfortably. "He's good now, right?"

"In a few days, good as new. Guaranteed." She winked. "Oh, I know. Hearing that from a fey makes you squicky."

"Thalia."

"It's fine," she said. "I'm used to it."

"That doesn't make it fine. It's my problem to get over." She shook her head and looked up at the brass chandelier above. "I owe you several apologies."

Her eyebrows lifted. "This is *not* like you. Should I examine you next?"

"Stop, or I'm not going to finish," she muttered. "I didn't know, but that's because I never really…."

"Bothered to get to know me?"

Cass nodded, her mouth setting to the side. "I made judgments and kept a distance instead. That was wrong."

Thalia smiled a little and reached out with one of her small, delicate hands and patted the top of Cass' head. "I forgive you. I did make a point of being extra strange on purpose."

"How much of that is an act?"

"Not too much," she confessed. "But now you know why." She pulled her bag further up her shoulder. "Well. It was nice to meet you properly. See you on guard duty."

She pulled the door open. Cass said, "Thalia. Let's get a drink sometime. It sounds like you have some stories."

Thalia chuckled. "Oh, just a few."

15

Brothers and Sisters

Once more, Cass woke in the middle of the night. This time, no one stood at the side of the bed and everything was as she and Alexander left it. She carefully detangled herself from his good arm and the blanket and scooted to the edge of the bed.

He must have been exhausted. Usually a hiccup in her breathing was enough to wake him, but tonight he stayed dead asleep until the bed made an unfortunate creak on her way up. He shot up. "Cass—!"

"It's all right," she told him quickly, settling him back to the pillows carefully cushioning his shoulder. "I'm going on watch, but I'll be back. Go back to sleep."

He blinked in the darkness as a little more of his present surroundings sank in. "Do you have to?"

She smoothed his hair from his face and placed a kiss to his forehead. "Yes."

"Godsdamned Demon Lord," he muttered blearily.

"Pretty much. Rest."

She tucked the blankets around him and dressed hastily and quietly before exiting and locking the bedroom door behind her. Out of habit, she checked the door three times. Didn't budge. On her way through the mist to relieve Gideon, she checked the windows, too. Newly reinforced, not going anywhere. She breathed out. She felt better about leaving, but she didn't imagine it would feel safe for a while.

She found Gideon perched on the estate wall, swinging his hooves idly and watching the street. She reached up and tugged on his tail like a bell pull. Without even looking, he said, "Careful. You don't know what that thing does."

He poked her between the eyes with the point of the spade and hopped down from the wall to meet her. She rubbed at her brow. "I'm here to relieve you."

"I'm relieved." He looped his arm through hers. "I'll take some walks around with you first, though. How's our girl?"

"Are you referring to me or Kaye?"

"Oh, definitely you. I'm not claiming that one."

"She's all right, you know. Just a kid. A little shit, but not the worst."

"I never have understood them," he muttered.

"Something that unsettles you," she chuckled. "Never thought I'd see the day."

"Everybody's got something. Don't dodge my question, love."

"I'm…okay. I'll be better once we have some solid leads."

He looked serenely across the lawn for any sign of anything out of place. Nothing. He steered them toward the bridge in the center. "You never did handle ambiguity well. But most humans don't. Having so little control over your world will do that."

"Rub it in, why don't you."

"I'm well on my way to joining you, dear heart. You had a difficult night last night. Has the day gotten any kinder?"

She bit her lip. "In that there were fewer mad dashes around the house, yes. I did find out that my witch and all around magic specialist is half fey. And not a word out of *you* about it for an entire year."

Gideon looked up at the stars. "It wasn't my story to tell."

"The fact that you didn't tell me says quite a lot, actually. You would have if it might have been dangerous."

"I would have. But it couldn't have been more obvious that she isn't. She's just lonely, like all the rest of us."

"Speak for yourself."

"I don't know if I can," he said shrewdly. "What was that with Jules earlier?"

Cass groaned and tried to pull free. "Is that what we're doing?"

Gideon reeled her arm back in. "Nobody wants to see their boss and her married lesbian life partner fight in front of them. It's traumatic."

"She's not…it's not like that."

"So what's it like? Because that got *heated*, and she was *real* upset afterwards. Like cried into two cups of tea and then didn't want to talk about it anymore upset."

Cass gritted her teeth against the weird swell of guilt and irritation mixed together. "She's like my sister. Do you have those down there?"

Gideon blinked, unimpressed. "Yes, Cassandra, I am familiar with the concept of siblings."

"So you understand how obnoxious and complicated they are to have."

"Not exactly. I'm an only child."

"I started out that way. And then Mum found Jules eating out of our trash after her dad kicked her out, and she gave her a job and let her stay with us, and it was like I picked up a sibling off the curb from day one."

"Must have been a strange transition."

"It wasn't. It was like she was supposed to have been there the whole time and we'd missed out." She shook her head. "I mean, we fought and shit, but that's what you do. You borrow each other's clothes without asking until one of you starts working out a ridiculous amount and stops being the same size. And your mum always sides with Jules because Jules doesn't complain about wiping down tables. But that's how it goes."

Gideon laughed a little. "I'll take your word for it. So what led to today?"

Cass growled slightly under her breath. "Do we have to?"

"Yes. We have to. The pent-up bullshit is not good for you or her or the family or for business, so let's make with a resolution, please."

"I hate you sometimes."

"That's fair." He took a quick look around them in all directions and advanced into the woods. "Well?"

"You haven't noticed her trying to get out of work? Or being anywhere but with Ellorin at every possible opportunity?"

"What? Absurd." Gideon tilted his head in concession. "All right, she's been scarce. But she is a newlywed."

"I don't think a year and a half counts anymore, Gideon." She shook her head. "All she wants to do is be a wife. And that's—fine, I guess. Ellorin is fine. Quiet, a little standoffish, but she's good to her and Jules thinks she hung the damned moon, so fine. But…."

He stayed quiet as they tromped through the mush of the forest floor, listening to what she wasn't saying. After a moment, he asked, "Are you jealous sissy isn't around as much?"

"Maybe?" She blinked. "This used to be so different. It was just her and me and whatever two blokes we could hire at the time. We would go, do the job, have a great time at the reception. I'd help her pick up girls, she'd try to get me to take someone, *anyone* home. Almost never worked." She smiled a little. "And then we would get up the next day and do it again. We never stopped. And then we got older, shit got serious. I got… entangled. That went badly. We hired regulars, started taking respectable jobs, living in places with actual ceilings. We still had each other's backs. Until she got married, and then it's like…nothing else matters. Not the job, not the clients, not Mum and me…." She pushed out a breath.

Gideon nodded slowly. "Have you tried, perhaps, talking to her?"

"Are you fucking kidding—of course I've tried talking to her. I'm not a child."

"Have you said the words, 'Jules, I feel abandoned since you've gotten married'?"

"No, because that's overdramatic."

"Is it?"

"Yes."

He rolled his eyes. "Okay, let's put on our big girl pants and break out the thesaurus, then. How about, 'Jules, since you've gotten married, I feel neglected'?"

"No."

"Why not?"

"Because it's not…it's not the issue. The issue is she keeps leaving us in the lurch because Ellorin has a tummy ache or might need a shoulder rub.

And it got people hurt. Me, and our client, and it could very well get worse. I have tried talking to her about *that* so many times. And it hasn't sunk in. Not even after last night."

"Because it's not the real issue. It's a serious one, but not the heart of it. You *miss* being close. Stop being stubborn, Cassie."

She hadn't realized that they'd come this far in this direction until she saw the familiar ridge emerge between the trees. The wind kicked up behind them and reverberated across the mouth of the open cell with a strange hollow moan.

He paused. "What is *that?*"

"It's, um, where they stash Alexander when the curse hits."

"They do *what?*"

"It's…not my story to tell."

"Touché," he said dryly. "He must *really* hate himself."

"He didn't start it," she muttered, turning her back to the cell and walking on. "But yeah."

Gideon trotted to catch up. "Wait. You're telling me his family did this?"

"Neither confirming nor denying."

His nose wrinkled. "That is despicable. That's the sort of setup they have downstairs."

"You mean in hell?"

"Obviously."

"I'd think that human depravity wouldn't shock you anymore."

"One would think," he sighed, glancing back over his shoulder. "Their *child*…."

"If you ask him, they were keeping him safe. I don't know that he's ready to see it any other way."

"That's the tricky thing," he said. "I saw plenty of people who did terrible things for what they thought were the right reasons. But then, that might be the human condition, too."

"You're cheery tonight."

He smiled a little. "I'm not tired at all this evening. Now I know why you lot are always so miserable when you can't sleep. It's all…ugly thoughts and mild panic."

Cass winced sympathetically. "Sorry. What did you do before?"

"I had nothing to compare it to! Bah." He shook his head irritably, then looked up at her. "Go on, go back to your lord. I may as well make my restlessness useful."

She looked at him sideways. "No, you should go see if you can sleep. There's an art to it you're going to need to learn."

"I don't think it's coming tonight. Let's just say I feel more devil than human."

Cass nodded slowly, sizing him up. The bags under his eyes of last night were missing, and he seemed as sharp as he might during the day. "It's not a straight shot to humanity, then?"

"Apparently not." He rubbed at the back of his head pensively. "I wonder if…? You can say no."

"What is it?"

"I thought I might seek out that Hubert fellow tomorrow. He seemed knowledgeable enough. He might have some insight on…." He gestured vaguely to the length and breadth of himself.

Cass nodded immediately. "Of course. Go."

"You're sure? I know we're busy."

"There is a distinct difference between taking some time to figure out what the hells your body is doing to you and fucking off shopping or whatever." She paused. "And if you had a mind, you could chat him up a bit about demon stuff."

He chuckled. "That's my girl. Multitasking." Gideon grasped her by the elbows and tilted his head down to look her in the eyes, jostling her. "Talk. To. Your. Sister. Like. A. Person. Okay. Good night."

Cass shook her head at him and went to let herself back into bed.

After all of that, it wound up being Cass who fucked off shopping. Alexander immediately had meetings, and with Bjorn handling the perimeter, Gideon away looking for answers with Hubert, Thalia resting or spying on the Knight Captain, and Jules probably being a wife, Cass was left with little to do in the meantime but take Kaye into town and find her some clothes she wouldn't hate. Humphrey had little experience buying things that weren't purely decorative, and Kaye was anything but. Alexander didn't really know how to shop for a girl. And thus, Cass found herself drafted. She didn't mind. Much. She found her up a tree when she went looking for her.

She was still mostly quiet. Cass understood. Even in the lower end portion of the Upper Ring, it must have felt like a different world. She also had to wear shoes, which made her walk stiffly. Cass stopped her at a little bakery and sat her at a table at the corner so they could watch people pass by.

"You know," Cass said, handing her a pastry the size of Cass' fist, "I don't know if I could have decided between going to school and a tutor."

Kaye glanced up at her and took the pastry with a little smile. "Thanks. What do you mean?"

"I didn't like going to school. Kids were loud and mean. But I also don't know if I would have liked spending all day with a person at home, either."

"I know," she moped. "Can't you talk to him? I'm not good at school."

Cass tilted her head. "The divide and conquer thing won't work, kid. He's your guardian, not me."

"But he likes you."

"And he likes you too, which is why he wants you to finish your education. It's really hard to do much around here without one."

Kaye observed Cass. "You fight. You don't need to have an education for that."

She laughed a little. "Sure, I fight. But you know what else I do? I keep books. I write contracts. I learned all about how the government works so I can comply with it. I study demons and fey and learn their tactics and skills, and I read a *lot* of books."

Kaye frowned. "What about that guy Bjorn? He tears trees in half. Did he learn that in a book?"

Cass was familiar with this kind of weaseling tactic. She'd need to embellish a little beyond what she actually knew. "Bjorn is a wilderness expert. Maybe not from books, but he studied a long time under mentors to learn how to track, how not to be tracked, how to survive, and—yes—how to tear trees in half."

Kaye drooped over the table, raking her hand into her hair. "So that's it. I have to go to school or be nothing."

"Nobody is nothing. But it helps a lot. What are you worried about?"

"Nothing," she muttered, watching a well-dressed woman and her kids walk past and frowning a little. "I just hate school, is all."

Cass nodded slowly. "Why don't you start with a tutor?" she suggested. "Someone to help you get up to speed. And then if you want to, you can always go back to school."

"Sure. Whatever."

"Wasn't there anything you liked learning?"

She thought, looking up at the clouds. "I guess…I don't know. There was a lady who taught singing. But they made me leave her class when…. You don't get to do the special classes if you go to the orphanage."

Cass' mouth set to the side. "That must have been hard."

Kaye shrugged. "It's life. I didn't stick around long, anyway. My sister came and got me and we went to the sewers. It was better there while she was around, even though she was kind of a—" She swallowed on her pastry, reconsidered her words. "Humphrey doesn't like that one. What's a different word?"

"What are you trying to say?"

"Well, she was kind of mean."

"You could just say she was kind of mean. Or you could say she was ornery."

Kaye blinked. "Ornery. That's a five gold word."

"You can have it for free."

"Ornery," she pronounced. "Yeah. She had it pretty bad when our dad was around, and it made her ornery. But she let me stay in her den and taught me how to do Rat stuff, and she didn't make me feel stupid."

Cass wanted to reach out and pat her hair and tell her that was the lowest possible bar, but Kaye's shoulders were hunched in on themselves. She knew that posture. She'd protect herself, even if someone was trying to be kind. Maybe especially. Noncommittally, she said, "Well, if you like, maybe I can show you a few things, too. Improve your form."

Kaye brightened. "Really?"

"Sure. But you have to promise you'll try with the tutor. Give it a good shot. Learn some more five gold words you can use instead of bitch."

She considered. "Deal."

"Good. Finish up and don't tell Humphrey I spoiled your lunch."

"Is he ornery?"

"No. He's just Humphrey."

She seemed disappointed with the explanation, but accepted it.

Humphrey took the bags from Cass at the door as Kaye immediately jettisoned her shoes and ran off to one of the numerous hiding spots she'd already found in the manor.

"I trust your excursion was successful?" he inquired, raising an eyebrow as she went.

"We're making progress."

"I'm glad someone is." He shook his head. "I don't know what Lord Alexander was thinking—well, I *do*, but frankly, I am too old to go through this again."

Cass laughed a little. "Somehow I can't see him being quite this rebellious."

"He had access to volatile alchemical supplies and he turned into an insatiably hungry wolf pup monthly," he said, weariness in his voice. "He was his own challenge. Speaking of which, I believe you'll find him in his study overworking himself already."

"Thank you, Humphrey."

He made a vague noise of tired acknowledgement and shuffled off to put Kaye's new clothes away. Cass made her way to the study and knocked briefly before letting herself in. He would know it was her by the sound of her gait from partway down the hall anyway.

Alexander looked up from his ledgers. His arm was dutifully still bound in the sling, but that was absolutely not stopping him from trying awkwardly to use it to hold his books steady as he wrote.

She cocked an eyebrow. "Should you be doing that?"

"It is damned near impossible to do without," he huffed.

"Then perhaps," she said, sauntering to the desk and gently relieving him of the book and shutting it, "taking *two days* to recover from *being stabbed* might be worth considering."

"Potentially," he grumbled. "It will all still be waiting for me when I do, however."

"I know." She perched carefully on the edge of his desk. "Maybe it is time to consider a clerk. Not an army, but one might do."

"Another person around to potentially find out? Hasn't there been enough of that?"

"How frequent a problem is it?"

"Since you've come around, much more." He paused, watched her face fall. "That...came out poorly."

"It's okay, I take your meaning. Since things got more exciting than you're used to."

"It was indecorous."

"Not everything has to be decorous."

He reached out with the unbound hand and put his hand to her knee. "You deserve decorous, or at the very least the sort of indecorous you appreciate. May I make it up to you?"

"Yes, please." She leaned forward and let him kiss her indecorously for a moment, then pulled back and kissed his forehead. "Speaking of indecorous and your work."

"Oh, dear," he laughed breathlessly.

Cass tucked a bit of hair behind his ear. "I had a talk with Kaye today while Humphrey sent us out shopping."

"Oh, thank gods," he said, relief flooding his face.

She leaned back. "You all right there?"

"No," he admitted. "I'm not qualified to have a child. Who let me have a child?"

"You let you have a child."

He took a breath. "I did. It was important. I suppose I'm having difficulty coming to terms with the sharp turnarounds in my life lately." Quickly, he said, "Not you—oh, godsdamnit, I've done it again."

Cass laughed quietly and tucked his hair back. "Most people have some time to think before adopting a ward."

Alexander nodded, his eyes wide. "My point is that I welcome your help readily, because dear gods, I have no idea what I'm doing."

"Well, we may as well figure it out at the same time, because neither do I. She's going to need someone gentle to tutor her. But she told me that when she was in school, she liked learning how to sing."

"Good to know. Perhaps that's the way in."

"I think it would have been," Cass said cautiously, "but it sounds like her dad died and they stopped letting her take any of the nonbasics when she went to live at the orphanage."

Alexander's expression shifted a few times, and at length, settled on stony. "Do you know which district she was in?"

"Not offhand. I can ask."

"You know, it doesn't matter," he said, tapping his knuckles on the desk. "That's the sort of thing we need a citywide audit for. You're right. I need a clerk. Maybe two. Maybe an army."

"Are you all right?" she asked cautiously.

"Honestly? No," he replied, looking about the study, distressed. "That is a degradation of the charter. *Every* child is to have access to all classes. That a school should be able to exclude a child based on a personal tragedy—and I was unaware."

"You can't be everywhere at once."

"No, you're right," he admitted. "But she is likely not the only one. And I need to know. But I'm stuck with this bloody wedding. That…likely came out wrong again."

She shook her head. "I see this a lot," she told him. "It's meant to be an honor. Instead, it consumes your time and peace of mind."

"It brought you, and I can't resent that, but…." He shook his head and looked at his desk. "I will not put the children on hold for a wedding. Even my best friend's."

She leaned across the desk again and kissed him. "Good."

"Thank you for telling me."

"I'm only sorry I told you today," she said. "I probably should have waited for that shoulder."

"Oh, I heard you," he said, brushing his lips against hers and setting his hand to her waist. "Recovering."

"Good." She intertwined her fingers with his and kissed him back.

The door opened abruptly behind them. Cass started and nearly slipped from the desk. Alexander caught her and turned sharply to see who'd arrived.

There stood a casually dressed, extremely surprised looking Crown Prince Ruhan, a frazzled Humphrey rushing up behind him. "My—apologies—Lord Alexander," he panted. "May I present His Highness—"

Ruhan's thoughts seemed to finally engage. His face split in a grin. "*Yes,*" he said.

Alexander's face reddened. "Please, can we not?"

Cass hastily got down from the desk and attempted a curtsey. Ruhan stepped forward and clasped her hand in his. "Please, there's no need for that. Cassandra, yes? My gods, I can hardly believe it. I mean, I can, you're lovely, but he's been a bachelor for so long."

Alexander sighed deeply. "*Ruhan.* We have talked about this. You have to knock when in other people's houses. They might be doing things."

"I…your point has been illustrated." He bowed to Cassandra. "I beg your pardon."

She rubbed at the back of her neck and stammered. "Of…course. I should probably…."

"No, please, stay. I had hoped to speak with both of you. I hadn't expected to find both of you here quite like this, but you know, I am actually delighted." He turned, caught sight of Alexander's arm in its sling, sobered. "So it's true. Gerund told me what happened. Are you all right?"

Cass' stomach sank. Gerund's name was enough to do that. Alexander sighed. "I'm well enough, thanks to Cassandra and her party. Have you come to fuss?"

"Yes." He folded his arms and paced a little nervously. "I don't like this, Xander. *Twelve* men? I let it go before, but you need guards."

That was the play. Gerund got the prince worked up. Alexander shot Cass a slightly alarmed look, then turned back to his friend. "Let's have this discussion somewhere more comfortable, shall we?"

Ruhan stopped. "You're going to refuse, aren't you."

"Did I say that? I just thought you might like to sit down before you wear out my floor."

"You said *discussion*. Discussion means you're going to be stubborn."

Alexander stood. "Just because you're used to people rolling over the second you walk into a room doesn't mean a discussion is automatically an argument."

"No, I just know better. A discussion is usually an argument with you."

Cass smiled slightly. Without the crown on his head and the whole audience thing, Ruhan seemed much more like a person, and they sounded much more like friends. Still, she couldn't help but feel Alexander's apprehension radiating.

As he led them to the sitting room, she caught his arm and spoke quietly. "Do you think he would really cast you out if he knew?"

Alexander glanced backward. Ruhan chatted easily with Humphrey, unaware. "He has no choice. He's still bound by the law, even if he is the prince."

"You don't think he'd look the other way?"

He faced forward again, troubled. He didn't want to test it. Cass ran her hand down his arm and opened the sitting room door. Humphrey opened the curtains. On the other side of the glass, a pair of knights stood, watching outwardly. Alexander seemed kind of resigned. Of course the prince wouldn't be allowed to come alone. At least they weren't in the room. She helped Alexander to a sofa and sat at his side with a respectable distance between them. Ruhan perched on a chair across from them and folded his hands in front of his chin. "All right, Alexander. What logic are you planning to flatten me with today?"

Alexander looked over at Cass. "I don't even know where to begin."

"There's a reason I tend not to tell brides and grooms everything," she said.

"I should let you wield your professional expertise."

"Unless you think a personal touch would be more appreciated."

The prince let his hands drop. "As adorable as this is—and it is; remind me to tease you about it later, Xander—would someone please tell me what happened here? Why are you harboring the girl who stabbed you? Why won't you let me send you guards? What the hells is going on?"

Cass looked to Alexander with a nod and took a breath. "Your Highness," she said slowly, cautiously, "my team is working on unraveling a complex series of threats which stem primarily from a demonic entity utilizing a network of supernatural and mortal operatives alike. Up until recently, we were hoping to keep a low profile. It seems that is no longer an option. Regardless of that, the fact remains that the entity's reach is long, subtle, and persuasive. Perhaps possessive. Opening the estate up to people outside this team is not a risk Lord Fremont—or indeed you and your bride yourselves—can afford."

Ruhan's eyebrows furrowed. "Are you suggesting my knights are untrustworthy?"

Well. That was not the right thing to say. She squirmed in her seat. Alexander pursed his lips. "It almost doesn't matter, Ru. The thing can corrupt with very little effort if they don't have the right protection. And if you put them around me, there is a fairly good chance if they're not corrupted, they will be."

"You dodged the question."

"You know very well what Gerund thinks of me."

Ruhan gripped the edge of his seat. Cass shifted her weight. Who was this anger for? "And you think he would allow that to impact his duty?"

"I think he already has," he said plainly.

"Alexander, that is quite enough."

He arced a silver eyebrow. "Not even willing to entertain the logic?"

Ruhan put his hand to the side of his head. "What I am not willing to do is entertain this…feud between the two men who saved my life."

Cass felt Alexander's hand clench inside the sling. He took a breath. "Regardless of how any of us feel about him," he said a little icily, "the point remains that inexperienced demon hunters are a liability. Cassandra's people handled the situation well before the knights ever showed up. Were it not for them, there would not be a best man any longer."

Ruhan's expression fell from stiff frustration to soft with guilt. He nodded and looked at Cassandra. "I…yes. Thank you."

"It's my job," she said with an awkward laugh. "Also I…sort of prefer him alive for selfish reasons."

"Even so. You have my gratitude. And you my apologies," he said to Alexander. "I…hadn't anticipated this."

In spite of himself, Alexander's mouth quirked up a little. "You hadn't anticipated having enemies. You, in training since before you could walk."

"I just…I'd hoped they would come for *me* and not those I care for in my place." A sudden thought gripped him. He turned to Cass. "Ifalna."

Cass held up a hand. "The situation remains unchanged. You and the Princess are safe until the day of. The entity needs you to make your vow uninfluenced. That means alive and unharmed."

He nodded slowly, his nerves settling visibly. His relief was incomplete. "Then why do they attack here?"

Alexander smiled grimly. "You can get married without me."

"No, I can't," he said. He looked around warily. "Hear me, demon? I won't. Not without my brother." He waited, listened to the silence. "That's what I thought."

"Don't go making promises now."

"It was a threat." The prince brought his hands back to the worn leather seat, rolled the palms over the piped trim. Cass tried not to watch openly, but it struck her that the prince was anxious. Always in motion in some way. It made a certain amount of sense; Alexander was also anxious.

They'd have been logical playmates. And yet Alexander held still, performed peacefulness, even now in the company of his best friend. Someone he called brother. Something was strange. Ruhan cleared his throat. "If you won't have guards, at least let me send something. Fortifications, weapons, someone trusted to stand in relief at Miss Cassandra's discretion. Please."

Alexander looked to her. "You know our needs better than I."

She thought. "May I think it over?"

"Of course. Have Humphrey send word when you've decided and it will be yours."

"I do have a question, if you don't mind, Your Majesty."

He nodded and smiled. "I shall do my best to answer, but if I'm being perfectly honest, half the time I'm struggling to remember which reports I've read."

"My magic specialist is a well-trained sorceress. In her preliminary investigation, she detected a fey charm of warding on the grounds of the Wyvern's Rest." She paused, watched him carefully. "Is that something you're aware of?"

The prince frowned. "No. That is…. You're certain? Fey magic is strictly discouraged within the walls."

"Quite. She was very clear on that, and I haven't known her to make mistakes. It's not a precise science, of course. The location is unknown, its purpose is unknown. I had honestly hoped you were going to assure me you knew exactly where it was and what it's doing."

"I'm afraid I can't," he answered, his knee bobbling. She watched. Was it a liar's fidget or a plain nervous one? "Do you think I should have someone find it?"

"It is of course entirely your prerogative," she said. "I would just caution that if you were to do so, you would likely wish to employ someone unconnected to your current household or the church to reduce the likelihood that you may be dealing with someone manipulated or corrupted."

He nodded. "What would such a device be used for?"

"A variety of things. It might protect someone against detection at its most benign. At its most malevolent it could curse any who enter a space uninvited. A particularly fancy one may have multiple functions."

Ruhan's eyes didn't grow any less troubled. As they shouldn't. No matter what it did, its unauthorized presence in his castle was cause for concern. "Thank you," he said. "This will be investigated. Would your sorceress mind if I called on her?"

"Not at all. I should warn you, however. She's, ah, not to everyone's tastes, but she knows what she's talking about."

Alexander started to smile. "You don't know anyone else like that, do you."

"Not at all," Ruhan said, chancing a smile back. Cautiously, he said, "About the girl."

The tentative smile fell. "She stays."

"Is that really what you want?"

"If the options are that or death, then yes, that is really what I want."

"That is what is offered by the law," he answered slowly.

Alexander frowned deeply. This time, it wasn't anger or frustration. Cass couldn't put a name to it, but he was stricken enough he barely breathed. At length, he said quietly, "Do you recall the day I inherited this place? The conversation we had on the balcony at the conference?"

Ruhan cast his eyes down. "I...I do."

"And what you asked me to do when you went too far?"

"Yes."

He stood. "You've gone too far. Cassandra, my dear, I am very sorry, but I am in need of a walk alone around the grounds. I understand this is a source of consternation."

But he *meant it*. He needed to be alone. Alexander was livid in a way she didn't think she'd ever seen. She nodded. "Bjorn should be circling the wall."

He leaned over and kissed the top of her head, then inclined his head stiffly toward Ruhan and left. The prince deflated. "I...beg your pardon. That must have been uncomfortable."

She put up a hand briefly. "Years of backstory. I understand."

"I see very much why he likes you. You're incisive."

"I hope that will not be a problem, Your Highness."

He took a breath. "No. Not for me. I do hope, however, you're prepared."

"For?"

Ruhan smiled, a wistful, slightly bitter thing. "Hundreds of years of backstory, beyond our own lifetimes'. Much as we try, these conversations will never be completely eliminated. Power has no place between hearts."

She folded her hands over her knee. "It seems to me," she said, her voice a little shaky, "that you're in a very good position to do something about that, Your Highness." She paused. That was such a stupid thing to say to the Crown Prince. But she didn't regret it. Unless he wanted to kill her. Maybe. "I'm—very sorry, Your Majesty. He also likes me because I'm impertinent. It's hard to turn off."

Ruhan looked at her a moment longer, and slowly, a real smile broke across his face. "Alexander couldn't have met someone better suited to him. May you drive each other mad for a long time."

16
Soulbringer

Gideon walked into the kitchen, an odd look on his face. "Was that—that wasn't the prince I walked past, was it?"

"Yes," Cass answered tiredly, extracting a peel from a potato in a long curl.

He plopped to the table next to her. "He put you to work? I thought being a lord's lady friend was about being in the lap of luxury."

"*I* put me to work. I needed something to do with myself." She nodded toward him and grabbed another potato. "How'd it go with Hubert?"

"Well, he didn't know much about me, but that's fine. He said he'd look into it. There's something more pressing, though."

"What?"

"Well, for one thing, the poor boy is absolutely smitten with me. We're going to have to put a stop to that."

She snorted. "The priest? With you?"

"It's more likely than you think. He keeps touching the back of his neck and blushing. Poor thing."

"You like the attention."

"I never denied that, but holy order, devil, definitely not going to work out. Secondly and more importantly, he's got some distressing news on the portent bell front."

"What's that?"

"Usually it only goes off when he's actively sounding it, right? It's just ringing any time he walks in the room now. But it's a different cadence. Not the Demon Lord tone." He shook his head. "We tried to make sense of it, but it's unfamiliar. At a guess, it's probably a demon he's got working for him."

"Do you think Hubert might be in danger?" She asked.

"Because he read the portents?" He rubbed at his chin. "I suppose it's a possibility, though simple revenge is sort of a waste of time for most demons. If it's on their way to do something else, they might have a crack at it."

"What are the other priests saying?"

He tightened his lips. "That's…of concern. They're writing it off as extra demonic activity due to the upcoming solar eclipse."

"That's a thing?"

"It's a thing. Eclipses loosen boundaries between magic sources. A demon might be able to seize a fey magic source, for instance, if they act quickly enough. But general noise is different than a clear, specific tone that only seems to ring for Hubert."

"Do we need to worry about the eclipse?"

He thought. "Maybe? The Knight Captain has a bunch of fey shit in a cupboard. We still don't understand how he's connected."

Cass nodded. "We need more from Thalia."

An arm leaned on her shoulder. "Did someone invoke my presence?"

She jumped. "I am *holding* a *knife,* Thalia."

She slipped her slight frame into the chair next to Cass'. "I would hope that you know what to do with knives by now."

"In general. Not when leaned on by surprise…fairy children."

"That's me." She leaned her elbow against the back of the chair and propped her face on her hand. "So good news, bad news."

"Great."

"Bad news is that Knight Captain Vainglorious Asshat keeps managing to punt me out of his vicinity. I think he's wearing the charm on his person."

"Wondrous," Gideon said, poking at a potato peel.

"Buuuut," she said significantly, "I made it harder and harder for him to do so and got some good looks around in the meantime. Obviously since he knew someone was looking he was careful not to say a whole lot.

He hurried some squirrelly little guy out of his room and told him to come back later."

Cass put the knife down and sat up. "Description."

"Probably about five feet, skinny, big teeth, pasty skin, brown hair, missing a chunk of his right ear. He was wearing robes. Like…churchy robes."

Gideon sat forward. "What color?"

"Purplish."

He looked over at Cass. "We need to ask Hubert who that is."

"I think that's a grand idea," Cass said, standing and collecting her potato peelings.

Thalia lifted her head. "That's not even the best bit!"

"What's the best bit?"

"Right before he pushed me out the last time, he unbuckled his armor to get at something on a chain. There was a mark on his neck."

Gideon sat up. "A brand?"

"Not sure. Could be that, or a tattoo. Either way, definitely magic. Our boy is meddling with somebody more powerful than the Rat Boss."

Cass paused a moment longer. "Thalia, tell Bjorn to keep making rounds a little longer. We're going to church."

The Amaranthine Church sat on a shelf just below the Wyvern's Rest, suspended strangely between the city proper, the harbor, and the castle. It was supposed to give the illusion of accessibility to both the upper and lower halves of the city, but in the end just made it a pain in the ass to get to. Gideon put his hands to his waist and puffed out a breath, his tail waving in irritation.

"Too many damned stairs for one day," he huffed.

Cass looked up at the tall purple glass building, spires reaching up for the Rest. "Best hope he's not up with the bells," she said.

"Oh, he's coming down to us," he answered firmly. "I am not negotiating those ladders again today."

Thalia skipped ahead almost weightlessly. "So people really go here to pray? Isn't the whole point of your gods that they're supposed to be able to hear you anywhere?"

Cass shrugged uncomfortably. "You're asking the wrong person. I stopped going after my mum stopped making me when I was maybe six."

Gideon looked up pensively. "People come here to think. The awe helps untangle things sometimes."

"Hmm." Thalia tapped at her chin. "Well, whatever gets you through, I guess. It is pretty."

She took the last few steps and grasped the gilded door handle. A pane of the glass pivoted open almost seamlessly. Cass and Gideon managed to straggle up to meet her and went inside. Cass had been on school trips, of course, but the sheer enormity of the place never stopped being over-whelming. The glass walls reached high a hundred feet into the air at least, refracting off of other glass panels in the late afternoon sunlight. Colors danced along the tile floor in beams. Priests moved through and attended to worshippers, who mostly stared up in the same wonderstruck way. Awe was a good word for it.

There were platforms and planters, and to the apse the bell towers, but they kept the nave mostly clear of furniture and iconography and clutter and let the light do the work.

"Whoa," Thalia said, a rare hint of appreciation in her voice.

"Welcome," a voice said from the side. A priest, a woman with her hair tied to the side of her head. She paused and looked at Gideon. "Didn't I see you earlier?"

He smiled. "Guilty. I'm afraid I have more questions of young Hubert and I thought my friends might like to meet him as well."

"I see," she said, her smile straining. "If you would kindly wait…."

"Anywhere you like."

She seemed relieved. "There is a garden around the side just through those doors. I shall send him to you."

Gideon bowed his head. "Thank you."

She hurried off. Cass watched her go. "Was she giving you a hard time?"

"She's fine. It's some of the others. Let's give her her deniability." He strode for the door and let them out to a small courtyard. A reflecting pool surrounded by small stone statues stood very close in the center. It seemed people were meant to enter through the gate and the church door was mostly for maintenance.

"Watch your step," he advised.

Cass shuffled a little to avoid being tripped by the gods. "If this isn't a metaphor…."

Thalia stooped. "Ohh, these are your standing stones? I wondered where they derived their power from."

"It's not like that," Cass said. "You don't get smote for stepping in the center like you would a fairy ring."

She stood up, surprised. "Oh. Weird. So what do these do?"

"They're art."

"That's…disappointing."

"I mean, you're standing in front of the depiction of Hilos, god of ice, sleep, and in-laws."

She tilted her head. "That's specific."

"Oh, yes." Cass made her way to a stone bench and sat, looking up at the building. It made her feel small, but like it was supposed to, somehow. She couldn't ever remember insignificance feeling appropriate before.

The gate creaked behind them, and Hubert hustled into the garden. "Mister Gideon, you're back—and you've brought others."

"Is that disagreeable?" Gideon asked.

Hubert raked his hand through his very short black hair. "Oh, no, not at all, I just…excuse me. Miss Friend, how nice to see you again."

"Hey, Hubert. Alexander says hi."

A little of the embarrassment faded in exchange for genuine excitement. "Oh, hello! Please extend my greetings to Lord Fremont in return. I hope he's well?"

"Uh, doing better," she said, wincing. "A minor stabbing."

"Oh," he said, eyes widening. "But he's all right."

"Yeah. Yeah."

"That's good. Hello, I'm Brother Hubert."

Thalia beamed. "Hi, I'm Thalia. I'm a heathen. I hope that's okay."

"Oh—oh," he answered. "That's fine with me. Is there something I can do to help?"

"Yes," she said confidently. "Do you have a priest here who's about yay big with a mop of brown hair and gigantic teeth and a notch in his right ear?"

"No," he answered.

"Oh," she said, disappointed. "Blast. We were so sure."

"There is an acolyte, though," Hubert said tentatively.

Thalia looked like she was about to burst. "*What* is the difference? Why wouldn't you just say yes—?"

Gideon reached out and grasped her shoulder to stop her. "Hubert, this is important. Is he here?"

Hubert hesitated. "Is…he in trouble?"

"Possibly. Possibly in danger. We can't know until we speak with him. What is his name?"

His shoulders slumped. "Lorenzo. He is…. Come with me."

Hubert walked quickly to the gate and led the visitors down a rocky path away from the church. It snaked around the hillside in the direction of the shore. On an outcropping below sat a few modest stone buildings arranged in an oval around a small garden. Two figures worked, starting furrows and planting seeds.

One of them looked up and spotted them coming and started to move around the building.

"We've got a runner," Gideon said.

Thalia laced her fingers together and stretched them backwards. "I can handle that."

"No damage," Cass returned by way of warning, picking up speed.

"I swear, no one lets me have any fun around here."

She waited for Gideon to grasp Hubert by the elbow and steer him clear of the area and traced a rune in the air, then tapped it and sent it in the direction of the fleeing figure. Cass watched a small purplish ball of energy flit through the air and sprinted after it. Most of Thalia's victims shrugged off the shock in a matter of fifteen or so seconds. This particular fellow seemed to be made of hardier stuff. He barreled through as though only nudged and started heading again for a path nestled in a patch of trees.

Thalia made an audible *ughhhh* sound from her spot higher up. She put up a hand as though to beckon, and the limbs of the trees unwound with cracks and groans and rearranged to make a sort of wall ahead of him. Lorenzo skidded short and doubled back to try to dart around, but Cass was ready. She closed the gap, reached out, and caught his sleeve. He slapped ineffectively at her fingers to try to get her to release him.

"We just want to talk," she told him.

"I have nothing to say," he hissed.

He wrenched his arm free and twisted to start running again. The air directly in front of him wavered, and Gideon appeared, his arm linked with a frightened and very flushed looking Hubert's. Lorenzo took another step backward, and Cass gestured with the point of a blade as Thalia strode in to join. "There's time to reconsider."

Thalia tilted her head, her illusory hair cascading over a shoulder. "What are you meeting with the Knight Captain so very secretively about later?"

Lorenzo's thick eyebrows lowered. "How…?"

"You saw all of the magic, right? Just assume that's always the answer."

Hubert folded his arms. "What is going on here, Lorenzo? I wanted *very* badly to tell these people it was nothing, but one does not typically run from nothing."

The acolyte lowered his eyes, his mouth pulled into an unhappy pucker. "*He* approached *me*, all right? I didn't want to."

"Didn't want to what?" Cass asked.

"I'm a dead man if I tell you."

"I hate to tell you this, but you're probably a dead man either way," she said. "If you tell us, we might be able to help."

He cast a disparaging look her way. "Yeah. Sure."

"The Knight Captain has a habit of disposing of his tools after they've outlived their use, even if they do exactly what he wants." She glanced down at his hand where it worried in and out of his sleeve. Scarred. "You were underground, yeah?"

He laughed bitterly. "That magic, too?"

"Different kind. He also hired a bunch of River Rats he polished off the other night. You're no Rat, which makes you a Templar or a Walker."

"Former," Hubert cut in. "Lorenzo has left his past behind. Or so he led me to believe."

Lorenzo looked away. "I—yeah. I was a Templar. I got out when things started getting…they asked us to…."

"Tell them," Hubert insisted.

He glanced up at Gideon warily. "Is he…one of them?"

Hubert turned, surprised. "One of…oh. No. Mister Gideon is a devil. There's a difference."

Gideon folded his arms. "If my presence is harming things, I can leave."

"No, you can't," Cass said. "He said one of *them*. That means demons. Gideon stays, because he's the one who helps me figure out how to kill demons. So let's hear it."

Lorenzo's shoulders slumped, and he nodded, rubbing absently at his notched ear. "I used to do some bad shit—uh, stuff. Sorry, Brother. I ran poppies and used to do hits for the Templars. Told myself it was okay, because the people getting addicted and killed were people like me. People who deserved it. I got the names of the targets from a box we were only supposed to check in the mornings, but me and some of the other lads got the bright idea to hide and see who was doing the drop offs." He shook his head. "It was a demon. Worst thing I ever saw. He caught us. Killed three of us right there. Told the rest that we might as well work for him knowingly now. And then the next targets were…different."

"Different how?" Gideon asked, leaning forward.

"Just…people. Not Walkers, not Rats, not even guards or Knights.

And he gave us these little balls...."

Gideon shut his eyes and swung his fist into his leg. He reached into the pocket of his coat and withdrew the sphere they took from Helshefzor. "Like this?"

Lorenzo backed away. "That's it. Get it away from me. Please."

He slipped it back into his pocket. "It's not mine. I took it off someone using it to make a deal with the Rats."

He nodded, wetting his lips. "Makes sense. The Boss was trying to get in good with...the Templar demon. He was using the Walkers, too. There's no...gang leaders anymore. They're all just him now."

Cass looked at Gideon, alarmed. Gideon too looked well off his axis, but there was something angry about it, not just afraid. "This demon," he said. "Describe him."

"He's *tall*. Like two of me. His skin is...purply red, and he's got these wings...they're...not right. Like they're made out of broken bones. His tail isn't quite like yours. It's got these spines, and if they hit you...." He shuddered.

"Not the one we've been looking at," Gideon muttered, walking away and back again. "A lieutenant."

"Are you sure?" Cass asked.

"Excruciatingly," he answered.

Oh. Cass wanted so badly to reach out and pull him into a hug, but the way his shoulders were hunched said that was very much not what he wanted, and they were still in the middle of asking questions.

Lorenzo looked at Gideon apprehensively, and Cass cleared her throat. "So you got away somehow."

"Yeah," he said. "I ran out on a job. Left everything behind, came here to try to...I don't know. Be better. But then the Knight Captain comes to pray and I'm helping him with the offering, and he tells me that I can either help him, or he can turn me over to Soulbringer."

Gideon turned sharply. "Fool, don't say the—!"

The air went strangely warm and sweet. Cass felt most of her senses dull, the sort of trade off that happened before sleep. Her mind went to

Alexander, his crooked smile, the beautiful curve to his shoulder, his hip, even the web of scars he took such pains to hide. She stood, transfixed, lost in the thought of him, the nearness. She reached out, felt for his hand, touched nothing. The vision of him smiled again and turned away.

A voice sounded, but it wasn't his. "Beloved," it said.

She gathered herself. Something was wrong. She needed her wits. Cass managed to blink, and Alexander was gone. Instead, there stood a demon calling out to Gideon, who kept his back turned. "Don't do this," he said, his voice ragged.

Cass tried to sharpen her vision. It was hard, still stuck in place, with her hand outstretched. She could only see the side of him. He was tall, about eight feet, muscular, clad only in a draping skirt. Misshapen wings with visible, throbbing veins protruded from his back, and when he walked, he seemed to drag with a limp, his breaths rattling like every motion was pain. He spoke strongly enough. "I am happy to see you, even if you can't muster any joy for me. Please, let me see you fully."

Gideon pushed out a breath. "And if I can't stand to look upon you?"

The demon smiled sadly. "I know you don't understand now, my love. There was a time I did not, either. Things change."

"They certainly do," he sighed.

"Are you well? Are you happy? Have you finally found your freedom?"

Gideon turned slightly, his face in profile. "I never wanted it."

The demon reached out with a clawed hand and surprisingly gently touched Gideon's shoulder. "You know I'm going to have to kill him."

"The priest? Don't. He'll grow out of it."

"And you?"

"I'm not in it." The claw stroked Gideon's hair. He hung his head and stepped away and finally faced the creature. "Laufit. Is it you in there, or is your ghost mocking me?"

"Beloved, there are no such things as ghosts. We talked about this."

"Well, you certainly remember some things."

"I remember everything," he said seriously.

"Then you should remember who I am," he said, his eyes darkening. "I love you. I always will. And I will cast you from this world."

Laufit smiled softly. "No, you won't, my darling. You don't have it in your heart to banish me."

Gideon shut his eyes against his tears, smiling too. "Perhaps not."

He traced his cheek. "I will go to keep you from wrestling with it. For now. But I will see you again very soon, and by then…perhaps things will change."

Cass' vision clouded again, and the chill spring air filtered back in as motion returned to her stiff limbs. She blinked. Hubert's arms were outstretched toward the space the demon had occupied, Lorenzo crawled on hands and knees toward it, and Thalia looked over her shoulder in a pining sort of way. A bit at a time, motion came back to them, too, but Gideon just stood stock still, staring at the empty space.

Cass moved through it to him and grasped his hands. "Let's go," she told him softly.

He nodded numbly and let her pull him away.

The other person tending to the garden had gone. She guided him carefully along the cobbled path to avoid stepping on carefully spaced starter plants. Gideon still stumbled, and she caught him, braced him like the posts holding up the sprouts as he buried his face in her shoulder. Cautiously, she avoided the point of his horn and held on.

"I'm sorry," she said at last.

He managed a step back, drew an arm across his eyes. "I knew. I knew I'd see him sooner or later."

"That doesn't mean you were ready."

"I was absolutely not ready," he laughed soggily. "But that isn't how these things go. He doesn't know what a gift he's given us by appearing now, much as I might not want it."

"What do you mean?"

"I know his true name, I know his weakness, and now, thanks to his performance I know his precise visage," Gideon said. "We can summon him and bind him."

Cass grasped his elbows. "Are you…?"

Gideon shook his head, his face contorted in disgust. "Of course not. I hate the idea. But you heard what he's doing. He has to be stopped."

"What do you need?"

"Time. A drink. Probably a few drinks. A bunch of shit from Thalia's house. I'll get it tomorrow."

Cass nodded. "Do you want company or quiet?"

Gideon looked down at the sprouts pushing their way out of the ground. "I think…I think I'm just going to try to sleep."

"Okay. You know where I'll be."

"Yeah."

"Whatever you decide to do," she told him, "I'm with you."

He smiled weakly. "Don't promise that. You may not like where it goes."

"I trust you."

"Thanks," he said, his smile strengthening a little as he started away. "That's a nice change."

Cass waited a moment to collect herself, then returned to Thalia. She was making large gestures with her arms toward the church, and both Lorenzo and Hubert looked vaguely uncomfortable. Cass said, "I'm just going to interrupt whatever's going on here."

Thalia said, "I'm just telling them how to safeguard their building now that Lorenzo's been made."

"Their methods are a bit different than yours."

"Featuring far fewer gizzards," Hubert supplied queasily.

Thalia shrugged. "Whatever gets the job done, I guess. But either way, friend, you are *not* going to want to sleep outside a warded house anytime soon."

"Probably not," Cass agreed, looking at Lorenzo. "What has the Knight Captain had you do?"

"Infiltration," he said, looking at the ground. "Mostly Lord Fremont's place."

Cass felt her jaw clench. "What *specifically?*"

"I don't—I don't know. Mostly he told me to go look around. One night he told me to get a window open and leave it open. A couple weeks ago he told me to try to get in when the place was all locked up and you were sneaking in. Then there were these weird noises and I bailed."

"How frequently have you been watching us?"

He shuffled. "Every couple of days or so. But—not like anything creepy. I haven't watched you do anything private or anything."

"Great. I'm so reassured." She stalked a few paces away and huffed out a breath. "Here's the deal. You're going to keep working with the Knight Captain. You're going to keep sneaking onto the property. And you're going to tell me what he's asking you to do when you do that, and sometimes, you're going to lie to him about what you saw when you leave."

"That…that's mad."

"You really think not showing up is safer?"

"Besides," Hubert said sternly, "the only reason you have had any opportunities is that Lord Fremont gave me mine. You will make amends."

Lorenzo seemed a little startled, and frankly, so was Cass. She hadn't known Hubert had this in him. She appreciated it, obviously. She looked at Lorenzo, her eyebrows raised. "Well?"

"You're really trying to get rid of the demon?"

In some capacity. "Yes."

"I'll do it."

"Good. There's a particular window on the sitting room that rattles. You'll knock three times on that one when you come by." She started to walk toward the path. "Oh, and Lorenzo…if you don't, she knows how to find you. We'll be by for another very long chat."

Thalia beamed. Hubert called after, "Be safe."

Cass paused, tried to formulate a thanks or an assurance or something. That was the hope.

It was well after dark by the time she closed the foyer door behind her, and Cass felt the weight of the last few days dragging at her. She locked the door and triple checked it, started the awkward process of shrugging off her coat and hanging it up without aggravating the slashes across her chest.

A door opened behind her and light spilled across the tile. "Cass? Thank goodness." Alexander hurried to her, a book still open in his hand, his clothes rumpled and his eyes bleary. He caught her and kissed her several times.

She patted his chest. "I told Humphrey to tell you not to wait up."

"It was getting late, and it...well, it felt off," he said, his face contorting. "Is everything all right?"

Cass sighed. "Well...yes. In a way, things are pretty good."

He watched her face carefully. "But they're also bad."

"In a way."

"Come eat and tell me. Humphrey kept a plate warm for you."

Confused, she turned, tried to get a look at the clock that sat in the hallway. "How—? Dinner must have been hours ago."

"It's, ah...something I made. I'll show you."

He ushered her into the kitchen with his hand to the small of her back and into the nook. He set his book down and lit a lamp behind her head before disappearing and returning with a bronze-looking plate with a cover balanced precariously between his one good hand and his chest.

She reached out and took it from him. It was still warm. "What is this sorcery?"

"Nothing of the sort. It's a particular alloy that traps heat at a specific temperature, so Humphrey lit the burner and let it cool until it reached that point, then set the plate on it. It will hold it stable for about four hours before it starts passing the heat back into the coil, and the process starts over until it passes out of holding range."

"That's incredible. Did you think of that?"

He slid into the seat across from her, flushing slightly. "I did, yes. Well, to clarify—the alloy was existent. I came up with the application."

"That is...." She shook her head in wonderment.

Alexander covered his face sheepishly. "Please, don't look impressed.

It was mostly to get him to stop fussing if I didn't get to something before it got cold."

"Necessity is the mother of invention. But I am impressed anyway. Thank you both for saving me this." She took the cover off and started in. "Hubert says hello. How'd *you* know him, anyway? You're not at all religious."

"Goodness, no. Hubert was one of a number of students who completed study very quickly. It's not uncommon for students in that program to undertake an apprenticeship in the time between the completion of the curriculum and the emotional maturation necessary for university, and he did his with me when I was working to expand the school in the northwest Market District block."

"Oh," she said, surprised. "How'd he go from there to the church?"

"I suppose it's just a different kind of teaching and administration." He paused. "Is everything all right with him?"

"Um…yes and no. His acolyte has been doing some shady business on the side. With…the Knight Captain." She sighed. "He's how the Knight Captain knew about me being here and the howling on the full moon and how the window got opened when Kaye got in. Gerund's been extorting him into trying to sneak in here and spy."

Alexander frowned deeply. "To what end?"

"It sounds like to catch you in the act of not being perfectly human, if I'm reading between the lines correctly."

"All of this — because of *that?*"

"No, there's more, it seems." She pushed at her forehead. "Gideon's husband is here and working for the Demon Lord. He showed up. That was not a good time. Gideon is understandably wrecked. But we know now that Gerund is acquainted with Gideon's husband, that Gideon's husband is effectively controlling all three of the major underground organizations in the city, and that while they are working together, it seems that Gerund maintains his own agenda. You appear to be a large item on it, and for the moment, it lines up with the demons' need to get the wedding party out of the way."

He rested his arm on the table and stared at the grain for a moment. "I knew he was a bastard, but demons and all out treason…."

"If I'm being honest, I'm a little more creeped out by the fixation on you," she said shrewdly. "Why does he hate you so much? It can't just be the title."

Alexander scowled into the corner. "I don't bloody know. I can guess, but fat lot of good that does me when it comes time to prove it."

"Guess," she urged. "It's just me."

He sighed, composed himself. "When Ruhan was very young, there was an assassination attempt. This is secondhand, mind. I wasn't orphaned yet at this point, which means I don't remember much of anything. I am given to understand that a man hired by the country of Prell entered the nursery and tried to throw Ruhan from the Wyvern's Rest. Gerund, then a squire, apparently heard the crying and broke into the room. He wrestled Ruhan back inside and then dispatched the assassin."

Prell. Cass thought. Historically the neighboring kingdom hadn't been fond of Amaranth. It took up most of the rest of the peninsula, and it always galled the rulers somewhat that the city-state was an independent chunk out of the edge of it. Still, outright killing the heir to the throne seemed a bit bold. "Did they ever find out who the assassin was?"

"Not definitively. It was chalked up to an all's well that ends well, Gerund was a hero, and has been a trusted and celebrated knight ever since. Even getting ready for that damned trip to the wilds, all I heard was how lucky we were to be learning from him, how he saved Ruhan's life at the risk of his own. But after the attack, it…nobody talked about him anymore."

"You think it's jealousy."

"It sounds so base when put that way," he said, vexed. "But really, yes. The veneration died back. I'm not suggesting I took his place. It just…the gossip vultures circled and the conversation changed. I think he'd become accustomed to being the most interesting person in the room. I don't…." He trailed off, squeezing his eyes shut.

She reached out and took his hand. "What is it?"

"The day my mother told the Queen, she tried to keep me with her, but Ruhan insisted on pulling me away, and it must have looked too strange to object. Gerund was attending the Queen, and when he heard what my mother had to say, he…." He rubbed at his neck. "I told Kaye. What I didn't say is that he attempted to make a…show of it. We were inches away from the court before the Queen called him off."

Cass' free hand tightened in her lap. She took a measured breath. "Love…."

"You forget I can hear your heartbeat."

"What the *fuck*," she exploded. "Who does that? Who—? And *Ruhan.* He fucking knew. He was there. That's why you took a walk today." She set her jaw. "I don't care if he's going to be king. Next time I see him, I'm going to—"

Alexander reached out and touched her arm soothingly. "I appreciate the fury, dearest, but please don't."

"How can you be friends with him? He's choosing the man who tried to kill you."

He sighed. "He *thinks* he's choosing neutrality. And why wouldn't he want to? In his eyes, Gerund is the protector of his family. He was with his father until the end, he was with his mother until the end, he stands with him now."

"And how does he reconcile that with what he tried to do to you?"

He looked into his lap. "A knight upholds the law."

"And if the law is wrong?"

"That's the argument we've been having for the last twenty years," he said with a wry smile. "He thinks you work within the law to change it. I think too many people wind up with swords to their necks in the meantime. And at one point, he acknowledged he was a bit too wrapped up in the law to see the people being affected by it. I hope he sees it again at some point."

Cass shook her head. "Alexander. You are worth a friend who believes you."

"He does," he said. "He doesn't want to admit it to himself yet. He still thinks he can believe us both. I told him today that he can't. You gave him a place to start to find proof. I suppose we will see what he does with that information."

"And will you keep risking yourself for him if he doesn't?"

"Ask me a harder question, why don't you." He smiled wearily. "And you? Do you still want to risk yourself knowing what you know?"

"I'm contractually obligated," she said somewhat darkly. "Laws are laws. He's not the worst person I've protected, even if I wind up resenting him the most."

He lifted her hand and kissed it before releasing it to free her to eat. "I hope you don't. I do still care for him a great deal despite his humanity."

"That's up to him," she muttered, stabbing a potato. "Time will tell."

17
The Days to Come

It would figure that Laufit wouldn't come when called. Gideon started out bemused but, as days wore on, grew agitated. He consulted books, drew and redrew chalk circles on the ground, attempted modifications, borrowed charms from Thalia, had her try to perform the ritual, and nothing.

On a night nearly two weeks on, Cass put her hand on his shoulder. "It's all right," she said. "We have other angles."

He leaned forward on his knees, his pale face reddening in frustration. "It's not all right. There's something. I *feel* it working, and then there's something pulling him back. Like someone else is immediately summoning him."

Bjorn looked up from his idle carving in his chair next to the sitting room fireplace. "You are thinking big demon?"

He shook his head. "There would be traces of that. It's definitely arcane."

Cass shifted her weight. She knew about as much about magic as she knew about advanced mathematics, but sometimes she remembered a little about each. "Didn't you and Thalia do some triangulation thing once to see where some magic was coming from?"

Gideon tilted his head up. "Cassie, my sweet, my darling, you are a genius."

"I scraped that out of the bottom of a dust-covered barrel in the corner of my brain."

He eyed the corner of the room and started thinking aloud. "So if the basic vibration started over there and decayed over there when it was it was about…half strength, I would say the destination point would have to be somewhere to the….” He pointed limply. “What's that direction?”

“Is north,” Bjorn grunted. “Mostly farms for the city.”

“The Walkers,” Cass said. “Their warlocks do protection rackets on the farmers. They probably have someone whose job it is to watch for summoning attempts.”

“Damn,” Gideon grumbled. “Well, that's something we're going to have to deal with if we want to take care of him.”

Bjorn perked up. “Oh, we are hunting warlock? My specialty.”

“Is it?” Gideon asked curiously.

“In Joranhelm, we do not like the wizards. It is forbidden to use the gods' gifts of nature for ourselves. This was my job.” He stretched, his large muscles bulging. “I find the warlock, I smash the warlock, the magic is left for the land. All is well. Until warlock uprising, and that….” He muttered something in Joran. “Well, I am shamed and I leave. I come here and find you *like* the wizards. That's okay, as long as they stay here. But I do like to smash them when it's time.”

“I see. Remind me never to do anything that requires smashing.”

“No, no. You are fine. Stay out of Joranhelm and do not hurt the weddings and I do not have to smash.” He put down his knife and leaned forward, a glint in his bright blue eyes. “We smash tomorrow? Full moon is best for smashing.”

Cass felt a bit of acidic panic rise in her throat. Shit, that was tomorrow. “I am unfortunately occupied. But if you feel like identifying the target and seeing if it's safe to smash, I'm all for it.”

“Yes!” he roared.

“Gideon's in charge.”

“Ah,” he grumbled.

“Take the other two,” she told Gideon.

“What about the perimeter?” he asked.

“I'll take care of it. I'm expecting Lorenzo.”

“I see,” he said. “You're sure you're all right on your own?”

“Yeah. Don't be seen. Last thing we need is another Walker vendetta.”

She looked out the window warily and started away. "I'll see you day after."

Gideon made a little salute and went his own way. Cass went to see to the rest of the house.

The door to Alexander's study was cracked, which usually meant an invitation. She came up close and paused once she heard voices.

Kaye snapped, "School is stupid and so was he. I'm not sorry."

Alexander sighed. "You're not at all sorry you threatened to set him on fire."

"It got him to leave, didn't it?"

Cass pushed open the door. "Excuse me?"

Kaye squirmed in her chair in front of Alexander's desk. "The teacher called me stupid so I said if he said so again I'd…," she mumbled. "Throw his books in the fire while he was still holding them."

Cass gave her a look. Alexander cleared his throat. "His precise words were 'stubbornly ignorant', which I agree were not the kindest, but in his defense you also refused to read any of the essays he assigned you."

"Because they were too boring. They were all—too long and complicated."

Alexander glanced at the open book on the desk and the single paragraphs inscribed on the page in large text. "Kaye, did you look at them?"

"I don't have to," she said, her face beet red. "I know I can't read them, okay? I can't read anything. Never could, even when I tried, so I stopped trying, and now teachers are just assholes about it. Are you happy?"

The room fell silent except for the tick of the clock. Alexander closed the book. "Why didn't you tell me?"

"Because everybody already thinks I'm a fuckup!"

"I don't. Kaye." He pressed the heel of his hand to his forehead. "When you try to read, do the letters seem to switch around? Run into each other?"

She sniffled, running her arm across her face. "Yeah," she said warily.

He stood and went to the shelves and searched for a moment. At last, he pulled down a book and brought it around the desk to her, crouching next to her chair. "Try this one."

"I don't…."

"It's a special type of writing. The copyist adds thicker lines to keep the letters distinct and help you see them. Try." He opened it and set in her lap. "What is this one?"

Kaye looked up at the ceiling, then set her jaw and looked down. "The…cat…went…home." She stopped, grabbed up the book, stared. "The cat went home. The cat went home? Is that what that says?"

"Well done."

She shrieked quietly, dropping the book back into her lap. Enormous tears rolled down her face. "I'm not stupid."

He grasped her by the shoulders. "You were never stupid. Bodies do what they do, unfortunately. It doesn't mean anything except you never had the right books, and I'm sorry. You should have."

Kaye crumpled and flung her arms around him. Alexander stiffened in surprise, but he held on anyway. Cass put her hand between Kaye's shoulders and patted softly until she came up for air again.

"Can…can I borrow this?" Kaye asked Alexander.

He smiled. "Of course. You and I will use it to practice together until you're comfortable. Just don't set me on fire."

"Or anyone, really," Cass said. "If it needs to be said."

Kaye nodded, wiped at her eyes again. "Okay. Thanks. Um…maybe tomorrow?"

Alexander's face fell a little. "Tomorrow. Ah. I don't think I've explained the quiet day yet."

"Quiet day?"

Cass looked at him. "I can."

"It's all right," he said, changing his weight from a crouch to more of a kneel. "When the moon gets full, the curse sets off whether I try to control it or not. The day of is extremely unpleasant. I keep to myself to keep from saying or doing things I may regret the rest of the month."

Kaye glanced at him with a little smirk. "Like setting people on fire?"

He nodded in concession. "The most important thing for you to know is that once the sun goes down, you are to stay inside and not leave unless the house is what catches fire. Is that clear?"

The smile faded quickly. "You're not joking, are you."

"Not remotely. What you saw earlier this month is unfortunately not the worst of it. I'd much prefer you never see it again."

She nodded slowly. "But you'll be okay, right?"

He glanced at Cass, who offered a smile. "I'll be keeping watch," she said. "Nothing to worry about, as long as you're nice to Humphrey while we're out."

Kaye's mouth twitched. "Yeah, yeah." She stood up. "I'm gonna—" She stopped, corrected herself. "May I be excused?"

Alexander chuckled. "Yes. I'll see you the day after tomorrow. We'll see what else the cat did then."

"Can't wait. Should be thrilling." She rolled her eyes, but she hugged the book to her chest, and she smiled. "Night."

Cass moved to help Alexander up, and he looked at her. "You're sure about tomorrow," he said, his own uncertainty radiating from every word.

"I'm not leaving you vulnerable when we know Gerund likes to send people on these occasions." She took his hands. "Besides, I'm not letting you out this time. What are you going to do to me except make a lot of noise?"

"I can't imagine the noise is all that much fun," he returned. "And metal is not infallible. I can be determined. Just because I haven't breached it doesn't mean I can't."

"Alexander. Please."

He let go of a breath. "It should be fine. You're cleverer than either version of me. Probably both put together."

"I don't know about *that*."

"The other one rolls in what's left of the deer carcass sometimes."

"Mm. Giving me something to look forward to, I see."

"Life in the Upper Echelon is not quite what you pictured, is it?"

"You know, somehow, I'm actually not all that shocked."

"Ah. That reminds me." He moved to his desk and retrieved a thick parchment envelope sealed with wax. "This arrived for you today."

"Me?" she said in surprise. "I'm getting mail here?"

"So it would seem. Humphrey of course believes it's some sort of incendiary device."

"Good instinct." She took the letter and set it down on Kaye's abandoned chair facing away from them, then eased a knife from a sheath and underneath the wax. In a quick motion, she swept the top of the envelope open and turned her face away. Nothing exploded, nothing burst into flame. Cass put her dagger away. "Due diligence done. Let's see if this needs to go in the threat box."

Dear Miss Friend:

I do not wish to trouble you when you are already so busy with all that is to occur, but I have hopes that you might loan me your experience. If you would be kind, please to meet me in the garden in the morning—perhaps at ten?

Yours in the bear's strength,

Ifalna

"Is it a threat?" Alexander asked anxiously.

"No," she said, offering the letter in his direction. "It's from the princess. She wants to meet with me tomorrow."

Alexander looked over her shoulder. "I'm surprised. I've yet to see Ifalna speak to anyone of Amaranth without Ruhan by her side. She's seemed quite shy."

She looked back at him. "You think something's off?"

"Not necessarily, although her timing is unfortunate."

Cass' eyebrows lowered. "There is that. Should I decline?"

"No, I don't think that's…."

Wise. Yeah. And even if she did, it was fairly late to do so. "All right, then," she said uneasily. "I guess I have a meeting in the morning. I'll try to make it quick."

"Shall we make it an early night, then?"

"I suppose we'd better."

It still didn't sit right. She sat on the edge of the bed and read the letter over again. Alexander emerged from the bathroom, also still lost in thought. "Are you certain it's from her?"

"I wondered that," she said, letting the paper drop. "But the writing is distinctly Joran. The way the vowels curve. Bjorn does that too. Either it's her or someone paying very close attention."

He stretched his left arm out carefully, testing the healing muscle and still wandering through his mind. "Perhaps it is a coincidence and we're making something of nothing."

"I'm very good at that." But sometimes she was right, and that sometimes was bothering her. She toyed absently with the neckline of her undershirt and tried to suss out whether it was even worthwhile to game out the possibilities.

Alexander sat on the edge of the bed at her side and took the note from her. He looked at it a moment longer, then set it on the bedside table. "There's no way of knowing," he said.

She nodded, sighed, leaned her head into his right shoulder. "I hate that."

"I know." He slipped his hand under her chin and lifted it. "And yet you seem to do best when the plan is out the window anyway."

"Good, because it usually is," she said.

"Gods know none of mine have stayed intact since your arrival."

"Is that good or bad?"

He drew in close. "Mostly very good."

He kissed her in the sort of way that knocked the breath back into her. She wrapped her arms around his neck and steadied herself, came up for air before pushing him back to the pillows and taking his breath in return.

This time he had no room for self-consciousness during. The urgency took them both over, and frankly she may have been just as lost in instinct as he was. She collapsed against his panting chest and lay still for a moment, her eyes closed. "You all right?" she asked.

"I...uh...wow," he answered, his voice gravelly, stuck between registers.

"Good wow or bad?"

"Mostly very good," he answered through a laugh. "I'm…a bit of a sight, though."

"I'm not looking."

She felt his hand close around hers, his thumb moving softly over her skin. There was a bit of a point to the fingertip, a little gnarled compared to the way it usually felt. "You…don't mind."

"Do you mind that I don't mind?"

"No, of course not…." He exhaled. "I should just let this be nice, shouldn't I."

She nestled in closer. "It's already nice."

Alexander relaxed against her. "Cassandra, you are the—"

He sat up abruptly, his words cut off by a growl in the back of his throat. She pushed her hair out of her face. "What is it?"

He listened a moment more, then breathed out, the fear gone, irritation persisting. "Your acolyte friend is here."

"Shit," she muttered. "He has the worst timing. I'll be quick. Stay out of sight."

He rolled to his side, pulled the covers up over his head and grumbled. "I thought that's what the fences and very tall trees were for."

"I know." Cass threw on some clothes and set a hand to the top of the lord-shaped lump in the bed. "I love you. You're wonderful."

"I…love you…too." Part of the blanket behind him started shifting like a metronome accompanied by a sort of sweeping noise. He sighed.

"Is that…?"

"I'd really rather not talk about it while it's happening."

"Right. Back in a moment."

Cass hurried to the sitting room. Lorenzo's silhouette against the window looked antsy, checking behind him. She went to the window and forced it open, the night air uncomfortably crisp. "What?"

"Hello to you too," he said dryly. He was not dressed in his robes today, but plain dark clothing. Pretty much the sort of stuff she'd wear if she went infiltrating.

"Not that I'm not thrilled to see you, but I'm not thrilled you've been sent. What's going on?"

He glanced up from his awkward spot down below, craning his neck to see her. "Gerund is coming here himself tomorrow."

The chill against her flushed skin grew colder. "What?"

"Says he wants me to watch in the morning and come get him when the deliveryman arrives like last month."

The deer. "And you're going to say the delivery never showed up, right?"

"He's not going to believe that."

No, he was right. Shit. Gerund was coming tomorrow whether she liked it or not. And she was going to be away. Damn it all. Terribly convenient. "Did he say what he wants out of the delivery?"

Lorenzo shrugged. "I think he's looking for an excuse to poke around. He kept using the word 'inspection'. And then I'm meant to watch to see if you sneak back in before dark."

"And is he having you watch at night?"

"No," he answered.

That almost unsettled her more. "All right. What does he have you doing here now?"

"He wants me to look for hiding places."

Was this what doing well when the plan went out the window looked like? She didn't feel that way. "Of course he does. Well, let me help you. There's a shed around the back, a little space under the bridge over there, and a detached cellar that's full of plants. That's it."

"Plants?"

"Everyone has to have a hobby."

"Sure, okay," he said slowly.

"All right, if that's all, I'd like to go back to sleep now. Leave and tell your boss nothing interesting happened."

His mouth twitched. "Got it. Night."

She shut the window on him and yanked the curtains shut, then hurried back to the bedroom. "I presume you heard that," she said to the

Alexander lump.

The covers shifted. "Yes," he said, dread in his not-quite-right voice.

She pushed out a breath and undid her quickly thrown together outfit. "Does the prince know you get sick even if you supposedly take this miracle binding?"

"Yes, but even that isn't going to cover for me if Gerund goads me into…which I suppose is precisely his plan. Ugh."

"Do you think you can hold it together to come with me tomorrow?"

"Not be at home?" he said, surprised. "Well…he would not expect that. I…it's a risk."

"It's a risk either way. This way, we may be able to work it to our advantage."

This morning, the carriage was necessary. Alexander spent the ride peaked, nauseated-looking, his head leaned against the wall, saving up his energy for making a show of seeming as well as he could when they arrived. Cass stayed quiet, silently hoping she had better gambler's luck than her father. Rain hit the window and ran down.

As they crossed the bridge, Alexander reached into the pocket of his vest and drew out the piece of paper he'd hastily composed something on at breakfast. He reviewed it, reviewed it again, then glanced up with a wan smile. "I don't know whether to be impressed or terrified by the deviousness of the three of you."

"In Kaye's case, I lean toward the latter. Possibly mine too." She tried to smile encouragingly. "Are you ready?"

"No," he sighed. "I can feel my father's apoplexy from the beyond."

"Let him keep it." If this worked, Alexander would have insurance — the kind Gerund himself had been enjoying so irritatingly all this time. If it worked, there would be eyes on many of the ills of Amaranth at the same time, the potential for forced change. If it worked, perhaps his friend might wake up and realize what needed to be done as a friend and as a king.

If it didn't work, he might be exposed then and there.

So much depended on where Gerund actually was. If he was at court, he wouldn't take the bait and waste time with Humphrey at the estate. If he was elsewhere waiting on Lorenzo's word, then it was up to Alexander. That in and of itself made them both nervous. Not only was he sick, his patience was preternaturally thin, and he knew it. Everything from the rattle of the carriage wheel to the collar of his shirt seemed to needle at his brain. He looked wearily at Cass. "I love you dearly, but I am going to say as little as possible today that isn't already written for both of our sakes. It's nothing you've done. It's just the fucking…piece of shit…moon."

Cass nodded. "Godsdamn moon."

"Tomorrow will be better," he sighed.

They hoped.

The crown prince immediately dropped all pretense at the sight of his friend and stepped forward to shake his hand, but also to brace him. "Alexander! My friend, I'm delighted to see you." He cast a worried look over at Cass, who just sort of nodded once. He turned back to Alexander and spoke in a low voice. "Are you well?"

He laughed slightly, a bit of an edge creeping in. "I am not a talented enough actor to pretend I am for the court's benefit. But there's a pressing enough matter that I am here."

Ruhan clasped his hand to Alexander's arm, his face uncertain, but at last, he nodded. "It must matter a great deal to you. Please. Speak."

Alexander steadied himself and retrieved his paper. He took a breath. "I am here today, with permission, to tell you the story of a girl. She is twelve. She likes to sing. She has a little bit of a sharp tongue, but it covers a soft heart. She didn't tell me that. She began her life in the Market District, not rich, not the poorest of poor, the last of three children. Her mother died giving birth to her. Her father was an accountant, until he lost his job. He began drinking heavily after that. This girl attended school at Northgable, which is why her story is of particular interest to me."

Cass scanned the room out of the corner of her eye. The other nobles were listening, a little stunned into silence by the look of it. Whether it was by his haggard appearance or the upending of the agenda, she wasn't sure, but they were paying attention, for once without formulating a response. Alexander didn't so much as glance their way.

"She learned her letters just fine. She could put them together to make sounds. But when the time came to form words, she struggled. When her peers were making sentences, she foundered. And when her teachers attempted to provide extra help and it didn't seem to make a difference, they decided the problem was with Kaye, not with what was being offered. They punished her for nothing she could help, and she learned not to listen to them. That was the first failure."

Ruhan started at the sound of the name. Alexander caught his eye briefly and returned to his reading. "They left her further and further behind and she was forced to keep going, told she was bad for anything she tried to do, over and over. She learned to give them nothing, go as little as possible. That was the second failure. The only thing she really enjoyed were her music classes. It seemed there was an instructor there who understood, or at the very least didn't prod at her. She went to school on music days. And then her older brother passed away—in your service, Your Majesty. He was a knight. Sir Heram."

Ruhan involuntarily stepped back an inch. Alexander nodded briefly. "A strange coincidence, I thought as well. Kaye's father took it very hard. A few nights later, he drank himself to death. Kaye was accordingly sent to the orphanage in Northgable's district and continued attending school. Her teachers gave her a little more leeway in most ways except one. She was barred from attending music class, because, and this is apparently a quote from the administrative records, 'students from orphanages do not have parents to pay into the enrichment allotments and funding is allocated elsewhere'." He lowered the paper, his muscles taut to the point of shaking. "The third and final failure."

Cass stepped forward and subtly as she could took his hand in the guise of handing him a handkerchief, the reminder. He nodded and forced a breath, tried to calm himself, used the handkerchief to mop at his forehead, read on. "Kaye decided, as I believe most reasonable people would, that the school did not have her best interests at heart. For lack of other options, she sought her elder sister—not quite at the age of majority, but she'd become estranged from the family and fallen in with a rough crowd. The underground element. That is how at age eleven Kaye became entangled with the River Rats, and at age twelve, they sent her to try to take my life."

The room filled with gasps, murmurs, mutters. "That's not the end of it," Alexander said over the noise. "Thankfully, Miss Friend acted quickly to save my life. She and her people subdued twelve malefactors in all. When the knights finally arrived, their only action was to attempt to kill Kaye in retribution."

Ruhan stepped forward. "Alexander…."

Alexander shot him a sharp, almost predatory look, and Cassandra quickly came forward to take the handkerchief back. He closed his eyes briefly, and continued, "In instituting rehabilitation, I have come to know Kaye. I have come to see and understand and mourn each subsequent reason for each poor choice. We *made* her. And I will not be responsible for making any more. I am here to announce that my office will be undertaking a citywide audit of all schools to ensure, first and foremost, that all students are receiving adequate instruction, taking into account all needs. We will be requiring even application of standards of learning across every school, regardless of district, regardless of class, regardless of student. I say we, because this will be impossible for me to do alone. I will be hiring staff to accomplish this, and I will be requesting your help, Ladies, Lords, and especially yours, our Prince."

Ruhan nodded. "A worthy cause."

"There are other requests not in my purview. Lord Evards will need to speak to the funding of orphans. I am, as you might imagine, eager to speak with him on that matter."

"He does not appear to be with us today, but I will ensure he is notified."

Of course not. Cass felt her lip try to curl of its own accord. Jules' fucking father. It was going to be a challenge not to want to punch him.

Alexander glanced back toward the assembled. "It will be an expansive project, with all of the meetings and events you might expect. In combination with the wedding, we will likely be scarce. I thank you for your understanding if my household is less responsive than usual at this time."

Ruhan nodded. "Of course, and you're still recovering as well. You are, as usual, setting almost too good of an example for the rest of us. Thank you for telling us, my friend. Truly. I think we will all be thinking of this for some time." He locked eyes with Alexander and smiled, a genuine sort of thing, then looked back to the court. "Excuse us for a brief recess. We will continue shortly. Please, Alexander, Cassandra, join me."

He led them to a hallway and waved the knights away. When the door shut and they were reasonably alone, Alexander sagged. Ruhan and Cass both lunged to grasp an elbow and haul him up.

"What the devils were you thinking, Xander?" Ruhan asked, leaning him against the wall. "You don't need to hurt yourself to make a point."

Alexander swallowed, his eyes shut. "Is that what I was doing?"

Ruhan grumbled something under his breath, then looked down the hallway to a door. "There. A place to sit. Come on, up you get, you great floury dolt."

"I heard that."

"You hear everything."

Cass bit her lip. She wasn't one to criticize playful teasing, but she was absolutely not sure where the line was today. Nervously, she said probably a little too loudly, "I really like your carpets."

"Thanks," Ruhan laughed. "They came with the castle."

"Oh, right." She balanced Alexander a little higher and held him up as Ruhan got the door open to a common room sort of place. Together they wrangled him into a plush armchair. She smoothed his hair down preemptively over his ears just in case. "Doing all right?"

He nodded blearily and grasped her hand. "Thank you. For minding me."

"Anytime."

Ruhan tugged off the ceremonial cape and tossed the crown aside and looked down at his friend. "Really, Xander, why today? I know what day it is. I know you need rest."

Alexander opened his eyes. "It couldn't wait."

"The city will still be broken tomorrow, friend! Even if you begin work right now." He shook his head. "Which…please don't."

Alexander laughed a little. "I did what I could today, I think." Cass stroked his hair again, and his breaths slowed. "I needed it out of my head before I could rest. I found out last night."

Ruhan knelt by the arm of the chair and looked at his friend, exhaling slowly. "Too good for us."

"No. Just a person. Mostly." Alexander's mouth quirked up. Ruhan cast his eyes down. "You keep track of my time of the month?"

"Of course I do. How could I not, knowing what you've taken on so I didn't…?" He stopped, picked his head up. "We've never really discussed it, have we."

"Euphemistically. Anything more would have given my father the vapors, and by now it's just habit."

Ruhan glanced up to Cassandra. "Do you…?"

"I know," she said. "I figured it out, after a few wrong turns. Don't take it out on him."

Alexander smiled crookedly. "She's too smart for her own good. But that's what I mean, Ruhan. The rigidity of the law…."

He nodded slowly. "I'm starting to understand. I don't…know what to do without it yet."

"You'll figure it out."

"You'll help?"

"When haven't I?"

He smiled. "No. You're right. You usually are. Except that thing with the ice sculptures."

Alexander's nose wrinkled. "I can admit I was very wrong about that."

Cass lifted an eyebrow. "Do I want to know?"

"It was not my finest alchemy project, and probably should not have been done on the champagne we stole as fifteen year old boys."

"It made a hell of a noise, though," Ruhan laughed.

"And it was probably the most interesting the midwinter social ever was."

"Assuredly." He gathered himself. "You set me straight. You've never been anything short of honest, good. The euphemisms are my doing."

Alexander flinched, sat up slightly. "That's not entirely true."

Cass set her hand apprehensively to his shoulder.

"You were right," he told her, patting her hand. He reached for his cuff.

Her back tightened. Of all the times and places for him to come clean, this was not the one she'd have suggested. If Ruhan didn't take this well, they were in his castle in a room with no windows and a single door, surrounded by knights. She was wearing her knives under her skirt, but that would do very little good.

Alexander rolled up his sleeve and exposed the scars, which were raw, aggravated, red and strangely silvery. Fine bits of fur broke out over parts. "There is no binding," he said shakily. "My mother lied to save my life. I never corrected the perception."

Ruhan slouched back to his heels, the leather of his boots creaking in the silence. "This whole time, you've — ? Every month?"

"Plus a few days in between if I'm not careful. I'm very careful. Usually."

"Murder attempts do make it harder," Cass put in a little defensively.

Ruhan shook his head, his eyes welling up. He took up Alexander's hand and clasped it in both of his. "Fuck," he burst out at last.

Alexander grinned tiredly. "Is that the second time you've ever said that word?"

"It is, and both times have been your fault. No. My fault and you've been around for it." He shook his head. "I am so…."

"If you're going to say sorry, stuff it. The fuck was worth it."

"It isn't, though," he said, anguished. "You've been cursed this whole godsdamned time, and I didn't know because you thought I might have you bloody *executed*. And you know what, you might not have been wrong if there weren't normal people around me from time to time. Gods. Fuck."

"I got two fucks," Alexander informed Cass just a bit deliriously.

"That's wonderful, darling," she said hastily. She eyed Ruhan firmly. "And what *are* you going to do now that you know?"

He looked up at her, startled. "You think I would…? Of course you do." He looked at Alexander. "You took on this burden for me. What could I do but look away?"

Cass couldn't help it. She felt her hand grip the back of the armchair hard enough to go numb. "You could fix the damned law."

"Would that I could. The outcry would be dangerous."

"Imagine how he feels having to hide all the time."

"I…can't. But believe me. He wouldn't be safe from that danger if I tried to ram it through."

"Cassie," Alexander said, tilting his head back to look at her. "I'm all right. This is enough for me. More than I hoped."

Her grip released a little. "It's just…less than you deserve."

"I agree," Ruhan said quietly.

18
Wolf's Troth

They left him to rest. Ruhan walked her down the hall under the guise that they were getting out of Alexander's earshot, but they both knew better, really.

"They will talk about him," he told her quietly. "But he knows that."

She nodded. That was rather the point, but they still weren't being quite that honest. "It was important enough to him."

"Thank you for accompanying him."

"It wasn't a question. Besides, I was actually already on my way here to meet with your bride."

He smiled fondly. "Ah, yes, she mentioned. Thank you for coming to speak with her as well. I have a great many things to thank you for, it seems."

"Going to be honest, seems a little weird, given that I've just sworn at you."

"I need that sometimes. I treasure the honest people I come across. I'm sure you can imagine they're few and far between here." He made a face. "I presume Alexander has said some things."

"You value honesty, don't you?"

"I do. It's one of the reasons we've been friends for so long. I also didn't say he was wrong."

"Are you trying to warn me again?"

"With…renewed vigor, knowing what I do now." He looked up at the ribs of the vaulted colonnade passing above them. "The announcement he made today. There will be some social gatherings that come with that process. The maneuvering is unfortunately unavoidable."

"Do you always throw parties when something needs reform?"

Dryly, he said, "Yes. Until the day everyone realizes that's part of the problem. For now, we pick our battles. Until recently, Alexander's disinterest in courtship has been taken for granted and the rumors long since grown dull. Be cautious. Don't underestimate the gossipmongers. It may seem like petty rivalry, but I have spies who are less adept."

Cass nodded slowly. She remembered on whose back the original information on Alexander was carried in. "What were the rumors?"

Ruhan looked her way, his head tilted scoldingly. "Cassandra. You're not one of them, are you?"

"No. But the right word or even appearance of encouragement to the right people can buy him some safety, even if it's not strictly true. I know how these things work."

He laughed a little and paused at the door. "All right. Perhaps I don't need to warn you. Humphrey must either love or hate you."

"It depends on the day."

"There were unkind suggestions that the attack and subsequent illness left him physically deformed. Whispers of dalliances with someone his parents disapproved of. Rumors that he took an undue interest in men."

Cass frowned. "All right, what is your lot's problem with all that? Honestly. It's a load of nonsense. People are people and they like what they like."

He rolled his eyes. "Guess."

"It's *not* about your damned heirs."

"Of course it is," he burst out laughing. "Everything is heirs and legacies and very little is to do with who we actually are. Have you ever seen a noble married couple together outside a formal function? A rarity, and for good reason. They tend to *loathe* each other. My parents did. As did Alexander's."

Cass wasn't certain that was a function of nobility so much as of marriage, but she managed to keep her mouth shut. "It seems you and the Princess are about to set a better example."

He broke into a furtive, genuine smile. "We were…very fortunate. I suspect she'll have more to say. I shouldn't keep you, and much as I wish I could, I shouldn't stay away from court much longer."

"That door will stay locked?" she inquired.

"No one else has the key," he confirmed, withdrawing a ring from the pocket inside his tunic lining, removing one, and handing it to her. "This is the only one. He'll be safe."

Cass held the heavy iron key in her hand and felt herself loosen a little. "Thank you," she said.

"For this?" he said, surprised. "It's very literally the least I could do after…everything."

"It matters, though. Very much to him."

He paused. "Will you be with him tonight?"

Cass looked at the tops of her shoes. "Is it wise for me to answer that?"

"I take that as a yes."

She stayed silent a moment longer, then lifted her eyes to him again. "The person who sent Kaye and the other eleven knows," she said. "They were given weapons specifically made to kill him. If they come back, I won't have him locked up unable to defend himself."

Ruhan stood, stricken. "How could they have…?"

"I think you know, Your Highness," she said carefully but firmly. "The question is what can be done, and what will you do?"

She skipped the curtsey and made a little bow instead to save her knee and walked out to greet his bride.

The rain didn't much bother Cass to begin with, but the glass awnings overhanging the garden made it downright pleasant, like water running down chimes. Ifalna stood at the edge where the decorative gutters spilled over in cascades, her eyes shut, listening. She wore a pale blue gown of a sort Cass had never seen—light draping fabric secured at the shoulder by a silver pauldron. Elegant and warlike. Instead of the usual two braids, her hair was piled atop her head in a series of intricate coils run through with silver pins shaped like stalks of wheat.

She carried herself differently in this. Her shoulders back, her face resolute, but calm. She didn't open her eyes at Cass' approach. "If I remain like this," she said softly, "I can pretend that I am home."

"You must miss it."

"Terribly." Her pink lips smiled. "Think of trees. Tall, taller than this castle. Gray rocks on green hills. It rains like this, and all at once, it stops, and the sun comes through and turns everything to gold. The shepherds call the sheep to home and they listen, across canyons vaster than the whole of this city. You may walk for days and never find the end of it. Long stone houses where we live with generations of families and tell our stories loud. Never lonely. And tonight, on Elkensfest, we honor our sister-warriors and give thanks to nature." She opened her eyes and looked at Cassandra hesitantly, the confidence melting away. "And here again, I am lost. May I seek your counsel?"

Cass nodded slowly. "Of course, Princess. Admittedly, I really only know about weddings."

She shook her head. "No, that is not —" A pair of lords emerged from the hall behind them, and she bit her lip. "Will you walk with me?"

"Sure."

Ifalna looped her arm through Cass', and they followed the awning around the side of the castle. She considered her words for a moment. "You…can fight. You are known for fighting. Celebrated. That is not the way for most women of Amaranth, is it."

Oh. Cass felt like bursting out laughing — not at Ifalna's expense, but at the apprehension she'd gone through last night about this conversation. "Not up here. Where I'm from, it's a little more usual."

Ifalna's light eyebrows lowered. "It is so…*frustrating*. Something happens and they immediately swarm on me like flies. As if I cannot handle myself. And I am meant to pretend as if I cannot! It is *ingrochte*."

Cass had no idea what that meant, but she'd heard Bjorn swear in Joran enough to catch the tone. All at once, Ifalna had opened like a book. "The prince asked you to?"

"No, he has not. He is much too kind to do that. But I am…." She sighed. "I am not my father's favorite daughter. He is already angered, thinking I have not made a good enough bride. If he believes that Ruhan's people dislike me, he will remove me."

Cass stopped. "Princess," she said, as diplomatically as she could, "you're happy marrying the prince, yes?"

"Very much, yes."

"Then your father can sit down and be supportive or I will make him."

A flash of a furtive smile broke across Ifalna's face, then vanished. "He is the king."

"And you're the bride. I don't care who he is. If he's not you or the groom, he's not required. I can make it look like an accident if it helps. People lock themselves in the bathroom all the time."

She snorted, then covered her mouth with a hand. "Excuse me."

"And that's the other thing. People will like you fine if you're you." She shook her head. "Gods forbid anyone find out the Princess is a *person*."

"Would you believe the same if it is you at the parties being stared at?"

She wanted to retort *yes, obviously,* but the words stuck in her throat. Up until today, she'd been sure there wouldn't be any parties. "I really hope so," she said.

Ifalna nodded, watched the rain pool in the grass alongside the path they walked. "Is it not womanly to fight for those you love and what you value in the Upper Ring?"

What a question. Cass laughed to herself and tried to piece together an answer. "I think it's not 'upper class' to care about something enough to be willing to die for it. That's my job. Besides, blood tends to clash with the kinds of frilly things that are in fashion these days."

She seemed perturbed by the answer. "I do not care for that."

"Me neither."

"Well. If you will permit me, I will honor you in my thoughts this evening."

"That's very kind. If it's not offensive, I'll do the same."

"No, that is very welcome." She smiled. "Thank you for bringing a bit of my home. I love my Ruhan dearly, and your Amaranth has many won-ders. But it does me good to know another sister-warrior. Cat's patience, bear's strength, wolf's troth, raven's cunning, and boar's fury to us both."

Cass found herself a little wistful over sudden memories of late nights preparing in taverns with Jules—very little work had actually happened in those days. "I'll drink to that," she said.

The rain slowed but did not stop by late afternoon. Cass looked out the window of the guest room she really only used when she wanted Alexander to sleep uninterrupted. No breaks in the clouds that she could see. She pulled her coat from the closet and added the muffler she'd brought from home just in case. No point catching a cold.

Kaye peeked out her door as Cass passed. "Psst. Can I help?"

"No," Cass said pointedly.

"But there's only one of you."

"Yep. Which means if something goes wrong, it's only me in danger. Stay here and listen to Humphrey."

"Nghhh." She leaned her head into the door jamb, went quiet. "He is going to be okay, right?"

"Yeah. He's been at this a long time. We're the new ones."

The unspoken fact that there were never people waiting around to try to kill him before went unacknowledged. Kaye nodded. "Okay. Night, then."

"See you in the morning, kid."

Kaye smiled a little and shut the door. Cass shouldered her bag a little higher and made her way to the foyer. Alexander's head whipped up the second she appeared in the doorway. "Just me," she said.

He breathed out, his sunken eyes calming slightly. He nodded. Humphrey glanced at Cass, then adjusted a bundle of cloth under his arm. "Thankfully, I was able to change arrangements with the butcher very quickly this morning," he said. "Several less conspicuous packages were delivered instead of the usual large one."

"Is that going to be enough for you?" Cass asked uneasily.

Alexander rubbed at his left arm. "Tomorrow isn't going to be the best day, but I'll live."

Humphrey said, "The Knight Captain seemed satisfied that nothing seemed out of place. But only after searching extremely thoroughly. And becoming quite frustrated."

"I'll bet," she said a bit darkly. "I'm going ahead to check the cell in case he left us any friends. Thalia already checked for magic. I'll range the area a bit, give you privacy but be close at hand, and then stay posted within visual range for the rest of the night. Humphrey will keep the key in case I'm subdued."

Alexander nodded again, his eyes nervous. "If I get free…."

"You won't."

"Cassie, please, dearest, I don't have much time." He took up her hand and placed something wrapped in cloth in it. "A good blow to the head wearing this should stun me. Don't worry. It won't poison me."

Beneath the cloth she felt the shape of a smooth ring. She held it, still in its wrapping, unsure what to say. "Alexander…."

"I know. Not how most people exchange jewelry." He reached into his pocket and pulled out a small brass vial on a chain and slipped it over her head. "And this is from Thalia. The contents, anyway. Now you're fore-armed."

She held his arm briefly, then reached up to kiss him and cradled his face for a moment. "I love you. I will see you soon. If you get there and anything feels off, turn back."

He held her hand in his damp, shaking one. "I love you, too. Be careful."

"Always."

Cass glanced to Humphrey, who just gave her a little nod. She kissed Alexander once more and headed out the door into the wet. She tucked the necklace underneath her muffler and pulled her collar up against the chill and disappeared into the woods.

Bjorn had taken her instructions to confuse the path and created a nearly unrecognizable terrain. It looked very much like a tree had fallen across it and gone uncleared—possibly months ago. She edged around it and found a few more inconspicuous blockages—downed branches, a boulder and a mud slick. She chuckled in appreciation. A bonus was in order. It wasn't often he got to use his survival skills, but when he did, he always impressed.

The cell appeared undisturbed. She leaned in to check the back corners to be sure. No dead deer today. Even the worn mattress had been removed in case Gerund came looking. Cass sighed, straightened out. She thought at some point she would get used to the idea that there was a cell on the grounds especially to contain her love, that he gave her a gift to subdue him, but even as it became less of a surprise, it never quite lost its distaste.

She climbed up the embankment, circled the tree he ran her up the month previous. His claw marks were still visible in the healing bark. Cass paused and listened for a moment, past the steady dripping of rain funneling down the leaves and needles to the carpet of decay on the ground. Nothing she could hear. She took a small loop of the area and checked above and below for signs of anyone but her. When it turned up nothing, she widened her path. The quiet was unexpectedly pleasant, even with the worry she might find someone on the way. She could come out here when she wasn't watching Alexander turn into a large wolf creature or watching for someone trying to kill him, she mused.

Who was she kidding? She wasn't going to do that. There was too much else to do.

On the return leg of her loop, she crossed paths with Humphrey, who tucked the cell key into his vest pocket and sighed. He looked up at her and pulled the bundle from under his arm. "It will be cold tonight," he said simply. "Try to stay warm."

"Thank you," she answered, holding the blanket close to her chest.

He nodded. "I shan't keep you, though if I might offer some advice, Miss Cassandra…don't listen to what comes next. You will feel like you should. But it won't help."

Cass bit her lip and looked at the ground for a moment. "Does it get any easier?"

"No," he said frankly, a sympathetic smile in place. "Stay safe."

He headed back toward the house. She held onto the blanket and fumbled around to try to feel what was bundled inside. Her fingers were a little too rubbery with the cold to accomplish much. She sighed and started in the direction of the cell.

Along the way, the moon must have risen. Alexander's voice rose in the distance in pain and panic. Cass tried to will her ears to stuff up or focus on the rain hitting the leaves above or literally anything else, but damn it all, Humphrey was right. She felt like it was…disrespectful, somehow, to pretend as if she heard nothing while he had to live through it. Unbidden, her pace quickened. Why, she didn't know. Getting to him wouldn't help him. All it did was make it easier to hear.

She nearly turned back around just to dull the sound of his struggling to breathe between warping screams. Was this what it had sounded like last time? Cass could barely remember. It must have; she'd thought he was a sacrifice. Her eyes stung, and she reached out for a tree trunk.

"Don't fight it," she reminded him quietly.

His voice quieted for just a moment. When it lifted again, most of what was familiar about it had gone. It was easier and harder to keep walking into the light of the lantern.

Cass knew by now that the way he was standing, his massive shoulders heaving, his shaking legs slightly bowed, meant that his form had settled. She slung the bundled blanket to the ground warily and waited for him to get his wind into him. He knew she was there. His ears twitched with her movements. It was just a matter of whether he was going to jump for the bars or not. "Hello, you," she said cautiously.

Alexander growled. His hide bristled with the wind that pushed into the cell, and he turned to glower over his shoulder at her. She put her hands up and gestured to the ground. "I'm just keeping watch. Nothing interesting."

He growled again, finished with a warning snap, and lunged. Cass jumped just out of instinct, but when he landed, it was nowhere near the bars. There was a pile of butcher's packages in the corner in lieu of the deer and he began tearing through ravenously. She snorted and lowered herself to sit. "Is that what you're on about? All yours, love. Don't want your warm raw meat parcels and the accompanying intestinal distress."

If he heard, he made no indication. That was fine. It gave her time to unroll Humphrey's bundle. A couple of canisters, both warm. One full of soup, the other coffee. She smiled a little and pulled the blanket around her shoulders and fidgeted with the ring on the middle finger of her right hand.

Anybody in the Upper Ring who looked would just see a pretty piece of jewelry. It was. Three silver flowers set among a spray of smaller green stones, solidly built on a sturdy band. It was very clever. The ridge of the petals was meant to take the brunt of a strike and direct the force into the object being hit.

Object. As if it was a thing. Him.

Cass sighed, pulling her hand to herself and looking into the cell. He'd made his way through the offering, as he called it, and was stalking the length and breadth of the cell, hunting for more. She stood and inched toward the mouth of the opening. "All done, huh."

He grunted, his breath coming out in hot clouds, his eyes fixing on hers. She edged to a crate a little ways off to the side. "I've got a little more, but we've got to make it last. It's a long night."

Cass honestly wasn't sure buying a shitload of meat wasn't any sketchier than buying a whole dead deer. She took out a few packages and came closer to the door. He watched intently, his muscles taut. Cass didn't like the looks of it. She tossed the meat in through the bars and watched him scramble away, took a few steps back. He was different than he'd been the night of the attack. There was less of him here.

When he finished, Alexander turned back to her, eyed her. She fidgeted with the ring on her hand and watched him, too. "Nobody's given me a ring before," she said with a bit of a laugh. "I've been engaged twice. Did I tell you that? Probably not."

He licked at his jowls and walked along the front of the cell again. Cass sat, crossing her legs, looking in. "There it is. That's the big secret, the sob story. Don't tell Gideon. You won't, because you probably won't remember it, and if you do, you're too much of a gentleman to bring it up again. The first time was…all right. He was boring, we were young, just didn't work. We're both better for not going through with it. But the second one? She did some damage."

Alexander watched her. Was he listening, or was he waiting for more meat? She couldn't tell. She leaned over and fished another cut out of the crate and tossed it in. He snatched it up and devoured it in barely a mouthful. "And then there's you. You gave me a ring so I could hurt you. You have to know that's…." She shook her head. "I don't know what to do with you."

More growling.

"Yeah, you know what you want me to do." She threw another package of meat in and put the lid on the crate. "That's going to have to do it for now if you want more later. I know. Self-restraint is not something you understand right now. And you *know* that, and that's why you gave me the damned ring. I just…." She stood, put her hands to her hips, sighed. "Maybe I'll get you some flowers tomorrow. That's what normal people in love do, right?"

Alexander scratched furiously behind his ear. Cass laughed weakly. "Yeah. I don't know, either."

Thank the gods for Humphrey and his coffee, because as the hours drew on, it was harder for Cass to keep her damned eyes open. Alexander did his best to make it interesting. Every so often, he decided that the cell was absolutely unacceptable and he needed to ram himself against the bars. Thankfully, they seemed sturdy and he was easily distracted by bits of meat, but eventually she ran out and her patience ran thin. She straggled up to the bars.

"Look, you," she said, gripping her container of coffee, "it is maybe five in the morning. I am *this* close to letting you bruise yourself to bits. Do you do this when Humphrey leaves you to your own devices, or is it just because I'm here? Hmm? I love you desperately, but I am tired, stiff, and *very* close to my last nerve. Go to sleep."

Alexander regarded her in a bit of bafflement. Cass stared him down and flung the last package of meat to the very back of the cell and started to stalk away. As she turned, Alexander's hackles rose and his growling took on a very different tone. She started to turn back to him in irritation, but a cracking branch in the woods behind her drew her attention, too. She let the coffee drop and grabbed her knives.

"Show yourself," she called.

A large shadow moved in her direction with purpose. Cass stood her ground and watched Gerund step into the clearing with his sword extended in front of him. "Should have guessed," he grunted.

"That's my line," she said. "You're aware this is treason?"

"That's my line," he returned, peering around her. Alexander, unfortunately, was not making himself terribly inconspicuous, forcing his snout through the bars, baring his teeth. "Doubly so. Move aside, or I will destroy you alongside that thing."

"Good fucking luck," she muttered. She darted forward, bringing a blade up toward his neck.

Gerund wasn't wearing his armor, likely to reduce clanking. He was clearly very used to it, by the way he quickly compensated to block her first strike. She made good use of it to make a second swipe at his chest. He managed to shirk in time to avoid getting too badly injured, but still took a fair wound. She brought her blades down in an X to block the downward swing of his sword and slid them open again to direct it away from her.

His position wasn't unearned. He was a strong fighter. He knew well how to use his superior size and strength to remain overbearing, and he pushed her back quickly to a set of rocks that she really disliked being shoved up against. Cass was quicker. She ducked a new swing, another, one more and maneuvered out and away from the rocks, then jammed a knife down into his collarbone. Gerund shouted, and she waited for him to stagger so she could retrieve it.

He didn't. He kept coming for her, the blade still stuck in him. Her eyes widened, and she stumbled backward. That missed step cost her a moment. He brought the sword down, and she just barely managed to deflect it. The point glanced off her shoulder, and her back hit a tree. He rolled his neck out and lifted the sword again.

From behind, the butt end of a pole arm cracked him across the back of the head, and he staggered.

Ruhan came from behind him and held his hand out to Cass, his chest pitching. "Come on," he said.

"We can't leave," she gasped. "He's going to kill him."

Gerund started to recover his feet, and Cass bit down hard against the pain in her shoulder and sent a fist into his eye socket. There wasn't much behind it, but he sprawled backward as if she'd hit him with a tree. Ruhan looked back at her in shock, and she staggered forward to look at Gerund.

Where her ring had struck his skin, a mark formed. Tarnish. He stared upward, dazed. She seized him by the collar and threw him face down, grabbing a set of manacles from her belt and fixing them to his wrists before digging a knee into his back.

"Why aren't you transformed?" she demanded.

He coughed into the dirt. "I don't know what you're talking about."

"Bullshit. The regular knife didn't hurt you but the silver did. How is the moon not affecting you?"

Ruhan stepped forward, staring down at Gerund. "Tell her."

Gerund tilted his head forward so he could breathe. Once he'd caught enough of a breath, he choked out a laugh. "Yours is not the most powerful throne I serve, Your Majesty."

Cass eased off and rolled him back over. "You have got to be kidding me," she muttered, yanking her knife free of his collarbone. "That bullshit story about the seelie queen and the wolf knights."

"It's never just a story," he answered.

Ruhan took a step back. "You're fey."

"I have a responsibility," he said, his eyes hardening, his head turning ever so slightly in the direction of the cell.

Cass' eyebrows furrowed. "*That's* why you want him dead so badly?"

"Descendants of the Wolven Queen are unrepentant abominations and must be removed."

"Oh, my gods, it's somehow even stupider than I thought it was, and I thought you were just jealous."

"Excuse me?"

"Buddy. Listen. Until a couple of weeks ago, he didn't even know what a Wolven Queen was. Still never been in contact with one. He got bit when he was a kid and has been doing his best to keep it to himself and be a good person, so you can piss off, and that is the last time I will tell you."

Gerund looked back at her sourly. "He has you deluded. Not that that seems difficult."

Cass contemplated punching him again, but Ruhan gave her a look, and she sighed. Behind them, Alexander gave a strangled sounding yelp. Cass looked up. It was hard to tell with the clouds still thick, but light was breaking. She looked to Ruhan. "Can you take Gerund to the house? Just —don't listen."

Ruhan glanced back uncertainly. "What about you? You're hurt."

"I'm fine. Just—get going." Alexander whimpered, and Cass added, "I —sorry. Probably shouldn't give you orders."

Ruhan laughed slightly and hauled Gerund up by the shirt. "No, it's fine, it's…is he…?"

"He'll be okay."

Gerund muttered, "He's paying the price for his failure to atone."

"You shut up." Alexander shuddered, and Cass moved in the direction of the cell. She looked to Ruhan. "Please. Get him out of here."

He nodded and prodded Gerund away as Alexander began to struggle in earnest. Cass put her back to the bars and kept her hands near the hilts of her knives in case Gerund wasn't alone. "Don't fight this one either," she told him softly.

He snarled his stubbornness again and and again until the guttural resonance went shallow and what was left was just…desperation. She fought to keep her eyes open against the sting and keep watching. Atonement.

At last, there was rasping, breath catching, shuddering. "Cassie," he called out, hoarse.

She turned. His hand reached through the bars not too far from the ground. She dropped to her knees, collected his trembling hands in hers. "I'm here."

Cass felt him strain to pull himself upward. It was hard to see in with the light starting to fill the clearing in earnest. "You're injured—you need…."

"I'm all right," she promised, reaching in to find his face in the shadows. His brow was clammy. "Hey. I'm all right. It's okay. Humphrey will be here soon and then we can both go rest."

"Did he hurt you badly?" he gasped.

"You remember."

"Some—ngh."

He collapsed against the bars. Cass caught him as best she could. "I've had much worse. Your gift made all the difference. Thank you."

He choked out a laugh. "I didn't think…it would work…on him."

"I know. Me neither."

"If he harmed you, I will…."

"Shh." Cass felt for his forearms to help him find stability and slowly got him to his feet, leaned him against the wall. "Hold on."

A figure burst through the clearing. "Miss Cassandra! Oh, goodness."

"Morning, Humphrey." She pulled off her muffler and crammed it into the shoulder of her coat to stem the bleeding. "Get that lock open, will you?"

His mouth fell open as though to argue, but at last, he nodded and busied himself with the cell door and helping Alexander dress. Cass took the time to give the wound a brief glance. It wasn't terribly deep, but it would need bandaging soon. She stuffed the muffler back in place then went to help Humphrey get Alexander headed back in the direction of home. "Did the Prince—?" she started.

"Yes," Humphrey said peevishly. "I am beginning to think we may need to add a jail to our grounds."

"We already have one," Alexander told him with a weak grin. "I can share."

"You're very chipper, Lord Alexander, for having been found out by the Knight Captain. The one person who can make your life very difficult and short."

Cass interjected, "It's…slightly more complicated than that."

"Of course it is!" Humphrey spluttered. "It used to be very simple. No one gets in. We keep to ourselves. Now some people know to various extents and others do not, and some are dangerous and others are not. I will need a *chart*."

Alexander smiled grimly. "I sympathize. Perhaps I'll make one later."

"Make sure it's in code," Cass said, distracted. Ruhan's silhouette was visible from the sitting room window, pacing back and forth in agitation.

"Oh, wonderful, there's a code now," Humphrey muttered.

"No, you'll have to make one."

"Even better."

"I have a few expired ones you can use if you can't be fussed to write your own. Let's…take the back door, shall we?"

Alexander followed her gaze. "Not resting yet, then."

"At least I'm not."

"I think I'd prefer to hear this myself, too," he added uneasily.

Humphrey sighed. "I suppose there's no talking you out of it. You're very weak, my lord. The prepared meats are just not sufficient."

"I'll drink the accursed broth while we do it."

Cass looked over at Humphrey with a tired shrug. "Willingly. That's pretty good."

"I suppose I'll take it," he sighed.

There was very little use pretending for Gerund's sake, but Alexander walked in under his own power anyway. Cass understood the desire, but still winced when he ran out of wall to brace himself on and needed to cross the precarious empty space to the sofa. Gerund eyed him significantly from his spot on his hard wooden chair.

"Lord Fremont. You look unwell. An uneasy night, I take it."

"And you look like you took a beating," he answered, lowering himself shakily to the sofa. Cass stood at the arm, watching with her arms folded. "Don't worry. It shouldn't kill you. It's a particular silver alloy. Just enough to stun."

"Look at you," he said. "A hollowed-out husk plotting against himself."

Ruhan looked down sharply. "All right, that's—enough. Both of you. For gods' sake, Gerund. I didn't want to believe you could be involved with any of this, but there were…too many signs, and I should have…." He looked guiltily to Alexander. "I should have listened."

Alexander's sunken eyes softened. "What *are* you doing here?"

He sighed. "I couldn't sleep, knowing what Cassandra would be doing." He looked to her. "Knowing why you were keeping watch. So *I* kept watch outside *his* chambers," he indicated Gerund, "to see if he left, and lo and behold, I followed him straight here."

Gerund's face twisted. "Vexing. How I didn't smell you or hear you, devils only know."

Ruhan smiled in quiet disappointment. "You taught me better."

The twist only deepened, a not-quite-right smile. "How careless of me."

"Unless you didn't," Cass said, setting her jaw. "How long have you been Gerund?"

"Oh, you are clever. Twenty years." Ruhan stepped back in alarm, and not-Gerund tilted his head. "Don't be dramatic. Your Gerund hasn't even realized he's gone. He's been having a fine time at the dance, and will until the end."

Ruhan looked fiercely to Cass. "Is there any reason to leave this thing alive?"

"Yes," she said tiredly.

"Smart," not-Gerund said again with a smirk.

"Does he need to *talk?*" the prince asked, his hands gripping the haft of his pole arm.

Alexander leaned heavily on the arm of the sofa. "Why?" he asked at last, no longer bothering to hide the exhaustion. "I have nothing to do with your Queen. Either of them."

The Knight Captain turned his head to observe him curiously. "So you do know, and still you've not sought her forgiveness."

"Is this what her forgiveness buys you?" Alexander asked, gesturing limply with a hand to Gerund's bound form. "Spending twenty years in someone else's court in vain hopes that maybe someday you might get to kill some spoiled noble brat?"

"Twenty years is but a blink to me, thanks to Her Grace. And what have they been to you? Torment. Punishment."

Alexander smiled bitterly. "Ah. Yes. My atonement. And what have I done, precisely? What did *you* do, for that matter? Did you plot the seelie coup yourself, or were you a wanderer like me? I'm curious."

Gerund seemed surprised. "That—"

"You don't know, do you?"

"The hubris of humankind."

"Are you willing to shoulder that all yourself? I'm not. There are many things for which I'll apologize, but that is one I just can't bring myself to grovel for. Least of all for my hubris as an eight year old." He paused. "So were you the Gerund that was there, or did you get sent out after the fact? Which came first?"

Suddenly the smug honesty with which he'd been answering was gone and he was silent.

Cass leaned forward. "I'd like an answer to that. I'm being polite, but I am very familiar with how to get fey creatures to tell the truth. I can be less polite if I need to."

Gerund's dark eyes flicked to her. Sullenly, he said, "I…was sent to hunt the Wolven Queen's operative lurking in the wilds."

Alexander laughed quietly. "Ah. Of course. I see now." Cass looked his way questioningly. He was smiling, but the way his eyes were creased looked very much like he'd just been struck in the gut. "It was never about me. The resentment was never *for* me. It was the fact that you couldn't manage to clean me up. I was the result of *your* hubris, and you have spent the last twenty years scrambling to make up for it. That's almost…more of a punishment than the original, honestly. I'm strangely satisfied."

He glowered fiercely, but said nothing. Cass found Alexander's shoulder. He shook, but kept himself upright.

Ruhan looked between Alexander and Gerund, fury building. "This cannot stand. If it weren't for him—"

"Careful," Gerund said. "Wouldn't want me speaking up in court, now would you? A werewolf in the Upper Ring, and the prince *knew.*"

"I should just kill you and have done with it!"

Cass shook her head and looked at the floor. "That would provoke the Seelie Queen," she said. "That is the last thing you want. Especially ahead of the wedding."

"So what are you suggesting?" he asked incredulously. "He can't walk free!"

"No," she said, sighing. She reached into her bag and pulled out a glass bottle. Gerund's eyes widened. So he knew what it was. "Don't worry," she told him, a little vindictively, "you won't even know you're gone."

She unstopped it and set the bottle on the floor in front of him. The bottle slowly began to revolve, building static against the rug, which climbed up the legs of his chair. Once the bottle picked up enough speed, there was a flash, and the chair was empty. The bottle stoppered itself with a ripe *plunk* sound and slowly spun to a stop, a flickering light inside.

Cass picked it up and inspected it. "That should hold him for a while. Not forever, but it will buy us some time until we don't have a demon lord to deal with."

Alexander looked at her, his heavily-ringed eyes a little wide. "Have I mentioned lately that you're mildly terrifying and I love you?"

Cass slid the bottle into her bag. "It's not harmful. It's like trapping a spider under a glass."

Ruhan nodded slowly. "How long do we have?"

"A year, a month, and a day, if the enchantment's still good. I'd recommend moving a little faster than that."

"What did you have in mind?"

"Diplomacy," she said frankly. "She's going to want him back, you probably want your knight back, you both probably want assurances you're going to stay out of each other's shit. I want assurances she's not going to keep sending people here for creepy…atonement reasons."

Alexander rubbed at his arm. "Yes, please," he said uneasily.

Ruhan furrowed his brow. "Making deals with the fey is notoriously tricky."

"Making war is much harder."

"You are, as usual, correct," he sighed. "Gods. Alexander, I…."

"I didn't see any of that coming, either, being honest."

"I still should have listened."

"You did." He reached out and took Cass' hand, his smile growing even as his weariness did. "When it was important."

She smoothed his hair. "Bed. Broth. All that."

"I think so."

Ruhan came to help prop up Alexander's other side, and they shuffled down the hall. At the door, the prince stepped back, regarded Cass and Alexander a moment, then stepped in and caught them both in a hug.

He stepped back again and cleared his throat. "I apologize," he said, "that was…."

Alexander laughed. "Human?"

"I was going to say *familiar*, but I suppose the effect is the same."

Cass smiled. "Thank you, Ruhan."

"My pleasure. I should go. Court will be starting."

Alexander said, "Ruhan. Come by sometime when things are less grim."

"I will. This time, I will." He looked down for a moment, then came back and caught him in another careful hug. "I'm an ass."

"It's all right. I've been an ass before."

"I don't remember that," he laughed, patting Alexander's shoulder gently and stepping back. "But I'll take your word for it." He squeezed Cass' hand. "Take care of him."

The prince walked away down the hall, and Cass opened the door to the bedroom. Alexander paused and turned. "Damn it, I forgot to ask him about the audit charter."

"Now, really?"

"You're right," he conceded. "Bed. Broth. All that."

"Good."

19

Wishful Drinking

Cass lay in bed and listened to Alexander's breathing for long while after she woke in the late afternoon. First, to make sure it was actually happening, and secondly, because the steadiness of the rhythm lent a little stability to her own thoughts. They kept trying to race on without her. She'd told Humphrey to tell Gideon and Bjorn she wasn't up for the farm country mission, but she was worried about them if they decided to do it. She was worried about *time* if they decided not to do it. She felt useless being inert here, but the drub of her shoulder told her running around wasn't a great idea.

And then there was the lurking sadness. She couldn't quite put her finger to it, but every time she thought about Ruhan and his hug this morning she felt this ache that gnawed. It wasn't him, not really, but the ease of those words. I'm an ass.

She threw the wrist of her uninjured arm over her head and puffed out a breath. It hadn't been easy. She could tell. But he'd done it. He'd shown up and he'd done it. Good for him. Must be nice to be that brave.

Next to her, Alexander stirred. "Cassie," he murmured.

"Did I wake you?" she asked, rolling to her side.

"Mm. No," he lied, but she appreciated the effort. He took her hand. "I don't think I'll be doing much today," he said tiredly.

"Good."

"Don't feel like you have to watch me do nothing."

"It's my favorite pastime."

"I know you take your work seriously, but perhaps it's time we find you a hobby."

She laughed. "Work is my hobby, love."

And again, that sadness, because frankly, that had once been true. At one point, she'd done this for fun, and Jules had been there.

Alexander sat up. "Are you all right?"

"Oh, I'm okay. My head's just busy and I'm not."

He nodded in familiarity, tracing her cheek. "I think you could use some time to unwind."

"I don't unwind."

"And I think that might be a problem, don't you?"

"Ha. Didn't you just try to chase down the prince about an audit before collapsing?"

"We have been over this. I am a hypocrite. I acknowledge this."

"I appreciate the honesty."

"I don't recall everything, but I don't…." He sighed, held her hand to his chest. "It wasn't a particularly kind night to you either. Do something kinder now."

"And you?"

"I'm not chasing down Ruhan about the charter, am I?"

Cass tucked her head in the hollow of his shoulder and smiled in spite of herself. "I suppose that's as good as I'll get."

"I can try to have a pleasant dream."

She leaned in and kissed his cheek. "All right. That's better."

Alexander looked up tiredly at her, his thumb tracing the dimple under her chin. "Cassandra…all this time you spend trying to convince me I am worth happiness, and you don't believe it of yourself, do you?"

She made an undignified noise. "That's hardly fair."

"Was it in our contract? Only the contractor is allowed to ask soul-cutting questions?" She made a face and scratched behind his ear. He twitched and held in a laugh. "Do me this favor, dearest. Please."

"I suppose I can make a deal," she said grudgingly.

"Please don't make it a combination work-fun thing, either."

"How did you…?"

He smiled, eyes closed. "A suspicion. Turnabout is fair play, my love."

Cass muttered under her breath and stood. "You owe me two good dreams for that."

"I'll…see what I can…do." His head hit the pillow and his breaths went shallow again. Cass dressed as quietly as she could before slipping out to hold up her end of the bargain.

She nearly walked away from the front door of the building four or five times, but the longer she waffled, the more likely it was that her mother might glance out the window and notice her, and it was still sort of damp out anyhow. She forced a breath and went inside the apartment building.

Most apartments in Amaranth had something just a little bit strange about them. In this building, it was that the ceilings felt just a little too short. It didn't help Cass feel any better about waiting after she knocked. By the time Ellorin opened the door, Cass felt very much like the hallway had compacted in on her.

"Hey, Ellorin," she said with an attempt at a smile.

"Oh, hi," she said, pushing her glasses up her nose and hiking her sweater higher over her shoulder. "How've you been?"

"Okay. How about you?"

"About the same," she said with a little smile of her own. "You must be looking for Julie."

"Yeah," Cass said. "Is she around?"

"Yes. I'll grab her. Do you want to come in?"

Cass rubbed a little at her arm. The shoulder ached a bit with the weird way she was standing. "Oh, I don't want to impose. Just a quick check in, is all."

Ellorin nodded. "Just a sec, then. I'll send her out. Did you hurt yourself?"

"What?"

She pointed to Cass' shoulder. The coat's shoulder was still torn open. Humphrey had managed to handle the blood, but he didn't know how to repair leather. Embarrassed, Cass grasped the gap. "I…kind of forgot about that, to tell you the truth. Just a little sword wound. Not too bad."

She tilted her head. "I might have a leather needle around. Want me to have a look?"

"You're so busy, I don't want to…."

She held out her hand. "It'll take me a few minutes. Come on."

Cass gingerly peeled off her coat and handed it over. "Thanks."

"What are saddlemaker's daughters-turned-lawyers for?"

She smiled and disappeared inside, leaving the door cracked open. It expanded the hallway by a bit, but Cass somehow still felt it had gotten narrower. She stepped away from the open door, walked a few feet to the window at the end of the hall, and looked out. She could see the lights of her mother's tavern from here, a bit of the street. It was a quieter corner of the city. She could never come back to live here, but visiting was nice every once in a while.

The door creaked behind her. "Cassie?"

She turned. Jules stepped into the hallway, dressed as she usually was at home—for comfort. Loose linen pants, soft shirt with sleeves rolled to the elbows, absolutely nothing that resembled structure. "Hey," Cass said, trying a smile.

"Hey," Jules said, kind of confused. "What are you doing here?"

"Can we talk?" Cass' words tumbled out in a rush.

"I mean, yeah, that's what we're doing?"

"No, I mean like…really." Cass steadied herself. "I mean I'm going to actually…say the things I mean instead of the shitty stuff around the edges, and you…talk to me." She shook her head. "You know it's been two weeks since we've talked?"

Jules laughed incredulously. "What are you talking about? I talked to you two days ago when we swapped shifts."

"*Really* talked."

"Ellie said something about a sword," she said, looking Cass up and down. "Are you feeling okay? This is really weird out of you."

"No," she admitted. "No, I'm not. But it's not the sword, it wasn't the injuries from the break-in, it's not even that you keep ditching work. I *miss* you. I miss being important to you. I miss just—shooting the shit with you, watching men try to arm wrestle you or flirt with you and fail at both, I miss going to bookstores with you. We don't do any of that anymore. We haven't since…. I know it's not her fault. And I can be pretty shitty about saying what I really think of it, and I'm sorry, I'm trying to get better at it. But gods, Jules. It's like my sister moved away."

Jules stood there silently, her broad face pensive. "I'm right here. I've been right here."

"You are and you're not." Cass shook her head, her eyes stinging. "I don't expect it to be the exact same. We don't have the kind of time we did, and we have different priorities. That's fine. But once in a while, I want to matter, too. Apparently."

"You…think you don't matter."

Cass folded her arms and looked at the ground. "Twelve guys, Jules. And the first thing you did was try to get out of watch."

"To be with my wife, in case they come here."

"To do what they had just done to me," she returned tautly. "I know! Of course you're worried for her! Of course you would be. But could you have spared a *second* for what had already happened to me? To my Ellorin?"

Jules cast her eyes to the worn tacky green carpeting in the hallway. "You really think he and she are equally important?"

"Yes," she said, staring slightly. "Don't you?"

"Yeah, I just…." She shook her head. "Never mind."

"No," Cass said. "Don't do that. This is what I mean. Let's talk. Tell me."

"I guess I always just kind of thought…you never seemed to like her. It was after Odelle, so I'd thought it might have…."

Cass reached out to the wall. "You thought I didn't like her because you're both women and you got married?"

"This is why I wanted to leave it," Jules said, covering her face.

"Jules, that's not it," Cass said. "I wish you had *said* something."

"Do you think that would have gone over well at the time?"

"No, probably not, but…." She sighed. "My shitty ex has very little to do with my feelings on your wife. Maybe I wasn't thrilled about going to a wedding right away, but that wasn't any of your fault. I like Ellorin just fine. I just don't love her like you do. I don't think you'd like it if I did."

"I guess…I guess not," she said with a watery laugh.

"I probably haven't…been as kind as I should have about her. I probably have been resentful. But it's because of…." She shook her head.

"Me," Jules finished.

"Not exactly."

"But pretty much." She looked at the ceiling. "I actually prefer that."

"I shouldn't have been shitty, though."

"No, you never did fight fair," Jules conceded with a laugh. She paused, looked down the hallway. "You want to finish talking this out over drinks?"

"Yeah? You're sure?"

She smiled. "Yeah. You're right. It has been a minute since I arm wrestled a guy. Besides. Ellie's been trying to get me out of her hair all day. She'll probably thank you for it."

"All right, then," she said. The hallway started to expand again. "Yeah. That sounds great."

The third guy's arm slammed into the table with a satisfying thump, and the people around the table erupted into cheers. There were always at least two who watched Jules humiliate the first guy that were so sure they wouldn't be the same. They were always wrong. Cass sat at the table across and laughed to herself over a flagon of something she'd probably once thought tasted pretty good. Jules rejoined her with her freshly earned drink. "You don't seem rusty."

"You're saying that because you aren't my biceps," she said, prodding gingerly at her upper arm. "I might have started slacking."

"Or you might have better things to do than tossing heavy things around for no reason all day now."

"Could be a little of both," she said, leaning her forearms against the back of the chair she'd butted up against the table. "I kind of can't believe we used to come all the way across town for this place."

"It was just because it was way away from Mum's," Cass said with a laugh. "Knew he wouldn't say anything to her."

"Not that we ever did too much."

"But what if we *did?* We needed the freedom to do something stupid free of bartender gossip."

"I think she'd still have found out anyway."

"Of course she would have," Cass snorted. "You'd have told her."

"Have you *seen* your mum when she gets scary?"

"She does that to get you to give in."

Jules shivered and drank. "It works. Hey, have you introduced Alexander yet?"

"Not yet. She's aware of his existence. I think that's as much as I can stomach for now."

"You know she'll love him."

"I do know," she said. That was the problem. "When it's time."

Jules nodded, watching her a moment longer. Gingerly, she asked, "Have you told him about Odelle?"

"No," she said heavily. "I mean…sort of. I'm not sure how much he remembers."

Jules' look grew odder with bewilderment. "What?"

"Magic stuff. Never mind. Point is, no, I haven't really gotten into what she did."

"Things seem fairly serious, Cass. Don't you think you should? I mean…especially since he's a he."

Cass downed a little more of her drink than she probably should have at a go. "Thalia checked, Jules. It wasn't a real curse. She was just being…her."

"I know, I know." She wrung at the back of her neck. "You know I think she's wrong, right?"

"What? Jules. We've definitely talked about this. I don't think you had anything…."

"I know." Her face reddened. "But I still…I don't like it. I left my entire life in the Upper Ring because I couldn't love who I was meant to love, because that sort of hate is bullshit. So she should know that kind of hate is bullshit, too. I don't know how she could put it on you because you were meant to love more than one kind of person. I just—I want you to know. We don't all think like that. Ladies who only love ladies."

Cass shook her head, tripping over her tongue. "I know, Jules. I never thought you were anything like her. Or even most. Is that why you thought I was upset you married Ellorin?"

Jules pushed out a breath. "You did get…different, then."

"Well—my fiance *had* just left me because I couldn't possibly have been telling the truth about fancying both men and women and being in love with her over everyone else. Everything was odd."

"That probably makes sense," she said ruefully.

Cass wrapped her hands around her mug. "Jules. I got you. I've had you since the beginning."

"I know. I just…." She shook her head. "I'm not kidding. I gave up everything so I could love the right person. Now that I got her, I feel like I have to…."

"Prove it?" Jules' shoulders drooped, and she nodded. "To who?"

"Everybody? I don't know."

Cass shook her head. "Believe me. We believe you."

"It's not *about* me, though. Ugh." She huffed out a frustrated breath and watched the heads bobbing across the dimly lit dive. After a moment, she chased a bit of condensation around the table with her finger and tried again. "We have this neighbor who calls us 'those real close girls'. And we can tell her over and over *we're married*, and it just doesn't seem to stick. So if you add her to my dad and half of Ellie's family and some of her coworkers…it just feels like we have to push to count as much as a husband and a wife. Even if maybe I don't have to push with you. Maybe it's habit."

Cass nodded slowly. "I don't think you're just 'real close girls'," she said. "You don't have to prove anything to me. Or any of us. I understand why you felt like you did. I love that you're happy, Jules. I love that you found the right person to love, and that giving up the Upper Ring was all worth it. I'm sorry I'm in my head too much sometimes to show it."

"You're just keeping us on track."

"Not all the time. Sometimes I'm just…in my own shit, and the work is just there."

Jules smiled a little. "Well, if you were going to pick an unhealthy way to cope, I guess the way that gets us paid is not the worst."

"I could have taken up parkour," she conceded. "Or alcoholism."

"Mercenary work could get you killed as quickly," Jules answered. "I…I am sorry. About the attack."

Cass shook her head and drank. "Even if you'd gone to the Rats that day…I don't think it would have been enough time."

"It might have been."

"Or they might have just made and killed you. There's no point in re-hashing. He's alive, we're all alive, and Kaye is alive, too." She slid the mug away from herself and leaned against the table. "I'm not mad that things are different. That drink is shit now, because we've had better."

Jules chuckled. "Yeah. Tastes like aftershave."

"I still miss you."

"I miss you too. I'm not gonna be so scarce."

"Good. And I know you're going to have to go sometimes."

"You will too, now."

Cass laughed. "That's…taken some getting used to again, yeah."

"So, *are* you serious?"

She groaned. "We're doing this?"

"I mean, we're supposed to be talking to each other openly, right?" she asked with a smirk.

"I guess I did say that. And don't mention the talking openly thing to Gideon, by the way. He'll be insufferable if he knows he was right."

"Oh, fuck no."

"Good." She swirled her cup around. "I think it might be serious, yeah."

Jules smiled. "Does he know you're scared of bugs yet?"

"Just the flying ones, and no. I'm keeping that to myself as long as possible."

"He's going to figure it out sooner or later. That noise you make is hard to miss. Maybe we should warn him."

Cass cocked her head. "Don't you *dare*."

"Tell you what. Let me get the next round, you get the one after that, I'll keep my mouth shut."

"Extortion. Always effective."

Jules stood, waited for Cass to finish the last of her drink, and swooped up the empty mugs with a practiced hand. "That's what family's for, yeah? Back in a minute."

Two rounds and a few more arms wrestled later, Cass found her way back to the estate lighter, still vaguely tipsy, more than a little sure she was not quite as good at endurance as she used to be, but content in the knowledge that the hangover would probably be worth it. She waved to Thalia briefly and let herself in the side door and tried desperately to be quiet.

Alexander miraculously didn't wake when she let herself in. She quickly stripped to her underclothes and attempted to ease into bed without disturbing it too much.

That, unfortunately, was wishful thinking. Alexander stirred. "Just me," she said quickly. "Sorry. I was hoping not to wake you."

"That's all right," he said sleepily, his breaths settling. "I was hoping to get to see you, and now I have, so really, I've come out the winner."

She kissed him, tucking in close. "How are you so eloquent at this hour?"

He rolled carefully to consult the clock on the nightstand, squinting. "That is a wee hour. You took that assignment seriously."

"It won't be a habit," she said, somewhat embarrassed.

Alexander set the clock down and rolled back over to hold her face in his hand. "I was going to say I'm proud of you," he said.

"I mean it, though," she groaned, shifting to her side. "I think I'm too old for it to be a habit anymore."

He tucked the blanket up to her arms and wrapped his arms around her from behind. "But was it fun?"

"Yes."

"Good. That's the important bit."

He kissed the top of her head and settled back to his pillow behind her. Absently, she let her fingertips play over the back of his hand, crossing healthy skin and scar alike. Cass felt his breaths grow softer on the nape of her neck as sleep threatened her, too, but she couldn't. Not yet. "Alexander," she said tentatively.

"Yes, dearest?" He mumbled.

"You said I deserve happiness. I want you to know I am happy."

"Oh—I didn't mean to imply."

"I know." She held onto his hand. "And you were right, too, but also… you should know. This is the happiest I've ever been."

Alexander pulled her closer and held on tightly for a moment, then pulled back and rose up to place a kiss at the join of her jaw and her neck, her ear, the top of her head. "I have no choice but to consider that a challenge," he told her, enfolding her again and settling back to the bed.

She fell asleep with a smile in place.

20
Rude Awakenings

Morning came obscenely, like a toddler given a drum. Cass clamped her hands over her eyes to try to block out the sunlight. It was futile. It was time to pay the piper.

She turned away from the window. Alexander was gone—probably for at least a little while, based on the fact that she couldn't feel his prodigious heat radiating from the sheets anymore. What was there was one of his covered warming plates and a note.

Today's deal: this breakfast, not necessarily in its entirety, we both survive the meetings, and I'll have a surprise (the good kind) at dinner. Yes? -Alexander

Cass sat back against the pillows and laughed to herself. Deals made via note were terribly one sided, but she supposed she forgave him. She could use the good kind of surprise.

She managed to hold up her end of the deal and took her time in the bath, trying to soak the drubbing headache away. It was mildly successful. When she finally got out and dressed—nicely but not too nicely—the signs of last night's indiscretion were thankfully invisible. She stared herself down in the mirror for a moment. Survive the meeting. All right.

Alexander's was in full swing. She heard it from down the hall. So many politely raised voices. It was a godsdamned miracle anyone in this portion of the city tolerated each other. Cass purposefully tried not to listen and made her way to the parlor instead, which sounded much more pleasant.

Kaye sat at the piano bench with her eyebrows furrowed and her tongue slightly protruding from the side of her mouth as she churned her way uncertainly through a simple song. Gideon sat on a chair next to her and turned the page. "That's a C."

"Right, okay," she said, bobbing her head.

"You two are getting along suspiciously well," Cass said.

"The spawn needed direction," Gideon said with a shrug.

Kaye wrinkled her nose. "Humphrey's helping Lord Alexander argue, so Mr. Devil is bored."

Cass looked at her sternly. "Use his name, please."

Gideon waved her off. "I got a Mister. I'll take it. Are you ready, Cassie?"

"Ready as I can be."

"Good enough." He tapped on the music sitting on the stand. "Keep trying this bit. You've almost got it."

Kaye nodded and set back to plunking at the keys. Gideon held the door for Cass, and they walked quickly through the house to avoid hearing or disrupting the arguments.

"Your lord told me you were out at all hours last night," he said slyly as they passed the threshold. "Look at you."

"I had three drinks and it knocked me on my ass," she told him. "It was mostly talking."

"Yeah, Jules told me. She's substantially less hung over."

"I would hope so."

"Good for you," he said, poking her in the side with the point of his tail. "Everyone needs to stay up late and be a little irresponsible every now and again."

"Maybe not this irresponsible," she said, checking her pocket watch. "Cutting it a little close."

"I would have gotten you up if it had gotten too much later, never you fear."

"Did you wind up doing the farm mission?"

"Yeah, about that," he said with a sigh.

"Don't like the sound of that."

"Oh, no, it went fine. Pretty easy. In, out, didn't even see a soul. There was a clever little device some wizard had made that picked up on my dear husband's resonance, and any time someone summoned it, it pulled a little lever that brought a crystal in line on his summoning circle. No one was even attending it."

"That would explain how it always seemed to happen so fast," Cass mused.

"Yes. Very cunning indeed. I hope they're paying that mage well and they didn't just steal his soul. But it—" He gritted his teeth. "Once again, it complicates things. We broke the device, which was poor consolation for our crestfallen Bjorn—he was so looking forward to hunting a wizard—but by the time we returned—"

"They had another."

He touched his nose, then pointed to her. "Somewhere completely different. My guess is that we could play this game for days."

Cass nodded, looking up past her hair. "I'm sorry, Gideon. I know you had hoped to stop him."

"I haven't given up," he said, setting his jaw. "I still think we need to take Laufit out of play prior to the wedding—sooner, the better. He's too powerful. We need a new angle."

Cautiously, she selected her words from a collection that all seemed wrong. She pushed aside a lump from her throat. "With Gerund out of the picture…are we certain he's still in play?"

"Gerund was a pawn. That your lord was targeted was convenience, extra incentive for him." Gideon passed through the open gate to the cobbled streets and took a quick look at how crowded they were. Neither abnormally busy nor slow. He still lowered his voice. "Gerund was approached by Laufit, not the other way around. I don't think Laufit was just doing an errand for the Lord; he'd send someone unimportant for that."

Cass nodded. And he'd have control of two thirds of the human assassins; the Demon Lord would need to go through him anyway. It would benefit Amaranth to take him out even if he wasn't directly involved in the scheme.

"All right, I can see that. What did you have in mind?"

Gideon traced a symbol in the air, sending purple sparks flying around them. They died back almost instantly, and the people around them walked on as if nothing unusual at all had occurred. Cass' hearing sharpened strangely, as though she and Gideon had entered a tunnel only they could feel. "We may not be able to summon him the way I want, but we can still draw him to us."

"A trap. Do you think he'd fall for one? He's smart enough to have people summoning him remotely."

Gideon laughed dully. "I think, depending on the bait, he won't be able to resist it. Becoming a demon comes with a great host of powers, but it also takes. You saw him, yes? He's practically feral."

Cass bit her lip. There was something familiar in the drive. The fixation in his eyes. Him, but not him. "Bait. Tell me you don't mean you."

He nodded. "The base layer of it. You have to really make it tempting for something as far gone as he is. You noticed, didn't you? He's not our usual fare."

"You mean the sort of demon he is?"

"Right. He's not feeding off contracts. He's feeding off emotions." He looked up at the branches of the trees in the park they passed, his eyes creasing. "Suppose I shouldn't have been surprised…anyway. I'm talking the big ones. Lust. Jealousy. Fear. Obsession. Heartbreak. Elation. Anything over the top. A seething mass of these would be catnip. Throw in a chance to harm your lord and get me back and he would never stay away."

"This literally sounds like the least appealing thing I have ever heard, but go on. Where would I get a seething mass of over-the-top emotions?"

Gideon raised a finger and gestured to the entirety of their surroundings. "These dramatic wastrels have a gathering every godsdamned week. Throw one. Their envious repressed hate-fucking could attract Laufit from three countries over. *Plus* the best man, *plus* me? Irresistible."

"All right. *Now* it's the least appealing thing I've ever heard, and it's going to be an incredibly hard sell to Alexander. How the hells do we keep an entire party safe? It's a little different from defending a rehearsed ceremony."

He shrugged. "I mean, if you're serious about hating them, we don't have to."

"Gideon."

"Keeping our options open," he said with a grin. "Seriously, though, invite the bride and groom, and keep conspicuously stepping away with Alexander. That'll keep their focus where it ought to be."

"Oh, dear gods," she said, pushing at her head. The ache was resurgent, event without help from the excruciatingly cheery sunshine. "This is risky. Even for us."

"I know. But the payoff is immense and immediate."

He was right. Even without any of the gang activity, it would put a damper on the Demon Lord's confidence to have a major lieutenant swiped from under him.

Cass took a breath. "I will talk it over with our employer," she said pointedly. "In the meantime, I want you to think about how to minimize that risk even further. Work with Thalia. Hells, ask Hubert. I don't care. Just demon-proof the hells out of everything. Even more than you already have."

He made a bow. "As you wish it, it shall be done. Easily."

"Yeah, you've left me the hard work. Convince my reclusive sweetheart to throw a party after twenty years of perfect solitude and figure out how to encourage 'hate-fucking' once we do."

He waved a hand. "That second part will happen naturally. Oh, speaking of which." He snapped his fingers, and the sparkles appeared again briefly, then dissipated. The sounds around them returned to normal. He gestured to the large wrought iron gate ahead of them. "That's the house."

Cass stopped and looked up. Out of the side of her mouth, she said, "Alexander's gate doesn't look this unwelcoming, and he's *trying* to keep people away."

Gideon squinted placidly and reached for the pull cord for the bell. "A fascinating commentary on the inner psyche, I'm sure. Lord Lomor, is it? I think I knew his father."

"Oh. Good. Maybe don't bring that up."

He waved her off. "Briefly. Erudite enough to acknowledge his wrongs. Ah."

The door opened, and a man in a tightly fitted black jacket raced down the stone path to admit them to the grounds. "Good afternoon, Miss Friend and companion. You are expected. If you would be so kind as to follow me?"

He didn't wait for an answer. Gideon caught her eye, waggled his eyebrows and mouthed *and companion.* She looked skyward and left it at that.

The foyer was…well-draped was the only description she could come up with. Every surface that could have fabric hanging from it did have fabric hanging from it, usually in several layers with fringe. It muffled their footsteps on the pink tile floor considerably, but it also felt unnerving, like Gideon's silencing sparkles hadn't quite gone away. The butler, tall and angular in contrast to Humphrey's plumpness, did not hold out his arm for any coats or really even pause. Instead, he led them between a pair of curving staircases and through a door nestled between them.

"If you would wait here, please."

"Thank you," she said. The butler shut the doors in response.

Gideon put his hands to his waist and looked around their holding chamber. It was a room with very little purpose. There was a sofa, and there were some bookcases for show. Cass knew they were for show, because the volumes were all old and meant to look impressive.

"So it seems Humphrey is actually the more pleasant of the bunch," Gideon said. "That's distressing."

She shoved him in the direction of the sofa and pointed. He sat. She checked the room carefully, quietly. No windows, not that she expected any from a room between two sets of stairs. She edged along the shelves, looking for books that didn't quite fit right, tomes a little newer than others. Nothing too strange. There was, along the wall, a lamp. Gaudy, oil-lit, with a bronze bell meant to look like the horn of an orchid. It had a little trap door that hadn't quite slid all the way away. Someone was listening.

She stepped back, traced the line up from the lamp up the wall to the floor above. It must have been a fairly large room off the top of the stairs.

She'd seen double doors, and an identical set on the other side. *Her Lady-ship,* she mouthed to Gideon.

Behind her, the door handle jiggled. He waved her off, and she turned to face the door. A lanky, tired looking man with graying black hair and a patch of stubble sprayed across his olive complexion appeared in the doorway. "Miss Friend," he rumbled gravely. "Welcome. I am Ferder Lomor, head of His Majesty's Grasping Hand."

The spies. Officially, Lomor was chief diplomat, but everyone knew what he really did. She bowed her head briefly. "Thank you for making time for us. This is my associate, Gideon."

Surprisingly, he didn't seem at all rattled, intrigued, or even really cognizant of Gideon's unusual features. He just nodded a greeting and closed the door behind him. "A pleasure. And it is truly no trouble, although I must say the request was something of a surprise."

Cass managed not to glance back at the uncovered horn behind her, but she felt it looming over her shoulder. "We deal in a unique business. Before we get too much further, if I might request—I've brought Gideon today as he's an expert in magical warding."

Lord Lomor rubbed at his stubbled chin. "Of course. Only prudent. You won't mind if I observe?"

Gideon tilted his head. "Are you a practitioner, my Lord?"

The slightest hint of a smile played across his serious face. "A poor excuse for one, but I know enough to tell a ward from a curse from a fire blast."

Gideon smiled in return. "Very well. I think you'll find the flavor a touch unorthodox, but the general methodology should be familiar enough. Please, feel free to chat. This will take a moment."

Lomor didn't look like the sort of fellow who *chatted,* but Cass also had a few questions she felt comfortable asking in front of the lady of the house and whoever else might be observing. "If I might ask—you are the one handling any political ramifications of the wedding, yes?"

He turned away from watching Gideon's circular gestures through the air. "I am. Is there something of concern?"

"No, thankfully, but it seemed a good time to confirm that as we start the final preparations in case something does arise."

Lomor nodded. "Your reputation is not unearned. I cannot say I was terribly surprised to see you at court after the changeling affair."

"Oh," she said, not bothering to mask her surprise. "I hadn't thought word would have gotten this far."

"There were some unseelie escalations after that."

She winced. "Ah. I should have guessed. Apologies."

"There are always unseelie escalations, Miss Friend. I'd much rather have them because an attempt was thwarted than because it was a success. When Lord Fremont first came looking for a list of candidates, I was happy to include your company."

"I…should definitely thank you, then."

"It was your work," he said with a brief shrug. "I think he happened to make a good choice." He paused, frowned as the shadows in the room began to escalate. "Is this…?"

"That's what he means by flavor," Cass said. "It's fine."

Gideon's eyes flared red, and the shadows licked up like dark flames to encompass the entirety of the walls. As they subsided, runes in shades of purple stayed behind, and Lomor relaxed. "Ah. You were right. That's more familiar."

"Magic is magic," Gideon said, glancing briefly toward the horn, then nodding to Cass. It was blocked up. "Now then. Let me just test this. Azorael, Lord of Demons, in life Dmitri Irividius, I call your presence to me." He paused, listened, waited. "We're fine."

Lomor's face went ashen. "What did you say?"

Cass sighed. That was probably not the way they wanted to break that piece of news. "The major threat to the wedding."

"That was the name you gave me."

"Yes."

"The dead man from Port Oranos."

"That's correct."

He reached for the chair across from the sofa and seated himself, removing a handkerchief from the pocket of his black satin vest and mopping at his forehead. "I see. Suddenly your request makes more sense. Some. Not much."

Gideon smiled kindly. "It's a lot to take in. Azorael is known to us post-descent-to-demonic-power through my connections, but his life before is an unknown quantity, and it seems he's utilizing some connections he made before. We hoped you might shed some light."

"Is that…common?"

"No. Not at all. Ordinarily those two phases of existence are much farther removed."

Lomor still seemed peaky, but he steeled himself and nodded. He turned to the table at his side and slid open a drawer, easing open a file. Cass recognized the type. Alexander had had them on his desk when she first met him. "Dmitri Ryustev Irividius. Second son of a minor merchant lord in Port Oranos. His father was caught up in an uprising and executed when he was young. His older brother ran the household. Went to military school, where he maintained a rather unimpressive record. He was mostly known for being quiet, keeping to himself, and spending all of his R&R in the port with figures older than he was."

Cass leaned forward. "His father's age?"

Lomor glanced up with a hint of appreciation. "I have no official confirmation, but by anecdotal accounts? Yes. These individuals tended to come and go, shipping out, never staying long enough to make much of an impression. And somehow, even after Irividius was deployed after his graduation, he continued to meet with them abroad."

"Did he see battle?"

"Yes. He made a name for himself as a guerrilla commander in the territory disputes with the nations of the peninsula."

"Nothing we or Joranhelm were involved in?"

"No."

Cass rubbed absently at her shoulder, achier today. "And the uprising? What was that about?"

Lomor flipped through his papers. "Power struggle between factions.

Nothing ideological."

She wanted a pattern. She liked patterns. She liked finding something to point to that said yes, this is the motivation, this is the how. Something he felt strongly enough about to persist after death. Everything seemed very lukewarm. Calculated, but lukewarm. She looked over at Gideon.

He sighed deeply. "Sorry. I don't have anything for you."

She tried not to grit her teeth. "Anything else of note, Lord Lomor?"

He consulted the notes. "He died in battle, age thirty-four. I'm afraid that's all I have as well. I'm happy to send this information with you."

"Thank you," she said. "It's deeply appreciated. We know you're very busy and won't take more of your time."

He stood. "Of course. It's my duty and honor. Do let me know if there is more I might help with—Alexander knows how best to contact me."

She bowed her head briefly in gratitude. "Thank you."

He opened the door and paused as Gideon's ward dissipated. "I look forward to observing more of your work, Miss Friend. You ask the right questions. Lord Fremont chose well."

Gideon lifted his eyebrows. "Well. That was mysterious."

Cass gathered the file and pressed it under her arm. "Fits right in with the subject matter."

"You are lucky," the butler said, appearing in the doorway. Cass grabbed at the back of the chair to keep from snatching up a dagger and throwing it at him in surprise. He seemed unfazed. "Lord Lomor does not express approval frequently."

"Ah," she managed. "Well. Thank him for me. We should…Gideon?"

"Yes, ready to go," he answered.

"Follow me," the butler said.

Before they were quite out of the foyer, a woman swept down the staircase to the left, trailing long light blue skirts, her blonde hair piled on top of her head in a deliberately carefree coif. "Oh, Anders, do give us a moment," she said.

He stopped and made a bow. "As you wish, my Lady."

She finished descending and watched pointedly until the butler left, then turned expectantly to Cass. "You must be Miss Friend! I've heard so much about you, of course."

Cass was absolutely sure she had, though what, she wasn't sure. She put on a smile. "That's me. This is Gideon."

She spared him a brief glance. "Charmed. I am Lady Danae Lomor, but please, call me Danae. I cannot believe my luck—I have been hoping to finally meet the mysterious young woman our Alexander brought to court. No one has had *any* success, and here she is, in my own house!"

"Oh—I've been…buried in work, mostly."

"Of course, of course, the wedding. I heard you spoke with our shy queen-to-be not so long ago. Tell me, tell me, what was she like?"

Cass didn't think she was quite prepared for the truth. "Very kind. Homesick, but excited."

The lady's crystalline eyes scanned Cass' features hungrily, searching for scraps of information she could seize on. "Yes, of course, the poor dear. Such a long way. But tell me more of preparations! I am dying to know something, anything. I live for social functions, and there are so few weddings these days. Although with Alexander changing his tune so abruptly, who knows? Perhaps there will be more."

Cass laughed nervously by reflex. She couldn't help it. The subject had changed so many times she could barely keep track, and yet she felt it had always been about her. "I'm afraid I'm not party to any of the good details at this point. Our work is much more centered on…."

"Evil," Gideon put in.

The look in the lady's eye said that that didn't preclude the details from being good. Gideon's eye clearly said *caution*. Cass felt strangely like she was flailing. She tried to collect herself. "But I do understand the ceremony will include a traditional Joran archer's blessing, which is a different sort of danger unto itself. A pretty one. But one we don't have to fight."

"Fighting," she said distastefully. "Right. And hopefully there will be none of that?"

"That is what the work ahead of time is hoping to accomplish," Cass answered. And what she was getting more and more nervous about actually accomplishing, but she wasn't about to say so to this particular Danae.

"Ah, yes, quite. I should let you get back to this. I'm sure you're terribly busy." She turned toward the staircase and looked over her shoulder. "I'll see you at the social this weekend, won't I? Of course I will. Who else would he bring? Do give Alexander my love."

"All right, will do," Cass said, forcing a smile and prodding Gideon toward the door. "Nice to meet you. Enjoy your evening."

When the door shut behind her, she looked over at Gideon, somewhere between baffled and irritated. He pulled at his cuffs and cleared his throat. "We should brief the others."

She was probably still listening. Of course she was. Her husband was the damned spymaster, and she was nosy. And apparently vengeful when denied the information she wanted. She had no doubt she'd get it another way.

Once on the street, Cass muttered, "I speak a fair amount of bitch, but that was beyond my comprehension."

Gideon sighed and took her arm and patted it. "Sweet, lovely Cassandra. You just took a master class in two and a half minutes. You're sure this is the life you want?"

He gestured to the Upper Ring, moving around them in its finery, its problems very different from theirs and yet somehow often the same. Cass looked to the dirt the rain had washed into the corners of the otherwise pristine walkways. "I'm not here for them."

"But he is one of them."

"No, he's not."

Gideon tilted his head and looked at her sideways. "Darling."

"What is it with you? First you're practically forcing me on him and now he's not good enough?"

"Oh, no, love, he's definitely too good for you. I just…." He sighed. "There are more where she came from, and you're not always going to be able to hide with him. Hells, he's not always going to be able to hide, and I think he's learning that."

She shook her head in irritation. "I got it. Maybe I was a little slow today. I'll hold my own next time."

"You will," he patronized kindly. "And it will be perfectly scathing, I'm sure."

"Ugh." She rubbed at her forehead. "I have too much *work* to do sullying my hands fighting in the meantime. Not that I have the faintest where to start on the Lord."

Gideon's general good humor sank. "I don't think there's any understanding him, Cassie. Believe me. I tried."

"What did you see?" she asked, trying to be gentle, but the curiosity and the frustration forced the words out.

"A boy, raging. Nothing more."

"About the war?"

"I don't think so. There was very little…" Gideon shook his head. "When he spoke, he was cold, smug, or irate. Everything about his life was cold."

"But he kept in contact with his dad's friends," Cass said.

"For a purpose, I'm sure."

"I don't doubt it." She ran her thumb along her bottom lip. "The harbor. Take Jules and Bjorn and see if there's been a docking lately. Do you know how long in mortal years he was down there?"

"Three," he said slowly. "And one more since he broke free. Cassie—Amaranth is an enormous trade hub. There will be plenty of dockings."

"But you're most likely looking at a ship from the Oranian Peninsula," she said. "Since travel from there just opened up again not but a month ago. Those sailors would have been held at port there for the last four years, if they met with him before his martyrdom."

"Which is likely." He paused. "And we know they would likely head to Laufit for shelter and orders. It doesn't seem like the bigger fish has physically manifested."

"Why would he? He has all these people to do his dirty work." She grasped his shoulder. "Let's start knocking some of them out from under him."

21
Surprise

Thalia was usually up a tree. It might have irritated Cass once, but now it made a lot more sense. With a hand to the trunk and her eyes closed, she could probably tell who was coming better than she could have on the ground with her eyes wide open. She tossed an acorn down at Cass before she even got close. "Get your own tree."

She put her hands up. "Don't worry. All yours. Can you come down so I can talk to you without permanently cramping my neck?"

Thalia made a show of standing peevishly on her bough, dusting off her backside and skidding down the trunk with barely even a pause. "You could have come up."

"You said—"

"I just said it was mine."

"Ugh."

Thalia smiled. "What's on?"

"Well." She reached into her bag and withdrew the bottle. "The Knight Captain is a little more than he seemed at first glance. Thanks for the bottle."

Thalia seized the bottle and squinted in through the glass. "*No.* You little shit—! All that time! Ugh. I guess that makes more sense than him stealing the charm, but I am *so* pissed I didn't see that coming."

"I don't think anyone did. He's one of the Wolven Guard."

Thalia gaped, her mouth pink and dangling, like a fish's. "You are *shitting* me. That's real?"

"Why did you tell Alexander the story if you didn't think it was real?"

"It's…things like this get complicated, okay. Sometimes details get lost or fudged or…." She peered in again. "Wait. Wait, wait, wait. If he's Wolven Guard…."

"Yeah."

"That's bad."

"The good news is he's spent the last twenty years trying to make up for his fuckup. He doesn't want the Fairy Queen knowing he didn't get the werewolf that bit Alexander—and he certainly doesn't want her knowing about Alexander. So it's safe to say she doesn't know what he's been up to. We've got time."

Thalia nodded. "Okay. Okay, that's leverage. Gods, you sure do know how to pick the complicated jobs, don't you, Cassie."

"What can I say? It's a talent." She pushed at the still aching wound in her shoulder. "Where's the safest place for this bottle till we can deal with this?"

"With you." She handed it back. "You're technically the one who caught him. If the spell were to be dispelled, he would still be beholden to you. Don't get me wrong; he'd immediately try to trick you into releasing him. But store him anywhere else and the wrong person gets wind, and that bit of edge is gone."

Cass pushed the bottle back into her bag. "All right, then. With me it is. Anything I should know?"

"The tree's mine."

"Right. I'm headed in." She started away, then paused. "Hey, just for my peace of mind?"

Thalia's lips twitched. "I sincerely doubt there's anything I can do for that, but go ahead."

Cass couldn't quite bring herself to look her in the face. She settled for folding her arms and looking up into the canopy of the very much claimed tree. "There definitely wasn't a curse on me, right?"

"Did you get bit? He gave you the water, right?"

"No—no, not that." She sighed. "Odelle."

"Oh," she said, blinking. "Wow. Okay. No. No curse."

"And there's no way it could have just been…hanging out, waiting for the next guy?"

"No. That's not how it works. The magic would have had to attach itself to you, and there was nothing on you. Not every vindictive thing someone says is a curse, even if they try to spook you into thinking it is."

Cass exhaled slowly. "Right. Okay. Thanks."

"What brought this on?" She tilted her head, illusory hair spilling over a shoulder. "I could have sworn we covered all this two years ago."

"Yeah, well, I do manage to pick the complicated jobs."

Thalia watched her a moment longer. "You don't have to worry. But if it makes you feel better, I could go over you with a ward before any questions get popped."

"That's not…I'm not planning anything anytime soon."

"Right."

"You know how I feel about marriage."

"Sure." She watched her unblinkingly. "That's definitely why you brought up a potential betrothal curse."

Cass felt her face heat up. "Ugh. Never—never mind."

"Cassie," she said with a laugh. "It's okay. Why don't we just do it? That way you're covered. Just in case you change your mind spontaneously. For no reason at all."

"What would you need?"

"Moonlight, some wormwood, an incense burner, you."

"Oh," Cass said, surprised. "That's shockingly easy."

"And a lock of your love's hair and five drops of his blood," she added.

"Never mind."

"He's got so much of it. I'm sure he won't miss a bit."

"You understand how strange an ask that is, don't you?"

Thalia looked at her owlishly. "I was raised by witches. No. I don't."

"I'll…I'll think about it."

She shrugged. "All right. Like I said, no magic on you anyway. But let me know if you want to do it. You know where to find me."

"This exact tree."

She grinned and vanished from sight, reappearing on the same branch high above. "For now."

Cass shook her head and sighed and made for the house.

She was barely inside the door when Alexander emerged from the sitting room, wrapped his arms around her waist, and fervently placed a kiss on her forehead.

"Hi?" she laughed.

"You," he said, peppering her cheek with a few more kisses, "are a sight for sore eyes."

"Those eyes must be extremely sore."

"They are. I see the self-deprecation attempt and as a master of the art, I appreciate it, but I don't even have the brainpower left to counter." He looked at her, vaguely haunted. "They *just* left. They have been in my house arguing all day. We got through the first article of the charter. Barely."

"How many articles are there?"

"Fourteen," he said, despair in his voice.

Cass patted his cheeks softly. "Let's talk about something else."

"Thank you," he sighed.

She took off her coat and froze mid-pull with the sudden reawakening of all of the nerves in her shoulder. Alexander hurried to help her with the rest of the doffing. Cass winced and rubbed at her neck. "It's strangely quiet. Where's Kaye?"

"I believe Humphrey may have drafted her into helping with tonight's dinner." He closed the closet door and ushered Cass by the small of her back toward the dining room. "She's learning the hard way as I did that one never complains to Humphrey about feeling uninspired unless one wishes to be immediately occupied."

"I see he and my mother trained at the same school for lovable hardasses."

Alexander pulled out a chair for Cass and seated himself next to her. "And we wonder why we have difficulty being idle."

The door from the kitchen pushed open, and Humphrey emerged

holding two plates. "And you're by far the most productive noble in the Upper Echelon, so I will take that as a complement. Hello, Miss Cassandra."

She laughed. "Hi. I did say lovable."

"Yes. Strange." He set her plate in front of her and gave her a suspicious look that might have been playful if he weren't so difficult to read. He straightened, tugged at his vest. "Well. I do believe Miss Kaye will be occupying *me* for the remainder of the evening, so please, enjoy."

He backed through the kitchen door. Alexander raised his eyebrows. "What on earth…?"

"This makes me somewhat nervous," Cass agreed.

He picked up his fork slowly and considered. "He did somehow manage to usher me into adulthood, and I had access to a fair few more flammable substances than she does. I trust him."

"Who let you have flammable substances?"

"An inattentive father with his own agenda," he said. "They're appropriately locked away now. That's the first thing I did when she got here."

"Thank you," she said fervently. "The very last thing I need is to be immolated by her curiosity."

"Curiosity is a good thing!"

"I agree. Most of the time."

"And it's never gotten you into trouble?"

"It *absolutely* has," she said, reaching for her wine. "It got you let out of a cell and me treed, and that was probably not the most dangerous trouble it's gotten me into." Cass paused to drink. "That reminds me."

"Oh, dear. Never a good transition."

"Danae Lomor." He made a face as though his roast chicken were entirely comprised of lemon. "Well, she sends her love."

"Wondrous. Please throw it it in the wastebin when you have a moment. I'd rather not touch it if it's all the same."

Cass laughed a little even though her insides roiled a bit and she couldn't quite name why. The chance meeting still sat strangely. Mostly because it hadn't been chance. It was so very pointed and purposeful. "She mentioned some sort of function this weekend?"

"Mm." He put down his glass. "Yes. I'd forgotten I let Humphrey talk me into the wretched thing. I have to go, unfortunately. It's an aspect of maintaining standing."

Cass nodded slowly, considering her words. "She made it seem like it was something I would…either be expected to attend or not welcome at. I'm not exactly sure."

His eyes widened. "Oh—oh. Goodness. No. Cassie, that's not it. At the time I'd accepted, it was still expected that I'd attend alone. I didn't correct the perception because I assumed this was not the sort of event you'd enjoy. I should have asked, however. I'm sorry."

"No, it's fine, I just…." She sighed and rubbed at her upper arm. "There are a few concerns. Namely your safety, and what happens if there's an attack there."

He deflated. "Right. Shit. I hadn't considered that, either. This thing's an even worse idea than usual." Alexander glanced over at Cass, still shrunken into herself, and rested his fork on the edge of his plate so he could turn to her. "Are you all right?"

"Oh, yeah," she said, forcing a smile.

"Do you want to go?"

Did she? The idea of a room full of Danaes didn't seem terrifically appealing. Being left off didn't feel wonderful, either. "I'm fairly competent, but I don't know that I'm enough if we get bombarded at a noble party."

"Cassandra," he said, unfolding her arms and taking her hand. "Forget the demons. Do *you* want to go?"

"I wasn't referring to the demons." She sighed. "I get the distinct impression that I will not fit in."

"I should say not." Her head whipped around to look at him, and he added quickly, "Cassie, these people are horrible. Not universally, I suppose. Ferder is a good man despite his wife, and some could be good if they gained perspective, but by and large: self-obsessed, vain, judgmental, and, most importantly, duplicitous. You are much more than them."

She took a breath and looked at her plate for want of something to do with herself. "They're still your peers."

"And they should treat you as one," he said with a frown. "I can have a word if you like."

"I get the impression it won't help."

"You're probably right," he admitted. "It's my fault, I'm afraid."

"Somehow I doubt that," she said skeptically.

"My unavailability for betrothal's fault, at the very least."

Suddenly, all of that made a lot more sense. "Okay," Cass said. "You're right. Wastebin."

"Entitlement is actually not her unsightliest personality trait, believe it or not."

"Is it the fact that she listens in on her husband's potentially confidential meetings?"

He looked startled. "She does what?"

"I have to assume he knows. It's fairly obvious."

"Sweet gods," he muttered. "A thought that will keep me up at night. You would truly not be missing much if you declined to spend more time with her. I believe I should do the same, much as Humphrey might like to turn my hide into a rug for it."

She nodded, then looked over at him. "Well, I have a suggestion that may either endanger your hide or save it, but at the very least ostensibly it'll boost your social standing."

"I don't know if I've ever been more intrigued yet apprehensive in my life," he said.

"I seem to do that to you a lot."

He leaned over and placed a kiss to the top of her head. "You do a lot of things to me. Not the least of which is make me want to put Danae in a wastebin herself. What did she say exactly?"

"It's best left."

"All right," he acquiesced with a grumble. "What's this frightening and interesting plan?"

"It comes courtesy of Gideon, so you know it's especially outrageous." She looked up at the ceiling. "I pushed back at it, but he has a point. I hate it when he has a point. His husband is a particular type of demon basically made to feed off of Danaes." A silver eyebrow lifted, and she raised her hands. "I'm *not* suggesting we feed her to the demon. It's just the sort of emotion he's attracted to. If we get a bunch of her in a room in an area we have decent control of, we could lay a trap for him."

He pressed out a breath. "So we would throw the party."

"Right."

"Good gods, I don't think there's been an event here in…. Well, I'm not *opposed* to the idea, but how do we keep him, hypothetically speaking, from eating Danae? It won't go over well."

"A few things." She ticked off on her fingers. "Invite Ruhan and Ifalna. Remember, they have to stay alive. The Lord will be pissed if his underling does anything sabotaging them. Also, if they're here—"

"The rest of the nobility will swarm them like flies."

"Right. It will be much less appetizing to do something indiscriminate. Next, Gideon. His husband is…." She sighed. "Well, he's not right. He remembers who Gideon is, and he wants him. If we keep Gideon away from the party itself, he will probably focus on that area—especially given that the house itself is warded, but the grounds are not. And then there's me."

"I don't like the sound of that."

"And you."

"That's only marginally more appetizing."

She shrugged helplessly. "He wants us both dead. He sent Gerund to send Rats to kill us both. If we keep his focus split, if he brings friends, that divides the forces. If they're human, they'll need to enter the normal human way and Ruhan's guards will snatch them from around the perimeter. If they're demonic, Gideon, Thalia, and hopefully Hubert will probably have something in place to neutralize a bit of that, and we can take care of the rest."

He thought, folding his hands and setting his chin on top of them. "You seem confident."

"This sort of thing *is* my job."

"Fair."

"I'm not going to lie to you," she told him, "I am worried. I've seen a lot of demons, but never one like him."

"How so?"

Cass tried to parse her thoughts, the memory of being frozen in place and yet drawn in by him, the visceral reaction to seeing his true form, the him that was not him.

"He warped my perception," she said. "All of ours at once, actually. To me, he looked like you. I don't know what the others saw. Demons can have a variety of powers—but to have something so uniquely suited to preying on humans is unsettling. I know his came from the Lord rather than the devils, so that has something to do with it. There do seem to be drawbacks, and I am going to push Gideon and Hubert hard on those."

Alexander nodded, disconcerted. "You wouldn't ask this if it wasn't important," he said.

"It is. He's doing most of the dirty work for the Lord. We remove him, we remove any assassins coming after you and me and any organized backup the Lord might have day of. We may also be able to get information from him before banishing him."

"Very well," he said, putting on a weak smile. "Let's throw a party and invite a demon. Why not. I love large social gatherings and demons."

She bumped into his arm with her shoulder. "I'm afraid that's life with me."

"Well, I do love you. Oh!" He jumped up as though his seat had suddenly grown teeth and ran from the room. Cass's eyes followed him out the door. She'd almost forgotten the promise of a surprise.

Surprises, in Cass' experience, were not usually good. They often had good intent but usually went awry somehow, like when her mother had thrown her a surprise party and invited everyone in her class, but hadn't known that everyone in her class disliked her. Her first proposal had been completely out of the blue, while she'd been helping him clean out his dead dad's house.

When Alexander returned with a small worn black velvet box the size of the palm of his hand, she felt inexplicable dread that she tried every-thing to keep off her face. He seemed excited, and she'd be damned if she was going to ruin that. He propped the box open on its hinge.

"I was rummaging through some of my mother's things today in the bottom of the desk in preparation for the meeting. The few things Humphrey hadn't catalogued and stored, or redistributed about the house." He withdrew a brass disk with a dial set along the top and checked it. "Good gods, it's been that long. Well." He twisted the dial around and the device made a plethora of metallic clicks. "Have I told you I can't look at the moon?"

"No, you hadn't," she said quietly. "What happens?"

"Dread. Deep dread that if I let go unchecked, turns into panic, which turns into—you know." He pulled a small glass hemisphere from the box and fitted it to the top of the disk. On the side, he pulled out a little metal drawer and began combining powders from a pair of little pouches. "So I don't look at the sky at night anymore, which was disheartening. I used to love the stars. So my mother made this."

He jumped up again to douse the lamps. Cass blinked in the dark, but as her eyes adjusted, light began to fade into existence in the base of the disk. Pinpricks formed on the ceiling, and a waning recently full moon, craters and all, came into being just shy of the chandelier.

"This is incredible," she said, recovering the breath knocked back into her. "She *made* this?"

"Yes. It can trace the phases of the moon and the exact position of the constellations for any date within a hundred years." In the faint light cast by the base of the device, she saw him smile, sad and happy all at once. "Sadly, it's the only invention of hers still in my possession."

"Why? What happened to the others?"

"She worked more closely with the Academy than I do. On her death they took ownership of everything contractually." She felt him sit next to her again. "It's what she'd have wanted. To have them studied and used by students, not gathering dust. Not to say I don't miss them."

Cass took his hand, still looking up at the light suspended in the air.

"I'm glad you found this one. Thank you for sharing it with me."

He looked up, too. "She'd like knowing you appreciate it. She'd have liked you. She didn't fit in, either. It was and is a good quality."

She squeezed his hand, trying to dislodge the lump from her throat. At length, she pointed up at the spray of stars that made up Ronos, the Hunter. "Look. Summer's nearly here."

"Do you like summer?"

She laughed. "Wedding season. I don't have time to like or dislike it. But it is hot, so less."

He reached out and twisted the dial. The stars and moon shifted around in a celestial dance, waxing briefly before diminishing and growing a few more times. "There. Winter again."

"Oh, don't back up," she said softly. "You weren't there in winter."

Time shifted forward—much farther forward. "Next autumn," he pronounced.

Cass leaned into him, still looking up at Ronos backing away in deference to Ilorus, the Shifting Wind. "Autumn is my favorite."

"I had a guess."

"Why next year, though?"

"I'm not sure," he said. "Partially to watch the light change. But I suppose I'm thinking a lot about the near future lately."

The lump was back. This had the ring of a surprise, and she wasn't ready—for a ring or a surprise. Nothing was ready. She steeled herself. "Me too," she admitted.

"So. It's the beginning of autumn next year. The leaves are beginning to turn and you, Cassandra, are doing exactly what you want to be. What is that?"

"Oh, ask me an easier question," she laughed ruefully.

"Tell me," he encouraged.

"It's silly."

"I doubt that. I don't think you've been silly once in your life."

"You'd be surprised." She took a breath. "I think I'd like to go back to school. I started, but I had to…Mum needed me."

"That's not silly at all," he said softly.

"I'm a good deal older than most."

"That will matter much less than you think." He traced her cheek in the dark. "You're brilliant. Whatever you put your mind to will only be better for it. What was your study?"

She felt her face heat up. "Arcanology. Demonology. Sylvan Studies."

"Three—goodness. I can see why you went into events. Those would serve you well."

"It's really not all that impressive. I only got halfway through."

"Cassandra, I went through university. One major was difficult enough. Getting halfway through *three*…. It meant something to you. You should finish."

"I'd like to. I don't know if there'll be time."

"There could be," he said softly.

"There's something I have to do first," she answered. "Something complicated."

"Is this to do with what you told me the other night about rings?"

"You…remembered that."

"Should I not?"

"No," Cass answered, laughing nervously. "Saves me a bit of explanation, but that isn't how I would have broken that if…I should really get better about what I say."

"Cassie. It's all right." Alexander tucked her hair away. "I'm sorry you were hurt. I wish that wasn't the case. I'm…not sorry you didn't marry."

She laughed. "No, me neither. She…oh, dear."

"You don't have to tell me."

"You should know. She's a witch."

"You did say she did some damage."

Cass laughed again, pushing at her forehead. "I mean that literally, love. Magic. And she was—very angry when she realized that I had previously been with a man, and had the capacity to care for one again. She believed it meant I had lied about caring for her. Because nobody likes both men and women."

Alexander stopped. He took her hands, held them close to his chest, his thumbs running over the backs of her hands. "I…know how that one hurts. I am very sorry, dearest."

"You don't need to apologize for her."

"I'm betting she never did."

"No. Quite the opposite." She took a shuddery breath. "In fact, she told me that she would be watching, and if I wound up wearing a man's ring again I would hear from her. I don't precisely know what that means."

He reached out for her and pulled her into his arms and held on quietly. "I don't think your team would let it come to that."

"No, but I won't risk anyone," she said bluntly. "Not if I can deal with her first."

"Cassie."

She closed her eyes. "I really thought that was that and I was going to be alone. I'd forced myself to get used to the idea."

"Sounds familiar." He slipped his hands down her arms, took her hands again. "I'll say the same thing you always tell me. The instinct is not wrong, but it's not all of you, either."

Cass nodded and reached out to kiss him. He wrapped her up again, and they ran down the alchemical reaction gazing up and wishing on next autumn's stars.

22
RSVP

A sudden and completely false malaise struck Alexander over the weekend. Humphrey resentfully extended his regrets and set about comparing social calendars with all the other Humphreys across the Upper Ring, the Corona District, a few in the Market District. He returned peevish and sniffling on a day the pollen hung thick in the air. "Two and a half weeks," he pronounced resentfully.

Alexander looked up from his writing. "That soon," he said, surprised.

Cass paused in comparing the ships' registers Gideon had procured in the dusky study.

"The following weekend contains the full moon," Humphrey said. "The weekend after has been spoken for. The weekend after that will be wedding preparation, and after that—"

He held up a hand. "I understand. Two and a half weeks it is."

"All due respect, Lord Alexander, but I am one man. An entire event in that time—"

"You're right. Hire whomever you need."

He lifted a finger as though to continue lecturing, then went slack. "I beg your pardon, sir?"

Alexander smiled ruefully. "Our household keeps growing, as do our respective workloads. We should keep up. And you deserve help."

"The…privacy…."

"It'll be all right, Humphrey. We can use the later model if you prefer."

He nodded, still a little stunned-looking. "I…will place advertisements. Excuse me."

Cass watched him go. "I think we broke him."

Alexander laughed quietly. "I think that was probably the last thing he expected to hear out of me. And after I told him to invite the entire Upper Ring to an event *here?* He may think I'm possessed."

She turned the page on Gideon's sheaf of hastily copied notes. "He knows who to ask about that."

He stood from his desk and stretched, regarded the mostly set sun, and made his way over to place a kiss to her cheek. "That is about all my brain can handle. I think I may see if Kaye would like to work on her reading. Are you going to keep working?"

"Mm. There's something here. I'm just…not seeing it yet." She unbunched her knees from her chest and frowned at the papers. "There's a pattern in the middle here. These two ships keep trading off. Why would there be a pattern if not…? I'm sorry. Thinking out loud." She lifted her eyes. "What?"

Alexander watched her with a fond smile, his gaze lingering on her bizarre posture in the chair and her furrowed brow. He leaned in for the other cheek. "You'll work it out. You always do."

"If only that were true."

"Someday you'll believe me." He tilted her chin up so he could kiss her on the lips, let his hand linger on her face for a moment, then smiled and left the room.

Cass' furtive smile stuck around too in spite of her whirling mind, and it took her a good moment to get her focus back. She exhaled and tried to get back down to business.

Two Oranian ships of interest that kept switching off. Within two days of one leaving, the other came to port. One had a regular route, three stops along the coast. She glanced at the manifest notes. Lumber. It was bringing lumber into the city for building projects. That wasn't inherently suspicious. The offloading was accounted for, and the captain appeared to be an Oranian woman whose title suggested retirement from the war.

Cass didn't know much about the conflict. It seemed on its face a traditional land squabble. Lomor's file suggested factions at play, but if she had to have a guess, most of the soldiers fighting knew nothing of that. It might be worth looking into this captain to confirm she'd never had contact with Irividius. Based on the other ship's departure time this evening, hers should be returning tomorrow or the day after.

That ship was less well documented. Cass bit her lip and shifted her weight to lean over the arm of the chair. The destination was unmarked save for the word *rendezvous*. The load was a very generic *construction materials—stonemasonry*. She frowned. The first ship's records said explicitly where the lumber was going. She turned to Gideon's copy of the manifest. Several tons of white marble.

White marble. That was the Wyvern's Rest. Even the Corona District, patterned after it, didn't use white marble, but an imitation. It was too expensive, since it was found only in the center of the wilds. The landlocked wilds. Which meant it wasn't *coming*, it was going. Her frown deepened. Where?

She turned back to the copied harbormaster's log and paged to the newest entry. The Oranian ship carrying the marble was slated to leave this evening in an hour. By the established pattern, it would not return for two months. And this time, it didn't say *construction materials*. It said *cornerstone*.

"Shit," she muttered, getting to her feet.

She pushed open the door to the parlor, startling both Kaye and Alexander. The former dropped her open book in her lap and the latter immediately jumped up. "Cassie? What's happened?"

"Why are pieces of the castle being shipped away?"

"The—Rest? Oh." He caught his breath. "I expect they're being sent as goodwill gifts to Ifalna's family per tradition."

"Whose work is that?"

"I…imagine Lord Maurier's men, as he's in charge of construction. Are you all right?"

Her mind raced. Maurier. His home was one of the few not located in the Upper Ring. He lived in the Market District to be closer to the docks. Maurier was also known, aside from Alexander, as the one lord who didn't play the society game.

In fact, he hadn't been seen physically in a long time.

"Fuck," she breathed, then ran for the door.

Kaye huffed. "Oh, it's okay when *you* say it."

Alexander rushed after her. "Cassie?"

She yelled over her shoulder, "I don't have a lot of time. I'll explain when I get back. Stay here."

Anders looked at Cass skeptically. "Lord Lomor is eating dinner. I will have to ask you to return another time."

Her insides had already been twisting about approaching the head of the Grasping Hand uninvited, but this just made it several times worse. "Look," she pleaded. "If I'm right—and I think I'm right—more than my employer is at stake right now. It could be the entire city. It could be more than that. Would you please just…ask him if he minds seeing me?"

The butler looked at her, unimpressed. After a moment, he said, "Wait here," and shut the door in her face.

Well, it could have been worse. He could have slammed the door on her to start. Her leg bounced up and down as she waited in the gathering shadows of the porch.

Minutes passed. She started to suspect she wasn't waiting, but was instead being left to twist. She started to formulate ideas about what she might do with her limited authority if that was the case when the door opened again, this time by a bemused-looking Lomor pulling his coat on. "Miss Friend. What can I do for—?"

She stuffed the harbor logs into his hands. "Right now, a ship might be sailing out with one of the castle's protective cornerstones. Did you know about this?"

He scanned the papers. "I can't say that I did. How did you get this?"

"We can be persuasive. If that stone leaves, that's an invitation for the Lord of Demons to do whatever he wants with the wedding, the prince, the city…."

Lomor shut the door behind him and started down the path, gesturing for her to follow. "Let us confirm."

"Do we really have time?"

He reached into his pocket and withdrew what looked like a typical silver pocket watch. The glass inside didn't protect a clock dial, but a sort of limpid cerulean haze. Lomor tapped on the glass with a finger and spoke across the surface. "Harbor agents, detain the vessel *Clarion Call*, all on it, and all contents for my arrival, please."

Faintly, a voice whispered back, "Understood, my lord."

All right, so they definitely had better things than she did. He smiled briefly at her. "If there is in fact a cornerstone missing, you and I have a more important target, I presume."

Maurier. Right. "Did you speak to him about this?"

"I did," he said, his jaw setting. "It was meant to be a quick thing to check off the list. A rather foolish tradition, frankly."

The things people were impatient to get over with were always the weak points. Cass kept it to herself, because Lomor seemed plenty irritated with himself as he opened a gate around the side of the Rest and led her down into the undercroft.

It was a strange space. It seemed like it should have been used for storage, or as a mausoleum, or to house a dungeon, but instead was mostly an open sort of marble basement. Occasionally there was an intricately carved relief in the walls, but the ground was just sheer rock.

"What is this?" she asked Lomor.

"Defunct sorcerer's warren," he said simply. "Occasionally used as a training ground."

It was a massive liability. If Gideon could see this, he'd be swearing up a storm in his devil tongue. Direct access to the earth, unprotected archways, and she was no witch, but even Cass could tell there was very little in the way of wards down here. The castle relied too much on its newfangled cornerstones for protection. Which Maurier would have known.

"I need to get my people down here," she said.

Lomor just nodded in defeat and gestured to a darkened hallway arcing off and up a flight of stairs. "It's been an ongoing argument. One I keep losing."

"Sorry to provide you ammunition like this."

He just shook his head and sighed. They took the stairs quickly and emerged into a chamber of scaffolding. Part of the walls were the same white marble as the hold, and some of them had been replaced with a dark green stone. Two new chunks stood out starkly. Lomor hurried past and pulled back a drape in the far corner.

They hadn't even bothered to put a piece of green stone here. There was just a large rectangular hole where the cornerstone should be. Lomor sighed deeply and picked up his pocketwatch again. "I was really hoping you were wrong," he told her.

If she'd been wrong, she'd have harassed a lord away from dinner and cast suspicion on a set of perfectly innocent sailors making a goodwill gesture, possibly getting herself fired. "Me, too," she answered honestly.

Lomor insisted on ringing the doorbell. Cass stood nervously at his elbow. There were guards dispersed unseen behind them, encircling the entire block. If Maurier ran, he'd be caught. It wasn't the running she was worried about.

The house was a strange thing, an estate out of the Upper Ring picked up and transplanted into the heart of the Market District. It was compressed—no sprawling gardens for Lord Maurier—but that didn't stop the house from being grand or well protected. The gate—eight feet tall, spiked wrought iron—had been left dangling open, and that made Cass nervous. She only spotted one light in the manor.

"This feels wrong," she said.

He rocked back and forth from the heels to the toes of his highly polished shoes and kept looking ahead at the house. "That's because it is."

"Then what is it we're waiting for?"

"To be invited in. Patience."

"You have men."

"Going in confrontationally is a good way to ensure a confrontation, Miss Friend." He reached out for the bell pull again and tugged firmly a few more times. He raised his voice. "Bertrand? It's Ferder. Are you there?"

A few more minutes of silence. Cass glanced backwards to try to spot some of the guards, ensure they were still there, and the door gave a click, a creak. She turned quickly again to spot a severe-looking man of middle age with a graying beard peering out at them.

"Oh, is that you, Lomor? It's quite late for visitors."

"I know," Lomor said apologetically. "There's a matter of great urgency. May we come in?"

Maurier's light eyes flicked briefly to Cass, but in the end he stepped back and acquiesced. They came into the dark foyer. It smelled strange, sickly sweet, like oranges left in the sun. Her hands wanted to hover near the hilts of her daggers, but confrontation begets confrontation, apparently, so she left them at her sides instead.

Maurier led them through to a sitting room—the source of the lone light, it seemed, from a fire burning in the hearth. The cloth furniture was all covered in white sheets. The coffee table had open letters strewn about it haphazardly, wax melted in layers throughout the pile. She shot another look at Lomor, who nodded once placidly.

"Now, then," Maurier began. "What is this urgent matter?"

"You remember the job we discussed the other day by post?"

He scowled. "Should have taken all of an hour. You came all this way to complain about that?"

Cass inched backward to try to get a surreptitious look at one of the letters on top, see if any of it made sense. Lomor kept talking. "It seems that your people may have removed a stone not meant to be removed."

"Is that so? The instructions may not have been clear."

"I believe the instructions were abundantly clear, Bertrand. Two stones. Not three, and certainly not a cornerstone."

She leaned a little forward. The handwriting on the corner seemed familiar, but she couldn't quite see around the wax. Maurier's eyes snapped to her. "I'll thank you not to read my private correspondence, Miss Friend."

She swung her head around. "I don't believe we've been introduced."

"You were at court, were you not?"

"I was," she answered. "But you weren't. How do you know my name?"

Lomor looked her way, then started to draw a rune in the air. Maurier leaned his head back and sighed dramatically. "Oh, *you.*"

The air wavered, went warm, still. Cass felt her breath arrested in her chest. She remembered this. Sluggishly, she turned her head to look at Lomor, whose expression had shifted into a wistful longing.

"Laufit," she managed.

"So he does talk about me," Maurier said, waving a hand dismissively.

The air around Cass grew less dense, less confusing, and she managed to take a full breath. "All the time these days," she gasped. ·

Maurier's borrowed face quirked up in a smile. Odd, with the frown lines permanently set in the skin. "You're *just his type,* I think. Strong. Smart-assed. Little bit damaged. But really, very soft."

Cass pulled for air again and tried to take stock. The area around her head, face, neck, parts of her chest and shoulders felt normal. Her feet felt absolutely stuck to the floor, and anything at the waist level felt like it could move by fractions of an inch. Okay, she thought. Strong emotions. Jealousy, lust, rage, fear. She'd have to starve him while she worked at it. A bit at a time, she closed the fingers of her right hand around the hilt of her knife. "Wrong girl," she said blandly.

"Oh, I don't think so." The warm air around him wavered, and Maurier lengthened and expanded into Alexander. "I saw what you made me in your mind last time," he said, a perfect imitation of his voice were it not for the flippant cruelty. "It's fascinating, really. Yours isn't the first lover I've had—not even close to the thousandth, really. Ten thousandth? Who cares. It's so interesting, though! You could have had him do *anything.* I could have given you pleasures that are physically impossible, forbidden by your gods, whatever, and all you wanted him to do was love you. That's tragic, actually."

She clenched her teeth and tried to drown him out. No strong reactions. Just breathing, dullness, bit by bit. The knife eased upward. "Do you have a point or are you just gloating before you kill me?"

"Kill you? No, that was before you kept *fucking everything up.*"

Vengefulness in Alexander's voice sounded terribly wrong. Cass turned her eyes to the ceiling and forced her breaths to stay even. "You need something from me," she postulated as calmly as she could. The knife was halfway out.

"Good girl."

He stepped forward and leaned his head down to level with hers in exactly the same way Alexander did when he was thinking about kissing her. Her heart lurched, and she turned her head away. Laufit took a step back—a small one. He examined his left hand, the scars peeking out from under the sleeve. Slowly, he started to roll it up, exposing the white and red webs of bite marks.

"He's been a challenge for me, your man. No one knows too much about him. Gerund told me about the curse, of course. And that's nice and all. Very damning. Could probably do some damage with that. He probably has done some damage, hasn't he?"

Cass kept her face blank. She started counting in her head, trying to remember her multiplication tables. She was as bad at them now as she had been as a child. Eight times seven had always eluded her. Eight times six she could remember, forty-eight, so adding eight....

Laufit whirled on her and snarled, his form bristling, bursting into a horrible wolf-man thing, clawing in her direction. She flinched, and the monstrousness faded away. "So he would hurt you if given the chance," he mused.

"Fuck you," she spat. The knife was free.

"Most I come across do," he agreed. "Am I wrong?"

"I am not telling you shit." Her damp left hand trembled, and she forced another breath. Eight times nine. Eight times nine.

"You are, though. Because that got a rise out of you, which means you want to defend him, which means, I think, he's a gentle sort. That's unfortunate. Those curses are always the worst."

She closed her eyes. Seventy-two. Eight times nine was seventy-two.

The knife was at her belt.

He started to wander, pacing away and back again in a wide loop. "So we have a young lord. Abandoned and adopted."

"Orphaned."

"Thank you. Already a shy lad. Gets bit by a nasty thing out in the wilderness, hides himself away for the most part, except he's still in charge of education. And it seems that he likes it. There are quite a number of schools, and it's getting harder to get the teachers to send the burnouts my way these days. Must be doing something right."

The knife was starting to move freer now. She firmed her grip and opened her eyes again. If she could get her hand to the free space, she could throw it, though it would have to be a good one to incapacitate him in any meaningful way, which would mean he would have to turn again.

He looked up at the ceiling, waving his hand idly in the air. "So what I don't get is where this prince fits in. We have this recluse lord who's scared of hurting people—guilt ridden, I think, and that's who the prince picks to throw a big wedding?"

"I suppose you wouldn't understand friendship," she said. "You weren't so great at love."

He stopped, chuckled, turned towards her. "Oh. That's adorable. Baby's first manipulation attempt."

"I'm just going off what I've heard. Like I said. He talks about you a lot these days."

Laufit stepped closer. Cass tried to collect herself, gauge the distance. A throw wouldn't have enough force with the bottom half of her body stuck in place. "You've given me the basics of his personality," he mused. "I don't need you around much more."

"That's not at all true. Ruhan will know the difference."

"I'll just say I'm out of sorts because I'm grieving you," he answered. Behind him, a tail rose, a stinger with an obsidian scorpion-like point nearing her.

She wrenched her arm up, bringing the knife up to Laufit's chest. "Your husband enchanted this dagger," she told him. "He's really great at killing demons."

He smiled serenely. "Go ahead. Stab your lover."

"You're not…." The overly sweet smell flooded the room again, and her head went foggy. She grasped at a fistful of his shirt, bore down hard. She had to do it.

Alexander stared back at her, his eyes wide, full of terror. "Cassandra, what are you doing?" he cried.

Her grip faltered. Eight times nine was seventy-two. She had to bring the knife down.

Alexander's hands grasped her wrists. "I'm sorry, my love, I'm sorry, please, I'm begging you, don't—"

Seven times eight…her eyes flooded, stung.

She dragged the blade across his neck and chest.

Alexander made a horrible sort of gurgling sound and dropped to his knees. A spray of something molten splashed across her knuckles, her chest, a bit on her cheekbone. Whatever fixed her legs to the floor unwound, and she dropped the knife, staggered back. Fifty-six.

Alexander lifted his head and stared up at her, a terrible smile on his face. "You are *cold*," he said, clutching his hand over the wound in his chest. "He thinks he's the dangerous one. Ha. Ha ha." He gripped the nearby coffee table and lurched upward, swiping an envelope from it. "I got your invitation today. Lord Maurier won't make it. But I'll see if I can pop in."

The air wavered, and Laufit disappeared. Cass stared into the empty space numbly for a moment, her eyes still spilling over.

Lomor finally unfroze, shaking himself out of the daze. "That…was a demon," he remarked.

Quickly, she dragged her arm across her eyes and returned the knife to her sheath, trying to ignore the burning of her skin. "Yes. That was in fact a demon."

"Are you all right?"

"No," she answered, probably too tersely. She took a breath. "I apologize. It's a manipulator."

He stepped forward and helped her up by the arm. "I can see that."

Suddenly, she went cold despite the burns snarling at her skin. "You were aware for that?"

"I heard it tell a great many untruths," he said passively. Cass wanted to seize him by the front of his shirt, demand that he confirm that he meant that he wasn't going to say shit about curses, but he looked back at her with a tiny smirk. "I would not be very good at my job if I didn't know what was happening in this city, and I would not be very good at my job if I weren't accustomed to keeping secrets. Let it lie, Miss Friend. Ah." He pulled his watch from his vest pocket and listened carefully. "The corner-stone is recovered. Very good. You have done the city a great service to-day."

She didn't much feel like it.

Once Laufit had been gone a minute, the sweet scent vanished in favor of the scent of decay. The guards came in and combed the place, and though she knew better, she stuck around. Maurier's body had been stuffed in the hall closet, shards of obsidian growing out of a puncture wound in his back. Cass had seen plenty of dead people by this point in her career, but this on the heels of everything else was too much. She turned for the outside and retched.

Lomor politely gave her a moment to finish vomiting the contents of her empty stomach and the memory of the poor hermit lord, his sallow skin stuck to his bones in his nightrobe. He joined her outside after she'd put herself back together. "It is going to be a long night here," he said, gesturing to the house. "Go get some rest."

"I can help."

"I am certain you could. From what I've seen you're a fine investigator. But you had a demon in your head and I think that's enough."

Cass opened her mouth to object, but her jelly knees and still watery eyes won out. "Yeah, all right," she said begrudgingly.

"Good." He started to head in. "Oh, and Miss Friend, I'll have Anders send the proper response, but we'll be attending the event. Let me know if there is any way I can be of assistance in the preparations. I haven't ever done demons before, but I can lend a hand with mundane things."

"I may take you up on that," she said. "Got a bit on my plate."

"I can see that." He nodded. "You're doing fine."

"Thank you." She paused. "What…did you see? When the demon charmed you?"

He seemed surprised. "Oh, that? The rest of my dinner. I hope Anders will keep it warm for me. Boring, but that's every spy's greatest secret. We're quite boring when it counts. It keeps us alive."

She was going to need to take some lessons.

The instant she closed the door, Alexander shot out of the sitting room and caught her up, his clothes rumpled and his eyes tired. "Cassandra. Thank gods. Are you all right, you're…burned. What happened?"

Cass sort of stood there, tired, disoriented. It was him. The smell of him, the frantic energy, the way his ears had gone slightly pointed with the worry, but then she'd been so sure…she set her hand to his chest and felt where she'd made the slash. There was a scar, but not from her. She tried to form words, but just stood there and stared at his alabaster skin.

At last, she said, "What kind of flowers do I like you to bring me?"

Confused, he said, "You don't. You prefer to leave them growing."

Cass looked up at him for a moment, then buried her face in his shirt and held on, her shoulders shaking. Still lost, Alexander collected her into his arms anyway for as long as she needed, then took her into a quiet, softly lit room and didn't press any further for the night.

23

In Dreams

Alexander knew something wasn't right. He'd gotten used to Cass' noises next to him in bed, even the light snoring she denied, but the previous few days he'd heard her start two, three, five times a night. Sometimes she got up and left if she thought she was going to keep waking him. Other times she tried desperately to get back to sleep. Sometimes she succeeded, but it still wasn't peaceful.

He turned onto his side and watched her curl in on herself, subconsciously pulling the covers tight to her chest. It didn't much matter if she stole the blankets; he was usually plenty warm anyway, but it was just more evidence.

He did what he always did with evidence. He made a list.

What he knew:

Cassandra had returned from an encounter with the demon that had formerly been Gideon's husband. She'd seen Maurier dead. Horrifying in and of itself.

Something about it had involved Alexander in a way she didn't want to talk about.

She'd told him previously that the demon had substituted his visage.

She'd been burned. Demon blood was hot, according to Cass.

Alexander sighed. The only logical conclusion was that she had stabbed the demon while it had looked like and presumably acted like him. Of course it stuck with her! It would haunt anyone!

Was he making it worse? He was probably making it worse.

He covered his eyes with his hand to block out the bits of moonlight fighting their way in past the curtains and rolled back to his back. People were not his strongest suit. In the past he'd have given up at that.

Not anymore. Not for Cassandra.

He did his best to push negotiations to end early the next day. Then it was a matter of politely shooing everyone from his house and dodging the new people Humphrey had brought on for the party. They were nice enough and good at what they did, but there was an awful lot of bowing that he needed to talk them out of, and by the time that was through, he almost needed to run to catch Jules before she headed out the door.

"Julia—er, Jules. Wait."

She turned and smiled. "Oh. Hey."

"Hi," he managed.

"Don't think I've actually gotten to talk to you in…what, fourteen years? Wild." She folded her very large arms and looked at him. "What's up? Everything okay?"

"Yeah." He caught himself. "Well, no, actually. Can I get you a drink?"

"Always. Lead on."

He took her through the house, dodged a few maids folding linens, and brought her into the parlor. "Please, have a seat."

"Don't have to tell me twice. I like walking in the woods, but I may have overdone it today. Twenty-seven loops in four hours."

He straightened and replaced the decanter. "Twenty-seven—? The perimeter is close to a mile."

"Ugh, I know."

"How are you functional?"

She shrugged. "I eat a lot?"

Alexander handed her a glass and tried not to stare. "That is…impressive. All right. Suppose I'd best get to it. You've noticed Cassandra is not herself, I assume."

She nodded, rubbing at the join of her neck and shoulder. "Yeah, that thing with Gideon's husband really threw her."

"Has she said *anything* about it to you?" He watched her face contort and added, "I'm not asking you to betray a confidence, I'm just…she hasn't spoken to me, and I don't think she's going to."

"Why do you say that?"

Alexander sighed and took a drink, then rotated his glass in his hands between his knees. "Because deductive reasoning has led me to suspect that she had to stab the demon while he was pretending to be me."

Jules sat up at attention. "Oh, shit, what? Yeah, that'd definitely screw with her head."

"I know!" He threw up a hand. "I know. But I can't…she won't talk about it."

"Yeah, that's Cassie."

"I *know.* My point…." He took a breath. "My point is that I don't know what to do for her. I've tried the usual things and run out. If I ask, she says, 'what are you talking about? I'm fine. Things are fine. It's fine.' And then she practically vibrates through the floor."

Jules snorted. "You do know her. It's like she's in the room."

"*Julia.* Sorry. Jules."

"It's fine. You can call me Julia. But just you. Anybody else starts and I'm punching them." She took a pensive breath. "Alexander, you can't solve this."

"What?"

"Mate." She leaned back, spread her arm over the back of her chair and gestured with her glass. "There aren't any magic words that can make her feel better about trying to kill fake you. I can tell. I can *feel* from over here how much you want her to feel better, and honestly, I like you a lot for it. But it's gotta run its course."

Alexander deflated, the ever present headache he carried since the moment he'd woken up from the shock of the blood loss thrumming as though trying to make a point. "You're…right," he admitted.

"But you want to try anyway, don't you."

"Obviously."

"The human condition." She looked up at the ceiling. "Maybe take her to see our—meaning her—mum. Might make her feel safe. She doesn't like to admit it, but she does like to go home when stuff happens."

He smiled. "She doesn't like to admit much."

"No. She'll take your secrets to the grave, though."

And that felt unfair, too. A lot to carry alone. "I feel like I'm interrogating her every time there's something to be discussed."

"Have to *tease* that bit of truth out of there like you're getting a splinter out. Yeah. That's our Cassie." Jules smiled. "She's doing better, though. I blame you."

"I…don't know whether to apologize or say you're welcome."

"Probably both." Her smile changed, strained. "Hey. Can I ask you a question?"

"Sure."

"It's okay if you don't know, but have you…?" She looked at the ground. "Have you heard how my brother is doing?"

Alexander's throat caught. That's right. She'd left behind a younger brother, now considered her family's only child. In all of his thoughts of her escape, he'd never considered that.

"He's good," he said quietly. "Just accepted to the Academy."

She looked up, her dark eyes shining. "Really?"

He nodded. "He'll complete his schooling this year and begin university come fall."

"Wow," she said, her voice cracking a little. "Shit. I mean…he's always gonna be eight in my head, but he's almost grown the hells up. When did that happen?" She sniffled. "Sorry."

Alexander fished in his pockets and found a handkerchief. He offered it to her. "No need to be."

Jules took it with a little laugh. "Perfect gentleman, you. Somebody paid attention during etiquette."

"Oh, barely."

"At least you showed up. I ditched completely."

"You always were braver."

"Or stupider."

He shook his head. "You left," he said. "Which of us was smarter?"

"Going to go with you." She looked around. "I mean, you're pretty happy, all things considered?"

He thought. Honestly, he hadn't given it much consideration outside fleeting moments, but he supposed she had a point. Strangely enough. "That…is a recent development."

Jules nodded. "Your dad was like mine," she said. "I could tell."

"Not as bad."

"Didn't he keep you cooped up in here unless there were official things on?"

"It was more or less for my own safety."

"You don't have to defend him," Jules said. "He can't hear you."

Alexander laughed sourly. Logically, she was right, but occasionally he still felt an odd compulsion to check over his shoulder to make sure his father wasn't going to round the corner. "Well, he didn't kick me out when he found me messing with a boy, let's put it that way. He just lectured."

"Oh. How gracious."

"Are you telling me you wouldn't take the lecture?"

She squinted into the distance. "My tolerance for that kind of bullshit is nonexistent. So no, none of it. I accept none of it. No dirty looks, no lectures, no kicking out, nothing short of what Cassie's mum did."

"What was that?"

"'I'm proud of you, clean your room.' That was it." She smiled. "I remember being so…jealous. You know how often anybody told me they were proud of me for anything I did, let alone for who I was? Well, Mum started after that, but before that? Zero."

Alexander looked into the alcohol in the bottom of his glass. "It sounds like we all just need Cassie's mum."

"She'll take you. Seriously, though, watch out. She'll put you to work." She drank. "Is my family coming to this party?"

Oh, gods, he hadn't thought of that. Now he felt like an incredible ass. "I…sent the standard invitations," he said with a wince. "I am certainly not above rescinding them, though, if you would prefer not to see them."

Jules shook her head and handed him her glass. "Nah, don't. I know you still have to be on polite terms with my dad."

"I wish I didn't," he said honestly. "Every time I see him I want to yell at him."

"Aww, that's nice. Thanks."

There were a host of reasons, most of them political, but she was in there too and she looked happy, so he didn't expand. "Will you be all right if you see them?"

"Me? Yeah. I'm going to be there with my hot wife doing my extremely interesting job for the prince with my friends who actually care about me." She grinned and shrugged a shoulder. "They can be sad and bitter with their friends who hate them and their unearned money. That's fine."

"I can get behind your concept of revenge."

"The best part, besides the hot wife, is that they're making *themselves* miserable. I'm not actually doing anything." She stood. "I have to get going, but listen…Cassie always talks. Eventually. When she's ready. Just be there—and don't tell her you're taking care of her. She hates that."

He nodded.

Cass returned with Kaye in tow not too much later. He heard the good-natured arguing long before they actually approached the house, but did his best not to jump up and greet them at the door immediately. Kaye said, "Look. Alls I'm saying is that shoes are stupid and I don't know why anybody wears them."

"You've seen what gets dropped in the street, right?" Cass said. "Nails. Broken glass. Bits of metal."

"That's why you get the bottoms good and roughed up."

"Nice try, kid. You live in the Upper Ring now. You wear shoes when you go out and when there are big fancy parties, which, by the way, I'm still not wild about you coming to."

Kaye made an impressive keening noise that jabbed him in the ears even from the other room. "I can defend myself, Cassie!"

"I know you can. I'm worried about you defending yourself into a feud with another household."

"I was talking about the demons."

"You're not going anywhere near the demons. You're going to stay with the prince and eat too much dessert and *wear your shoes the whole time.*"

Alexander smiled to himself and rose and set his book aside. Cass told Kaye, "Wash up for dinner. With soap."

Kaye grumbled away, and Cass turned and nearly walked into Alexander. "Oh. Gods. Hi."

He caught her by the arm to steady her and kissed her on the cheek. "Hi. Good trip?"

"Found a dress she doesn't hate."

"Good. You know, I don't particularly care if she takes her shoes off."

"I don't either," she admitted. "But Humphrey might faint."

"We should spare him," he agreed.

Cass smiled, then glanced up. As had been happening lately, she must have seen something in him that reminded her, because immediately she began tamping down discomfort. She brushed a bit of hair away from her face and turned slightly. "I should—"

"Cassie," he said softly, taking her hands, careful to avoid the still healing burn across her knuckles. "It's all right. Ask me something only I would know."

Her eyes caught his, startled. Yes, he wanted to tell her, I figured it out. We don't need to talk about it if you don't want to. Tentatively, she asked, "You…don't mind?"

"No. If it makes you feel safer, anytime." He held her hands to his chest. "Ask."

She still hesitated, as if she wasn't sure this was something she was allowed to do. Guilt. He knew the feeling. After a moment, she asked, "What's my most egregious abuse of power?"

Alexander smiled wryly, took her finger, and set it behind his ear. Cass smiled weakly and gave him a bit of a scratch. The strange leaping feeling in his gut took hold, like an electric line from his ear to his leg. He lurched and swallowed a laugh that could well have turned into a yelp. "How'd I do?"

"That's the one," she said, her posture relaxing a little. "I told you

you'd regret telling me that."

"Not remotely. It makes you smile."

She did, holding onto his hand with both of hers. At length, she looked up. "I knew it was you," she said quietly. "I just…."

"I take no offense to an occasional check."

Cass looked up at him. "How did you know I…? Did I say something in my sleep?"

He shook his head. "I put it together from what you'd said about your previous encounter with it."

"You don't forget things. I forget sometimes."

"That's not true."

"You don't forget details. You forget circumstances."

"I suppose that's more true," he conceded. "But it's only because a lifetime of lazy study has trained me to retain shreds of information that may or may not come in handy later."

"Is that lazy or effective?" She squeezed his hand and went to put her coat away.

"Cassie," he started, uncertain.

"Mmm?"

Part of him want to blurt that they'd been so close to actually talking about it, but the other part of him saw that she was more relaxed than he'd seen her for the first time since she'd come back from the Maurier house. Instead, he said, "I have a presumptuous favor to ask."

Her eyebrows lifted. "You? Presumptuous? I might need to ask another question."

"I know," he said somewhat nervously. "It's unlike me to impose."

"Go on."

"I was hoping…that you might introduce me to your mother."

Cass stared. "You…want to meet my mother?"

"Is that all right?"

"I mean—yes, but…." She blinked, as if still trying to wrap her brain around it. "Why?"

"Well, for one thing, I love you and she's your mother."

"Right," she said, "which means you've heard me talk about her. And how nosy she is. And pushy. And how she means extremely well but quite frankly she's going to be pressuring you to propose from the second you walk in that door."

Alexander's mind whirled. Damn, he'd forgotten the circumstance. She could smell an excuse from further away than he could smell blood. "That's not so terrible."

"I don't think you understand. My mother would trip you so you wind up on one knee and then make it too awkward to get up."

"I…." He glanced up at the portrait of his own mother behind her. It felt like a low blow, but it wasn't at all a lie, either. "Also, honestly, I miss having one. I've shown you what I have of mine. I'd like to meet yours."

Cass' face fell and the suspicion dropped away. She reached up for his face. "Okay," she said with a sad smile. "We'll go."

Good gods, he felt like such an ass, pulling out the dead mother card. He wished it could be as easy as, "let's spend some time with your mother and build your spirits back up," but he knew! He knew that there was a party upcoming at which she was anticipating a reprise of the demon, and even when things were good, she didn't like not working. He knew she wouldn't want to be taken care of.

He felt his father's portrait's eyes on the back of his head. It was the sort of thing he would have done. He wouldn't have felt a twinge of guilt about it.

But she did sleep better that night.

Alexander was certain that his colleagues were absolutely mourning the fact that he'd cancelled their deliberations for the day. *He* certainly wasn't. The audit was proceeding apace and losing a day wouldn't harm anything, and Cass' mother worked during the evenings. That was how he wound up leaving the Upper Ring during the day for the first time in… goodness knew how long—and remembering exactly why he didn't do it frequently.

The Market District was a sea of sounds and smells, and he was drowning. It was also irritatingly bright and a bit warm out. Every time he thought he had his bearings, a new person would wander through with their own musk they were absolutely unaware of, and his focus would be pulled in yet another direction.

The one he knew by heart drew closer. Linen, lightly rose scented soap, a hint of exertion, always a little old blood. Cass took his hand and pulled him away from the main thoroughfare. "Alexander," she said, as though she'd been calling his name for a minute or so and he had yet to answer. He winced. "Are you all right?"

He shielded his eyes and took stock of where they were. A backstreet, mostly made of bricks. A few people made their way through, but nothing like the crowd they'd come from. He could still hear the vague murmur like a buzz not too far behind. "I…yes. Sorry. I…get overwhelmed. The noise and the smells."

Realization dawned on her face. "I'm sorry—I hadn't even thought of that."

"Neither had I," he said. "I do it so rarely I forget."

Cass pulled him even further away, threading his arm through hers. Was he that unsteady? "How will you do at the wedding?"

"I'll need breaks," he said.

"And the party?"

"The same."

"So it's not just being shy."

"No, I legitimately cannot stand being in the same place as a large number of people," he answered, trying not to sound agitated. He felt agitated. Prickles all along his spine—hackles trying to come through. He took in a deep breath and tried to focus only on the nearness of her scent and the sound of their own footsteps bouncing back against the buildings. "Father seemed to think it was something I should be able to learn to tolerate. Mother thought I shouldn't have to. I don't know what the answer is."

"Do you think you'd have any desire to be in a crowd even if it wasn't overwhelming?"

Alexander tried to think, to separate the two things. "I would like to enjoy my friend's wedding," he said. "The autumn festival always looked like fun."

"You've never been?"

"Ah. No. There are a great many things I haven't done. Even at university, I didn't attend large classes." He glanced over at her. She barely kept the pity on her face contained. "It's hardly kept me from living a full life."

She looked away, embarrassed. "I…sorry. It's insensitive."

Alexander's irritation melted. It wasn't her. It was never really her. "No, say it," he said softly. "I'm curious."

"Do you really feel that way?" she asked quietly. "That you haven't missed out?"

He wanted to retort that she only thought he had because all she saw was the isolation, the high fences, the single butler. He'd had an occasional friend, he'd studied, he'd had a few youthful indiscretions.

But then he thought of his mother building a machine to bring the stars inside, and he didn't know. "I never knew anything else," he said at last.

"It just…seems to touch everything."

"It does," he admitted. "It changed everything. But I don't…." He blinked, considered his words carefully. "There are only a few things that I feel truly unable to do, and those I'm sad about, but I don't truly mourn. Everything else I resent because I feel that I *could* do them, if only people could understand. Make an allowance here and there. Stow their damn judgments and trust that I know my limits."

Cass stopped and took up his hands, lacing her fingers through his. She smiled a little, then met his eye. "That's the first time I've heard you say that."

His chest pitched slightly. It was probably the first time he'd ever said it. It wasn't wrong, though. He knew when he was on the edge of something. He knew when something was going to turn dangerous. He'd spent twenty years in this body and had learned it, what every funny bump and jolt and odd hankering meant and he'd learned to master them, and he was even learning how to subdue the other form. Gods, if anyone had told him he'd *remember* anything that happened on a full moon, he'd have told them they were mad. He couldn't bring himself to say it out loud, though, so he just nodded.

Cass stood on the balls of her feet and kissed him. She let her hand slip down the back of his head to his neck. Without thinking, he leaned into it, and the prickling started again along his back, a different way this time. He pushed out a breath and closed his eyes. "We should…we should go."

Cass tucked his hand into hers and led him the rest of the way to her mother's inn.

She kept warning him. "Really, it's nothing spectacular," she said for the third or so time as they entered the correct district.

"Cassandra," he said, stopping her, squinting against the sun. "Why are you apologizing preemptively?"

"I'm…not," she said, twisting her weight over her knee in a strange way. Her heart was hammering furiously. She was that nervous?

He set his hands to her shoulders and looked to the ground to try to gather his thoughts enough. "I've a title now, but I was an orphan. There's no judgment."

A little guiltily, she looked up. "You say that and I know that you mean to mean it, but I don't…you'll see." She took up his arm and pulled him a few more doors down, took a breath, and ushered him inside. "Mum?" she called tentatively.

The room was empty. It was a modestly apportioned tavern, well-kept and clearly well-liked. He could smell the faint hints people had left behind, and plenty of them. Recent. There was rattling coming from somewhere up above, and at last he noticed a ladder propped up behind the bar and a board slid away from the overhead crawl space.

Cass' hesitation slipped without delay into a scowl, and she stalked over. "Gods, Mother, what have I said about the ruddy hole?"

A hefty thump and a muffled voice. "Cassie? Oh, good. Hand me the cheese."

"I am not handing you the—get out of there."

"I am *not* old enough for you to forbid me from climbing around the inside of my own ceiling, young lady."

Cass started up the ladder, glowering deeply. "The doctor said—"

"Oh, the doctor wouldn't know his ass end from his mouth if the tailor didn't tell him which was the shirt and which was the pants."

Alexander covered his mouth to quiet his laugh. Cass turned her glare to him, but it wasn't enough to arrest it. It was impossible not to hear where Cass herself had come from, and she knew that, too. She shook her head and ascended a few more rungs. "I will bait the damned traps, Mum. Get out of the bloody ceiling."

"I'm already here! Just get the cheese, girl."

"If you fall, I'm not going to give you sponge baths," she muttered, stomping down and swiping a block of cheese from the counter and shoving it up through the hole.

"Oh, I wiped your bum for three and a half years. You can manage the sponges."

Cass buried her face in her hand. "*Mother.* I brought—"

"Yes, yes, I'll be right down. Fuzzy little blighters. I'll get you this time."

Alexander turned away and pretended to be very interested in the paintings on the wall to avoid incensing and/or embarrassing Cass further. Most of them were the sorts one could find at weekend markets—Academy students looking to make coin reproducing work of the masters, things of that nature. There were a few that did genuinely catch his interest: some yellowing pencil sketches, carefully pressed behind glass. A woman who had Cass' proud cheekbones and soft dimples and a wild mess of curls to her shoulders, holding a little girl in a rocking chair. They grinned at each other. The same girl, a little older, unmistakably Cassandra, reading a book in a window seat. In the large window, the sails of a ship passed. She'd lived near the harbor? She'd never mentioned.

There was also a painting. Cassandra, sometime between the ages, perhaps four, squatting to pick—no, to *pet* flowers in a well-appointed garden. In vivid colors, it was easy enough to tell the fabric was satin. He turned, a little surprised, and Cass looked away and up the ladder.

"Mum, are you almost done, or…?"

"Hold your horses, Cassandra Marina."

"How many horses do you think I have?"

"I don't know, you tell me." A cloud of dust billowed out from the crawl space, followed by a flurry of skirts, and Cass hurried to help a woman down the ladder. She set her hands to her hips and stretched out her back. "Oof."

"I *told* you. Get me or Jules or hire somebody."

"Oh, and where's that money going to come from—?" She caught sight of Alexander and froze. A bit of cobweb swung from where it was stuck in her hair. "Oh, goodness me, hello. Cassie! Why didn't you say something? I was in the bloody ceiling! Is that—?"

Cass looked skyward. "I *tried*, but you were busy sassing me. Mum, this is Alexander."

He stepped forward and extended his hand. Nervously, Mrs. Friend looked at her daughter and grasped fistfuls of her skirt. "Lord Fremont. Do I…?"

"Please, don't," he said gently, taking her hand and placing a polite kiss to the top of it. "Just Alexander. I'm very glad to meet you. I've heard much."

She smiled in exactly the same way her daughter did when taken off guard. "Lyriana. Pleased to meet you at last. I've not heard as much as I'd like. Please, make yourself at home."

"Thank you. Ah, yes." He awkwardly proffered the flowers Humphrey had insisted were necessary. "I hope that Cassandra's penchant for leaving flowers where they are isn't a shared one."

Lyriana laughed brightly, scooping the flowers into her arms. "Nope, don't know where she got that! I have no qualms about beheading 'em. Thank you, they're lovely. Let me fetch a vase. Cassie, sweet, maybe you'll help me get some cobbler?"

"Oh, sure," she said. She touched Alexander's arm and said very low indeed, "You may want to plug your ears. She's going to assume you can't hear us."

"Wouldn't be the first time."

"Yes, but this time it's my *mother*."

Lyriana looked back. "Sit!" she told Alexander before disappearing.

Mortified, Cass yelled, "Mother, he's not a dog."

"It's all right," he said with a laugh. "I took the meaning."

"She's just—forceful with her hospitality."

"Cassie," Lyriana called from somewhere around a corner.

Alexander kissed her cheek. "Go on. Perhaps I'll teach myself to roll over while you're away."

Cass slapped her face into her hand and groaned. "This was a mistake. I should never have put you both in the same room. I'll just get teased into oblivion."

"I love you."

She smiled at him and went to join her mother. He sat at the table nearest the painting and considered it a while longer.

Cassandra and her mother were not the same person, but it was very clear that they were fluent in the same language. He felt like an amazed scholar documenting a unique and long-established society—somewhat lost, but content to be. Despite the bickering, he watched the tension leave Cassandra's shoulders. She leaned into him as she told stories to her mother, to him, to both. It was good to listen.

It was always borrowed time. The headache crescendoed to a blinding crackle, and despite his practice at remaining staid, he grasped at his forehead. Cass sat forward. "All right?" she asked.

"Just…the market catching up with me," he managed.

Lyriana tilted her head. "What's wrong, dear?"

Cass explained quickly, "He gets bad headaches from loud places. We should probably head back before it gets too much worse."

Alexander shook his head. "No, please, not on my account."

"I've just the thing," Lyriana said, standing. "A little of my headache tea and a lie-down and you'll be good as new."

"Mum—" Cass started.

"That sounds perfect," he said quickly. She shot him a look, and he told her, "I'll try anything once."

"That is absolutely not true," she retorted under her breath.

Lyriana bustled away. Over her shoulder, she called, "Cassie, show him to your room, please. You can take him the tea when it's ready."

"I don't think he'll fit," she called back.

"Very funny."

"I'm not joking." She sighed. "Well, come on, then. Watch your head."

Cass pushed open a very narrow door to a staircase up to what was assuredly meant to be an attic. Low beams cut across diagonally, and the door at the end was a tight squeeze, but at last they emerged into a room roughly the size of the tavern below, albeit with a very low ceiling and a few more treacherous beams.

Two small beds, one to each side. One had flowers painted on the light purple walls next to it, the other had aging posters for various fights pinned above. Both had a decent stack of books. There was a single window draped with moth-eaten lace curtains. She made a face and cracked the window open. "I don't think this window's been open since I moved out."

He moved to the bed which was obviously not Jules'. "Did you paint these?"

Cass rubbed at her neck. "It was a long time ago."

How long? he wondered. The flowers had definition, shadows, the appropriate number of stamens and leaves. He touched an iris. "You're very talented."

"Well, thanks. I don't really…do that anymore, though. Not since I was—I grew up."

Alexander turned to look at her. She fidgeted with the latch on the window, which seemed to have gotten worn with age. "He was an artist?"

Cass dropped the latch, her shoulders slouching. "Was, yeah. Pretty good, right?"

"They're lovely pictures."

"Yeah. It's confusing, because he did love us. Wasn't enough." She sighed. "Yeah, he was the best in his class, did a bunch of big gallery showings for your society types, bought a big house by the harbor, married Mum, had me, and then pissed it all away starting shit over his conduct with a patron. She busted her ass to save ours, used the last of everything to buy this place. He just stewed."

"She did well for you," he said quietly.

"Yeah. She did. Best she could. Wish I could convince her she has enough to hire somebody for the mice now, though." Cass looked up at the rafters. "Ah, godsdamn it, the birds got in again. Every damned spring."

It wasn't terribly difficult for him to crane his neck and see up into the nest. "There are eggs," he remarked.

"Guess they can have it," she said begrudgingly. "Jules and I aren't using it. The tea's probably done. Speaking of which. Since when are you eager to try out new remedies?"

"You know…occasionally it's obnoxious enough I'm willing to try something out."

She cocked an eyebrow. "You talked to Jules, didn't you?"

Alexander knew he shouldn't be shocked at this point, but he still stared. "How…?"

Cass came over to him, set her hand to his chest, and kissed him. "She wasn't wrong and neither were you, but you are not very good at sneaking. I love you too, and I apologize in advance for the bed."

She left, and he tested the edge of her bed. It wasn't the worst thing he'd tried to rest on, but there was a spring attempting to break free. Gingerly, he avoided it and turned to the wall to look at the flowers she'd left perpetually blooming here.

It was the same sort of dream he'd had a thousand times before. The setting changed. This time, he was standing in the middle of a vast hall with an expansive purple carpet down the center, waiting. Music churned from an organ somewhere unseen. Ruhan stood next to him, exuberant even before all these faceless people watching them. How was he able to stand them—enjoy them, even? The sound of their very breathing with so many layered on top of one another felt like an assault.

Doors somewhere in the vague distance opened, and the bride came in, her face covered by a veil. Ruhan beamed, and for a moment, Alexander forgot the pressure in his head, the feeling of those featureless faces turned in his direction. This was why he'd agreed to this. They'd shared in enough of each others' pain, it was about godsdamned time for some joy.

A massive black crack snaked across the floor, and the uncontrollable fear rose in him like a tidal wave. The tension built along his spine, twisting, tendrils of pain ripping through skin and muscle and bone alike. Alexander clutched his arm to his gut and tried to back away only to bump into Cass from behind. "I have to get out of here," he gasped, his voice already warping.

She looked back. "I'm sorry," she told him over her shoulder. "There's no way out."

"Cassie, there are so many of them." He could hear them all, the thunder of their blood in their bodies, the weak ones shielding wounds or taking shallow breaths. It would be simple to pick them out, rip them free. The iron preemptively watered his mouth.

She lifted her blades, blocked something behind them. "Love, you can handle it."

"I...ngh!" He dropped to his knees, the hunch breaking through the back of his shirt. "I can't."

"You can't stop it. But you can handle it."

He looked back at the people. His prey. It would be so easy to take them. And that was the thing he tried so desperately to block out—that secretly, he didn't think he'd be very sad if they were gone. Amaranth wouldn't miss them.

He crouched, leaned into the thought. Because fighting it was what was keeping him from being free. Alexander closed his eyes and allowed the pain to ravage him in a rush.

And just like that, it was over, and he stood there, panting, ready, mouth still watering. Take them, his pulse demanded. Rip tear claw—

No, he reasoned. He could hear another pulse—hers. A reminder. There was another him, and he was expected. Perhaps he'd not miss them, but he'd not live with himself for removing them.

He would handle this. He had to.

He awoke with a start. Quickly, he felt for his face. A normal, human-temperature nose, reasonably shaped teeth. Alexander pushed out a breath and collected himself. That was not typically how those sorts of dreams went, nor was a shallow nap usually the sort of sleep that brought them on. He waited for his heartbeat to slow and sat up. Strands of silver fur drifted off his shirt. Well, he thought, cringing as he tried to gather what he'd shed, at least it seemed he'd kept his claws to himself.

It occurred to him as he finished stuffing the last bit of his fur into his pocket and started making the bed back up that something else was off. He frowned and pushed at his forehead in case it was one of those pressure things and he wasn't just at an odd angle. It wasn't.

He gingerly made his way downstairs, avoiding beams and spider-webs, made a last minute check to ensure there weren't any unsightly left-over wolf bits, and emerged into the tavern proper. Cass and her mother appeared to be arguing over whether or not Cass could accept something in a bag draped over a table, but they ceased the moment he appeared.

She stood up, looking at him uncertainly. "Hey. Are you all right?"

"What…was in that tea?" he managed, looking at Lyriana.

She looked up at the ceiling. "Anise, bit of ginger, forest mint, spare root, some herbs out of my window box. How'd it do?"

"I don't have a headache," he said, baffled.

"Oh, good," she answered, pleased. "It usually does the trick."

"It's the first thing that has in twenty years." He blinked around at the room at large in disbelief, at the sun coming in through the windows without stabbing him in the eyes. He turned to Cass. "Make a loud noise."

She laughed and smoothed his hair over his forehead. "Let's not test it that rigorously."

She was probably right. Too sensible. Still, the relative freedom—he felt like he could stand a symphony, or perhaps even attempt the market again. It felt as though parts of the world had opened up. Lyriana smiled and took the teacup from him. "I'll send you with some bags."

"You are a miracle worker."

She patted his arm. "And you know how to butter an old lady up. I like this one, Cassie."

She rolled her eyes. "Oh, good. I was worried."

"You should be," Lyriana said, walking back toward the kitchen. "I have your school portraits around somewhere."

"You're cruel, woman." She touched Alexander's chest. "You're sure you're all right?"

For the first time, he felt like he could handle it.

24

Preparations

The closer the party drew, the more frenetic Humphrey got. Cass had seldom caught him eating before—he claimed, as a servant, it was not his place to be seen having bodily needs, which she told him was patently ridiculous—but now if she did, he also tended to be scrubbing something simultaneously.

She leaned over to one of the new people. "I will give you five gold to go and point out that he got mustard on the spot he just cleaned."

The young man folded his umpteenth napkin and shook his head with a grin. "Couldn't pay me enough to do that."

Gideon grabbed her by the elbow and pulled her into the slowly metamorphosing ballroom. "Stop torturing the new kids."

"What? He was having fun."

"Yeah, in the *my boss's boss's lady friend is joking with me* sort of way. Now leave him be." He folded his hands on the recently unearthed piano and cast an appraising look around the room. Cass looked, too. She hadn't known this was here, to be honest. There was a door that they never opened and a space that was theoretically unaccounted for, but it hadn't even occurred to her to be curious. A few days prior Humphrey had led a small squadron of servants to attack the layers of dust and dirt and Alexander had walked past wearing a wistful sort of expression, but nobody really elaborated, so she'd left it.

Gideon said, "Starting to shape up."

"How's our bit?"

He gestured to Bjorn, balancing Thalia's narrow feet on his shoulders so she could affix ribboned bundles of herbs to the chandeliers. "Proceeding apace. Once they're done, she and I'll make rounds and ward it."

"Good. And making it look festive to boot."

He grasped his tail and pretended to curtsy. "Full service demon-banishment. We live to serve."

She glanced at him. "How're you doing?"

He kept beaming. "Miserably. You?"

"Oh…that's not relevant."

"I think it is." He leaned over the piano, looking out the window. "Jules told me."

"Damn it," she muttered.

"I appreciate you sparing my feelings, doll, but you should have just told me what happened at Maurier's. I'm the only one who knows what you're dealing with." He fidgeted with a knot on the piano lid. "That was his job. He manipulated. He found what gets to you and got to you bad enough you repented. I'm actually surprised you're sane."

There were times she doubted, but it was getting easier. "How can I tell?" she asked quietly. "If it's him, or…?"

Gideon breathed out. "If he's seen who he's turning into? You can't. Not by looks. If he's observed who he's turning into for a substantial amount of time for their behaviors, their voice, you can't. Your only hope is to touch him."

"Touch him?"

"Yes. And really touch him. He can make you think you're touching him. But if you actually do it, you'll know."

She paused, as an uncomfortable thought wormed through her guts. "Gideon. What do I always tell you before I leave the office?"

Hr smiled a sympathetic, lopsided smile. "Wondered how long it would take. 'Don't burn the place down.'"

It was him. The relief wasn't too complete. Cass tried to find her breath, at least enough of one to make words. "Is this even possible, Gideon?"

He reached across the piano and grabbed her arm gently. "Hey. I know he shook you up. But that's what he does. And that's most of what he can do. We keep our heads straight, we do our prep work, we stay smart—we can do it."

"Yeah, there's a problem with that," she said, rolling out her neck.

"What's that?"

"None of us are straight except Bjorn."

He looked at the ceiling. "I walked into that one. Straight into it. I hate you."

She smiled, a little of the trepidation melting off. "Eh, it was pretty good. Come on."

"You're the worst."

"I'm actually pretty okay."

"Yeah, yeah." He shot her a little smile. "So Bjorn will live and the rest of us will die, and that's just how it is."

"Shit."

"Nah." His smile faded, and he found a reason to be really interested in the way the dust was scrubbing off the large, many-paned floor-to-ceiling windows. "I've got one big trick up my sleeve. A planar web."

"What's that?"

"An enchantment that I can lay outside. When he makes contact, he will be temporarily held to the earth. If Thalia can sustain it, I can focus all my energy on ensuring he's properly banished. It's enormously powerful, but short-lived, so we'll need to time it well."

"All right, so where do we put it?"

"That is the question, but I turn it back on you, o tactical genius." He rubbed at his chin. "Obviously outside."

"If Alexander and I are bait," she said grudgingly, "we can use that. The patio. Close off the bedroom wing and set the trap right before the patio but slightly away from the house. We'll step out for some air."

"Good. Yes, good. And the patio is a hard surface, which makes drawing the lines much easier. I like the way your mind works."

Cass let her fingers run softly over the keys—not hard enough to produce notes. "I am worried," she said. "He was very aware that this was a trap."

Gideon smiled lopsidedly. "The final bit of bait. He won't be able to resist outwitting it."

"Game night must have been fun at your place, huh."

"Oh, love, you have no idea."

"I'm—sorry. That was probably insensitive."

"No, actually." He folded his hands on the piano lid and fidgeted with a golden ring that Cass didn't remember ever seeing him wear before. "It helps. Remembering him the way he was. Sometimes it's easy to feel like I imagined him. Telling you there were certain games we didn't play when friends came to visit because of his competitive streak makes him feel real."

She smiled a little. "Which ones?"

"Liege's Folly. A little like your chess, but with four players and a tiered board. Oh, and never *Temet*. That was a good way to ensure a blood feud. A cordial one. But an enduring one." Gideon sighed, his fondness cracking at the edges. "Can you believe me, having endured him now, when I tell you he was once a good man?"

"I can. You wouldn't fall for a bad one."

"You put too much faith in me." Cass shook her head. He insisted, "Yes. I knew there was darkness there. I looked past it because I was taken with him."

"Who doesn't have some?"

"You're right about that. To see it control him is…not something I'd have expected of the man who couldn't let the hellhound sleep on the floor." He laughed ruefully. "Scorch marks on the sofa. He was the one who'd been worried about them to start."

"Is…a hellhound cute?"

Gideon tilted his head. "I'm not sure you'd think so. Then again, you're not most humans. She does drool a sort of magma slurry."

"Ew."

"Most things are less flammable back home," he said as though that helped.

"Gideon…you know it's not your fault, right?"

He stared at the surface of the piano lid and smiled slightly. "Most of me does. It's a little maddening, though. Reliving the conversations, wondering what was real, what wasn't, what I could have said…."

"It was all real, and you couldn't."

He nodded quietly. "Yeah."

"If you banish him…is there any getting him back?"

"You know what banishing does to a demon, don't you?"

She shifted her weight. "Discorporates him and sends him back to the infernal wellspring."

"Right. Where he will slowly and painfully reconstitute over the course of decades."

"But in theory—couldn't you reconstitute him as a devil again?"

"Even if I could, Cassie, it wasn't the transformation that killed him." He sighed heavily. "I'd like to believe in redemption. That was my duty, supposedly. But really, I brought people to neutrality. I don't even believe *that's* possible after the choices he made, the manipulation he's been through, after betraying him like I plan to. Besides. I may not even live long enough."

"What do you mean?"

"He'll be banished from this plane, I'm banished from his." He grinned mirthlessly. "Mortal now, remember. I might die before he's reborn."

Her heart sank. "Gideon."

"I'm all right."

"No, you're not."

"No, I'm not. But this is the way it is. And the last kind thing I can do for my husband as I knew him is to make sure he can't destroy anyone else. That's what I have to do."

"Is there no other option?"

"I'm sure I'll try to reach for one. If I do, he's getting to me, and I need you to remind me what I came here to do." He held her gaze. "Promise me."

Cass didn't want to, but she nodded. He glanced up and over her shoulder, a grin forming on his face. "Oh, this looks like fun."

Alexander struggled into the ballroom balancing a large wooden case roughly the size of his own torso. Cass rushed forward to help him steady it, and with her help he eased it to the piano. "Whew," he breathed out with a sheepish laugh. "Heavier than it looks. Hello, dear."

"Hi," she said, looking curiously at the mahogany box with its brass fittings. In this house, she knew well by now that meant a piece of machinery. Usually a marvelous one. "What is it?"

"An entire orchestra," he answered, patting at his pockets and at last coming away with a key. "Ah. Here we are."

The front of the case swung open to reveal a set of brass cylinders behind a pane of glass. She recognized the pins and the little tines, admittedly on a much smaller scale. "A music box! An…enormous one. Wow. Was this hers?"

"Yes and no," Alexander answered with a smile. "Mother didn't make it, but she did love it. Inherited it from her father and trotted it out every chance she got. I swear it was half the reason she liked having parties."

Gideon reached out as if to poke a finger between the teeth, then thought better of it. "Mortals and your machines. How do you make it go?"

"Oh, there's a crank on the side there. Give it a whirl if you like. Six or seven times should do it for one song."

Gideon tentatively wound the mechanism, which fell into place with a weighty click. Bright plucked music sounded from the cylinder and reverberated through the piano and out into the grand room—much bigger than her mother's little jewelry box, but familiar enough it made Cass smile. What she wasn't expecting was a tiny section of woodwinds to join in, and something that sounded like horns, and even a little set of drums. Alexander noted her delight and took her by the waist, pulling gently toward the center of the floor where the acoustics peaked. "A very small orchestra."

"So small," she exclaimed, turning her face up to hear the sound bouncing off the domed ceiling. "Where have you been keeping these diminutive musicians?"

"Storage," he answered, taking up her hand and keeping the other at her waist.

"That is just cruel."

"I am a monster," he agreed, slowly entering them into a waltz.

She glanced down. "Are we dancing right now?"

Alexander smiled at her. "No, we're just testing the ballroom before we bring other people into it."

"Good. Because if we were dancing, that would void the contract."

"Technically, I didn't ask."

"Oh, so you *did* read it."

"Enough to figure out how to skirt it."

She let her forehead thunk indelicately into his shoulder. She'd forgotten to ask him a question, but it was him. "I don't know how to dance," she confessed.

"That's all right. I was forced to learn. Some good will finally come of it."

And he did seem to know what he was doing. It wasn't terribly often he carried himself with confidence, and it was…somewhat less terrible to be hauled through the motions of these inscrutable steps she could never quite figure out, because it was him. Still made very little sense, and by the end, she felt dizzy; but dizzy in his arms she could handle.

The music box ticked to a stop. She looked over at Gideon, who gave her a smile and a nod and then went to check on Thalia's progress. "Doing all right?" Alexander asked.

"Yeah," Cass said, managing a smile. "We're as prepared as we're going to be."

He tucked her hair back behind her ear. "Knowing you, that means we're well-prepared and that you're still chasing what-ifs."

"That's about right." She straightened his rumpled vest and hesitated. "Don't go far from me tomorrow."

"Darling, you know hosting has particular expectations. I'll have to be moving. Talking." He made a face. "It's horrid, and I'd rather be standing around with you, but once in a while I need to pretend to be what I'm supposed to be."

"I know. I know. Just…I might need to grab you every now and again."

Perplexed, he said, "Always."

Cass crossed her arms insecurely. "Is it a…problem if I'm near you?"

"No—no, of course not." He took her by the elbows, trying to coax her shoulders down. "What I mean to say is that these things tend to move strangely. I expect to be strong-armed away often because of my duty and my reticence, and then organic conversations form and…." He stopped himself. "You know that you're there as an equal, don't you?"

"I don't think it matters," she said plainly. "I've got a demon that can look like anybody, and he wants to be you. Apparently I can only tell you and him apart by touching him—or you." Her face heated and she didn't notice the rise in her voice's volume. "My hurt feelings or Lord Whatshis-face's are the least of our worries. Just let me check on you, for shit's sake."

Alexander nodded slowly. "Cassie…."

She shook her head. "Sorry. A little…a little worried."

He took her hands. "I won't be far," he promised. "We'll take care of him."

Gods, she hoped he was right.

25
Host

Strapping an entire armory's worth of knives underneath it was no problem, but securing the closure of Cass' mother's dress was proving difficult for her. She cursed under her breath and tucked the vial of Lightspring water further down the bodice so it would stop hitting her in the face as she twisted to try to catch the clasp. Her rib cage was a touch wider than Lyriana's, which didn't mean she couldn't wear her clothes, it just made it harder.

Alexander called from the door, "Are you all right?"

"Just wrestling a dress old enough to have babysat me," she stewed.

He was good enough to keep most of his amusement to himself. "May I assist?" he managed with only the smallest chuckle.

"Please," she sighed.

He entered the room in a lovely suit of plum and midnight blue details and set a bundle of something on the bed before moving to handle the fastenings. "This fabric," he said.

Cass smoothed down the green taffeta of her skirt, watching the way it refracted the light like the shell of a beetle. "It's Amaranthine gem silk," she confirmed quietly. "My uncle wove it. She had it made and wore it to a gallery back then. Probably could have sold it, but it was a hard thing to let go of."

"I can see why," he said, finishing the last of the clasps and turning Cass toward him. "Stunning."

She'd told her mother repeatedly that she couldn't borrow this, that there was every possibility she'd bleed all over it. Lyriana had responded that it would ensure that Cass kept her blood in her body.

"Well, it's why Humphrey's letting me get away with wearing something twenty-five years out of date," she said with a laugh.

"I believe the term is classic. Which reminds me." He leaned over to the bed and retrieved a worn velvet box from a silk wrapping. "I'd very much like you to have this."

Tentatively, she accepted the box and moved to sit on the edge of the bed to balance it in her lap and open it. Inside sat a delicate silver necklace—almost a lace drape for the collarbone hung with three teardrop shaped moonstones capped with pearls. She'd seen this before—the late Lady wore this in her portrait.

"Oh, I couldn't," she breathed.

He picked up the ends of the necklace and fastened them quickly around her neck. "She'd want you to have it. She wore it every time she hosted something. You brought parties back here. It's only fitting."

She turned. "Alexander, I—" She paused. "Did you just burn your fingers touching that?"

He smiled lopsidedly. "Only slightly."

Cass smacked his hand gently, then took both of his in hers and held them. "It's beautiful," she said. "And I'm…beyond honored. But people will recognize this. Think about what you're saying to the people attending this thing."

"I know exactly what I'm saying," he told her, holding her gaze.

She flushed. At length, she brought his hand to her lips. "I should brief my people."

"I love you," he insisted.

"I love you, too. I'm not sure your colleagues are ready for that."

"They don't need to be," he answered, kissing her forehead.

She held onto his hand as long as she could get away with. As he had predicted, they were separated by groups who wanted to talk about different things, and with the audit on, Alexander was unexpectedly popular this evening. Cass kept as much of an inconspicuous eye on him as she could from where the natural drift of conversation had pulled her.

By now she'd checked in with Lord Lomor, traded uncomfortable pleasantries with his wife, met a few more nobles whose names her brain promptly discarded in favor of noting Gideon's movements back and forth across the room, and lost track of how many times she'd seen Kaye and the band of well-heeled kids she'd somehow rallied into misbehavior sneak back and forth from the dessert table.

In this brief moment without a conversation partner, Cass chanced a breath. The warm, buzzing room made it a little hard to steal one. She'd never been nervous in a crowd, even with something at stake before. This felt different. There were eyes on her for once.

Two of them were glowering. Lissa stalked over, Jules' arm firmly clutched in her grasp. She still smiled, but her voice, just barely loud enough for the pair of them to hear, was furious. "I cannot *believe* the pair of you," she whisper-exclaimed.

"Hello to you too, Lissa," Cass said, scanning the heads to ensure she could still see where her particular lord had gotten to.

"After everything I've done…all the teas, all of the information—and not *one* word of warning."

"About what?" Jules asked blankly.

Lissa gesticulated tightly to Cass' whole form. Cass smiled wryly. "I'll try not to be offended by that."

"Oh, you know what I mean," she said crossly. "There were rumors, of course, that Lord Fremont had taken up with some city girl, but you could have at least told me first."

"I was a little bit focused on the supernatural entities I'm trying to keep from interrupting the prince's wedding, but you're right. Next time I have a piece of personal news, I'll drop everything to tell my noble informant."

"See that you do! I had to hear it from Danae Lomor. The insult." She glanced around the ballroom at large. "I will say, though, if this was your doing, well done."

"Oh, it was all Humphrey—"

From behind her, Humphrey spoke up. "Miss Cassandra's modesty is one of her many charming traits."

She started. "Good gods, you've got to start being louder."

"I'll do my best, madam." He bowed in Lissa's direction. "A thousand pardons, my Lady, but I'm afraid the hostess is needed."

Lissa's mouth quirked up. "Of course. Don't let little old me keep you. Ta, Cassandra, dear. I'm sure we'll see much more of each other. Julia, you're not off the hook yet."

Jules slumped slightly. Cass followed Humphrey to the periphery. "What modesty? You literally did all the work."

"The party was your idea," he said as though it was the most obvious thing in the world. "I put it on at your behest. Therefore, I acted as your proxy, and it's as though the work was your own."

"Well—that's—" She glanced around at the proximity of all the other people and kept her actual thoughts well clamped down. "Delightful. Thank you, Humphrey, for that edification. What is it you needed?"

A hint of bemusement chased across his face, then vanished as he lowered his voice. "Mister Gideon wishes me to inform you that there has been a…'fiddling of the ribbons'."

Cass cast a look up to the chandelier. Sure enough, some of the knots on the warding charms had been undone. The one in her throat tightened a little. "Where is he now?"

"The garden."

"Good. Find Thalia and send her his way out the back, please."

"Is this…?"

"I don't know," she told him, her voice as calm as she could make it. "But whatever happens, stick close to the prince."

He watched her appraisingly a moment, then nodded. "Good luck, Miss Cassandra."

She was going to need it, by the sounds of it. And maybe a drink. She clasped his shoulder briefly and took off through the crowd.

Cass made eye contact with Ifalna, who excused herself demurely from Ruhan's boisterous conversation with a gaggle of nobles and came to greet her with both hands.

"Our Cassandra," she said loudly enough to be noticeable. It wasn't hard. Anything Ifalna said publicly was noticeable. "Thank you for having us."

Cass bowed her head. "It's our pleasure, Your Highness."

More quietly, Ifalna said, "Is it time?"

"It seems that way."

"Then we begin the dance," she said with a nervous little smile. "Raven's cunning to you."

She pulled away and returned to Ruhan, and a few moments later pulled him onto the ballroom floor. This, of course, meant most everyone else fell over themselves to follow suit, which meant more people away from the edges. Cass tucked her elbows in and headed upstream, back toward Jules and Lissa, this time with an increasingly tipsy Ellorin.

Ellorin did not like social gatherings but, like Alexander, had to accept them as part of her professional landscape. This one was one of the few where she was not surrounded by colleagues, so Jules kept her in champagne flutes, it seemed. "Cassie!" she exclaimed.

"Ellorin," she laughed. "Having a good time?"

"Yes. Thank you for inviting me." She looked around the room in an ever so slightly drunken wonder. "It's a lot more fun when I don't care about anyone here except you two! Oh, and the others, of course."

"Of course. Hey, speaking of which. I need to borrow your wife."

"Bring her back in good condition," she said warningly, shoving her glasses back up her nose with a finger.

Jules glanced back towards the windows. "Is it on?"

"Seems so."

"All right, then." She stripped off the lace shawl previously covering her sleeveless black dress and handed it to Ellorin, rolling out her neck. "Time to spike Gideon's husband back to hell where he belongs." Lissa put her hand to her chest, and Jules assured her, "He's a demon. I mean that literally."

"I don't think that helped any," Cass told her.

Jules shrugged and turned to move for the front door. "I don't see why—" She stopped short.

In front of her stood a couple, finely dressed and frowning, and a gawky teenaged boy, all of whom shared Jules' brown hair. The boy looked back and forth nervously between Jules and his parents a few times. Jules, ordinarily so confident, seemed to wither.

Cass touched her shoulder. "Lord and Lady Evards," she said. "Welcome. I'm Cassandra Friend."

"I know who you are," the Lady snapped, not taking her eyes from her daughter.

"Do you? You're well informed." Cass stepped closer, lowering her voice. "So am I. I've heard a lot about you."

Jules took Cass' elbow. "Cassie—it's okay," she said. She steeled herself and faced her parents. "Mother, Father. Hey, Marco."

"You were told not to show your face in these circles again," Lady Evards said, her voice lashing like a serpent.

Cass gave her a sharp look. "Your daughter's presence was specifically requested for these events due to the skill, competence, and intelligence she's cultivated in the time since you've told her not to show her face in these circles. She is an honored guest. As are you. But more importantly, she is critical to the success of this evening, so I will thank you not to cause trouble."

Lady Evards' eyes—so similar to Jules', and yet wielded so differently—burned, and she turned and stalked off. A pocket of strange silence hung over their corner of the ballroom. The chatter and scuffling and music continued around them, but it didn't seem to properly permeate.

At length, Jules lifted her gaze to her father. "What about you? You going after her or what? You were the one who told me not to show my face, after all."

He couldn't quite look back. With his gaze directed over her shoulder, instead he saw Ellorin. "Is that her?" he asked quietly.

"Yeah," she said. "That's my wife."

"She's…a lawyer?"

Jules looked a little taken aback. "Prosecutor. And if you try anything, she will make sure it hurts your standing so badly our ancestors will be divested of their titles. So I wouldn't."

"No, that's…." He shook his head, swiping a hand over his mustache. "Julia, I…you seem well."

She looked at the ground and laughed. "That's it?"

"I am trying," he told her quietly.

"Keep at it. One day you'll figure out how to apologize."

His face went a little red. "You weren't exactly a model daughter, either."

"I was pretty okay," she returned. "I got in a few scraps, I talked back, and I didn't like boys. That's it. I turned out pretty good. I *seem well.* Actually, you know what, I *am well.* I'm happy, Dad. I live in a shitty apartment with my beautiful wife and a million cat pillows and work a weird job with my best friend where it's not only okay to be myself, people *like* it. People hire me to do it. The *prince* hires me to do it. I'm really well. Wish it didn't go the way it did, but you know, thanks. Couldn't have done it without you."

She stalked a little ways forward and stopped in front of her brother, who looked back at her, both awed and terrified. Her fury subsided a bit, and she smiled lopsidedly. "Hey, kid. Sorry you had to see that."

"I-it's okay," he answered. "It was a bit vindicating, actually."

"That's a five gold word. See you've kept reading the dictionary."

He laughed a little. "Almost through X now."

"You'll get there." She put her hands on his shoulders. "I'm…so glad to see you. Gods, you're huge."

"*I'm* huge," he snorted incredulously. "Look at your arms."

"Oh, that. Got bored in university. Started lifting bookcases."

He suddenly dropped the stiff teenager affect and threw his arms around her. "I missed you," he said into her shoulder.

"I missed you too," she answered into his hair.

"You should come visit."

"I don't think the parents would like that." She squeezed him and took a step back. "You're still living with them. Holding up the legacy and all that. I get it. But I tell you what…there's a red-headed kid running around here somewhere. Probably ditched her shoes. Got the same wild-eyed look I did. She knows all the good places to sneak in here, in case you need to slip away."

"Okay," Marco said. He waffled a moment, then added hesitantly, "Maybe I can visit you?"

"Probably the same problem, but…maybe."

From the corner of her eye, Cass spotted a purplish flash. Gideon's magic. She pulled Jules' arm. "We have to go."

"Shit, right," she blew out a breath and mopped at her face. "Demon."

Marco's eyes widened. From a little ways behind, Ellorin called, "Break him in half, sweetheart! That's my wife. I'm married to her."

Cass patted Jules' shoulder. "Yeah I know, terrible timing. You okay?"

"I got this," she said. "Might be good catharsis."

Already starting away, Cass told her, "Go get Gideon from the front. I'll grab Alexander and get to the drop point."

"Be safe," Jules hollered back.

Cass dodged a few dancers and tried to locate Alexander's silver head again across the room. He'd drifted quite a ways while her attention had been pulled, and he was walking with a purpose in the precise opposite direction she needed him to be, his expression that familiar mask of calm he always wore when he was trying not to be extremely nervous.

She hurried to head him off, grasping him by the elbow. "We need to go," she told him, out of breath.

His face sank. "Right now?"

"Yes, right now," she answered. "Why? What's happening?"

"Of course Lord Welles has picked *now* to start signaling he might budge on the third-to-last article of the charter," he told her, casting a nervous glance to a gaggle of nobles off to the side. "And if I don't play nicely right now, I could be scuppering *weeks* of work. All of this negotiation. The kids."

"I understand, love, but there is a time-sensitive plan on, and I need you."

"I know, I know…." He squeezed his eyes shut. "Two minutes. Two minutes to salvage things. Please."

Cass took a deep breath and looked to the window again. No more flashes, which was either a good sign or a terrible one. She saw Jules dart past the bushes, neither looking alarmed nor relaxed. "A hundred and nineteen seconds," she agreed.

"I will be *right* there," he promised, holding his hand out as he backed away toward the waiting negotiators.

She hazarded a look at them. The one who greeted Alexander, Welles —she'd seen him at court. An antagonizing sort of fellow. One of the vipers. The wards would protect the house against any shapechangers, but nothing would keep a human conspirator from walking in.

She couldn't control that. She could only work on what was happening outside. Ruhan and Ifalna were inside, and the guards and Lomor were there to keep an eye for assassins. Her job was demons. She turned and moved for the blocked-off bedroom wing.

Emerging into the night air was both pleasant and horrible at the same time. The cool was a relief after the stifling shared body heat of the ballroom, but without anything to cover her shoulders, Cass shivered. She stepped to the very edge of the patio—the invisible beginning of the planar web. Gideon had assured her that should she or Alexander cross it, it would not entrap them, but she still didn't want to risk springing it too early.

The lawn was quiet, dark. The clouds obscured much of the waxing moon, and the lanterns had mostly been lit to draw the guests toward the front of the house rather than the back. Cass gritted her teeth. She needed Alexander's ears. Of all the times to have to be a proper noble….

She cupped her elbows against the wind and tried to seem as though she'd just stepped out for a breath. An overwhelmed hostess. That was partially true. There was too much happening in there, out here, too many layers of deceit. She could navigate it, but it didn't feel good.

It had to be getting close to two minutes.

Was it shitty to take that literally? Probably. She felt herself instinctually backing for the door again, ready to go drag him out here by his hyperaware ear and put him to work properly. And then *she* heard something. A small cry, a thud, crunching footsteps in the dark. She reached under her skirt and pulled her knives and moved in that direction.

Her heart leapt into her throat as she watched Alexander straggle up to his feet, clutching a wound in his abdomen. "Cassandra," he gasped.

"Gods, Alexander—!"

He held out a bloodstained hand. "Stay back! Stay…unh." He stumbled, his shoulders arching, bulging. "I can't stay here. I can't…."

"It's—it's all right. What happened?"

"Something in the…dark." He swallowed hard on a mouthful of blood. "Like a…scorpion."

He stumbled again, and she hastily sheathed a knife and reached for him. "Please, darling, let me help you."

He stared back at her, eyes hollow, haunted. "I don't want to hurt you again."

She looked back at him. The look was familiar enough, but it wasn't lost on her that he wouldn't let her touch him. Was it worth risking—? Gods, she hated herself for even thinking it. At last, she just said quietly, "Okay. Okay. Come on. I'll get you away from here."

He mustered his strength and followed down the path where she indicated. She looked back over her shoulder into the darkened woods. "Bjorn?" she yelled. "Thalia?"

"What are you doing?" he gasped. "Don't call more here—I'm not strong enough—"

"We still have to keep the house protected while we're away, love."

Tromping footsteps broke through the woods, and Bjorn appeared, red in the face. "Cassie! Lord! Lord is injured. I can carry him."

"You will do *no* such thing," Alexander snarled, teeth bared.

Cass put out her hands to separate them. "No—it's fine, it's fine. Bjorn,

I'm taking Alexander somewhere safe. I need you to stand watch right there." She pointed to the walkway a little ways toward the patio. "Where are the others?"

"There were sneaky humans," he answered, jogging to where she indicated.

"There were?"

"Yes. We have handled them. Gideon chases the last of them now."

Distraction. "Signal them," she said.

Alexander shook his head. "Cassandra, I'm barely hanging on—"

"I know, love, I know—just two minutes, right?"

Bjorn reached around his belt and blew into a horn he plucked from it. Cass heard the same resonant blare only the Company would. One of Thalia's tricks. Alexander looked at it, between pained, baffled, and stressed. She stepped forward and gestured toward the house. "This way."

"That—that's the house."

"I know. We're short on time, so we'll use the safe room."

"Cassandra—we can't. There are so many people in there."

"Hey—hey, it's okay," she said placatingly, ushering him further toward the door. "I have the route secured just in case."

"They'll hear—"

"Alex," she said pointedly. "I need you to trust me."

He looked at her. "Of course I trust you, beloved, but—"

Behind her, Cass heard several sets of footsteps approaching. She gathered herself with a breath. Short, but powerful. She had to make this count. "He's always hated Alex," she told Laufit before lunging for his center of gravity to knock him into the center of the planar web.

A few things happened at the same time. First of all, she understood exactly why he wouldn't let her touch him. He felt like warm sand constantly slipping through her fingers. In fact, she pretty much fell straight through him.

Her force was still enough to jostle him into the the web, but only just. Gideon yelled, "Cassandra, *move.*"

She looked up. It was hard to see past the arcane sparks looping in their eye-searing purple concentric circles, but Laufit's form was…unstable. His Alexander shape kept flickering into the demonic form and out again, and his tail thrashed out wide. He might not have been able to leave, but he could still move, and he was *pissed*. His hands clawed for the air and he let out a scream, somewhere stuck between rage and agony.

She scrambled to recover her feet and hurried to the edge of the circle, only to watch it flicker. Thalia shrieked. "Step back! Step back!"

She did, and the lines flared back to life. Laufit screamed once more, but quickly it turned into a hoarse chortle. "Oh," he said. "That's perfect. You smudged it. Now you have to stay in here if you want your little *trap* to hold. We're in it together now."

Gideon rushed forward. "Laufit, don't—"

The tail lashed out. Cass blocked with her blade, straggling backward, trying to remember where the bounds of the spell were. The lights flickered again, and she rushed forward once more.

"Gideon," she called out, trying to sound more confident than she felt.

He put up his hands, staring at the creature. "Your presence is revoked from this plane…"

"It won't work," Laufit said gently. "Your heart's not in it."

"In the name of the sacred…"

Another tail strike. Cass blocked again. This time, the knife went flying away. "He's stalling you," she shrieked. "He's just playing with us."

"Oh, no, Cassandra," Laufit said. "If I were playing with you, I'd do something more like this."

The tail whipped out again, but this time, changed directions midstrike. Cass saw it well before it happened. It was moving for Thalia through the edge of the web, her hold on the spell already tenuous.

Cass swallowed hard and darted forward.

Sorry, Mum.

The stinger caught her between the ribs on the front left side, inches from the edge of the web.

It was very much like being back in the ballroom in that strange bubble of silence. The temperature, the sounds around her all remained, but they seemed muted in favor of the nothing happening in her vicinity. Her blood pulsed with poison, a vague drubbing she could feel working its way through her entire body. She could hear the others screaming, feel herself hoisted on this tail, hear the owner speak. "You know what happens when I withdraw from this wound," he said. "If you remove me now, her soul is forfeit."

Numbness overtook most of her. Not even pain, not even fear. Just numbness and a resolve that she didn't think she would have had even a few minutes earlier.

Somehow, she managed to turn her head. "Gideon," she said. "You have to do it."

He looked back at her, his eyes wide, his cheeks wet, his hands still caught between a half-mast state of alarm and action. "Cassie."

"Do it," she told him with a bit of a smile. "You came all this way. Finish it."

Gideon's wet eyes closed, and his hands pulled into fists, withdrew to his chest.

Laufit said softly, "It's all right, my love."

"Is it?" he asked tersely.

"You are kind, and that is why I love you. You will forgive yourself this failure in time and come to see it for the kindness it is."

Gideon lifted his head and regarded his husband. "I love you, too," he said. "Desperately. Permanently. Irrevocably. Even after all you've done."

"I knew you would—"

His hands shook, the tears kept coming, but in a steady voice, he said, "Away from me, Ezethrea."

There wasn't much time for the shock to properly register on Laufit's face. He melted into flame that seared Cass' entire consciousness, and she knew nothing more.

26

Drink Life, Drink Death, Drink Glory

Even with Lyriana's tea, the headache was strong today. It was inevitable. Too many clustered in the same room, too much chatter, too many perfumes, colognes, general scents, too much bloviating. Welles had always been deeply unpleasant, and Alexander had expected plenty of it today given that he'd been holding up funding for updated childrens' textbooks pursuant to Alexander's agreement to certain content restrictions. Now, here, tonight, in front of everybody else, he was ready to appear to change his mind.

"It seems to me, Fremont, that printing the extra mathematics in those districts is a waste of money, but if you're set on it," he said.

"I am indeed set on teaching children completely." Alexander handed off his champagne flute to one of Humphrey's new helpers, who seemed rather amused by the whole exchange. He honestly didn't blame him. How ridiculous this all must seem. "I am grateful for your flexibility, Lord Welles. Perhaps we might set up a time in the coming weeks to flesh this out more fully—"

Everything was sort of muffled past the general noise of the party, but this sound cut through. Cassandra's breath, knocked back into her, a terrible gasp, a rattle. She spoke briefly—not strongly. Then someone else did. And then she…fell. Cold dread choked him.

"Would—you excuse me, please."

Welles might have objected—he didn't know. He couldn't *care*. He couldn't do a single thing except walk very quickly for the front door and negotiate strenuously with the urge to break into a run on all fours because his body intrinsically knew that would be faster.

Not right now, he negotiated with himself in the way she'd suggested, as he let the door swing shut behind him and broke into a two-legged run. Both halves of him were in complete agreement. This was…terrifying. It only got more so as he left the noise behind and he could hear heightened voices arguing, could smell blood—*her* blood. But he needed himself for this. She needed this version of him. So he choked down the wolf and he ran.

Her people were all crouched around someone on the ground so thickly he couldn't see who it was, but he didn't need to. "What happened?" he demanded, his voice catching.

Jules stood up to stop him, the makeup running down her cheeks. She tried to answer, but in the end, she just said, "It's…bad. It's very bad."

Hackles. He pushed them down. "Is she…?"

"No. But it might be worse." He turned, and she caught his arm. "Do yourself a favor," she pleaded. "Don't look."

He felt his teeth clench, the jaw trying to shift, the growl trying to rise in his throat. He breathed. As gently, as he could, he managed, "I might be able to help. I'm an alchemist."

Jules looked dubious, but in the end, she nodded. "The demon hit her with a stinger before he got banished," she said. "It had a…poison on it, and it's fucking with her…soul. That's all we've been able to figure out."

He swallowed hard and moved into the space Jules had given up. The smell of Cass' blood intensified, and he shut his eyes and waited for the nausea and shuddering to pass as he grappled with the inability to ignore it. He shouldn't, he reasoned. It was why he was here. He just needed to turn it to productive purpose.

He managed to open his eyes and immediately saw why Jules had told him not to look. Cass lay on the scorched patio, her skin strangely gray and ashy, her head limply laying to one side. The blood was coming from a deep puncture to her side, out of which seemed to be growing large black crystals. Her chest rose and fell shallowly, like she was only asleep. But when he grasped her cheek and turned her face toward him, her eyes—terrible, ink black, all pupil—stared open and glassy.

"Cassie," he murmured, trying to vainly elicit a response, a reflex, anything. "Cassandra."

"She's not here," Gideon said, his voice thick.

"Well, then where is she?"

"At a guess? Either I just banished her to hell along with my husband, or…." He put his face in his hand. "Limbo."

Alexander stared. He could feel his ears shifting, but at this point, it was a concession. "What the hells is that?"

"The in-between plane the Demon Lord's been hiding in." He dragged his hand down his face. "Mortals cannot physically access it. Unlike the other two. It's *unusual* that hell is the best case scenario. Godsdamn it, Cassie."

"If mortals can't go there, how would she be there?"

"She doesn't count right now. But none of this matters if we can't save her body, which we can't do with this…."

"No," Thalia spat from her position at the top of Cass' head. "We're not giving up. She didn't give up on the plan. We're not giving up on her."

"What did you have in mind?" he said, gesticulating wildly at Cass' limp form. "Every second that necrotic curse just eats more—"

Curse. Alexander sat up quickly and reached for Cass' neck. The second necklace on top pinned the chain down too tightly. He gritted his teeth against the acid-like burning as he unfastened the clasp and set it aside, then pulled the vial necklace free.

He held it out to Thalia. "Will this work?" he asked urgently.

Her eyes widened. "Bless you, paranoid lord," she murmured. "I don't know, but it's the strongest shit my people have got. Let's give it a try."

"Doesn't it need to go in the wound?" Gideon asked.

"Shit. You're right."

Alexander gingerly touched the spikes of rock growing from and effectively plugging the gash. With little force at all, some of it splintered away around the edge. "Obsidian," he murmured. "Heat. Can you make fire?"

Gideon nodded and, with a gesture, a purplish flame appeared in the palm of his hand. Alexander reached out and directed his wrist toward the center of the crystal. A long crack formed, snaked its way down toward her abdomen. With his other hand, he gestured to Thalia and started to unknot his cravat. "Get it unstopped. Quick."

She did, and he let go of Gideon's wrist. In the same motion, he grabbed the vial and seized a portion of the hot rock with the hand wadded in cravat. It pulled free, and the godsdamned intoxicating smell of her very lifeblood washed him over again. He took it for the reminder it was and poured the lightspring water in before the obsidian could grow over again.

At first, nothing happened. Despair strangled him. He remembered how immediate the relief from the silver had been, how quickly the poison had retreated from him.

In an instant, the remaining shards of obsidian shattered, and the stark black veins around her eyes began to retreat. Thalia yelped. "It's doing something! Oh, shit, get that wound covered."

Alexander rushed to push the cravat into the pulsing hole in her side. He shivered again, pushing away another wave of nausea.

Gideon leaned forward, checked her eyes. "No—she's still—"

"I can treat the wound now," Thalia said, hopping to her feet. "There'll be a body to get back her back to. Let's get her inside."

Alexander stooped and pulled her close to him. Bjorn approached. "I can carry her, Lord," he offered.

It was probably the smart thing to do to hand her over. Bjorn had much more stamina and was far less likely to try to eat her. He still couldn't bring himself to let go. "I have her," he said. "Get the door, please."

He hurried ahead to do so and found himself foiled. "It is locked," he said, frowning.

"Godsdamn it," Alexander muttered. "Can any of you pick it?"

"That was Cassie's thing," Jules said quietly.

Shit, shit. He looked down at the cravat, now brightly soaked through with red. He couldn't carry her through like this. The panic it would cause. "We need a distraction."

"I can do this," Bjorn said. Thalia, Jules, and Gideon all turned to stare. He shirked. "You are not giving me the confidence."

"No, it's not that, it's just…social stuff usually isn't your thing," Jules said diplomatically.

"I have it this time," he insisted. "Big distraction. No one will miss."

Thalia and Gideon swapped looks. "Well, we're both needed," she conceded.

Jules nodded. "I'll…help out. Come on, Bjorn. Tell me your plan on the way."

Alexander waited on the other side of his front door, listening, cradling Cass' inert body against his chest. Jules had gone rounding people up for some reason, and the chatter had hushed. After a moment, knuckles brushed against the door. "You're good," Jules whispered on the other side of it.

Gideon opened the door and ushered Alexander and Thalia through. Alexander stopped in front of Jules. "What is he…?"

Bjorn's voice boomed across the ballroom. "Lords and Ladies, I am Bjorn Torrenson, Huntmaster of the Eastern Watch. You are wondering—who is loud man who is talking to you? To you, I am no one. In Joranhelm, I am…a little more than no one, but still mostly no one. But here—I am one of two proud Joran people."

Thalia's eyes went briefly wide, but she crept along ahead anyway. Gideon muttered, "I'll be damned, he's giving a toast."

Alexander had to hand it to him. There were few things nobles loved more than pretending to appreciate long-winded speeches and giving toasts, because it meant an opportunity to tack one on afterwards and potentially outdo the first. They could be at this all night. He edged after Thalia, still keeping well back in case someone got bored of waiting their turn.

Bjorn rambled on. "In Joranhelm, when our princess weds, our warriors weep. And you have met her now. You see why we might, yes?" Polite clapping. "Our leader. She is strong." His voice went a little sodden.

"She is brave. And cunning. And wise. And faithful. And I hope that you will join me in singing traditional…wedding toast."

"Oh, gods, there's singing," Thalia mumbled.

"As in times of old, we raise our glasses highhhhhh," he bellowed. "Drink life, drink death, drink gloooooooryyyyy."

There was some uncomfortable shifting from the direction of the ballroom, but even so, Alexander heard Ifalna gasp. Not a happy gasp, not an offended gasp, but a realization. He couldn't make it out over Bjorn and the nobles starting to awkwardly get into repeating the refrain, but he heard her say something in a hushed voice, and heard Ruhan answer.

As they hurried out of sight underneath the sash blocking off the bedroom wing and rushed into the bedroom, the call and response picked up. More voices added in as nobles lost their inhibitions or gave way to peer pressure or just decided why the hell not. Under any other circumstances, this would have probably been the best one of these miserable things he'd ever been to.

Thalia pulled the covers back unceremoniously to make room for Alexander to lay Cass down and immediately took over staunching the wound from him. "Good. Gideon, get my bag. Your Lordship, take a walk."

"Beg—your pardon?"

She glanced at him over her shoulder. "You're struggling with the blood. It's about to get worse. Go catch your breath and come back."

Alexander stared blankly for a moment. She was right—the most useful thing he could do would be to remove himself for the moment, but he couldn't stand the thought of being anywhere else. At last, he managed, "If there's any change—"

"You'll hear it."

He nodded. It was completely unimportant, but also somehow imperative before he left to lean down and brush the curls from her eye. "I'll make you a deal," he told her quietly. "Anything. Just come back."

There was, of course, no answer. He kissed her forehead and left.

The hallway was dark, save for the tiny bit of light coming from the end of it. Safely concealed, he sank against the wall and allowed himself to cry silently into his hand.

A door opened down the hall, and he stood bolt upright. Darkness was not an obstacle for his eyes, and Kaye's scent—mostly dirt and sugar—was familiar enough. "Lord Alexander?" she asked tentatively.

He cleared his throat. "Kaye. I wasn't expecting anyone."

"I came to get my twig collection. Are you…?" She caught sight of the blood stained across the front of his vest and took a step back. "What did you do?"

She thought he…his eyes found the scars cutting across her eyebrow and cheek, lighter now, but still very much there. Of course she thought. He shook his head. "Not me. The demon."

Her face shifted as realization hit. "Oh—oh. What happened?"

What *had* happened? He'd never really gotten an answer. There wasn't time for one. If he'd been there in the first place, he wouldn't have needed one. He stopped himself. Kaye was waiting, her eyes wide and fearful. He needed to be the adult. "He attacked Cassandra, and she's…well, she's quite hurt."

"Is she going to be okay?"

"They're doing everything they can for her."

Kaye's face hardened—not anger, or frustration, but a sort of stoicism Alexander recognized too well. She folded her arms and looked down the hall toward the light. "I'm going to go," she said.

"Kaye…."

"Everybody always leaves," she said, a hint of frustration cracking into her voice as she started away.

He swallowed on the lump in his throat, fully intending to give her space, but she only got a few feet before words burst out of him unbidden. "Kaye. Wait. Listen to me. I know. Believe me. I have lost two sets of parents, every friend I had except one. And now…." He couldn't finish that thought, so he left it. "And if you want to be alone to think about this, that is all right, but I am not going to let you walk away from me feeling like you *are* alone."

She turned, giving him a look that started out angry, but was really just pure panic. Alexander stepped forward to bridge the distance. "I know you've known a lot of loss. But I'm making you a promise right now. No matter what happens, there will always be someone here for you."

Kaye looked up at him fiercely for a moment, and then her lip quavered, and she flung herself at him, her skinny arms clinging to his midsection. He patted her back as it shuddered with quiet sobs. "I really like her," she cried.

"I know. I love her very much." He closed his eyes against the stinging tears. As much for himself as for her, he added, "She's never given an inch on anything without a hellacious fight. Let's not count her lost yet."

She nodded, still clutching. He let her.

A moment later, there came another set of footsteps, this time from the direction of the party. Alexander pivoted, still holding onto Kaye, this time more protectively. Ruhan materialized in the dark. "Just me," he said, worry written in his face. "Is everything all right?"

"No," he answered honestly. "How did you…?"

"Ifalna told me. The song was a vigil, not a toast. It's Cassandra?" Alexander nodded wordlessly. "Gods, I'm…."

"Don't finish that," Alexander said dully. Ruhan apologized enough for things that weren't his fault. He couldn't stand to accept one for this. It would feel too final. "She and her people managed to banish the demon running all three of the criminal enterprises in the city and the primary present obstacle to your wedding. She's not sorry."

Ruhan set his mouth to the side, but nodded. "What's being done?"

"The witch and the demonologist are…." Scrambling. Doing their damndest. In over their heads. If they were, anyone else would have drowned by now. "Stabilizing her and trying to control the metaphysical damage."

"Metaphysical—?"

He nodded grimly.

Kaye looked up at him. "What does that mean?"

He hesitated. She was a smart kid. She knew when people handed her bullshit. Even so, he barely felt qualified to have moderately difficult adult-to-child conversations, let alone begin discussing whether or not Cass' soul was at risk.

It was probably very wrong, but he felt strangely relieved along with alarmed to be interrupted by a loud crack sound from the vicinity of the bedroom. "What was that?" Kaye shrieked.

"I don't know," he answered. "Stay with Prince Ruhan, okay? I'm going to find out."

"Alexander," Ruhan said, his eyebrows lowered. "Let me help, please. What do you need? A doctor? Clerics?"

He shook his head, his body instinctively angling toward the bedroom. "I have the experts already. Just—if you can deal with the damned party. Don't let on."

"Of course," he answered uncertainly. "For gods' sake, be careful."

Alexander just nodded and dashed back into the bedroom, barely able to breathe until he took stock of the room. Cass was exactly where he'd left her, now sans dress and extensively bandaged. Gideon was slumped against a wall, clutching his head, and Thalia looked torn between continuing to work on Cass and going to check on him.

"What the hells was that?" Alexander croaked, moving to Gideon. "Are you all right?"

Gideon winced, blocking the light from his eyes. "Fine. I think. I just…failed to pull her out of Laufit's clutches. I'll need to do some divining in a bit, but…ugh." He pulled his hands away from his head. Alexander froze. At the base of his horns, black stone crystallized, slowly winding its way around the organic material. Gideon looked at him sideways. "What?"

Alexander grasped him by the arm and pulled him up, tugging him toward the mirror. Gideon leaned forward and touched the obsidian. "Well. Shit."

"What does it mean?"

"I don't really know," he admitted. He paused a moment longer, then turned away from his own reflection and walked back to the bed. "It doesn't matter right now. All I know is it's definitely not simple possession. There was an element that I did end, but there's…something else seething in there."

"What do you mean?"

"It's as if they've…combined several forms of magical intervention." He set his fists to his hips and breathed out, trying to steady himself. "I think it's misdirection."

"Well, what are we supposed to do with that?" Thalia demanded, throwing a bloodstained rag aside. "I can't cure misdirection!"

"Thalia," he said gently. "We're doing what we can. You got her stabilized. We have time now."

"It's not—it's not enough." She tossed some tools back into her bag, muttering something under her breath even Alexander couldn't make out —not because she was being particularly quiet, but because she was speaking something incompatible to the ear. When her head bobbed back up, she fixed Gideon with an accusatory look. "And I suppose *you* don't feel any additional responsibility at all?"

"Of course I do," he said with an unhappy laugh. "He's my evil husband. Was. You, on the other hand—"

"She took it for me," she snarled. "Stabilizing her isn't good enough."

Alexander deflated a little. "Is that what happened?"

Thalia's bloodied hands balled into fists at her sides, and then went slack. Her lips wavered. "Yes," she answered, her eyes spilling over. "And I can't…and I'm so…."

Gideon shook his head, his own grief pulling his voice hoarse. "It was a calculated move, Thalia. He did that on purpose, to see what she would do. If she let you take it, we'd have lost the web. If she took it, he had a bargaining chip, a chance to manipulate me. Either way, we were going to lose something. She made sure we still won the battle."

Alexander lifted his head. "She'd have done it either way."

"What?" Thalia asked soggily.

"She doesn't…." He shut his eyes against the stinging. "She doesn't play the game. Not with people. She'd have taken it for you either way.

It's just what she does."

Gideon laughed into a handkerchief and blotted at his nose. "Suppose so. Never did understand why she hurt her knee for that—"

"Assbiscuit," Thalia concurred.

"Not a hero, my devil-tailed ass," Gideon mumbled to Cass' unconscious body. "Sometimes selflessness is a curse."

Alexander tried not to take offense at the colloquialism. People never really meant anything by the comparison. He felt for Cass' hand at her side, absently running his thumb over the scraped-up back of her hand. Today, though, the comparison didn't feel like so much of an over-exaggeration, and he couldn't precisely name why. He glanced down at Cass, her stricken, dark eyes still open, slightly pained looking. The persistence, he realized. How many things they'd tried.

"Hold…hold on," he said weakly. "Demons don't do curses, do they?"

Gideon's head swiveled toward him. "They absolutely can. Why? You don't think…? No. They're usually focused things. They'd have to concentrate, and he's not…but then…." He paused. "If it's not *his* curse, and he's just delivering it—that may be why I failed to interrupt it. Not because Laufit is still holding her, but—"

Thalia perked up. "You think he's linked to the Demon Lord?"

"We *know* he's linked to the Demon Lord. He was given the name Soulbringer."

Alexander glanced to Thalia. "Shouldn't the water have taken care of that, though?"

"No, the water does poisons. Venoms. That's why it can't take away your curse now that's it's established, but if you got to someone you bit in time, it could help them." She stood bolt upright and yelped. "OH! Oh oh oh oh! That's it! Oh my gods, I can't believe it was sitting in front of me the whole damn time. You don't mind going through with the decursing, do you?"

"The—what?"

Thalia started rummaging in her bag. "The thing with the blood and the hair—she asked you to do it, didn't she?"

"I'm getting the impression not," he said, bolstering himself against the bedpost. "You're several steps ahead of me. Please slow down."

She sighed heavily. "Damn it, Cassie. Leaving me to explain your baggage. She had a fiancée."

"No, she told me that. And about the curse, but she said there was something *she* had to do. What is this about?"

Thalia puffed out a breath. Her illusory hair drifted overdramatically, and she looked irritatedly at Cass' still body. "Typical. Couldn't ask for a favor, could you. I gave her an easy way out. Quick, dirty way to shrug off pretty much any curse aside from the kind you carry and certain generational things. The only catch was that she'd have to ask you to contribute some things, and that's *weird*, apparently."

Urgently, Alexander prompted, "What things? Can they be done now?"

"If you're willing to part with some hair and a bit of blood, yes."

"To get her back? My hair, my blood, my heart—take it."

Gideon glanced at him uneasily. "Careful who you say that to, Your Lordship. Invoking sacrificial magic is powerful. Thalia, you're sure—?"

Her head bobbed up from her bag. "Not even remotely, but we're at the try everything stage. Stay with her. Come on, Lord Fremont."

"Where are we going?" he asked, falling in.

"Asking the moon for help," she answered.

For the most part, Alexander avoided the woods. It reminded him too much of the monthly ritual. Tonight they skipped the cell and instead went for the clearing a little ways past it, which Thalia led him to with so much confidence that he knew she'd been mapping the woods for some time these past few months.

"Perfect," she said, surveying the sparse, grassy hilltop. "Could have done with a full moon, but…well."

"Good luck getting blood from me then," he said uneasily. "What…do I do?"

She held up a finger, then set about placing stones in a ring around the top of the hillside. At the center, she placed a little lantern, whose door she opened. Inside she set some bundles of incense, which she lit and quickly enclosed behind the door. Smoke poured from a slot at the top of the lantern, onto which she set a bowl. Then she gestured for him to come. "Sit," she said.

He edged closer, careful not to disturb anything she'd set out, doubly careful not to look up at the naked moon above. It bathed everything in crisp silver light that his entire body took as a warning. Alexander sat gingerly on the damp grass. "Before we do this…is there any chance it could backfire?"

Thalia waved a hand. The antlers and wings and short-cropped hair flickered back into view as though he'd just blinked on a piece of dust. She turned to look at him. "There is always a chance," she said seriously. "But if we do nothing, she stays gone."

He nodded, but the disquiet lingered. Gideon had been so perturbed. "Just…what might happen?"

Thalia sighed and came to perch on her knees across the burning lantern from him. "If we were to attempt this and she wasn't your true love, there could be curse amplification. But that won't happen. Right? You're disgustingly in love."

Alexander took in a deep breath. Why hadn't she mentioned this—? No. There wasn't time, there wasn't room for this now. He looked back up at Thalia, who pulled a knife with a bone handle from her belt and held it out to him. "Well?" she asked quietly.

He took the knife and shut his eyes for a moment, then sliced across his palm and let the blood run into the bowl. Prickles broke out along his spine in response to the pain, and he breathed it out. Not tonight, he told the moon. It would get enough of his attention in the next week. Tonight, for once, it could help him.

He reached back and pulled his hair forward and raised the knife. Thalia held up her hands. "I appreciate the gesture, but I don't need that much. Here." She pulled out a small pair of shears and separated a piece from the front. A length of silver strands coiled and settled atop the blood, and the remains of the lock fell somewhere just below his chin. She handed him a cloth. "Here. No need to lose any more blood, either." She glanced up at the moon. "All right, then. Here goes. You sit there and think about her. I'll do the rest."

That wasn't difficult. Aside from general nervousness, it was the only place his mind could go at the moment. He pressed the cloth into the slash in his hand and tried to steer his thoughts from the rigid, blank-eyed version of her, even from the beautifully dressed, harried one he'd thoughtlessly sent away earlier. Two minutes, he'd said. What he wouldn't give to have those minutes back.

Instead he thought of the Cassandra who had tried unsuccessfully not to smile when Kaye had brought a frog inside the house and lost it. The one who had captured said frog so Humphrey didn't have to. The one who had badgered her mother out of the ceiling. The one who absorbed new information with curiosity and a hunger and appreciation. The one who had insisted on talking to him even if he was more likely to try to tear her apart than listen. The one who had stared down a demon with not a single waver. The one who had walked in with a contract and some flippant remarks and had walked out with his attention entirely.

In his pocket, the other, smaller velvet box weighed heavy.

Thalia spoke. "Three times speak I, three times heed me. In the name of the wind and wood, relinquish the beloved of this blood and bone. She is not yours to hold."

He almost wanted to cut in. She wasn't *his*, either. She was her own, and that she let him hold her was a gift. She gave him many, and he'd turned from her. His eyes shut, and he felt wetness trail down his face. The wind picked up, carried away the tears, played with the newly cut bit of hair.

Thalia said again, "She is *not* yours to hold."

The playful breeze turned vicious, whipping at their clothes. Alexander opened his eyes and looked around. Thalia's eyes glowed with a vibrant amber energy, and the stones she set out rotated around them. The contents of the bowl burned with a cold fire that seemed eerily comprised of the moonlight itself, but no matter how long he looked at it, nothing in his body threatened to give way. His eyes still watered, both thinking of Cassandra and against the sharpened air, but he made himself look.

She would want to hear about this, he knew. She would have so many questions when she woke up. And he would have very few answers, but at least he could describe this as well as he could, feed that curiosity of hers as well as he could.

Thalia slammed a hand to the ground, and the moonlit flames licked high. "Call her to you," she told him.

Alexander thought of her again, the light in her eyes in the Corona district every time she found a new corner in which to press him gently against a wall and kiss him. Maybe she wasn't his to hold, but he was hers. Unreservedly. "Come home, my love," he said quietly. "Please."

Thalia kept one hand pressed to the earth and drew the other up in front of her chest, pulling something faintly shimmering from herself and sending it into the flames. She opened her eyes and regarded the world sternly. With a final admonition, she told whoever would listen, "She is not yours to hold!"

But he was hers. And he would hold his arms out to receive her.

27

Face to Face

Cassandra was everywhere and nowhere.

Her body felt transcendent, limitless, and yet *awful.* The poison still ravaged her bloodstream—or so she thought. Did she still have blood? She felt no pulse, no breathing. For that matter, she couldn't see. Everything was darkness.

She took a step. A step—she was walking. With that step, the blackness rippled as though she had disturbed a very shallow pool of water. She still saw no evidence of her own form. Another step, two, three. Cass started to run. The ripples intensified into waves, gently ebbing off into nothingness. She didn't know where she was going, but there was no point in standing still.

The void stretched on. She looked as she went for a hint of anything—a door, a flash of movement, even a patch of slightly lighter darkness. At length, in the distance, a small flare of red appeared.

Well, there was literally nothing else here. She headed for it.

It glowed brighter and brighter as she went, but never seemed to draw closer. Cass focused, reached out. This time, in the vague radius of its glow, she saw the outline of her hand, seemingly comprised of the same shadow as everything around her, but rippling outward at the edges, displacing the dark the same way her footsteps did. Disconcerting.

"You are beginning to realize, then," a low voice said from somewhere in the dark. "You are nothing. The same inconsequential chaff that makes up everything else."

Cass reached down to her sides and came away with nothing. Either her knives didn't come with her, or there was no point in trying to access them. "Big talk for somebody hiding amongst the nothing."

"And yet you are drawn to me," the voice said. The red glow flickered.

"Ha." She took another wary step closer, trying to get a better look in perspective at the source. She could make out something at the base of the light—a brazier? "Is that you?"

"It is an aspect of me. My gatepost." Cass felt as though she blinked, and all at once, she stood right next to the flame. Alongside it, the shadows were nearly distinct now. The ground seemed gray, and there were… walls, it seemed, in various shades of purple. She herself was deep blue. A door swung open and the flame flared brighter. "I am extending you an invitation, insect. You've been a particularly annoying gnat. But perhaps once you've seen the swarm you'll understand. Come. See what I have built."

On the other side of the door, a new light flickered into existence. Then another, and another, and another, beckoning, pulling. Even if she'd wanted to retreat into the blackness, something prodded her forward. She crossed the threshold hesitantly and emerged into a dusklit street.

Purple buildings rose into a black velvet sky, red stars sprayed across in constellations she couldn't name. The flames burned in lanterns and torches set just out of arm's reach. And all around her were…people. Just like her. Blue, largely featureless, save for black eyes, not quite solid-seeming, but there. They noticed her, but didn't stop their work, their…conversations. If she could call them that. Heads bobbed, hands moved wildly in gestures, but she heard nothing but hissing.

Involuntarily, she stepped back. A few of the figures cocked their heads curiously, hissed in her direction. She put her hands up in front of her. "Don't mean to interrupt," she said uneasily. "Don't mind me."

"They don't," the voice said. "They do what I tell them and nothing more. And so will you, once your body dies and your soul is fully mine."

Oh. Cass felt her backwards shuffling falter. She didn't know who else she had expected. All of the flames flared with her recognition. She turned slowly. At the place where the horizon met the end of the road rose a ziggurat, and atop that on a jagged obsidian throne loomed a demon.

The demon in question. The one who named himself a lord immediately on shedding his humanity, and rather than allowing the rest of the demonic hierarchy to laugh at his insolence for it, he proved it.

"Dmitri Irividius," she said. "I didn't think you'd show yourself until the end."

Another blink, and she was at the base of the ziggurat. The figure rose, kept rising. He was broad, bulky, eight feet at least from head to clawed feet, but instead of resting on those, he slid forward on a massive serpentine tail that jutted out behind, nearly doubling his height. The scales were mixed obsidian and garnet, wending their way up most of his body and ending in very large protruding spikes from his shoulders and down his spine. His horns, unlike the gentle spiral of Gideon's, curled outward and up in four points.

It occurred to Cass, looking at him, that she really felt she ought to be more intimidated by the look of him than she was. Everything about him —his dragon-like clawed hands, the pointed fangs, the strange horizontal pupils—seemed like it was deliberately selected to scare. Like a children's story.

He slid to a stop on the steps a few feet in front of her, still careful to stay above. "Mortal fool. It *is* the end. Look around you. Look at yourself. You're formless. A whisper in the dark. All that remains is a formality."

"Then why are you going through all this trouble to impress me?" Out of habit, even here, she leaned back to take the weight off her knee despite feeling nothing. "You're not stupid. You made a plan to die, didn't you. Held firm through all those tortures hell had in store just to get to…this." She gestured to his body. "So I don't think it possibly could have escaped your notice that you only managed to down one of five of us contracted to stop you. It's not the end. Not even close."

Until now, the Lord's face had remained smug and impassive. Now it soured. "Kneel."

"I wasn't finished."

He closed the rest of the distance and reached out with a clawed hand, raking the fingers through her form. "You *will* grovel."

The same urgency that had hurried her into the city of dusk brought her to the ground, her forehead pressed to it, arms spread out in supplication. Damn it. He already had some sort of sway over her. If her body died, it would be complete.

Thalia was good. She'd hired her not because of her sorcerer's academy credentials or who her mothers were, but because she thought differently than any other witch she'd come across. She had to believe Thalia would take care of her.

That meant her job was to find out what she could and buy time and hope to gods they'd figure something out.

Gideon was good, too. She had no idea why she'd hired him at first, to be honest, but how quickly he had proven himself. How good a friend. How much he'd given, and how good an example.

"All right," she got out, picking her head up. "I groveled. I assume you want to use me to get at them."

"I will use you in whatever manner I see fit."

"It would go a lot more smoothly if you would just *talk*," she answered, getting to a knee. "If you were assured of your plan, you wouldn't bother with the theatrics. But I can tell you a good honest offer goes a lot farther than trying to frighten me into submission. I'm listening."

He observed her shrewdly. "You would betray your comrades and your contract so willingly."

"Believe it or don't. Either way you save yourself some energy."

"After all that effort to banish Soulbringer."

"That was personal," she said tersely.

"I did take that personally. He was rather instrumental to me."

"Because of his management of the underground, right? His playing with the fey creature posing as Gerund? His smuggling of your old Oranian resistance friends to take the cornerstone?" The smugness was about to fall away again. She headed it off at the pass. "Soulbringer was *sloppy*. More to the point, he was deliberately so, because he *wanted* us to find him. I'm telling you. Make me an offer. I will bring along the four others and then it will actually be the end."

Irividius slithered around her in wide loops, eying her appraisingly. He pulled up and came to stand on his lizard-like legs in front of her. "If you know of my Oranian allies, you know of my goal," he said. "Your delicate Amaranthine sensibilities take no offense?"

It was good that he assumed she knew. He might take the opportunity to elaborate, to hear himself talk. But his goal didn't matter—they'd stop him before he could get even close to it. "We're mercenaries," she told him. "Not heroes."

He chuckled to himself. "I believe the devil among you would disagree, according to Soulbringer."

"He might. But he doesn't have to know."

"Curious." He folded his arms. "Everything Soulbringer told me of you said you were calculating. Clever. But soft."

"For those I care for." She shrugged a shoulder. "Assure me and mine safety and prosperity and we'll already be doing better than we are now. You should know. You fought a war about a better life."

"Idealistic men fought a war about it. I fought a war to fight a war."

"You and your father both died for the cause. I'd have thought you'd have more respect for it."

His lip curled. "My father died for idiocy. I died for *my* cause."

"And yet you still employ his men."

He turned to look at her over his shoulder, the smugness completely gone in favor of ire. "Your insolence is not unnoticed. You may be of use to me, but to speak this—"

"All right, all right," she said. "Just an observation. It's my job. Look. If I'm this irritating, I'll start the bidding. Send me back. I'll finish out preparations. When the time comes, my people won't move and you can take what you want as long as you leave us alive, unharmed, and with a place in what you're building. Counter?"

Irividius turned fully to face her. "I would have no cause to trust you."

"No, but that's all right. You've never trusted anyone in your life except yourself."

His mouth twitched. "How would you know that?"

She shrugged. "I'm good at what I do."

And she knew that scared, puffed-up little shits like him were every-where. She couldn't believe she hadn't been able see it. Under all of the mystique and tall tales, the time they'd spent trying to untangle his motive, he was just an overgrown brat who liked to cook ants under a magnifying glass and scare the other kids at school. Even at eight feet tall and mon-strous, all she had to do to rile him up was suggest that maybe he had feel-ings about his dad.

It would be funny if it wasn't pitiful and world-endingly dangerous.

Irividius worked his jaw, still looking at her with his weird amber eyes narrowed. He turned to say something to her.

Before he could, a brilliant flare of silvery white light interrupted the perpetual dim. Cass raised her translucent arm to try to shield her eyes, but it wasn't much use. The other blue figures retreated, and Irividius re-coiled.

She heard Alexander call to her. "Come home, my love. Please." In her head, or...? She blinked into the light. A pair of hands extended from it. His?

Cass glanced back at Irividius. He was struggling with—something. He writhed, strained against the light. She turned and sprinted toward it.

"No!" he shouted. "You *will* get back here, you insignificant—!"

She felt his will tugging at her, pulling her back toward the ground. It still held some sway, and she stumbled, but she gritted her teeth and pressed on. No, she wouldn't. She was getting out of here.

Alexander's hands reached even further, fingers spreading out desper-ately. She strained to meet them. The demon lashed out and struggled to keep her bound to his strange not-earth. She tossed him a look. "I'd rather keep my options open," she eked out, and wrenched upward.

Her hand made contact, and Alexander grasped her wrist and pulled.

This time, all she could see was light.

28

Blue Moon

By the time Thalia and Alexander had managed to dash back into the bedroom from the outside, Cassandra's eyelids fluttered heavily. Alexander scrambled to the bed and scooped her head under his arm. "Cassandra. Cassie."

She blinked up at him, her irises back. They should have been brown, but he'd take this new blue, even extremely bleary. "Hey."

He leaned his head back against the headboard and let go of a shuddering breath. "'Hey'…yes, that is the customary greeting after returning from bloody limbo. Good gods, Cassie." He kissed her hair about a dozen times to remind himself that she actually had come back.

She rolled her forehead into his chest. "I am…so tired."

Alexander collected himself, gripping her hand hard, as though if he dared ease up it might go slack again. "Of course. My gods. You're back."

"You thought I wouldn't be?" she mumbled.

"You had me a bit frightened there, yes."

Cass patted his chest, her eyes sinking shut again. "I'll always come back."

"Is that a deal?"

"If you eat breakfast," she mumbled. Then she stopped moving again.

Alexander sat upright in alarm, but Thalia pushed him back down. "She's asleep. Relax."

Yes, certainly. Relaxing was high on his list of things that he could do. Cass was back, yes, but not unscathed, not quite the same. He looked at Gideon. "What…happened to her?"

Gideon peered down at Cass and cautiously lifted a lock of her hair—

now a vibrant midnight blue. He let it drift back down and drew a circle in the air, populating it with runes and steering it over Cass' now lightly snoring body. "What the hells," he murmured to himself.

"Going to need better assurance than that," Alexander said uneasily.

"No, she's fine, it's just…." He gestured impatiently for words to catch up with him. "She brought some of the plane back with her."

Thalia peeked over at Cass. "I thought that was only possible for you lot and the angels."

"Yeah, I did too," he said. "I suppose if he tried to bind her to it and we didn't really separate her before pulling her back…."

Alexander shook his head. "What does this mean?"

"Well, that's the question," Gideon said. "It's a very small amount of planar energy. It won't hurt her. But, apart from that…."

"You don't know."

"Afraid not."

Thalia rocked on her small feet. "But there's no more creepy demon stuff, right?"

He nodded. "It's only just the bit of limbo."

She rubbed her hands together briskly. "Well. She needs to rest. She's probably going to sleep a lot for a bit here. Curses are tiring. Oh. You know."

Alexander tried not to nod too sardonically. "And the wound?"

"I don't think it's going to make any more trouble tonight. But I'll stay the night in case that changes."

Changes. He was somewhat numbly uncomfortable with that word.

He waited and watched for a while with Gideon, while Thalia took the opportunity to retrieve more clean supplies, but all that happened was some very deep sleep on her part. After some indeterminate length of observing that, Humphrey's prim knuckle-brush knock sounded at the door. Alexander sighed, his headache redoubling. "Enter."

The door opened. "Lord Alexander—oh, dear gods."

Humphrey wasn't a fan of blood. This was not the best household for him to have worked for in those circumstances, but he was just as stubborn as all the important people in Alexander's life, so he still came into the room despite the pallor to his face at the sight of Cass' bandages, Alexander's shirt, and the many, many discarded cloths Thalia was collecting. Alexander smiled grimly. "I assume you're here to chide me for being a bad host, but as you can see it was somewhat urgent."

"I can see," he said, his voice going gentle. "Nevertheless, I must try to prevail upon you to make an appearance at the farewells."

"Humphrey. Do you honestly believe I can bring myself to give a solitary damn what they think right now?" he asked, his voice cracking.

"For Miss Cassandra's sake," he said firmly. "There will already be talk with her absence. If it's you as well…."

They would automatically assume there was some sort of scandal afoot, and moreover, that it was her doing. Because he was *raised better.* He gritted his teeth in resentment. "Very well. I'll manage."

Gideon stood. With a quick gesture, he somehow banished the bloodstains from Alexander's shirt. "I could use a distraction myself," he said. "Best find yourself a new cravat, though. I don't think there's enough magic in the world to save that."

Humphrey made the mistake of glancing down at what remained of the scarf sitting crumpled at the bedside and immediately drained of what little color he had left. "I…had best confer with the coat attendant. Excuse me."

Alexander sighed and began putting himself back together, at least visibly.

Gideon was a master. To look at him, no one would have guessed he'd been in a fight with several men, banished his own husband, and been hit with a rebuke from a demon lord, apart from the still-present crystals encasing his horns.

On the way down the darkened hallway, Alexander asked quietly, "Are you holding?"

"As well as I can." He smiled, but held his gaze straight ahead. "It was a game he liked to play, before. Would I choose him? or whichever thing I cared for those days? It had never been a person before. I am very—very sorry it was Cassie."

"Wasn't it Thalia or him?"

"It was. And it wasn't. It was both."

Alexander watched the floor pass under his feet. "Well. I am relatively new to this love thing, but I do know that isn't how you're meant to do it. Testing it."

"You are very right," Gideon murmured. "And yet I always chose him. Until tonight. Well…in a way. I did, and I didn't. Both. Cassie helped."

"That's what she does," Alexander said, holding up the sash so Gideon could pass under.

"That's what she does," he agreed.

A little at a time, the ballroom began to clear. Alexander kept his bandaged left hand behind his back and shook with his right and let Ruhan do most of the effusive talking. He watched the Evards family awkwardly split as Marco rushed to give Jules a genuine hug goodbye. She made brief eye contact with her father, who gave her a strained nod. Lady Evards pretended not to have seen any of it and rushed the boy out by his shoulders when he rejoined them.

Alexander excused himself to Ifalna and made his way to Jules, who looked away, trying to disguise a sniffle as a cough. He put a hand to her shoulder. She whirled. "Oh. It's you. It's—you. How's our girl?"

"She's going to be all right now," he answered, and for the first time, it set in. "There are still plenty of questions and I am not the right person to answer any of them, but she'll be okay."

"Oh, thank every last god." She grabbed him up in a hug and Alexander got the distinct impression that if she wanted to, she could toss him around like a child with a doll. Thankfully, all she wanted to do was squeeze. "Thank you."

"I did very little."

"I really doubt that. Oh." She flushed and set him back down, looking at the few nobles remaining in the ballroom. "Sorry, that was *improper.*"

He laughed. "Hang improper. You and Bjorn did a wonderful job."

"It's going to his head."

She jerked a thumb toward the corner of the ballroom. Bjorn stood telling a story illustrated vividly with hand gestures to a small crowd of lingering nobles. Alexander couldn't quite tell if their expressions were intrigued or disturbed. Possibly both. Alexander's mouth twitched. "It's good to make friends, I suppose. What about you? Are you all right?"

Jules started. "Me? Oh. Them. I—it seems wrong to talk about that right now."

"I don't think Cassandra would agree."

"Oh, you're absolutely right about that." She raked her hand through her hair and sighed. "Well, it didn't go how I expected. With my father, at least. He seemed…regretful."

That surprised Alexander, too. Evards was a hardheaded bastard in most every regard. His wife usually seemed more reasonable, if not a terrible gossip. He had no doubt that there would be fourteen vicious rumors circulating by morning to take pressure off of the ones about her family. Some of them would be about Cass. He tried to push that from his mind.

"Is regretful sufficient?"

"No," she answered frankly. "But it was surprising as hell. And maybe a start. Maybe. We'll see." She paused, a rueful smile inching across her face. "Cassie *may* have offended my mother mortally. Sorry. Tried to signal her, but she was in vengeance mode."

He laughed quietly. "I expected that might be the case. It's all right."

The staff spread across the room and began snuffing every third candle, the universal passive-aggressive sign that anyone left should get going. Bjorn's new friends inclined their heads as they filed out past him, ending their conversation—lingering to talk more after the dimming of the lights was the greater faux pas.

Jules waited for them to leave, and anxiously, she said, "I don't know, Alexander. My mother's vengeance mode can be just as bad, and Cassie is…."

Conspicuously absent. Vulnerable.

Ruhan strode over and set his hand to Alexander's shoulder. "Easily dealt with," he finished. "Tomorrow at court I'll commend her bravery for the injury she sustained putting down the threat at the party and thank her for her discretion in not causing a panic *and* her mannerliness in not taking attention away from my lovely bride."

Jules smiled a little and made a completely incongruous-looking curtsey. "Cleverly done, Your Highness."

"Nothing that isn't thoroughly true."

Ifalna came up next to Alexander, her expression uncertain. Quietly, she said, "This maneuvering. Your whispers, the secrets. The message in the song, the stiff dances…this is how battles are fought in Amaranth?"

Ruhan took up her hand, tendered it in his. "It's not a *battle*, dear heart, it's—"

"Then why does Cassandra lie wounded?" she demanded.

Alexander couldn't help but blink in surprise. He didn't think he'd heard Ifalna's voice rise much above a polite murmur—in fact, he hadn't thought her capable of anger, but her slate gray eyes flashed in a way that struck all three of them pretty well silent.

Bjorn, on the other hand, seemed summoned by it. "*Korjesta*, Princess. The fighting is secret here. It is pretended not to happen—but it happens with words, or with magic, or with poison, or with hired grunts, and then in the shadows. They do not declare it, unlike home."

"*Brost!*" she shouted, her face flushing pink. "And you call *us* uncivil! We fight when there is cause to fight, and we do so with honor. *We* name our troubles! *They* slink like snakes. The ravens take their eyes and their tongues and cast them into the sea." She turned to Alexander and wrested a golden bracelet from her wrist. "Please—give this to Cassandra to speed her healing and honor her bravery. One of the few proper warriors in this place."

He fumbled to take it from her, still flabbergasted. "I…thank you, Your Highness. I will."

"You. Bear-hunter."

Bjorn stood with his shoulders squared, looking down at her fiercely.

"I am in exile, my Princess. I have no claim to this title."

"You speak with honor. It is remembered. Do you carry the branch axe?"

He reached inside his coat and eased a hand axe from his belt. "It is my honor," he said, holding it by the blade and extending the haft to her.

She held it, a resolve hardening her face. She turned to Ruhan, axe in hand. "I walk myself home," she told him, and stalked to the door.

One of the guards posted at the door to the ballroom shifted his weight uneasily, but Ruhan waved him off. Ifalna fixed him with a look, and moments later the front door closed heavily.

"What…?" Alexander started.

"That was Ifalna," Ruhan said with a rueful laugh. "The real one. I'm sorry. She's struggling with court intrigue and being restrained."

"She is not at all wrong," he answered. "You know that."

"I…."

"Tell me you haven't been making her act tame."

"No, gods, no. That was her father's idea, and it—well, it wasn't a bad one."

Jules shrugged. "I mean, that's a long tradition of not letting girls be themselves much. Or anybody being themselves, really."

Ruhan's mouth fell open to object, but Alexander lifted an eyebrow, and in the end, he shook his head in concession. "It felt safer," the prince said. "I love her for every fierce bit that she has, but not everyone would."

Bjorn chuckled. "Princess can handle herself, Prince. Ask her axe."

He rubbed at the base of his neck. "I know. But…." He looked to Alexander. "You know."

He did. Unfortunately. The vipers had noticed that his cravat wasn't the same. "Even…even so. We aren't helpless, are we, Ru."

"Xander…."

"We're not children any longer," he persisted. "There may be unpleasant consequences should we buck tradition, but it's not impossible. There is a choice to be made now. Let's not pretend it's wholly out of our hands."

Ruhan considered, tracing the edge of his jaw with a thumb. At length, he laughed quietly. "You always were the braver of the pair of us."

"And you're full of it," he said with a tired grin.

The overall tone in the air fell somber, and Ruhan said, "How is she?"

Alexander looked for words to answer that and found that he'd used them up on Jules.

"Her physical wound is stabilized if not still fairly serious," Gideon said, stepping in smoothly, as if he sensed the imminent breakdown of Alexander's cogs. "She will require rest. The bigger threat was the abduction of her soul to the liminal plane known as limbo."

Bjorn tilted his head. "That is the wedding dancing game with the stick, yes? Bending over back?"

Jules shook her head. "Different kind of limbo."

Gideon chuckled, the general damper on his demeanor still not quite enough to stifle the amusement. "The game is more fun, if you can believe it. Limbo is nothing. A dimension that exists only to protect the planes from one another. It drifts there and occasionally picks up refuse jettisoned from this world, the hells, or the heavens. And that is where our target has been hiding."

"How is that possible?" Ruhan asked.

"Someone in hell gave him the secret to opening up the void during his takeover."

Jules wrinkled her nose. "And that's the sort of thing somebody just… knows how to do?"

"It was…sort of a refuse disposal," he said defensively. "It's beside the point. The point is, until the Lord of Demons, nothing was there that didn't accidentally find its way there. Very little of it has been studied — just enough to ensure it doesn't constitute a metaphysical threat."

Ruhan nodded. "This I'm aware of. Our scholars watch it. They call it the dusk."

"Euphemism. How very human." He rubbed at his head. "I expect they will have lots of questions for Cassandra, given that she's the only person alive to have ever experienced it personally."

Alexander's chest tightened. "They'll have to wait."

Gideon started slightly. "Yes—of course. She needs to recover before anything else. The Lord of Demons taking possession of her soul was taxing and seems to have…left some sort of planar abnormality behind."

Jules stepped forward, her fists clenched. "What?"

"What does that mean?" Bjorn demanded.

Gideon held up his hands. "Can you please—? It's very hard to explain with you muscly people looking like you're going to break me in half for doing so. Right now, mostly that certain parts of her turned different colors and kind of shimmery. Other than that, I don't know."

"Does that happen often?" Jules asked, her voice pitching abnormally high.

"Dear, nothing like this happens often. But it's not…out of the question, for devils and celestials in particular, to get touched by certain planar influences. It seems limbo has the capacity to do that to humans."

"She still *counts* as a human, right?"

Alexander turned away sharply and walked aimlessly to the edge of the ballroom. Distance wouldn't be enough to save him from the conversation, but old habits. He spotted Kaye, asleep facedown on one of the stiffly upholstered lounges around the outside of the room. Too much party.

He glanced back at the others, still deep in discussion. Gideon pushed deeply at his clearly weary head. "…every possibility that that's all it is. Or there may be additional effects. The point is we won't know until further observation is done, and *panicking* about it helps no one."

No. It didn't. Alexander scooped Kaye up and draped her over his shoulder. She stirred a little then fell immediately back asleep. "Good idea," he told her quietly.

He carried her down the darkened hallway until he couldn't hear Jules fretting or Gideon talking Ruhan out of calling for scholars. Kaye's room was dark, quiet, and just a little bit messy. He didn't know how she managed that with Humphrey following around behind making beds and tidying, but it didn't seem like it would be hers if it was pin-neat. He removed her box of assorted twigs and pine cones from the tangle of sheets and set it on the bedside table.

He hadn't wanted to offend her by providing too many toys. She was at that precarious age where she was both a child and assuredly *not*, depending on the day you asked her. And the life she'd had…well, she'd had to grow up quickly. But when he set her down on the bed, he found the stuffed bear there, clearly well used. He tucked it in the crook of her arm and went to remove her shoes. He needn't have bothered. They were already gone. He smiled to himself and pulled the covers over.

At the doorway, he nearly ran into Humphrey. "Dear gods, how do you manage that," he breathed, shutting the door behind him.

"Years of practice," he answered with a small smile. "You left so quickly, I grew concerned."

"I was just putting Kaye to bed."

Humphrey nodded. "It's been an adjustment for me, Lord Alexander. I've watched you grow from a boy, and it seems, almost overnight, you have a family of your own to care for."

He reached for the doorframe. "I know it isn't the way anyone expected it to be. It certainly isn't the way it would have been even if I had been a normal lord. I know there has been no courtship, no nursery days, no— trappings."

"My boy," he said with a small laugh. "I do not mean to give the impression that I am disappointed."

Alexander looked at him, confused. "This…wasn't the plan. *Any* of the plans anyone had for me."

"The plan." He folded his hands behind his back. "Do you know what it was?"

"Raise me to succeed my mother and father and take my place in the line of lords?"

"That was the table dressing. It was to give you a home. That was what your mother wanted above all else. To make sure you had a home." He cleared his throat. "Now. Even if one is no longer a boy himself, one might still find himself in need of comfort. That is not a disappointment, either." Alexander opened his mouth. Humphrey tilted his head warningly, and Alexander shut it again. "I have thanked Miss Thalia for her diligence and care and prepared some evening's refreshments so that you may rest yourself. You will need it."

Bemused, Alexander found most of his protests useless. At length, he said, "Thank you, Humphrey."

"It is my distinct pleasure, sir."

"Please, see to it that anyone who would like to may stay as long as they need to see to Cassandra."

"Of course."

"She…doesn't dislike you."

"I know, sir. We have a very different outlook on the same goals." He reached up to pat Alexander's arm. "Perhaps not all the same. She has decidedly more interest in certain aspects of your Lordship's life I would rather know nothing about."

"*Humphrey*. Did you just—?"

He wiped any trace of humor from his face and bowed. "I should see to the rest of the cleanup. Rest well, my Lord."

"She is not going to believe me if I tell her you said that. I'm not sure I believe that just happened."

Humphrey disappeared around the corner. Comfort indeed.

Days of fleeting consciousness for Cass, and constant low-grade worry for Alexander. The point to his ears never really smoothed out again. Fine, because he wasn't in a state to accomplish much, and with Ruhan's carefully dropped information, people reached out to him to reschedule. And send flowers. So many flowers.

He brought the vases into the bedroom mostly because he didn't know what else to do with them. The flower murdering had already taken place; it was too late for Cass' primary objection. They made the room feel a little more cheerful at least.

It wasn't that she couldn't wake up. It was that she was too exhausted to stay up. Thalia hadn't said anything, but Alexander knew she'd begun to worry about the lack of progress. The lack of understanding.

He sat on the edge of the chaise he'd been sleeping on at the bedside. In the daylight, her hair could almost be mistaken for black again at the right angles. Straight on, though, there was no mistaking that something had changed. Unless he looked hard, he could no longer make out individual curls. Instead, it seemed like a warping nebula made fibrous, almost satiny in its luster, with tiny hints of silver like pinpricks of starlight. If he looked carefully, he found hints of the same blue in the undertones of her skin—like very faint freckles that collected more noticeably at the corners of her eyes, her lips, now hued vaguely bluish, sprayed across her nose. That wouldn't be what people noticed.

Alexander, on the other hand, needed to learn it. He of all people. He put his face into his hand for a moment and tried to suppress the urge to snap at himself. He wasn't sure why it was proving so jarring to him, not having what was in his head match up to what he saw. He needed to get past it.

Alexander pulled his hand from his face and looked at Cass again. She slept as she usually did, with her mouth slightly open. After the bandages had stopped soaking through, Thalia had put her in a robe, which had gotten rumpled with her usual tossing and turning. Not everything had changed.

Her hair gave off the faintest bit of light against the cream colored pillow case. In wonderment, he reached out softly and touched the whorl above her ear. It felt oddly like placing his fingertips into warm water—comforting, indistinct. He went directly for the curl that always went a bit wild and tried to tuck it away. That felt more as he remembered.

Her fingers wound around his, and his eyes flicked to her face. Cass' eyes were open—heavy-lidded, but open. She smiled tiredly. "What're you…doing all the way…over there?"

Alexander leaned forward and kissed her—cautiously, but fervently all the same. "You may have missed it," he told her, "but there's a hole in your side, my love. I'd rather not bother it."

Cass shifted stiffly and patted the bed next to her. "Oh, I noticed. Come here anyway."

"Cassie."

"Please. Before I fall asleep again."

Alexander smiled in spite of himself and carefully climbed onto the bed on her other side. "You make it very hard to say no to you."

"I did…almost get trapped in…." She blinked, considering. "Well, first it was nothing. But then it was a city."

He positioned himself up on an elbow, propping his cheek on his fist. "A city?"

"Mmhm. But not a real one. Like a reflection of one. I wasn't properly real either, but more than the others."

Alexander lifted his head. "Others."

"Other people. Sort of. Once. They were…living isn't the word. Wandering the city. He kept saying when I died I'd become one of them, but you made sure that didn't happen. Thanks, by the way."

"He. The Lord of Demons? He was there? You saw him?"

"Oh, yes." She pulled a wan face, her nose wrinkling. "Plenty of gloating and threatening and trying to get me to sell out the others. He's made himself plenty dangerous, but he's really just…well, it pissed me off, really. Everyone in that room last night had daddy issues. It's practically a staple of Amaranthine culture. You don't see us doing genocide about it."

Alexander choked on a laugh briefly. "Darling."

"I'm including myself in that," she said defensively.

"It's not that." He hesitated. He knew very well how overwhelming the bedside talk was. To have everything dropped right after coming around. It could very easily be too much. But she was strong. She'd want to know. "It's…been a few days, actually."

Cass blinked, disconcerted. "How long was I in there?"

"In limbo itself? An hour or so, perhaps. You've been asleep mostly since."

"Is that where I went? Huh. I couldn't…it was hard to tell how long. It seemed like eternities."

"I am sorry it took so long," he said quietly. "We struggled to figure out what had happened."

"Oh—Alexander, no, that's not what…you saved me. You pulled me out." She turned her head stiffly to look at him in that earnestly stern way she did, the new blueness to her eyes more familiar somehow. Her gaze caught on the bit of his hair now too short to quite make it to the tie-back with the rest of it, and her fingers reached out and touched it. "What's happened here?"

"A hole in your side and a trip to limbo and you're worried about my hair?"

"You also gave Thalia some blood, didn't you."

Alexander shifted his weight and showed her the palm of his hand, the slash still healing. "It was how we got you back," he told her. "There were so many different types of magic—we tried just about everything."

Cass looked at the slice across his hand, her expression difficult to read. Crestfallen? After a moment, she took up his hand and placed a kiss into it. "Thank you, love. I'm sorry it came to that."

He shook his head vehemently. "Cassandra. It was nothing. You know I would give that and more for far less. Don't you?"

"You shouldn't *have* to. It was my problem—"

"You're not on your own," he told her. "You don't have to be. If you think for a minute I'd leave you to a demon or a curse when I could do something—" Her eyes darted away, and his throat tightened. He *had* left her. He hadn't been there. "Cassie."

"There isn't…any point," she said. "If he hadn't been able to be you, he'd have been…Kaye, or someone. It'd have gone the same."

"That doesn't mean I—"

She reached out for him and kissed his forehead, then pressed it to hers, running her thumb through his hair at his temple. "Please, love. I don't know how much longer I'll stay awake."

He nodded, squeezing his eyes shut. "I am sorry," he said softly around the stinging wetness. "I'll leave it there."

Cass nodded too, still absently stroking his hair. Her thumb caught the tip of his ear. "What's this?" she asked, then pulled back and laughed gently, tracing the tears spilling down his cheeks. "And this? Darling."

"Is it that shocking to find I've been terribly worried about you?" he asked with a laugh, mopping at his face.

She pulled him back to her and kissed his cheeks. "Oh, I'm just fine. None the worse for wear, and after a little while, no one will even know it happened." He hesitated, and she pulled away again. "What? What don't I know?"

Alexander took a breath. He'd hoped for Gideon's help to explain this, perhaps some time for her to recover a little more. But she was inquisitive. There wasn't going to be any deflecting. He'd always hated waking up, feeling terrible, and having a series of realizations dumped in his lap, a string of wondering to follow.

He walked to the vanity and retrieved a little-used hand mirror from the drawer and held it to his chest for a moment before returning to the bed, this time propped up against the headboard. "There seem to have been some aftereffects of your presence in the plane," he said carefully, handing her the mirror.

Her shaky hands—weak from days of eating little but broth coaxed into her in brief periods of waking—struggled with the heft of it. He helped her lift it, which was good, as she would have dropped it again. "Fuck, I'm still—" she blurted.

"Still what?" he prompted gently.

She poked at her hair. "No, no, I'm solid. Okay. Okay. That's okay. Probably."

"Cassie, what's happening?"

"When I was there, I was all…this color. And see-through. So were the other souls. Things just passed straight through, unless they were also made of the same stuff." She prodded uncertainly at her hair again. "But it still seems like hair, just…weird."

"Gideon says this happens sometimes, with the heavens and the hells. Just from being there, sometimes people will change in slight ways."

She nodded, still a little wide-eyed, but she smelled less like acrid panic now. "Yeah, okay, sure. That makes…no sense, but it's better than being partially dead or possessed or whatever. I'm still talking normally, right?"

"Yes," he said slowly.

"Good. Okay. Good."

"Both he and Thalia agree that you're perfectly regular apart from that little bit of extraplanar magic you're carrying around."

Her breaths slowed a little, and she nodded again, her head thumping back against her pillow. "Do I smell different?"

"Do you—? No. Goodness, no. You smell like Cassandra."

"Well, I assume extraplanar beings smell different than humans," she said, tossing a hand up limply.

"Somewhat, from my limited experience. Listen." He set the mirror aside and took up her hand. "It doesn't matter. You remember what you scolded me for those weeks ago? It's as true for you as it was for me. You're a person. Even if you wind up…not being entirely human, or never coming to a decision."

Cass paused, attempted to sit up, immediately figured out why that was a bad idea. Alexander lurched to lay her back down, and she settled with her head in his lap. "Did *you* ever come to one?"

"No," he answered frankly. "Either way felt wrong. So I left it."

She gazed up at the ceiling. "That's brave," she said absently. "We like to have answers to things."

"Sometimes a non-answer has to serve."

"I like that." They slipped into quiet for a bit. She fussed with the longer end of the piece that swooped over her ear, just barely visible to her over her eyebrow. "It…seems a silly thing to be fussed over," she said sheepishly. "He had my soul and there's still a wedding to do and I'm hung up on my hair changing color."

Alexander shook his head and smoothed her curls back. "It's very personal," he said quietly. "Mine was red."

She glanced up. "Was it really?"

"A little darker than Kaye's, if you can believe that. And quite short. There's little point in keeping it so any longer with certain nervous tics, but it did rather feel like the choice was taken. I understand. It isn't truly about the hair."

"Will I get used to it?"

"You will," he assured her. "With time. It may not feel completely right, but it will stop feeling wrong."

"I can scarcely imagine you with red hair."

"Me neither, anymore."

"My mother is going to lose it." She paused. "My mother. You didn't tell my mother, did you?"

"I…did."

"Oh, no."

"We were concerned you wouldn't wake up for a while."

"No, you're right, it would be worse if you hadn't." She took in a breath through her teeth. "Oh, I'm not going to hear the end of this."

"You have literally just lived through worse, I promise you."

"I don't know, you haven't heard Mum's *what did I tell you about messing about with demons* lecture yet."

"She may be right."

"Obviously, but we don't *tell* her that." She blinked heavily. "Ugh. It's coming back."

"What is?"

"The sleep. I don't want it to."

"I know." He stroked her hair gently and watched her eyelashes flutter again. "A short rest this time. I'll try to wake you in a bit. All right?"

"You'll stay?" she mumbled.

"Yes. I'm not leaving this time until the moon makes me."

"The…moon."

"It's coming on soon, but that's not for a few days. Rest now."

Her hand curled closed around his as though to subconsciously make sure he kept his word. Alexander leaned his head back against the headboard and stayed.

Longer bursts of wakefulness, still not long enough. She started to get strong enough to eat. Humphrey kept her in soups and Lyriana brought bitter smelling tea that seemed to help her stand long enough to use the bathroom.

Alexander ranged the room, trying to ignore the gnawing at his gut. It was extremely premature today and all the more irritating. He could not possibly have eaten enough to get it to stop, but he really would have preferred his wits about him, so he'd tried. Practically three breakfasts' and two lunches' worth. Cass snored lightly, having managed most of a meal. Better than she'd done in a while. A study in contrasts.

A soft knock at the door, and Jules poked her head in. "Hey," she said. "Is now a good time?"

"Of course. Please, come in."

She slid in as though opening the door any wider might somehow wake Cass up, and she looked around the room. "Wow," she said. "This is weird. It's like being in trouble as a kid all over again."

Humphrey had updated most things about the room when he'd insisted it was finally time for Alexander to take it over. It would have been terribly disturbing to sleep in the master bedchamber unchanged since his parents had used it. He still knew what she meant. The space could be dressed differently, but it still felt the way it did those years ago at times.

"No, not in trouble."

She glanced over at Cass. "And…she's not either, right?"

He nodded and sighed. "A little at a time. Slowly, surely, getting better."

Jules set her mouth to the side. "But not quickly enough."

Alexander rubbed at the back of his neck. "I think she's going to have to be the one to come to that realization. But perhaps the pace will pick up. Thalia is quite the healer."

Jules didn't look convinced. Yeah, Alexander didn't believe himself, either. He sincerely doubted Cass would ever voluntarily sit out a wedding, let alone this one. He didn't want to be the one to suggest it.

"So," Jules said mock-brightly. "Cassie-sitting. Lay it on me."

"Right. Yes. It's really not terribly difficult. She's mostly been asleep. When she comes round, try to get some food in her. That can be a bit of a race."

"Like, literally?"

"No, no. She just falls asleep very quickly sometimes. It's rather a coin toss if you can wake her purposefully. It's been longer stretches lately and more frequent wakings, but still…." He gestured to the bed. "Mostly this."

Jules nodded. "Anything else I should know?"

"Yes. The wound. It's mostly closed and healing well, but there's a very specific regimen. Thalia has instructions, but it's probably best if I show you." He paused, considered Cass. She'd fidgeted in her sleep a few times, which usually meant she was closer to the surface of waking than not. He held up a finger to stay Jules and went to the bedside. "I prefer to get permission if I can."

"Of course," she said with a bit of a smile.

He sat on the edge of the chaise and turned Cass' face toward him gently. He'd learned by now that if she wasn't looking at whoever was doing the waking there was usually a startled moment, and when she regained her strength that could potentially turn dangerous. Today just that motion was enough. Her eyelids shot open. "Who's…?"

"It's me," he assured her quickly, running his thumb softly over her furrowed brow. "Jules is here too."

"Hey, Cassie-cat," she said over his shoulder. "You're looking better."

Cass blinked drowsily. It was a slow waking, this one. It usually was, if it wasn't her body's idea in the first place. "Which bodily function is it this time?" she grumbled.

He laughed a bit. "None in particular. If it's all right, I was hoping to show Jules how to take care of your…"

"Demon hole."

"If you insist, dearest." He reached for the covers and began to pull them back. "Is that all right? She's going to be with you tomorrow night."

Cass caught his arm with a surprising amount of dexterity. "Tomorrow—what's tomorrow?"

Alexander tried not to glance nervously back at Jules. She'd politely not asked for any details of what prevented him from being here. He knew she was vaguely aware of *a* curse—that much had been unavoidable. Well, his wasn't the only one that involved the damned orb in the sky. "The moon, Cass."

She opened her heavy eyes wide. "That's—already? I'm…not ready. Who'll be with you?"

"I've done it alone before, my love."

"There weren't people trying to off you before," she said, hoarse voice rising. "I can…if I can just wake up…."

Alexander sat forward in unease. There was something strange—the acrid smell of panic starting to alert him to easy prey mingling with an electric feeling in the air. "Cassie, it's all right. For right now, this is more important."

"Not to me," she answered, frustration in her voice. "I want to *be there.*"

He started to reach out, but before he could touch her hand, there was a flash of blue light. When his eyes cleared, the bed was empty.

He leapt to his feet, his heart pounding against his chest wall. "Cassandra!"

Jules sprinted to his side. "What the hells happened? Where is she? Did he take her back?"

"I don't—" He stopped. There was a smell lingering in the air, faint. Like ozone. Some sort of energy transfer. No, it was something that had happened to her state. At the same time, a sound from outside caught his ear. It was Cass' voice, but just for a second. "No, she's still here," he said, dashing for the door.

A few more moments of quiet, and then another short burst of Cass' voice further away in the distance, definitely alarmed. When he threw the back door open, her scent hit him like a tree branch to the face. That panic mingled with the ozone smell. He doubled his speed and followed the trail. The damned woods again. "This way," he told Jules.

"How do you know?" she demanded.

"Now really isn't the time!"

And if he wasn't careful, she was going to find out firsthand. The impulse to fall to all fours for the superior speed was strong. He pushed it down and kept on toward the woods.

The energy state smell grew strong. Several hundred feet ahead, another flash, and Cass' silhouette appeared. Just her silhouette. The whole of her was the same blue of her hair apart for some silver flecks scattered like stars. Her posture was tense, frightened, and she seemed to grasp for a nearby tree. He called out, "Cassandra!"

She turned to look his way. "Help—!" she got out just before she flickered out of view again.

Jules' jaw dropped. "What in gods' name…?"

A few moments later and a few hundred more feet ahead, the blue form reappeared. "She's teleporting," he panted.

"Is that good or bad?"

"You know about as much as I do, Julia!"

"Apparently not!"

He bit back a rising growl. He hated how quickly the irritation came on the days before. "I'm theorizing as I go," he explained as patiently as he could muster between breaths.

And he was pretty sure she knew where she was going. Each reappearance brought them closer to the cell. Once he was fairly sure that her trajectory wasn't changing, he indicated a little clearing between the trees to cut around. It got them to the mouth of the cell just as she solidified inside.

Her hands clutched at the bars, and she looked around with her solid silver eyes frantically. "Alexander?" she called desperately.

"I'm coming," he shouted, skidding down the hill. Gods, did he have the key to this? The wolf wouldn't have been clever or dextrous enough to unlock it, but he could see his father telling Humphrey to keep the key away from him. Shit.

He ran up to the bars, and she peered out at him, shaking. "Am I dead?" she asked urgently.

Alexander fumbled around his pockets. "No, you're not—"

"Are you *sure?* This is how I looked."

He stopped his fishing for his keys, looked at her semi-transparent fingers clenched around the iron bars. "Give me your hands," he said.

He held his out to her. Hesitantly, she uncurled her fingers and reached through the bars. Cass let her hands hover above his for a moment, her just-barely visible mouth set nervously. At last, she closed her eyes and let them drop.

They came to rest on his palms. His hands closed around hers. The same warm water sensation washed over his skin. He smiled a little and brought her hands to his lips. "See? Real."

Cass stared at their hands, the solidness of the contact. At last, she looked up at him. "I'm still—I'm not tired. I can't feel my side."

Disconcerting, but he made an effort to keep his face from showing it. He squeezed her hands. "We'll figure it out," he promised. "But we have to get you out of there."

"Should you? What if this is him?"

"I don't think it is," he answered, returning to the search for his keys. "I think you did that."

"Great," she said shakily. "Good. That is a thing."

Jules put her hands to her hips. "I mean…you could stab a whole bunch of demons really quick. Be over here one minute. Over there another. Sounds pretty good."

"I don't even know if that's what I'm supposed to do!"

Alexander finally fished the ring from his pocket and handed it to Jules. "Please start trying keys. It's not these first three." He turned back to Cass and found her hand again. "I don't know if there's a *supposed to*, darling. What happened?"

"I—I just thought of you out here alone and it scared the shit out of me," she confessed. "Then it—I was back there."

"Limbo?"

"Sort of?" she said helplessly. "It was all…backwards. The city was backwards on one side, everything here was backwards on the other, and I just kept—bouncing back and forth."

"Backwards."

"Like when you look in a mirror looking in another mirror and they keep bouncing off each other." She looked down at her hand, examined the way the shadow of the cell bar could sort of be seen through it. "Oh, what the everloving *shit.* Am I stuck like this?"

"One thing at a time, Cassandra. Can you do it again?"

"What—go back through the mirror-thing?"

Jules glanced up from her key-testing. "Oh, hey, that's a good idea. Maybe you can get yourself out."

It was, again, hard to make out much of Cassandra's expression, but he knew very well that it was dubious, bordering on incredulous. She tilted her head up toward the ceiling of the cell. "Oh, dear gods. Okay. Um."

Her shape flickered briefly, and Alexander felt his grip on her hand shift through it. Immediately, she solidified again. "Something happened," he said.

"I didn't move," she said, vexed.

"First try. It's all right. Come on. Try to come to me."

She closed her eyes and focused. Her form blinked in and out of existence for a solid minute before she came back and stumbled against the bars. "It's no good," she gasped. "I can't get past the godsdamned cage."

Alexander sighed. "Because of me?"

"I am *apparently* staying here until you get in."

Jules looked up. "Wait. What? This is for you?"

Cass' translucent hand flew up to her mouth. "Fuck."

Alexander felt his hands tighten around the cold iron, certainly not for the first time. The panic shrilled out of habit, but by now there was a sort of acceptance. There was too much going on to avoid referencing it. "I will explain when I can," he said as evenly as he could manage.

Cass began, "Alexander, I am so—"

"It's all right," he said, his voice steely and calm. "Let's just solve this. Please."

Jules stared at him in a manner that suggested that she was about to solve this by putting him in a headlock until he confessed what was going on. He looked vaguely in her direction, avoiding eye contact.

"Agreed?" he prompted, a little of the stiffness diminishing. She nodded curtly and went back to fidgeting with the key. He turned back to

Cass and softened entirely. "You may not feel it," he said, "but you're still injured."

Cass looked at him hesitantly. "I…."

He reached through the cell door and brought her forehead to his. "I know. I know you want to safeguard…but there is a reason they put me in here. I'll be all right. But I can't lose you again."

Her hands wrapped around his arms and she closed her eyes. Another bright blue flash made him shut his eyes, too. He felt Cass' grip falter, and he flung his hands out blindly to catch her. When he could ease his eyes open, he realized he had her barely draped—nearly normally tinted and definitely exhausted—over his hands. "I've got you," he said, lowering her slowly toward the floor.

She breathed hard, blue eyes wide. "I…guess it's all right for me to leave," she mumbled, collapsing a bit at a time as he eased her down. "Not that I'm up to…walking out. Now I feel it."

"We'll take it from here," he said.

Something metallic clicked. "Got it," Jules exclaimed. "Back up, will you?"

Alexander squeezed Cass' hands. "If I let go, will you fall?"

"I think I have it."

The confidence was not doing much for his. He dropped one hand, then the other, waited. She didn't go careening toward the stone, so he stood to let Jules swing the heavy door open enough to get them inside. After an awkward moment of shoulder-jostling, they both made it to Cass and took an arm each.

Jules observed Cass a moment. "This is usually the part where I'd give you shit for scaring us, but you seem pretty freaked out yourself."

Cass lifted her head and looked around at the gray, stained cell. "A bit."

Alexander found himself in the uncomfortable position of self-consciousness. It was not unfamiliar at all, but it carried a different edge now with people in the know. In various states of in the know.

Jules wasn't there yet. She glanced at him suspiciously. "Yeah…can we talk about this yet?"

"I'm a bloody werewolf," he blared. "Yes, I know how it looks. I put myself in here because I *don't* like hurting people. Can we get on with it now?"

Wordlessly, she took Cass' other hand and slung her over her shoulder. "I…see."

Slightly winded, Cass said, "Jules. Don't do that."

"I didn't say anything."

"Very loudly," he muttered.

"And you," Cass said wearily, pointedly, "go a little easier on her, given that dropping this accidentally and inconveniently is my fault."

"I wouldn't say—"

"That's because you love me. But if you're going to be cross, be cross at the right person, please."

He glanced at her guiltily. "I…ngh."

"And both of you, stop talking about me like I'm a child. I'm sleeping all the time and suddenly turning non-corporeal, not a toddler." She folded her arms. "Now…carry me back, please. It is far too cold for my lack of pants."

Jules burst out laughing. Alexander's mouth twitched up too, and he placed a kiss on Cass's cheek and led the way back to the house.

Gideon returned from his errands not too much later. Errands were a euphemism for having mostly taken over the investigation and coordination of the warding efforts while Cass recovered. Nobody quite seemed ready to acknowledge that. He listened to the account of her bouncing between planes with bemusement, rubbing at his chin.

"Well, congratulations, Cassie," he said with a chuckle. "You seem to have found the strangest use for limbo I've ever heard of."

"*I* didn't," she countered, struggling to keep her eyes open. "It just…happened."

"Well, you made it happen. Whether you meant to or not."

"That's good news, isn't it?" Alexander asked, taking her mostly empty bowl of soup from her. "You were worried it was him."

"If I can manage to…keep from doing it on…accident," she mumbled.

Gideon tilted his head. "You'll learn to control it."

"You think?"

"Oh, I'm not comforting you. I'm commanding you. Unstable magic is a recipe for disaster." He smiled fondly, prodding at her forehead with the point of his tail. "We'll work on it."

"Great. Magic. I do magic now."

"Anybody can do magic. It's just about opportunity." He lifted an eyebrow. "Exposure to raw planar energy doesn't hurt. I mean, it could, but it didn't."

"Hey, what happened to your head?" She pointed. "On your horns."

"You're just now noticing?"

Jules touched Alexander's shoulder. "Hey. Can we…?" She gestured with her head toward the door.

He nodded and rose, listening to Cass and Gideon chat on for a while. He opened the door to the lounge, and Jules walked in and sat on the couch, patting the seat next to her. Alexander blew out a breath and joined her.

"I…apologize," he said. "It becomes somewhat difficult to control my temper in the hours before. It is not an excuse."

She nodded, leaning her elbows on her knees. She turned her head toward him, her voice quiet. "So, that hunting trip, huh."

"Yes. That's when it…yes."

"I'm…sorry. For not noticing."

He laughed a little. "My parents worked hard to ensure no one noticed."

"What illness turns a little kid's hair silver? Why did they keep you inside? We all knew something was weird on some level. It was just easier not to look too hard."

"And how old were you? Ten?" Alexander shook his head. "There are better places to put blame."

"Yeah." She wrung out her neck. "They didn't really put you in there, did they? Wait, our dads were friends. Yeah. They did."

"It's not…." He sighed. "You knew what the word meant when I said it. That means you must have some idea what I'm capable of."

"I also know that Cassie trusts you," she said, looking at him significantly. "That means either the stories are exaggerations or you're maybe not as scary as you think."

"Well," he said with a small laugh, "the former is certainly somewhat true. The latter…may be becoming more true. Thanks to her."

"She has a way of knocking sense into people. Or maybe stuffing you in a prison wasn't the right thing to do. Probably both."

Alexander rubbed absently at his arm, trying not to think too hard about the lump of guilt in his throat. "I hardly fault them," he said. "When your child starts going absolutely feral at least once a month and it's either that or risk limbs or worse…."

"Oh, horseshit." She stared at him intently. "You look me in the eye and tell me you'd do that to Kaye. Could you?" He set his jaw, tried to summon words, and she shook her head. "No. You'd find another way. And you've only been taking care of her two months."

Alexander sat quietly for a moment, folded and refolded his hands a few times. "Tell me," he said at last. "What's changed? Now, I'm probably not as scary as I think. Earlier you took Cassandra from me, and frankly, I suspect were willing to wreck me to do it."

"If the stories I heard are true, I don't know if I can."

"Depends on your equipment."

Jules considered her words. "You were honest," she said at last. "If not slightly cranky about it. You didn't need to be. Could have told me to fuck off. Probably should have, actually. But you told the truth in a…familiar way."

"What's that?" he asked, laughing slightly.

"You're tired of hiding."

He looked at a flower on the carpet so long that it blurred into a vague blue and pink spot rather than a bloom. "Until this precise moment," he said, "I thought I would be just fine with a few very specific people knowing and keeping up all of…this." He gestured to the the roses out the window. "But almost every accidental revelation has perversely been a weight removed. I've been raised to fear it more than anything, and it's only been…relief. I still don't know what to do with that."

Jules nodded. "Funny how that works. Anyway. Look. Cassie's really worried about you and tomorrow. Enough that she's apparently bending metaphysics. Maybe, if you're okay, we change the agenda to lord-sitting."

He pressed out a breath. "Oh. Hmm. That's very kind. And extremely embarrassing."

"You think I'm going to judge?"

"I think it's impossible not to."

"Everybody's got bodily functions, friend. Yours are just…." She searched for a word. "Fucking weird."

He smiled in spite of himself. "You're not wrong."

"For her."

Alexander thought. It was far more honest than he was used to being. He'd only *just* gotten used to it with Cass. Barely.

The thought of her worrying her way back and forth between planes was enough. "For her," he agreed at last, even through the unease.

Humphrey looked up as they walked. "Next month we won't need the lantern," he remarked as he did every year.

Despite the electric humming in his veins, Alexander smiled fondly. Every year, the sun stayed out later in the spring and summer, and every year, Humphrey was either surprised by it or acted well. "Strange how that seems to happen annually."

"It *is* strange how it always seems to creep up."

"Speaking of creeping up," Alexander said loudly without turning around, "Kaye, I believe you were told to stay inside with the doors locked."

Her padding barefoot steps grew louder as she scurried to catch up. "I know, I know, I just…." She managed to fit a few of her short strides into one of his long ones. "I just finished this and wanted you to have it before…you know."

She held out a lumpy red velvet rectangle about the size of his palm, stitched together unevenly with blue thread and stuffed with sawdust and something fragrant and oddly soothing. He took it from her. "Thank you. It's quite nice."

Kaye excitedly withdrew a large leather bound book from under her arm and started flipping pages. "Thalia's been teaching me to spot plants. Look!" She pointed to a drawing of an herb with long, flat leaves. "They call it Hound's Slumber. They use it when they want to move guard dogs. It gets them kind of sleepy. I know, I know, you're not a *dog*, but maybe it might help?"

Alexander looked at the sachet in his hand a moment, then back at her. She stashed the book back under her arm and peered back hopefully. He managed a smile and looped her into a quick hug. "Thank you, Kaye. It's very thoughtful of you."

She beamed. "See, Humphrey? I sewed."

He looked very much like he had something he wanted to say about the quality of said sewing, but Alexander sent him a look, so he just nodded. "I am glad you are practicing, Miss Kaye. But Lord Alexander was right. You must hurry along inside now. This is not the night to dawdle out here."

Kaye looked at the ground, then chanced a brief glance at Alexander. "You'll…you'll be okay?"

He set his hand to the top of her head for a moment. "Just fine. Go on. Keep Cassandra company for me, please. She'll need it tonight."

She nodded, gave him one more hug, and ran back in the direction of the house. Humphrey watched her for a moment. "I didn't think there was anything that could possibly compel her to practice needlework."

Alexander continued on toward the wood. "It wasn't that long ago I was refusing to do things that didn't have a practical application."

"I suppose not." He fell in. "Will it work?"

He kept his voice low. "Hound's Slumber is a soporific in large amounts. It's also somewhat poisonous long term, which is why they never tried it."

Humphrey's eyebrows lifted. "Dear *gods*, why are you holding onto that? And the witch certainly knows that—"

Alexander held his hand up. "In this quantity, it's little more than potpourri. A nice gesture. She's just giving the girl a way to feel helpful. Not everything is an attack on me."

A bit at a time, Humphrey unruffled. "I…apologize. For a time, many things were."

"I remember. We have friends as well as enemies now, Humphrey." He looked down at the little red pouch in his hand. "It's a lot to get used to."

In the dark, blood-soaked stone room, alone as he was every month. It didn't matter how many times it happened, how familiar the scene, the apprehension never stopped overwhelming him. He knelt on the battered, stained mattress and set his clothes aside, folded neatly as he'd been taught.

He froze. He'd been taught to fold his clothes carefully in the cell where he underwent experimental treatments for his lycanthropy as a child.

Thoughts like this occurred to him monthly, too. Usually he pushed them away. There was enough pain at hand. Today he heard Jules' regret in his head. *It was easier not to look.*

One hand curled tight around Kaye's sachet, the other against his knee. His head dropped forward, and as the invisible tether between the moon and him snapped taut, the cry that came out of him wasn't just agony.

Fury rampaged through him as things twisted, bent, snapped, stretched. There wasn't much room for thought, but snatches of memory flared like fevered dreams. His small body shivering, the taste of something so sour he nearly ejected everything he'd eaten across the cell, his mother comforting him from outside it. *I'm sorry. I tried to talk him out of it, but it's the way it must be.*

His claws tore into the mattress. She was meant to be the good one, the one who loved him. She'd let it happen just as much as his father had made it. Alexander's spine arched, hips tucking under. He screamed — partly in frustration, partly in anticipation of the abject misery that always followed this, the worst part.

This time, though, the pain was different. Present, certainly, but dulled somehow, turned to raw adrenaline, anxiety, purpose, driving the rest of this wretched process. He huffed, the last of his sweat disappearing. Confusion. Cass joined the fevered parade of memories. Don't hold on, she'd told him.

Was that it? Had he stopped? And would she still think the same now that she knew the inside of this place?

It was over strangely quickly. He stood on his paws, panting, barely cognizant, but *cognizant.* That was new. He felt the breeze from outside ruffle his hide and could for the first time appreciate it. His heart beat quickly, and again, he felt the urge to *go*, be somewhere, do something.

Not particularly easy in here. As if by rote, he started a lap around the chamber. The smell of the carcass in the corner pulled like a siren still, but he felt a higher call. The lope turned into a run now. No way out. He knew this, of course, but it seemed his body needed to confirm it. He slowed, paced the back for a bit, sank to his haunches. No wonder the wolf got frustrated in here. They'd been foiling this ready-made drive for years.

And the moon was still calling. He'd thought it would stop once the transforming was done. It was still beckoning, demanding his adoration. Tempting, to actually look at it. So much noise in this quiet little room, and that wasn't even counting the crickets, the wind in the trees, the call of the night birds outside, and all the inadvertent noises of the woman who was keeping an eye on him.

What was her name…? He'd known her for years, longer than this room. His other half cared for her deeply. Names were hard like this. He supposed it didn't matter. He knew her smell and she was drawing closer. His stomach turned over.

Best to get to the deer before she arrived.

He turned and found the corner obscured by darkness. Confusion. He could see perfectly well in the dark. The shadow began to roil, tendrils curling outward. He backed up, his ears flattening, hackles rising even with no input from him. In the center of the darkness, a familiar dark blueness began to grow. No, it couldn't. He didn't smell her.

A large figure slipped silently from the darkness. Alexander startled. No heartbeat. No breaths. Not a rustle to give him away. The slick of darkness faded, leaving him crisp in all his frightening detail. He leaned on a long golden staff and blinked down with his split pupils at Alexander.

"The best man," he said blandly. "Wouldn't know it to look at you, but a stroke of luck all the same. Your maid of honor doesn't know what's she's done. So many times over."

Fear and fire both flared in Alexander's chest at the same time. The demon who'd held his other half. He didn't need the wolf's help. A growl burst from his throat, and he lunged.

Almost instantly, he slammed into the wall. The demon reappeared behind him, wreathed in shadow, brandishing the staff with a flourish.

"Let's see if you're as indestructible as they say."

Alexander snarled and recovered himself quickly enough to dodge the point of the staff and a few broadsided blows. A point somehow extended from the ground and jammed into his ribs, knocking him away and into the bars. He blinked away the specks of light the impact made on his vision. A stalagmite of obsidian stuck up out of the ground where he had been. Like what he had removed from his other half's side. He snarled his rage and tried to scramble back to his paws.

The smear of darkness in the air appeared before him and the demon brought his staff down on his head. "Fascinating. Barely made a puncture. So it is true. You're well protected. Surely not from *everything.*"

Alexander wrenched and clawed out at the demon's tail, leaving a trail of strange, warm ichor he knew instinctively to be blood. His body, hungry though it was, rejected it. The demon barely blinked, but slipped backward. Alexander freed himself from the staff and lunged again.

Again, no demon. Instead he hit a new piece of black crystal, his snout sliding underneath. Something white hot hit his haunch. He yelped and pulled away. "*Very* interesting," the demon commented. "It hurts, but it doesn't *harm.* So theoretically…you're the perfect candidate for torture."

He freed his muzzle and darted behind the obsidian, his sides heaving with the exertion. The usual thoughtless bloodlust was threatening his mind like storm-swollen waves on a shoreline, but he forced a breath. I know, he told the wolf. I want to rip his throat out too.

But the fact of the matter was that he probably wasn't going to in here. Not alone. He lifted his head and howled in desperation to the woman. His friend.

Somewhere not too far off, he heard, "Alexander! I'm coming!" Her steps broke into a run.

The demon didn't seem to notice. He reappeared on the other side of the crystal, his tail wrapping around Alexander's body and constricting. Alexander tried to lash out with his claws, but the scales seemed very much like armor. The demon brought his face closer to Alexander's, but just far enough away that snapping his jaws did nothing.

"I'm so curious. Does disrupting your blood flow make a difference? Choking the oxygen out? I know you can't answer me right now, but fortunately I'm patient. It *was* you who pulled her out, wasn't it? Thoroughly irritating. Of course if she hadn't had the will to go herself, it would have done nothing, but you did offer her the opportunity."

Alexander growled again, gnashing his teeth, trying to avoid the urge to whimper. It was starting to feel much like the transformation, all the compacting in ways his body shouldn't bend.

"Ordinarily things would have started breaking by now," the demon mused. "And it *is* hurting you, but you're clearly breathing. I am impressed. You've blundered yourself into some serious life insurance. Just as your Cassandra blundered herself into power. Very useful. Of course, it did enable me to come back to this plane…straight here to you. I wonder if she made that deal with me after all."

Cassandra. His other half. His eyes closed as his pulse thrashed against the demon's hold. What *had* she done?

The demon's grip lessened ever so slightly, and he raised Alexander's body higher. "One more thing. Indulge me." He snapped the staff in half, revealing a stiletto-like blade attached to the top half. "I wonder if you can withstand a piercing to the jugular. Even you shouldn't be able to."

He brought the knife down, and Alexander diminished with the panic. The wolf took over. His jaws clamped down around the demon's arm. This time, the demon threw his arms and head back, screaming in pain. His tail released Alexander by reflex. Hot ichor filled Alexander's mouth, and instantly, the wolf in his mind subsided in favor of the man, who let go and dashed toward the gate, trying not to retch. The ichor was slick across his fangs, like no blood he'd ever tasted.

The woman finally crested the hill, her breaths ragged, her eyes wide. At the sight of the demon, she called out, "Dmitri Irividius, I cast you—"

Before she could finish, the demon flung out his uninjured arm. Shards of obsidian went flying. They peppered Alexander's skin with little more than stings, but they hit the woman—Julia; no, Jules—much harder. She fell back, the iron spike of blood piercing Alexander's senses. The demon eyed Alexander and sent another shard of obsidian, this time at the lock. It crumpled and fell away. "Well. I was here to kill you, but instead I'll thank you for the education. And the insurance. Good night."

He vanished in the same blue-black smear, leaving the gate swinging open.

Alexander's pulse practically vibrated. Jules. She didn't move. The blood—gods, he could barely stand it. But what could he do—sit here and wait? Pretend the cell was still locked? Eat the deer?

That sounded stupid, but it was possibly the best idea. He hurried and scarfed down as much as he could bear, then slowly approached.

She was breathing. A smear of blood pointed to a wound at her temple. She'd been hit in the head. The scent of it threatened his clarity, but he bargained. Not her, he said. More deer, or maybe a rabbit or something. The wolf grumbled in the background, but Alexander managed to approach.

He nudged her open hand with his muzzle. Jules groaned. He nudged it again more insistently, whined. She stirred, turned her head, and jumped when she saw him. "Oh, *shit.*"

He knew what that meant. He backed away, keeping his belly and head low to the ground and his paws crossed over his snout. Not going to touch you, he hoped it conveyed. She sat up suddenly, then grabbed her head and cringed. "*Ow.* You're…you're *you* right now, aren't you?"

How on earth was he supposed to respond to that? He just sat there. She seemed to take that as an affirmative. "I'm sorry, I thought it was supposed to take longer. Oh, fuck, Alexander, you bit him. Does that mean he's…?"

He closed his eyes. He assumed so. Insurance. He heard Jules stand up, move toward him. He edged away. She said, "Hey, it's okay. You had to…you did what you had to. What…what now?"

Alexander took a breath. He stood and started loping down the path toward the house. After a moment, he looked back over his broad shoulder. "Oh, you want me to follow? Okay. I'm coming. Give me a minute, though. Still kind of dizzy."

Which was the only reason he hadn't turn and run the exact opposite direction yet. It still nagged at him, the blood and the wood and the moon, all pulling him in different directions. He didn't like the way she wobbled, though.

At last, they hit the lawn with the windows in sight. He looked back at her, picking her way through the grass.

"What's the matter?" she asked.

He looked very pointedly toward the house, then back at her again.

"Oh. What about you?"

Alexander turned his gaze briefly toward the wood.

"Cassie's not going to like that. What if he comes back?"

If he came back, it would be a fairer match out in the open, and no one else would have to get hurt. He couldn't say that, so he didn't. Instead, he turned toward the house and let go of a piercing howl. At length, a light went on. He looked to Jules one more time, and she bit her lip.

"I don't know—are you sure…?"

He let out a brief growl, a huff, and took off into the tree line. He heard a door open back at the house and the devil call, "Jules, what the dickens happened? Come here, let's get you cleaned up."

Good. She was safe. The smell of her blood faded as he put more distance between them.

He didn't know where he was going; only that he seemed to need to go upward. His breath spilled out in fog in the moonlight in front of him, and despite the terror of everything and the general discomfort, a guilty little eddy of exhilaration pulsed through him. All this time in the cell, he'd never known that running felt like flying.

He dodged trees and boulders and buried himself deep in the woods where he'd played as a boy, far from endangering others, far from others endangering him, and when he finally crested the hilltop, there it was, finally real. The moon, full, round, white, holding court among scattered stars. As resentful as he might have felt of it, the awe eclipsed it. He sat and howled an ode, unbidden, for once, the wolf and man in full agreement.

29
Fray

"The cat went up the hill."

Cass' eyelashes fluttered. Someone was speaking.

"The dog met her there. 'How now, Miss Cat? What shall we two do?' Why does the dog talk like Humphrey? Actually, why is the dog talking? I guess this book is meant for little kids."

She forced her eyes open. The light burned a little, but for once, it didn't seem to make her want to immediately shut them again. Slowly, she turned her dully aching head. Kaye sat in bed next to her, her book propped open in her lap, a mostly eaten plate of cookies at her side. "Two is a hard one," she commented idly. "If you read it the way it's spelled, it looks like it should be like t-whoa. But it's really—" She stopped and tossed the book aside. "Cassie!"

In a dry voice, Cass answered, "Hey, kid."

Kaye flew across the bed and threw her arms around Cass' neck. "You're okay! You can't do that anymore!"

"Do what?" she asked, confused.

"You went back to sleep. The bad sleep. Don't you remember?"

She searched her sluggish mind. What was the last thing she remembered? There had been the zipping across the estate and into the cell, being brought back, talking. There was something after that…. "Not really."

"No? You got some bad news," she prompted cautiously. "And then you sort of…passed out?"

Bad news. It couldn't have been Alexander; she wouldn't be this calm. What bad news…?

A flash of gray mottled sunlight in her mind, a memory of Thalia sitting on her knees. On a scale of one to ten, how evil do you feel right now?

Shit. That was it. Some lingering connectivity with the damned demon lord. "Right," she said, reaching up for her forehead. "That's right. I'm okay."

Kaye looked at her skeptically. "You're sure?"

Cass assured her, "Yeah. I'm feeling pretty good, actually. Look." She eased herself up on her own power, and her side only complained the tiniest bit. "Sitting up and everything."

"You're sure you're not just trying to get Alexander and the others to put you back on the wedding?"

She braced herself on an arm. "Wait—what?"

The four of them and her love had stood around the bed, sharing concerned looks she couldn't read, speaking hesitantly. I don't know what the ramifications are, Gideon had said. Until we can find out for sure, I think it's probably best for you to stand down.

Please, Alexander had added.

"Oh, hell," she sputtered, and disappeared.

Oh, it was strange. Like she'd left her stomach back in the bedroom. To go from the warmth and comfort of the bed to the relative nothing of this vacuous space felt like being sucked into a hole in sand giving way to the ocean. This time, there were no little stops. She was propelled straight forward through the darkness, the dusk city flying by to her left, passing through walls and hallways on her right. She re-emerged in the sitting room doorway with a jolt, the blueness dropping away from her like water.

Three other nobles sat on the couches holding teacups, their eyes wide. Alexander, already standing, lowered the tablet on which he'd been writing, his face draining of its color. He looked to the assembled. "Would you…kindly excuse us for a moment," he managed, dropping the tablet to a table. He rushed over and guided Cass to the door by her lower back.

Once in the hallway, she turned on him. "What are you doing?"

"What am I doing—what are you doing?" He pushed her hair from her face and looked her over fretfully. "I'm thrilled to see you up and about, but you shouldn't be pushing yourself like this, and frankly I don't know how I'm going to explain that, my love."

She pulled back. "I don't care how you explain it," she said, shaking. "And I don't feel like you're welcome to call me that with what you just pulled."

He lowered his hand slowly, closing his eyes. "Cassandra…." His breath leaked from him in a slow, wounded-sounding hiss, and he glanced back to the sitting room door. "Let's not do this here."

She folded her hands under her arms and laughed acridly. "Right. Wouldn't want to affect the old reputation."

"Please don't—"

"Am I wrong?" she asked pointedly. "I think it's only fair they know you're in breach of contract."

He looked up, eyebrows lowered. "I'm not, actually. I can show you the subsection if you like."

Her fists clenched. "You think I'm compromised?"

Alexander turned his face away. The genuine sorrow written across it made her want to cross the space between them and throw her arms around him and also to scream, and it roiled her so badly that those impulses were so firmly intertwined. "*Now* might we move this discussion?" he asked quietly.

Not for his reputation. Not wholly. There was a healthy dose of that, but hers, too. Some of her ire lowered to a simmer. At length, she nodded. He pushed open the door to the lounge.

They sat across from each other, distant, quiet. His eyes kept traveling to her as though he wanted to move to her, but he was wary. Why? What had she done? She folded her arms, tucking her robe closer.

Alexander steadied himself visibly. "When we spoke last, you were unwell," he said. "How much do you remember?"

Cass thought. Vague shapes, vague words. Mostly feelings, mostly the same as they were now. Confused, hurt, furious. At length, she just shook her head.

He folded his hands. "The night of the full moon…three days ago." Her gut wrenched. So much time lost. This waking was different, but the sleep had been too. Alexander continued, "The Lord of Demons appeared in the cell. He attacked me, and I couldn't do anything to him, until…."

Her blood went cold. "Tell me. Tell me you didn't."

"I…I can't."

Shit. She jumped to her feet, paced the length of the space in front of the couch, her hand to her forehead as though trying to hold her racing thoughts in. If the curse worked on demons, which…other curses certainly did, so why not this one? Azorael was now next to impossible to kill.

They almost never really killed demons. Too many ways for a determined soul to come back or enterprising enablers to call it back. But to truly and properly put one away in the weave of fate, they needed to capture it in the moment of a mortal blow. To be so limited in how to inflict one…she turned to Alexander.

"And you think taking me away from this is a good idea—why? I think I've proven plenty trustworthy."

He stood and cautiously took up her hands, leading her back to the couch. She sat, stiff, awaiting the answer as he perched on the ottoman in front of her.

Frankly, Alexander said, "There…were things that didn't add up. Gideon said after Laufit's return to the hells that the Lord of Demons should not be able to return to this plane. And then he did. Something for which he credited you."

Cass stared. "You can't possibly think…."

Alexander didn't look at her. "What deal did you tentatively strike with him?"

She laughed in disbelief. "I was bluffing."

"It seems that he didn't take it that way, and that that matters when dealing with demons."

"Well…of course that's a possibility, but…."

Now he looked at her, his eyes uncomfortably hard. "You knew there was a possibility that you might have entered a contract with a demon?"

Cass' fingers curled into the couch. "My soul was trapped in an extra-planar dimension and being threatened with eternal servitude as some sort of terrible…husk. I knew I could handle it, all right? I know contracts. I'm practiced. I'm capable. I know what I'd need to do in order to word things carefully—"

"Apparently not! He was locked out of this world, and now he can get back in! You had to know we'd come for you."

"Oh, what, you wanted me to sit tight and wait to be rescued? It was my problem to solve. My work to do."

"Ah. Right." He glowered into a corner. "The other missing piece."

"What was that?"

He folded his hands and pressed them to his forehead with a sigh. "No—that's…not part of this. I shouldn't have brought it up."

"Well, it's brought up. What are you talking about?"

He uncurled his hand and showed her the scarring cut across it. "All this time, I could have removed any lingering curses on you, if any, but you said nothing. You are very capable, Cassandra. You say what you mean. But what you don't say means things, too. I wish you'd…just told me you didn't want to marry."

"You think—?"

"What else am I to think? The solution sits before you and you hide it from me? I would have done…anything."

Her eyes stung sharply. "Except come when I needed you when there's deals to be made."

Alexander reeled back as though he'd been slapped, his eyes growing wet. "Cassie."

"You think it was such a foregone conclusion that you'd come for me in limbo? An entire event planned around this specific thing and you put it on hold to speak to someone you can't stand." Her fingernails dug into her damp palms. "I get it. You don't want this. This wedding is an unwelcome distraction for you. But for me? It's my work. My work is my life. It's all I had, until…so for you to swoop in and take it from me…." She pointed a shaking finger in the direction of the sitting room. "And *still* put it second to these people you despise so much…put me second. You rushed me out of that room so fast. Like a godsdamned mistress. You say you hate them, but in the end…you are them."

His eyes darkened in the way they did when he needed to take a walk before things turned dangerous.

Honestly, Cass couldn't bring herself to care. She glared. "I'm terribly sorry to be such a distraction," she said. "Let me remove that complication for everyone."

She heard him call out her name as she disappeared into the in-between space and dashed all the way to the gate. Cass reformed just in front of it, allowed herself a moment of extremely ugly crying, and then pushed it open.

She had work to do.

First it was to her apartment for the first time in a very long time for a change of clothes. Difficult, with the throbbing spot on her side. Perhaps walking all the way across the city hadn't been the best idea. Before she could get to the clothes, she had to deal with the fact that she'd forgotten a few things in the pantry when she'd started spending every day with—

No, she wasn't thinking about that. She disposed of the moldering remains and propped open windows so the place could air out while she went and did yet more ill advised walking to the Cathedral.

This time, when she got there, she realized she'd probably overdone it. She leaned against the wall and felt for the throb in her ribs. Nothing overly warm or swollen. Just aggravated. She blew out a breath and looked up at the zig-zagging staircases cutting up towards the glass ceilings. How did she think she was going to manage that?

A priest approached her. "Good day, Miss. Blessings be upon you. Is there something the Amaranthine Church may offer you? Healing, perhaps?"

That obvious, huh. "Um, thanks, but no. I'm looking for Brother Hubert."

She smiled. "Very good. If you would—"

"Miss Friend," a voice interrupted in surprise. Hubert's head peeked down from one of the many staircases above. "Good gracious, it is you."

She held out her hands. "Surprise."

He took a few more flights. "Thank you, Sister. I'll escort Miss Friend from here. What in the blazes…?"

"You're particularly effusive today, Hubert."

He dismounted the staircases, huffing out a breath. "I should…I should say so." He straightened his robes and looked at Cassandra, his face mystified and somewhat anxious. That boded well. She steeled herself. Well, that was what she was here for. The other priest gave him a strange look as she stepped away, and he continued again, his voice lower. "I heard your coming. It's very, very rare that a mortal develops their own leitmotif."

Cass folded her arms insecurely. "I don't know what that means, but the word rare keeps getting thrown around a lot, which is why I need your help."

He nodded. "Mister Gideon sent word of the…."

"Contamination?" she muttered darkly.

"I wouldn't use that word."

"Seems to be what they're worried about."

He tilted his head. "And you?"

She pressed her lips together. Aside from sleep-logged, achy, pissed off, heartsick, weak, naked-feeling without the blades she'd left behind when she fled the estate, she didn't feel much different. Surely if there was something hidden inside her, she'd have noticed. That directive inside the duskbound city to come, to supplicate—she'd felt that.

No, of course not. She knew better than that. "I'm here to clear myself," she said stiffly. "That's it."

Hubert watched her a moment longer. At length, he nodded. "Come with me."

He started to lead her up the stairs. She managed all of two flights before the pain in her side became too sharp to ignore. She glanced up. "Are we going all the way?"

"Yes," he said regretfully.

"Is there anyone else up there?"

"Not at present," he answered, confused.

She took a deeply hampered pained breath. "I hope this isn't blasphemous," she said, and went into limbo.

The gods didn't strike her from the church where she sort of stood, so there was that. From behind her strange midnight veil, she heard Hubert call out in surprise. She went up a few flights and briefly reformed on the landing. "I'll meet you there," she told him, then took as many more flights as she could stand.

Interesting. It wasn't unlimited. She seemed to have strained herself making it all the way from the lounge to the gate. Each time she reappeared, it seemed a shorter and shorter distance, but still far easier than trying to coax her busted normal body up twenty odd flights of stairs. Hubert caught up, panting. She froze, about to try to force the form away.

"Wait," he gasped. "Can you sustain it?"

"I don't…really know," she answered. "I've only done it twice."

He nodded, pulling his normally pristine collar loose to free his throat. "Remarkable."

It occurred to Cass for the first time that this outline of her didn't really seem to reflect clothes. They were virtually transparent while the rest of her was dark blue. It didn't follow her every curve—more of a suggestion—but it still felt more vulnerable than she'd like. "Don't…stare."

"I apologize. No one has ever…."

"I know, I know. First of my kind. Gideon seemed to think up until now that it was just the dusk that did it. That I'm just some sort of weird mortal. That's what I want to make sure of."

Hubert nodded again and gestured her into a large wooden loft laden heavily with brass instruments, leading her further in. "Mortal I can assure you of, whether or not that's a comfort. Your bell rings a heartbeat. You are no demon. I hope that's to your liking."

"If I said no, would you have to destroy me?"

"In the interest of transparency, yes."

"Then yes, it's to my liking."

He smiled. "You came seeking reassurance, whether you said so or not. I figured it would be. It's about to get very noisy."

They emerged into a vast room hung with a panoply of bells—some vast, wider than some of the buildings below, some small as her hand. When she took steps, they echoed off the insides in shades of the tones they'd make when moved by the wooden masts they were attached to. Instead of ropes as ringers, there were delicate silver cords, fed into a device that housed a large roll of paper. A large web for a very strange spider.

Hubert led Cass to a metal partial dome in the center of the room, just large enough for her to sit cross-legged inside. He leaned in. "Now then," he said, his voice bouncing back to them in a variety of notes from above. "I will begin the transcriptor so we have a record, and then I will offer the supplication. The bells will do the rest. Do you have questions?"

She craned her neck around to look at him. So many. What was she doing here? What would any of this do? It wasn't that she didn't believe in the gods, exactly—she'd seen what Hubert's bell magic had done in summoning Azorael the first time. She just...didn't think they gave a shit. About her, any of it. He just looked back at her earnestly, though, so in the end, she shook her head.

He smiled reassuringly and disappeared to go do...cleric things. She was left looking at the strange reflection of the dim light she was giving off in the highly burnished metal. In a little disbelief, she reached out and touched her cheek. The reflection prodded its cheek, too. The strange, mostly featureless entity was her, freckled with silver.

The silver. She wondered if that would have been there if he hadn't come for her. None of the other blue things had borne any silver.

Her eyes stung, and she turned from the reflection, facing the only little bit of the dome that could see outside.

Hubert's footsteps came to a stop. His voice rang out amongst the bells, clear and loud, as if vying to be heard in between their all-consuming fervor. He sang a few repeating lines of grave, pleading notes, whose words she couldn't quite make out within her little shell, but the resonance filled it, filled her chest. Shortly the bells picked it up too, repeated it. She almost wanted to cover her ears, so loud were they, but at the same time, the wonderment, the near-euphoria kept her listening.

Underneath was a steady thumping—a heartbeat. He was right. There was a pulse. After a while, the prayer fell away, leaving a melancholic-sounding tune with rising playful sections. Cass leaned against the dome, her breath arrested. Was this—her? It shifted, moved, changed directions at times, sometimes picking up, sometimes becoming fragmented, but the basic sounds stayed the same. She knew very little about music, but it felt so familiar she could almost cry.

And then she did. At the very bottom of the register, a familiar pattern, one she had first heard just before the fire had raged and he had made himself known.

The blue light of her flickered out, leaving her dull and aching against the side of the dome. They were right. She hated it, but they were right.

She was compromised. She'd led him back here.

How? she asked herself, sending a fist into her good knee. How could she have done that? Even there, her thoughts had been on how to draw him out so they could finish him, how to back him into a corner. She'd known fully what she was doing.

And he'd used that.

Why. It came back to why. He collected power, he collected people to use, despite drawbacks. He wasn't attached to any of them. He didn't bother to attach them to him, really. He used fear and subjugation. Means to an end. Was he not planning on enjoying any of it?

No, it was to prove he could.

Cass' stomach curdled as her portion of the song picked up again. Of course. That was familiar, too. That bitterness, that something to prove. He was nothing who had come from something—someone who had squandered his potential. Dad could have provided a leg up into the world, but instead, he'd blown it. Cass acted out. Dmitri became a soldier. Neither of them needed anyone, but needed everyone to know they could do it. Whatever it was.

The song ground to a resolution, still ringing around the chamber. There was a ticking sound that wound down, too, and Hubert approached with a long roll of paper under his arm. He held out a hand. She took it, wiping fiercely at her eyes.

"What do I need to do?" she asked, her voice low.

"What do you mean?" he asked.

"He's in there. You heard it, didn't you?"

Hubert unfurled a bit of the roll, observing small punched rectangles in the fading sunlight. "I heard it. But if I'm not mistaken, that's a pentatonic. Let's have a look."

"What does that mean?"

He led her back to the first loft to one of the many instruments mounted on the posts. He fed the long sheet through a slot and shifted a brass slider over, moving a few markers. Cass wandered the floor for lack of anything constructive to do with herself while he worked for minutes.

"You were all correct," he said at last.

"What," she managed.

"You did in fact reveal much of your hand to the Lord of Demons by attempting to bluff your way through a deal. Your hubris is what will allow him to wreak chaos before the wedding. This, however, is not what allowed him to return to this plane." He shook his head. "Your accidental connection to the dusk—a quirk of fate—is what did that. He has purposely bound himself to the dusk in order to hide there."

"It…it's a fluke," she repeated numbly.

"Yes."

"Are you allowed to believe in those?" she asked shakily.

Hubert laughed quietly, withdrawing the roll from the instrument. "Miss Friend. The fabric of faith is full of them. I merely bear witness to a few hundred thousand."

Cass covered her face with a hand for a moment, feeling the wet saturate the space between the two. "I…sorry."

"That's all right. You knew you were innocent, after all."

"No one likes a smarmy priest."

He smiled and folded up the paper. "I can send this with you, if you like."

Cass shut her eyes. "Can…can you forward that to Gideon at Al— Lord Fremont's, please? I can…here." She fished out a piece of gold and put it in his hand. "I'm sorry, I'm just not…."

"I understand." He glanced at her. "I can have someone look at your wound."

"No, thank you. It's been seen to all it can be. Just something I'm going to have to deal with." She started toward the stairs.

"Be well, Miss Friend. I hope matters improve."

She did too, but she heard the song. There was a ways to go, and ultimately, much of it was sad.

In her apartment, still vaguely scented of produce past its prime, she sat on the bed and cautiously removed her shirt. The bandages around her midsection needed replacement. The wound was old now and mostly left to its own devices, but too much walking and the foolish attempt at stairs had cracked at an edge of the scab. Her job had been sloppy, owing to the fact that she could only really see most of the damn thing if she looked in the mirror.

The cracked, dusty mirror that had seemed good enough when she'd lived here, because she hadn't really lived here. She put her arm down and sighed.

It was like seeing it for the first time, except the first time she'd really seen it, she'd said "this will do". The hole in the ceiling plaster, the barren walls, the shutters she hadn't ever bothered opening until today's fruit fly expulsion. It wasn't that she'd spent the last three months living in luxury, although honestly, feeling the several years-old mattress under her rump, there was a bit of that reminder. It was that she'd never bothered to make this a home. Or try to make one anywhere else, either.

Even before this job, she hadn't been that broke. She could have afforded something like Jules' place. It was that this would do, and it did, because she didn't…have need of even a small comfort. She'd thought.

Now, having had hot chocolate with Kaye on a porch swing, or sat with a book on a window seat with sunlight coming in, or sat in front of the fireplace next to—

No, she wasn't finishing that thought. Changing the bandage. She had to have bandages in this place. There would have been a need for those.

She rummaged through the underside of the sink until she found a roll, along with a comb she hadn't used since her hair was much longer and a bottle of perfume her mother had given her for her twentieth birthday. That would do.

Cass went back to her bed and unwound herself more carefully than she had wound herself the first time. It stung. She winced. "Shit."

A knock sounded at the door. She looked up at the ceiling and mouthed the word shit instead. Her spare knives sat under the bed. It was likely the landlord checking on her, since the windows had been opened and she hadn't been by in a while, but she kept a box of enemies for a reason. Either way, she was shirtless and bleeding, so she kept quiet and hoped they'd go away.

No such luck. Another knock. This time, a voice called out, "Cassandra?"

Her heart flew into her throat. Alexander. How—? Shit. It would take her a while to cover the blood up, and no one needed an angry werewolf in an apartment building.

"Cassandra, please, if you can hear me…I know you're angry, and… you've a right to be. But we're all worried, and I can…smell blood. If you can, just—"

Oh, for gods' sake. She shut her eyes and blinked her way to the door, staying blue once she got there. She flung it open and pulled him inside, putting a finger to where her lips probably would be when he could see them again. "Quiet down," she warned him, her voice low. "I know you're not used to places like this, but the walls are thin. My neighbors really don't need to know you're a werewolf."

He looked at her. She looked at him. He looked, quite honestly, terrible. His hair was pulled back away from his ears, very much pointed, his eyes sunken, reddish. The nice clothes from the meeting were well-rumpled, jacket cast aside, vest open. He shook his head, searching for words.

"Let them," he said finally. "Cassandra, I…."

She felt such an urge to stop him talking, but what was the way? Was she angry? Did she want to kiss him? Tell him she was sorry? No, she wasn't. But she was. She gripped her upper arm and asked, "How did you find me?"

"We've been looking everywhere," he said. "Anywhere you might go. We were beginning to worry we wouldn't be able to find you."

Cass laughed a little. "I guess it says something that it took until now to find me here, huh."

"You're not one for staying home," he conceded with a little smile. "Are you safe, are you…?"

"I'm fine," she answered. "I was just trying to change out the bandage." She gestured to her general blueness. "This just…paused the bleeding. So we can talk."

"Right. That's…a good idea."

"It's not too uncomfortable?"

"No. No, of course not."

Cass took a faltering breath and swept the discarded bandage from the bed and went to stuff it into the bin in the bathroom. "It's not much, but you can sit."

He didn't. "It's cozy."

She snorted. "No, it isn't. But thank you for trying to be gentlemanly about it."

Alexander turned back to her. "You…you were right. Very right. I've lived my life in disdain for my fellows and yet…." He shook his head, setting his jaw, smiling in contempt. "But I need you to understand, Cassandra. I have never…never once hidden you because I am ashamed. Not today, not ever. I have hidden you because I want them nowhere near you, because you are too good, too pure for them. Because I have watched money and power soil everything they touch by conniving or by corruption. Myself included."

"Alexander—"

"I did not want you near me when I am like that," he confessed. "I wanted to be…me. A foolish conceit."

"You're not…."

"I am," he said. "We can pretend that it's for noble means. And perhaps in a way it is. Education is noble. But to play their game, even to help, I must consent to it. Even as I gripe at Ruhan for doing the same, I protest nothing. I am part of it. You were right."

Cass looked at him. Alexander's hand was tight around the back of a chair. She knew this look. "What will you do?" she asked quietly.

"Sponsor reform. The assembly should elect individuals to the stations currently occupied by nobility, not families. And they should be able to review and remove individuals working toward their own self interests. Kings included."

"That will earn you no friends," she said.

"No. No, it will not." He smiled a little. "But they're not really friends now, either."

"I don't think you'll be able to return to a quiet life after the wedding if you do this."

"What was there to return to? Hiding? Humphrey will be disappointed, but no. I can't do that any longer." He looked toward her, his quiet smile turning to an aching thing. "I can't do either without telling you that I am…so sorry. I…on that night…I should have been with you."

"Alexander, please—I shouldn't have said—"

"I knew it," he said. "I knew it immediately. I chose, and wrongly. I did break your trust."

"I…I know it seems like I hardly extended you any," she admitted. "It's little wonder you thought I sold everyone out."

"And that's…I should have…I took his word over yours."

She shook her head. "You were right, too," she said, her voice distant. "I knew better, and I let him in. I gave him what he needed to get to all of us. It sure looked like I could have done it. Even I believed it by the end of the day."

Alexander looked at her, his eyes pained. "Would…? Never mind."

She drew closer, took up his hands. "No, not never mind. Don't let it go."

He set his forehead to hers. "I'm just grateful you're safe."

"And that's why we're here," she said. "We keep…not talking. Neither of us likes talking. We're just relieved to have each other and it's not the same. Tell me."

He closed his eyes. "Would you have taken it?" he asked quietly. "This false deal."

Cass went quiet. "Maybe," she admitted. "If…it felt like the only way. I felt so alone." She felt him slacken a little. "Alexander…."

He pulled away, paced a bit, rubbing at his chin. "The whole world at stake, you said."

"Yes."

"Why?" he asked, turning to face her. "Why would you take the chance that you'd have to face me at the end of it?"

"For the chance that I could still fight to save you," she answered, her voice breaking. "I needed to get back to you."

Alexander froze, seemingly lost for words.

Cass, on the other hand, found both words and tears pouring out in embarrassingly equal measure. "And it's shitty that I'm the way I am, because I just—the more I want something, the more it looks like I don't, because I get all…nervous, and distant, and try to pretend that I don't think about it, but I really think about it all the time, I just never *talk* about it. Until it all comes out at a stupid inconvenient time, and people get hurt, like it did with Jules. Like this."

"Cassie—"

"Of course I wanted the curse broken, if it even existed, which I have my doubts about, I just—how do you do that? How do you go up to the person you love most in the world and go, 'hey, you want to go do a creepy ritual in the woods with my weird friend so we can get married someday? Oh, yeah, just need a bit of blood and hair, hope that's all right with you!'"

Alexander crossed the room again, his own cheeks wet now. "Cassie, you have heard what I've had to ask. You've been through much stranger on my account. Whatever it was, I would have understood."

"I know," she said, viciously wiping at her eyes. "But when you pay the last bit of rent with money you make delivering milk when you're ten and you don't get birthday gifts so the kids down the street can have socks for the year, you're a lot more used to giving help than asking for it."

He took up her face in his hands, gently pushing away the tears with his thumbs. "I understand now," he said quietly. "No, no I don't. I didn't have to. I was privileged."

"But you listen," she said with a soggy laugh. "That's something. I… need to talk."

"We need to talk," he agreed.

"I think we did."

"Yes."

He pulled her close. He still somehow felt warm, despite the fact that she didn't notice any other temperature while she was blue. "I'm sorry," she said. "I'm sorry."

"As am I." He looked around. "I…don't wish to sound like a judgmental ass, but may I take you home?"

She laughed, probably freer than she meant to. "I wish you could. Really. The second I drop this, though, I'm pretty well done for the day. I was not quite ready for the grand tour of the city plus the bell tower."

"I could carry…no, blood. Damned inconvenient—" He looked up at the wall and stopped himself before saying much further.

"It's all right," she said, touching his cheek. "I'll be back tomorrow… assuming you'll have me."

"What kind of question…?"

"Maybe you'll think better of it in the daylight."

"Cassandra." He shook his head. "I am already having a terrible time imagining tonight without you. I can only imagine that would get proportionately worse with time."

She laughed a little, then looked up at him. "You…could stay a while longer, then," she said. "If you don't mind the strangeness."

Alexander leaned in and kissed her firmly, his hand on her hip. "What strangeness?"

"I am in some sort of transdimensional state at the moment, if you hadn't noticed," she answered, kissing him back.

"Are you you?"

"As far as I know."

"As far as I'm concerned, that makes you perfect."

Cass smiled. "I'll try to live up to it."

30
Mend

It was very little use. Cass felt Alexander drift off behind her, his arms still wrapped around her, and she laid there awake for gods knew how long. It wasn't a mind-racing sort of thing; in fact she was strangely at peace for the first time in a very long time. It was more that she just…couldn't. She opened her eyes and held in a sigh to avoid waking Alexander. It followed, she supposed—in this form, she couldn't feel tired, or pained, or cold. There was, so far, no need to eat, and she didn't bleed. Sleep was probably on the list.

A few more futile minutes, and she gave in. Softly, she ran her hand over Alexander's arm, the very fine patch of fur that had broken out over the outer edge of the forearm. "Hey, I'm going to plan C," she said softly.

Blearily, he stirred. "Mm. No good?"

"Dusk Cass doesn't sleep, apparently."

He kissed her shoulder, the faintest hint of pointed canines glancing across her softly illuminated skin. "You're sure. I can still head home."

"No, you can not."

"Sure I can. Lend me a cloak, I'll put up the hood and keep my face shadowed and no one will be the wiser."

"Love. That only works in stories. Guards will immediately want to know why you're lurking in the shadows with your hood up." She paused, trailing her fingers over his slightly clawed ones. "Also, how do you plan to get the tail…?"

"It's…been done before."

"I won't ask."

"Thank you."

"Left pocket?"

"Left pocket. Small red pouch."

Cass slid out of bed and picked her way through the dark apartment to the chair over which Alexander's clothes were neatly draped. She found his jacket and fished around until she came away with a small, mildly lumpy herb-scented sachet. The needlework looked like it could have been hers ten years ago, to her mother's chagrin. It was a bit better now. She turned it over between her fingers as she brought it back to the bed. "Kaye must like you. This is very much not her speed."

"Amazing what listening to children instead of talking at them will do," he mumbled.

She reached out to tuck it next to his pillow. "Go figure. Still, does this stuff even work? I thought it was a…." She glanced over and found Alexander fighting to keep his eyes open. Not a myth, then. She ran a hand over his hair and he gave into sleep at last.

Cass stayed and made extra sure before rising again. He didn't even stir when she stood. On Hound's Slumber, she stood corrected.

She went to the bathroom mirror and tried not to wince too much at the sight of herself, too much like those entities in the duskbound city. The trails of silver specks helped, and her eyes—silver, too, not the blackness of the void. She leaned on the sink briefly to see into the other room. Alexander hadn't moved.

She took one of the knives from the underside of the bed and ran the edge along a finger. The pain was the same as it would have been any other day. Cass flinched, nearly dropped the knife, did drop to a knee. Her side ached, dripped warm with blood. When she lifted her hand to examine the cut, her skin was brown again, and red ran down her finger.

"Huh," she said to herself.

A grin burgeoned on her face. It seemed like it shouldn't—like this discovery should be a disappointment, but really, the fact that she could be wounded like any other person felt like a damned blessing. She wasn't like any other person, but she was still a person, and that was the third best news she'd gotten all day.

She bandaged herself quickly and thoroughly, threw on some sleep clothes, and returned to bed alongside Alexander. Her person, most unlike any other, yet still a person.

Her apartment smelled strange again. First she thought that something else had gone putrid that she hadn't discovered, but quickly she realized there was a smoky element to it.

Fire.

Cass shot up, pain snarling through her ribs in response. She reached out to grasp Alexander, but the bed at her side was empty, and quickly she started to realize that the apartment wasn't filled with smoke, really, but the smell of bacon.

Alexander spun, pan still in hand. "Cassandra, are you all right?"

She blinked, still trying to get her brain to come to terms with the sunlight soaking the floor instead of flame and the fact that she wasn't quite in mortal danger. Also, a lord had set her table. There was even a little flower in a pot in the center of it. Where had he…? "Are…are you cooking?"

"Yes," he said, confused.

"So they're not trying to smoke us out."

"Who is *they*, and should I be concerned?"

Cass tossed the blanket aside, shaking her head. "Never…mind, apparently. Where did you find bacon? It probably should not be eaten if it was anywhere in this apartment."

"No, gods, no." He set the pan down and doused the stove. "I went to the market."

"You…what?"

He cast a bemused look over his shoulder. "Is it really such a surprise that I might be able to handle breakfast?"

"Ye—I mean, no," she said. "I just hadn't realized you got up. Or that it was morning. Or that you knew how to cook. All right, yes, I'm surprised. Grateful. But surprised."

Alexander laughed and set the plates out and pulled out a chair for her. "What is alchemy but very volatile cooking?"

She eyed the battered toast warily. "This won't explode, will it?"

"I've left my black powder at home." He sat. "I liked watching Humphrey in the kitchen. He begrudgingly taught me some things."

"*That's* what I was trying to put my finger on," she declared. "It was less that you were above cooking and more that I couldn't see anyone letting you."

"Only on the rare occasion I convince him to take a leave these days. He's at least comforted by the fact that I can manage to feed myself." He glanced up at her across the table. "How are you feeling? You were, in fact, rather sound asleep again. I'd thought it best to let you lie in."

Cass took stock. Tired, but she was usually tired when she woke, and much less today than previous days. A little weak. The ache in her side had dulled. "Strangely, fairly good," she answered.

"You're not just telling me what I want to hear, are you?"

"Since when have I ever done that?"

He smiled in concession. "Not to make it strange, but you didn't lose much blood."

"That is…a bit strange."

He looked down at his plate. "I had been—afraid. You'd seemed on the mend, and then…very much not."

Cass tried not to sigh too loudly. She had her own questions about that, and it chafed a bit to not understand, especially not now. His unspoken question hung over the cute little purple pansy in its pot. How long would this upswing last? "This feels different," she said. "I feel clear. Really damned tired still, but much more…here."

"Good," he said, and a little of the apprehension softened out of his shoulders. "That…is good."

The other question hanging in the air was probably going to wilt the poor pansy. She took a breath. "So…can I have my job back?"

Alexander looked up, a little alarm behind his eyes. Not alarm—more that panicked jackrabbit caught in the hunter's lantern light look on the rare occasion that he wasn't prepared to smooth over a conversation.

"Mm. I…I know it's very important to you."

"Yes," she said, lifting an eyebrow.

"You take great pride in seeing your work through to completion."

"This makes me think you're going to say no."

"I…am not," he said at last. "Because I have no right to. You are not compromised and therefore, I will not break the contract. Moreover, I don't control you."

She tilted her head. "I mean, *technically* you do. You could tell me to do something and if I didn't do it, you could jail me by your birthright."

"And that would make me a complete shit, and I know we're in agreement on that front," he said pointedly. "I *am,* however, going to point out that you are still injured in ways we don't understand."

"Yes, dear, very much aware."

"You have a tendency to only care after it has become harmful to you."

"It gets the job done."

"And is that still the most important thing?" he asked, his eyes locked onto hers.

Cass stopped. Alexander wasn't dodging. Neither would she. "No," she answered at last, "but it is still important."

"I respect that, I do, but—"

She grasped his hand across the table. "I'm sticking around," she said. "I'm a mercenary. We look out for number one."

"No," he said with a small smile, "you're not."

She supposed it would be hard to argue that, all things considered. "New deal. I'm going to do this. For you, and Kaye, and the others, and Mum, and all the people I've never met. But I'll stop short of giving everything."

"How am I to hold you to that if you breach it?"

"I'm sure Gideon knows someone who can help."

He looked at her flatly. "I'm sure you find the implication that you're planning to go to the hells hilarious. I find it less so."

Cass ran her fingers over the top of his hand. "I suppose you'll have to trust me," she said. "I can give you some collateral. I'll train appropriate amounts. Rest. Let Thalia fuss. Let Gideon study."

He looked at her sideways. "You forget I'm still not withholding permission. It's not mine to give or deny."

"I know. I'm not making this deal with my employer."

"It's not mine as your lover, either."

"I'm not asking permission," she said. "I'm asking your blessing. It's important."

She held out her hand to shake. Alexander looked at her a moment longer, the mask of anxiety cracking into a bit of a smile at last.

He took it and placed a kiss on the back of it instead. "You should eat," he said. "You have a meeting to get to."

She beamed.

He'd hovered at her elbow most of the walk back across town and insisted on carrying the bag of the few things it was worth bringing from her apartment, but otherwise he kept his worry in check. Cass held the little pot with the little flower between her hands in the warm late morning sun as they passed through the gate.

"The tea is really that helpful?"

"Yes," Alexander said, disbelief still in his voice. "I managed the market just fine. It was overwhelming, certainly, but—" He stopped, his eyes distant.

Cass knew this look. He was sensing something beyond her perception. "What is it?"

"Kaye," he said, hoisting the bag higher. "Come out, please."

The cedars a few feet ahead of them shook, and out crawled Kaye, barefoot, dirty, foliage sticking out of her hair—and pure fury in her eyes. "Where *were* you?" she demanded.

Cass glanced at Alexander. "This is not usually the direction the 'what time do you call it' conversation goes."

Kaye was patently unswayed. "You were both gone *all night*."

Alexander stepped forward and brushed a twig out of Kaye's hair. "I told you I was going to look for Cassandra," he said gently.

"Yeah, I know. That's fine, but you could have at least sent word."

"I'm sorry." He paused. "You weren't waiting here, were you?"

"That…no," she said defensively. "That would be…stupid. You're stupid."

"How did you get past Humphrey?"

She looked at him as though he was, in fact, stupid. "I'm staying in *your* old room, right?"

He closed his eyes. "The…chimney grate. I didn't board up the chimney grate."

"You gave it some really nice hinges."

"It used to squeak otherwise."

"This is adorable," Cass interrupted, "but you, miss, are not supposed to be wandering the grounds alone."

Kaye's eyes snapped to Cass, the fury back instantaneously. "And *you* weren't supposed to leave."

"I can come and go as I like. I don't need to explain myself."

Kaye threw her dirt-stained hands up in the air. "Oh. Okay. You just disappear after being really sick without saying anything. That's not shitty *at all.*"

Alexander took a breath and looked pointedly at Cassandra. "I believe what Kaye is saying is that she was worried."

Cass nodded slowly, turning her gaze back to Kaye's rage-mottled face. "I just needed some time to think," she said. "So I went home for a bit. That's all."

Kaye's mouth pulled down. "This is home," she said, and turned and stalked back toward the house.

Cass watched her crumpled dress flap in the light breeze and ran her hand through her hair. "That…could have gone better."

"Diplomatically put, yes, it could," Alexander said, putting his arm around her shoulder. "Have you tried *not* escalating with her right away?"

"It's just so…*difficult,*" Cass blustered.

"Why?"

"She's testing boundaries."

"And you aren't an expert in doing so?"

"I never said I wasn't. That's precisely why it's got to be nipped in the bud."

"Did that work on you?"

She sighed. "No, it did not. It's like looking in a…particularly aggravating backwards-aging mirror."

"You haven't known many children, have you."

"Not since I was one."

"Try again later," he urged. "She needs you to."

"Are you sure?" she asked uneasily. "Seems like she needs me to back the hells off."

"For a minute. Maybe a few minutes. But not longer than that."

Cass set the pansy down alongside the laid brick path and stood up a little stiffly, setting her hand to her waist and breathing out the pain. "I will do my best. I think she might get angrier."

Alexander took her hand and brought her inside the house. A flustered looking Humphrey appeared in the doorway with enormous dark circles under his eyes. "Lord Alexander. There you are."

"Here I am." He set the bag down and helped Cass off with her coat. "Is something the matter?"

"No, not at all. Just missing an entire household one moment, and then they all return the next. That's—that's quite all right. Correspondence on your desk. A lot of it, following yesterday's excitement. The bridal party is where you'd expect them to be. My nerves are somewhere…else."

Alexander winced. "Have you considered a holiday, Humphrey?"

Humphrey stared at him. "Have you gone quite foolhardy, Lord Alexander? With the state of this house? Absolutely not. The girl would be on the roof, one or both of you two would be bleeding, perhaps fatally, and I would be driven to drink."

Cass covered her mouth to keep from laughing, swearing, or both. She didn't know whether or not to be touched that she was included in Humphrey's fussbudgetry or impressed or concerned that he'd dropped his pretenses somewhere in the past twenty-four hours. Alexander grasped his shoulder. "Perhaps after the wedding."

"See to it that you both survive that long," he mumbled. He glanced up. "I am pleased to see you still live, Miss Cassandra."

"Thank you?" she said. He may have been angry with her on Alexander's behalf. It was hard to tell with Humphrey.

Alexander started to lead him down the hall. "I think you could use some sleep."

"Everyone had best be here when I wake up," he muttered darkly.

"That should be the case, yes."

Cass smiled a little ruefully and headed toward the parlor. She could hear the edge of Bjorn's bass from down the hall, interjected by the lightness of Thalia's voice. She paused at the door, steeled herself, and waited for a lull in their conversation.

They had already been quiet, but the second she walked in, somehow the room went even more silent. She stood awkwardly in the doorway, watching her friends watch her. "Hi," she said.

Jules stood up and seized her in a hug. "What the hells were you thinking?" she asked, squeezing.

Cass, winded, reached up and patted her arm. "I...sorry. Can I...breathe, please."

"Oh, right." She let her loose and steadied her while she caught her breath. "Seriously, though. We thought you might have gone somewhere he could have snatched you."

Cass set her hands to her hips and filled her lungs. "I know. It was not my best idea."

"More than that," Gideon said, looking up from where he sat on a footstool. He looked about as tired as Humphrey. He held up the folded hole-punched transcription of the bells she'd had sent to Alexander. "It was careless. He can track you."

"I...found that out, yes." She bit her lip. "I just...I couldn't stay. I needed to find out."

"If you had stayed, you would have found out that this was all we wanted," he said, looking at the sheet.

Despite her best efforts, Cass felt her face heat up. She turned, tried to keep from blowing up. That wouldn't help. "Yeah. On a practical level. And I get it. Usually I'm pretty practical." She felt her eyebrows pulling down and shut her eyes instead. "But it's not exactly…easy, getting held hostage by a shithead demon, then coming back and finding out something big changed about you, and then having everyone you love all of a sudden think you might have screwed them over…."

She had to stop. Her throat clogged up, and she felt her eyes stinging. When did she get to be such a crier? Jules' hand found her shoulder. That alone made her want to go back to yelling. It was easier to yell.

Instead, she took a breath and finished, "I got emotional. I am sorry about leaving. Not about feeling, though."

Gideon leaned back on an elbow, regarding Cass for a long time. At length, he laughed slightly. "Huh. If I didn't have your bells in front of me, I might wonder if you were possessed. Did that come out of our Cassie?"

She rolled her eyes. "Shut it or it'll never happen again."

"That doesn't mean you should disappear and start using unquantified magic willy-nilly."

Bjorn scratched his chin. "What is this phrase?"

Thalia looked up at him. "It means…haphazardly. Recklessly. All over the fucking place."

"Ah. Yes. This is true. Cassie-duck should not disappear all over the fucking place."

"I hate to break it to you, but that's sort of what I do now," Cass said. "I'm starting to get the hang of it."

Gideon couldn't help himself. Curiosity took over the disapproval in his expression. "Are you?"

"I think I can use it to our advantage." She tilted her head. "I'll let you take a look if you promise to be slightly less mad."

"I might be able to manage."

She gave him a brief smile and vanished, appearing just on the other side of Bjorn and grabbing the horn off his belt. He twisted, and she dissipated again, reappearing to briefly hand it to Thalia before landing behind

Gideon and tapping him on the shoulder.

Jules grinned. "Shit. I knew that would be useful."

Gideon just about fell over himself to face Cass, readying all sorts of runes and analyzing intently. "Well, hells," he said at last.

"Is that good or bad?" she asked nervously, fidgeting with her blue hands. "Because I have to tell you, I'm already feeling pretty weird about all this. Hence the emotion."

"Magic isn't good or bad. It just is. It's what you use it for." He looked through the transcription again. "You seem to be gaining control, I'll give you that. But you still shouldn't push it too far."

"What's too far?"

"You'll know. Trust me."

Thalia bit the edge of her thumb, her leg bobbling. "It doesn't feel good."

Cass looked sidelong at Jules, who just shrugged ever so slightly. She looked back at Gideon. "I'm willing to learn if you are."

He watched her a moment longer. At length, he smiled. "Ah, what the hells. I hate being in charge anyway."

Thalia cut in, "But you're taking what I give you even if it tastes like bog farts."

Jules added, "And if you take off again, this time I'm letting Mum find you."

Cass laughed a little. "Fair enough." She leaned her hip on the edge of a sofa and folded her arms. This felt better. Like a usual meeting. "Where are we?"

Gideon answered, "Finishing up the final wards on the undercroft, the chapel, and the gardens."

"Wonderful. Any activity?"

Jules said, "Not that we've noticed. Ever since," she started, then glanced briefly at Gideon and said carefully, "their leader went away, the gangs have been too busy trying to figure out who takes over and hiding from the guard. And with what you found out with the shipping, the cornerstone is back and the Oranians are detained."

"He could well be working alone at this point," Thalia said. "Which would explain the last ditch effort to make himself harder to dispatch."

The bite. Cass deflated. The blue washed off of her, and without even meaning to she glanced to the door to the study. "I'll…work with Alexander on that. In the meantime, I don't think there's much chance of drawing him out before the day."

Gideon shook his head. "He seems too canny for that."

Jules looked to Cass. "Can we go to him? You can go there. Maybe you can take us with you."

She thought. The possibility was appealing. An uninterrupted wedding was obviously ideal. There was just too much they didn't know. "He controls the place pretty completely. And he has these…blue soul people. They may be able to fight for him."

Gideon turned to her abruptly. "Wait—what?"

"Yeah. They looked…sort of like the blue me, but no silver. Just black eyes. They don't talk, they hiss. He said they were souls he owned."

Gideon deflated. "The souls the gangs were killing and collecting. They weren't energy fodder, they were literal…he made them vessels out of the dusk."

"What…does that do?" she asked hesitantly.

"Well, for one thing, he commands their dusk-bodies completely while there."

"And while here?"

He frowned. "I…don't know. I don't think they'd be terribly stable. If they were destroyed, he would lose control of the soul."

Cass paced a bit. "Oh," she said at last, her eyes widening. "Oh, oh, *of course*. We've been looking at the whole thing backwards."

"Then we would not be able to see," said Bjorn sagely.

"We assumed he became a demon to more easily conquer the world," Cass said. "But he didn't just want to be, he *had* to be. He's not just going to conquer it."

Gideon jumped up. "He wants to use the confluence in the undercroft to send the whole thing through to limbo, which he wouldn't have been able to do unless he had demonic power."

She snapped her fingers, moving to the table on the edge of the room. Cass grabbed a blank sheet of paper from it and a pen and started writing. "The cornerstone removal wasn't to make it easier for him to come through. He's got me to anchor, and if he hadn't gotten me, he'd have had Laufit. It was to tear a rift. Did they get it reinstalled?"

"Yeah. It's still going to be somewhat vulnerable."

"They need to put everything they have into bulking it up. I'll send this to the prince and let him know."

Thalia looked at Gideon. "We might be able to help with that."

He looked at her appraisingly. "That would be a lot for your source. Are you sure you can handle it?"

"What do I care if the wood's pissed? Not like it ever liked me much anyway."

"Translation?" Cass asked.

Thalia sighed impatiently. "I'm fey. I draw my power from nature. For me specifically, that would be the wood out there." She gestured vaguely to the east. "I can lend some of that power to the enchantment of the cornerstone, but it's not exactly my specialty. Fey magic is very…tit for tat."

"You'll be punished."

"Maybe," she said, irritated. "Or maybe the damn wood doesn't want to go to limbo and will see reason for once. I know I don't. Sorry, Cassie, but it didn't sound like a great time."

"It really wasn't." She looked to Gideon. "What about you?"

"The hells really don't care what I do. Especially now," he answered. "Someday it might just turn the tap off. Who knows?"

"You all are okay with a lot more ambiguity than I can handle," she sighed.

Thalia shrugged. "The fey are big on *things aren't what they seem.* Mostly they seem like assholes, and they are."

Jules shifted uneasily. "I don't like this. You two are going to burn yourself out on a pillar?"

"Maybe the most important pillar in the world," Gideon corrected.

"And hopefully not. We'll let the clerics get as far as they can get."

Bjorn too seemed uncomfortable. "I am not liking, either. Demon is still…." He made a fanged motion with his fingers.

"Well, that's good news for you," Cass said with a weak smile. "You get to go shopping for weapons."

"And on a quest," Thalia said. "I'm going to be busy. But you lot can get water from the Spring of Light. I'll tell my mothers I sent you. Just in case he gets rude with those teeth."

"Well," Cass said, folding her letter. "I suppose we have work to do."

Jules smiled and patted her on the shoulder before joining Bjorn near Thalia to get directions. Gideon stepped up next to Cass, who glanced back at him as she sealed the letter. "Thank you," she told him. "For keeping this going while I was out."

"Someone had to," he said with a little smile.

"It was in good hands."

"It's in better ones now."

"I don't know about that." She ran the letter's edge over the corner of the table absently. "Those souls. What happens to them if we win?"

"That is a good question," he said. "They won't be bound to him anymore."

"Will they move on, or…?"

"I'm not sure. Either way, it will be better than what they have now."

"You're sure?"

"Absolutely." He looked at her, pained, resolute. "You know a little of what containment felt like. Laufit did it to you. He just didn't quite finish the job."

The aching numbness, the nothing. The visceral terror of being everywhere and nowhere, and then suddenly channeled into someone else's will, as though her own had no meaning. He was right. "They can feel it, then."

"Acutely. While being able to do nothing, and feeling their resistance slip away until giving in is almost a relief. It is, in some ways, worse than anything my hell could conjure."

She had been repulsed by them, unnerved by their being. It was misplaced. "We have to win."

"Yes."

No small order.

31
In Training

"Come on," Jules goaded, keeping her fists high. The late afternoon sun was warm, and sweat was accumulating on her forehead. Cass felt it plenty herself, her fingers sliding along the grips of her daggers. "You know you want to do the blinky thing."

Cass wiped at her brow and panted, "That's probably the least impressive way to refer to it I've heard so far."

From the sidelines, Gideon commented, "I can think of worse."

Jules took the opportunity to swing for Cass. She ducked instinctively, mundanely. Jules' eyes crinkled in disappointment. "You're no fun anymore."

"Me," Cass protested. "You're the one with all the cat pillows."

"Hey."

She grinned and took a wide swipe toward Jules' left side. The left side was always a little stiffer than the right for whatever reason. She didn't tend to react as fast. The blade came a few inches from actually touching her, and Jules sighed and put up her hands. "All right, that's three for you, two for me. Seriously, though. Where's the blinking?"

Cass threw her knives down into the lawn and paused for a drink of water. "I just want to make sure I can still do it without," she said.

Gideon stretched lazily on his coat spread out on the grass. "You think it won't be available?"

"I mean, he does control the dusk."

"From inside it. I don't think you've much to worry about. Although I'm reasonably sure neither Thalia nor your lord will much care for the way you're wearing yourself out right now."

"I'm good," she answered, watching a puff of white cloud pass overhead. "I mean it. A little tired, but this feels pretty good for two and a half weeks lost. And if I were to use the…blinky thing…I'd be in even a better spot."

"So let's see it," Jules said, holding her hands out. "Or do you want me to actually start hitting you?"

Cass sighed, grinning. "You asked for it," she said, slipping from the plane and running around Jules' other side.

Jules whirled, keeping her fists close to her chest. Cass didn't bother staying long. She darted through both planes to Jules' back and tapped her on the shoulder with the hilt of a dagger. "Four for me."

"Told you it'd be useful," Jules said. She spun with a leveled fist, pulling back and just touching the knuckles to Cass's flinching forehead. "Three for me."

Then she dropped to a knee. Cass was about to make some sort of snide comment about not having to concede so formally, but out of the corner of her eye she spotted a retinue of guards clustered around Ifalna.

Cass bowed her head, but refrained from much more than that. "Your Highness." She couldn't keep the surprise completely out of her voice. "To what do we owe the pleasure of the visit?"

Ifalna looked over at her guard in irritation and waved them away. When they finally dispersed to her satisfaction, she came over to clasp Cass' hand. "I had come to see if you were well. Well enough to scrap, it seems."

"I am, thank you. Thanks to everyone." She indicated Jules and Gideon. "I am working up my strength again for this weekend."

Ifalna nodded approvingly, walking around Cass as though appraising her armor. After a moment, she drew a golden cylinder from her sleeve. "If everyone else is getting to test this new blessing of yours, perhaps you would allow me the pleasure?"

Cass held out her knives. It was good to have them back. "Please. By all means."

Gideon cleared his throat. "Cassie, are we perhaps verging on overdoing it?"

Probably. But Ifalna had been keen for a fight since the moment she got here, and Cass needed to know what she was in for if she did overdo it.

With a flick of the wrist, Ifalna extended the the cylinder into a long, delicate golden spear. Probably not much for heavy opponents like Bjorn, but if wielded with precision, pointy enough to serve as a decent offense and a good defense against weapons like Cass'. She lifted it in a salute and brought it around toward Cass' shoulder. "My father comes tomorrow."

Cass blocked with both blades and stepped back. "That early?"

She scowled and swung back, aggressive, without pause. "He is one to encumber a host with his presence early and late. He comes to judge Amaranth, and therefore Ruhan."

"I see. And I take it you must entertain him for diplomacy's sake?"

"If he were to withdraw his blessing—"

Cass frowned, then disappeared, reappearing behind Ifalna, who whirled, caught her just before she touched her upper arm with the flat of the blade. "Would you do as he said?"

"That *is* a blessing indeed," Ifalna admired, letting the haft of her spear scrape down the blade and withdrawing a few steps to recover herself. "I would not condemn your people to suffer his wrath for my own desires, and if Ruhan did…I wouldn't have agreed to marry him in the first place."

It wouldn't be the first horrible family member she'd kept busy. "So we keep him happy, or at least distracted."

"And you believe you can do this alongside the preparations?"

Cass watched Ifalna lift the spear to swipe for her shoulder—an awkward move, because ordinarily she'd be striking for the rib cage. She was pulling her punches. Cass melded into the dusk and came back out on the opposite side of the arm, letting the point of the spear land impotently in the dirt. She lifted her knife—careful to keep it away; the guards were still watching this—and said, "It is my job."

Ifalna looked hard at the knife and at Cassandra for a moment, her jaw set. She wasn't used to losing. In a moment, though, she grinned, bringing the spear back against Cass' ankles, just shy of tripping her. "You should declare your victories promptly, Cassandra. Losing on a technicality seems the sort of backhanded thing the Amaranthine nobles might favor."

She glanced down. "Well played, Your Highness. You'd be correct."

Ifalna withdrew the spear and held it to her side. "Thank you for indulging me. It's been too long."

Cass sheathed her blades. "Thanks for the practice and the reminder."

"Oh, that it need not be so constant," she muttered.

The practice wore her out, but it wasn't a bad worn out. It felt like she'd accomplished something, and therefore she didn't feel too bad lying on the sofa in the lounge with her head on Alexander's lap while he read something that'd have put her to sleep ages ago. The educational standards, she thought. Every so often he made a note of something, but mostly he reviewed it like a novel. She didn't know how he managed.

His hand moved absently over her hair every so often. The low light from the fire and his warmth and softness lulled her into forgetting the ache of her muscles and almost everything else.

Almost.

Her eyes fluttered open again. Damn it, why did she have to remember now? "Alexander," she said hesitantly.

"Yes, my love?" He answered without looking up from the book.

"May I ask a horrible but necessary question?"

Now he lowered the book, shut it, set it aside. "Always an enticing beginning to a conversation. Go on."

Cass took a breath and sat up, her sore everything protesting. She turned to face him, but couldn't quite manage to look at him. "If I were to need to kill someone with your curse…is silver the only way to do it?"

Alexander coughed slightly. "Ah."

She cringed. "That…was probably not the best way to ask that question. Irividius. Obviously."

"Of course."

"I just—it seemed like the sort of thing you would know."

He laughed a little darkly. "You're absolutely not wrong."

"If you'd rather tell Gideon, or Jules…"

"Cassie." He pressed out a breath and took up her hand, tendering the fingers in his. "I'll tell you, and gladly. I just…need a moment to come to terms with it."

She held his hand tighter. She'd grown to take his candor for granted. "As long as you need."

The leg not supporting her head bounced a little, and he took another breath. "It's not the most pleasant thing, to be a kid and have a cleric rattle off everything that'll do you in, but at least it will finally be of use. No. Pure silver is not even the most effective way to kill me. It's just the best known and the most accessible."

Cass felt like she should sit up and take notes, like this deserved the appearance of complete attention as well as the reality of it, but the exhaustion was a good enough deterrent. Alexander didn't seem to mind, still vacantly patting her hair for want of something else to do.

"Arcane magic or demonic and celestial magic won't help much, but fey magic will be extremely effective. Thalia is a very good bet, assuming her bloodline will allow her more than one spell at a go. Her other skills and Gideon's are better put to work disorienting and distracting, which are easily done using concussive noises and overpowering scents. You, Bjorn, and Jules will have the hard work."

He helped Cass sit up and took a notepad from the side table and balanced it in his lap. His eyebrows lowered, he started writing, a string of symbols and numbers she found incomprehensible, but recognized well enough as alchemical formulae. "This is an alloy that combines silver with a few rare earth minerals and is far deadlier than silver alone and has the added benefit of looking more like steel. I'm certain that he's heard the old wives' tales about silver and would work hard to avoid that. This would confuse that impulse."

Cass nodded and accepted the paper from him. "Are these minerals obtainable?"

"Not cheaply, and possibly not for all three of you on short notice, but it's worth the try. I have a classmate who has gone into specialty alchemy in the Corona district. If she can't get it, she may be able to make up something loosely equivalent." He winced. "Not without asking three thousand questions about why on earth we want *this* particular formulation."

"Is it worth raising those questions?"

"I believe we're talking about the entire world pulled into a void if we don't take every opportunity afforded us, yes?"

She nodded. Damage control could come later. They had to make sure there was a plausible later.

Alexander sighed. "One more thing." He rolled up his sleeve, exposing his scars. He pointed to the lightest, a raised oval the size of a shirt button, and looked at Cass a little uneasily. "If you can, one of those blades directly to the bite will end it very, very quickly. With me, there's…confusion, because there were other—I got fairly torn up. That mark is what you're looking for."

"Alexander," she said quietly. "I'm not looking to kill you. You believe that, don't you?"

"I…yes." He let his arm fall into his lap. "I don't believe I left too much other damage."

"Where was it?"

He laughed slightly, looking down at his arm. "You know…the same place. I hadn't realized that before now, I don't think."

"Love…."

"Oh, I'm not extending my sympathy," he said. "I got my arm bitten trying to protect my neck. He got his arm bitten because he was spearing me and that was all I could reach to get him to stop. I still wish I hadn't."

Cass leaned against his shoulder and took up his hand, her free fingers carefully trailing over the lines on his ravaged skin. "What were you supposed to do?" she asked softly.

"At least finish the job," he muttered. "Am I a bloodthirsty animal or not?"

"I think you know the answer."

"Well, his blood tasted terrible."

"Was it that magma shit?"

"Hot sludge, yes." He made a face.

"No, I wouldn't want that in my mouth." She settled her hand on his arm. "Thank you. For telling me."

He leaned over and kissed her head. "Thank you for listening. Always." He sat up straight, alert, then looked back at the darkness beyond the cracked door. "Kaye," he sighed.

"That girl's eavesdropping."

"You did sneak onto this estate when directly forbidden to," he reminded her.

Cass stood cautiously, waiting to make sure she had her feet under her. "And picked the lock and set you loose to chase me. Yes. I know. I'm going to see if she's ready for that conversation now."

The look on his face clearly said *are you?*, but he was kind enough not to say anything. "I'll be along to bed in a bit."

She leaned over to kiss him. "Not too late."

"No."

Cass followed the dark hallway to Kaye's bedroom, light still spilling out from underneath the door. She knocked. "Go away," Kaye called.

"How'd you know it was me and not Lord Alexander?" Cass inquired.

"I didn't. You should both go away. Humphrey too."

Cass leaned her head on the door jamb. "Nah. Not buying it. You don't tell Alexander to go away. You have a soft spot for him. You'd say 'don't talk to me right now' or something equally prickly, but you wouldn't tell him to go away, because you wouldn't want him to actually *do* it."

"What's your point?"

"I'm just curious. Tell me how you knew."

"Why do you care?" she snipped.

"Maybe because I know a talented observer when I meet one. Maybe because I train investigators. Maybe because I'm impressed."

"Bullshit."

"You swear at me, but not him or Humphrey. Why is that?"

"You can take it," she said.

Cass laughed slightly. "It still doesn't feel good, you know," she answered. "I know you and me, we pretend not to care. But it doesn't *really* stop it from hurting, right? It just makes people who aren't paying attention think it doesn't bother us. And it's kind of embarrassing to admit when something hurts. But I do pay attention. I'm sorry I hurt you. I needed space, but I shouldn't have left like that. Not then, not without saying something."

Silence for a few seconds, and then the door flew open, an agitated nightgown-clad Kaye in the doorway. "For an investigator, you're pretty dense."

"I'm missing something. Help me see."

"Why should I?" she demanded, retreating into her room. "Does any of this even matter to you?"

Cass blinked and remained in the doorway. "I'm…sorry?"

"You keep saying you're onto me because you were like me." She glared intently. "I don't think you stopped, did you. I know this trick. If you run off before people run out on you, you get to pretend it was *your* idea."

"What are you…?"

"You've been looking for ways out all over. You got yourself stabbed. You keep poofing out of the house. Now you're talking about killing Lord Alexander, and he'll bloody let you, because he's so damned moony for you. All so you don't have to say this is home."

"Oh—oh." Cass shook her head. "You heard…no. There's a different werewolf to fight, Kaye. Lord Alexander was helping me. He knows how to do it because he knows how *not* to die. I want him very much *not* dead."

Kaye eyed her sideways. "Then why'd you leave him wandering all over town on his own?"

"I didn't think he'd come after me." She paused. "I should have probably known he'd come after me. Didn't think he'd *want* to, but—that's beside the point. I'm home now. He brought me back again."

"Home?"

She nodded. "I've brought the rest of my things. No going back now."

"You're not frightened?" she asked, a little curiosity taking the place of some of the prickliness.

"It can be a little frightening, loving, being loved," Cass mused. "I can't say I'm not at least a little."

Kaye crossed her arms against her chest. "Still?" she asked, her voice strangely small.

"I had many years of practice being scared," she said. "But even so. It's worth it."

She considered a moment, turning one of her skinny ankles in. "You're a lot quieter when you walk. Like a Rat," she said at last. "Alexander doesn't know where his knees and elbows are and Humphrey does this weird little shuffle thing. See you in the morning."

The door shut quickly in Cass' face again. She stood there, hands on her hips. At length, she just laughed. "Well done," she yelled to Kaye, and went to bed.

32
Maid of Honor

Cass could get used to having the run of the Wyvern's Rest. She could see why people found power addicting. People got out of your way when they knew you had important shit to do instead of getting in it. She got from the main hall—where the banners and overly floral decorations were being hoisted under Jules' watch so as not to disturb the wards—to the undercroft in a matter of minutes, and that was even accounting for her still-sluggish pace. She leaned an arm on Gideon and observed Thalia, whose tongue defiantly stuck out as she manipulated some runes in the air in the direction of the cornerstone.

"I just got *saluted*," Cass said. "Do you have any idea how odd that is? How goes it?"

He glanced over at her, bemused. "I'm sure your ego will recover. It's…going. Hard to replace thousands of years of accumulated magicks with two fools and a handful of clerics over the course of a few days."

She nodded. He looked utterly exhausted, his eyes sunken. His pure white skin was always sallow, but today it lacked…depth, somehow. "Should…you have slept last night?"

"I'm getting that impression. This is more important." He lowered his voice and grasped Cass' elbow, angling her away from Thalia. "Besides. She's worse off."

"What's going on? The source thing?"

"It's been…stubborn."

Cass glanced back. Thalia leaned toward the smooth marble obelisk with its carved runes, holding her hands out as though trying to move it with nothing more than the force of her mind. A vein stuck out starkly against her forehead, her neck. The illusion of her long hair flickered briefly, wings appearing, disappearing, just quickly enough to make anyone who passed by think they might have imagined them.

Gideon folded his arms. "Better to have someone standing by in case anyone gets too curious."

"Do you want me to see if I can make sure nobody gets too curious?"

"That's a good way to *guarantee* somebody gets too curious."

She nodded in concession. "Just…don't spend yourselves. All we can do is delay him. I know we want to give ourselves the best possible chance, but —"

Gideon nodded. "We'll let the clerics take over in the afternoon."

"Good. Then get some food in you and *sleep*."

"Look who's talking," he snorted.

She glared. "I've been doing nothing *but* for the past gods know how long, all right? Cut me some slack."

"I was just thinking you seem to be doing well."

She was just thinking she wished she had a chair, but she wasn't about to say so. "Going to check in upstairs again. Let me know if you need me."

He gave her an overdramatic salute, and she gave him an obscene one back. He grinned. She braced herself for the stairs.

Back in the main hall, Bjorn arrived and searched the crowded room in confusion. She lifted her hand and tried not to appear visibly out of breath. He nodded and approached. "Cassie-duck. Good. I am returning from alchemy wizard."

"Not a wizard," she reminded him for the third time. "How'd it go?"

"Very good. She can do knife for you and axe for me. Jules is out of luck."

That was fine. Jules preferred to use her hands anyway. "Good, good, good," she said absently. "That'll do nicely. She can do them in-house?"

"She has smith friend nearby. Fancy weapon friend. They return our blades."

Across the room, movement caught her eye. Ruhan, Ifalna, and Alexander, meeting with a large man whose upper body was decked out in ornate armor. He had the same sandy hair as Ifalna and a similar beard to the one Bjorn kept—though much more intricately braided. The King, she presumed. Alexander made a practiced, measured bow. The King seemed absolutely unimpressed.

She glanced back to Bjorn. "Wait, they're making all-new weapons?"

"They cannot simply coat our blades," he said, handing her knife back. She slipped it back into the empty sheath. "Something about…reaction…I did not understand."

"How long will that take?" she asked anxiously.

"They will have it done…day before."

Her stomach jumbled. "Cutting it close."

He put up his hand. "She swears it to me. It will be done."

Cass pushed at her forehead, unsure she wanted the answer to her next question. "How much did *that* cost?"

"Very…very big number. She says she collects from Lord later."

Wondrous. Billing him for weapons that would most efficiently murder him. He'd love it. Probably a little too much. "She…didn't ask too many questions, did she?"

"Oh, plenty. Why he asks, where he gets numbers, how long he spends getting numbers, what did she say… 'what crackpot books has he been reading lately'… she says she will ask again when she sends the bill. She likes the 'crackpot' word. What is crackpot?"

"Uh…out there. Fringe theory. Kind of wild, kind of not."

Bjorn nodded, then followed Cass' occasional glances. "The King," he said reverently.

"Have you met him before?"

"Once. I was a younger man."

"What can you tell me?"

"He is chief among men in our lands. The word 'no' has never been spoken to him."

"That…seems highly impractical."

Bjorn squeezed his eyes half-shut in a sort of mirth she didn't see on him often. "Oh, Cassie, being silly. He would not get far if no one ever said *no*. No one *denies*. That is the difference."

"Oh. A metaphor."

"Yes."

No wonder Ifalna seemed nervous. "And is he reasonable?" she asked.

"Ehhh." He tilted his head. "When no one denies, his is a different sort of reason. Good for what he is for. We are good for what we are for. He respects this and gives respect to us if we give respect to him. That is reasonable."

Interesting. Cass wasn't sure she agreed, but it seemed a little better than the nobles here thinking they knew better than everyone about everything and mucking about in it. Maybe. Bjorn guffawed. "Of course, if you disrespect, he cleaves skull in half."

"Please tell me that is also a metaphor."

"Silly, silly Cassie-duck."

Why did she ever get her hopes up? "Right."

"Oh." He lifted his chin. "Here comes Lord. He is quick for skinny man."

Cass turned, and Alexander caught up her hands, only barely masking his fluster. "Good. You're here. Are you well?"

"All right," she said with a bit of a laugh. "What's going on? Is everything all right?"

He started walking, taking her with him, his voice low. "I haven't time to explain, but whatever happens, play along."

"Oh. Good. I love it when you whisper sweet worrying nothings in my ear."

"Everything's fine. Should be. As long as this goes well. Skip the curtsy, grip the arm, hold eye contact until he breaks it."

"Alexander."

"I'm sorry, I know, I'm terrible—" He picked his head up, his perfect mask back in place. "Your Exalt. It is my honor to present Ser Cassandra of the House of Masks."

It was everything she could do not to turn and stare her daggers into his perfect face, keep her own perfectly placid as though she hadn't just been introduced as a knight of a thousand-year-old defunct order. Ruhan didn't budge, either. He was in on it. What the damned hells—?

The King of Joranhelm approached, and whether or not she meant to, she made eye contact. The man was *massive*. He wasn't as tall as Bjorn, but he made up for that in sheer bulk. Some of it was likely the ceremonial leather armor—the pauldrons and bracers both bore fin-like spikes jutting out—but in between were slabs of muscle. He reached out a large hand and she returned the gesture, barely fitting her own around a third of his forearm. When he made contact, the whole of her body rollicked, sending white hot pain through that damned demon hole in her side. She choked it down.

"Well met, warrior," he boomed. "I see scars of war."

"Yes, sire," she managed.

"It is good," he said, releasing her arm.

Ifalna leaned forward. "Papa, Ser Cassandra nearly bested me in *ovepakte* yesterday."

His eyebrows lifted. "*Ech?*"

"It was very close."

Cass wasn't sure whether this was good or bad, so she just smiled briefly and bowed her head toward Ifalna. The King looked at her curiously. "Let me inspect your weapons."

Ruhan nodded. Cass went for her knives slowly, trying not to look as panicked as she felt. This was where the whole charade fell apart. Her blades were no knight's weapons. They were functional—decently made. She'd taken to wearing the silvered one she'd confiscated from Kaye and her weighted off-hand blade, but even these were not the fine things any titled person would carry.

"They're nothing special," she said, handing them over. "Sentimental, I suppose."

He observed them in the bright light spraying in from the large windows. Those windows made Cass nervous. Their wards would protect the guests from most anything physical or magical spilling over from a fight on the day of the wedding, but there was very little to stop glass from spraying from above should the Demon Lord choose to break them. One thing at a time, she tried to remind herself.

"Well-kept," he remarked.

"Yes, sire," she said. "A dull knife does no one any good."

"You clean them immediately."

"When I can."

"And yet…." He squinted, lifted the off-hand and pointed to the scorch mark near the hilt. "What is this damage?"

She watched Alexander and Ruhan tense, but Ifalna didn't. Cass answered, "What remains after gravely wounding a demon in haste, Your Exalt. The blood is hot."

Alexander watched the King carefully a moment. When he didn't immediately burst a vein at the mention of demons, he ventured, "Ser Cassandra specializes in hunting demonic and fey malefactors."

Ruhan nodded. "Indeed. It was her service in this area that earned her the knighthood. Now she serves as a key advisor to the throne on such matters."

The King didn't smile, per se, but there was a general loosening of his features. He held the daggers back out to Cassandra. "Very good. I am eager to hear your battle-stories. A respected crude weapon is better than a fine one left to rust."

Was it her imagination, or did he look at Alexander and Ruhan when he said that? Ifalna quickly grasped his arm. "And you'll hear them after the strategy meeting. Come, Papa. I'll show you to the training grounds, and the overlook. You'll like to look on the harbor."

He made a sort of affirming grunt, and the two walked away. A bit at a time, Alexander's shoulders edged downward, and Ruhan swiped a hand over his face. "Sweet merciful gods," he said fervently.

"I don't think it went all that badly," Alexander said.

"Only thanks to Cassandra, although I fear if you keep it up, he may try to marry her off to *you* instead."

Cass settled the knives back in their sheathes and hooked her thumbs idly through the straps. "Well, Your Highness, you have one up on me in that you own quite a bit of territory and I'm a commoner. Until a few minutes ago? Is this the part where an explanation is forthcoming?"

Alexander glanced over his shoulder to check the occupants of the room. "Presently, but elsewhere. Ru, if you wouldn't mind…?"

"I would be delighted to be anywhere but here," he said, holding a sweeping hand out in the direction of a door behind the throne. Alexander took Cass' arm and let her lean on him as they went through and up a set of wide, purple carpeted marble stairs. Guards stood every few feet—different guards from the main halls of the castles. Knights, dressed as the false Gerund had been. They were heading into the private residence portion of the Rest. Cass felt strange, somehow, about that, like she was invading somewhere she didn't quite belong.

At the top, they emerged into a large receiving chamber, with plush couches arranged in a ring around a stone table with a map of the world engraved into it. The windows were vast, floor to ceiling, looking out of the harbor, the spires of the Cathedral just barely in view in the lower corner. "Wow," she said, unbidden.

Alexander, in the process of sitting as though this was just another day, looked too. "I'm glad it's a clear day," he said with a bit of a smile. "Making its best impression."

"You're joking, right?" she said, gaping at the white sails on the ships against the blue sky, the endless water. "Gray, blue, storming, I don't think it could possibly make any less of an impression. How could this ever get old for you?"

Ruhan looked to the guards at the top of the stairs. "Thank you. Please leave us." They clanked away gamely, and he shed the crown and the cape and slouched to the sofa like, well, a person. "I think you can get used to most anything if you marinate in it long enough."

She shook her head. "Absolutely not. Not something like this."

He sat up slightly. "Want to test that?"

Suspiciously, she said, "What are you getting at? Um. Your Highness."

"Please. No need."

Alexander glanced over at his friend. "It's really no good being cryptic with her."

Cass frowned in his direction. "I am sitting right here."

"It's a compliment, darling."

"And *you.* 'Play along'? I did owe you one, but now we are *solidly* even. Did I sleep through the knighting to a long-dead order, or was that just a lie on a whim to an extremely dangerous king?"

Alexander's smile grew fonder. He shook his head and laughed. "Of course you know what the House of Masks is. This is what I mean. She's too sharp. If we avoid answering long enough, she'll put the whole plot together."

"I'm not a parlor trick, Lord Fremont."

He grimaced. "I'm getting titled. I suppose I earned it."

Ruhan chuckled and leaned forward, rubbing at his forehead. "My soon-to-be father-in-law is, er…well…."

"He thoroughly kicked Ruhan's ass," Alexander translated.

"That seemed to be something he approved of," Ruhan said. "And I held my own. But during said ass-kicking, it became immediately apparent that he does *not* approve of hiring people to fight for you."

"Oh," Cass said. "I can see how that might constitute a problem."

"Ordinarily, one does not call attention to differences of that nature during diplomatic exchanges," he said, standing, pacing around the table. "There are bound to be philosophical disparities between any cultures. However, we were somewhat backed into a corner by the demon problem. Lord Lomor felt it prudent to warn the King of the situation."

Fair, Cass supposed. If she were a visiting monarch and she found out after the fact that there was this sort of danger, she'd feel fairly offended about being kept in the dark. "So you wiped the mercenary off."

Quickly, he said, "Now—please don't take it the wrong way. Were it not for the tenuous nature of our betrothal agreement, I'd insist on agreeing to disagree. But honestly, I'd already been considering ways to honor your company's great service to the city in neutralizing the leader of three crime rings, particularly your sacrifice in having done so. This…seemed doubly prudent."

"If not expedited."

"I hope it's not entirely disagreeable."

Cass fidgeted. Was it? She didn't know much of anything about knighthood, aside from the fact that it came with requirements Alexander seemed to dislike.

She picked up her head in realization. Alexander. It would put her on more equal footing with him, societally. She'd been trying not to think too much about it, but with the contract drawing to a close, she would lose the authority to act on his behalf unless they were married. If he needed her protection, or even just to reach out to another household, they would need to go through Humphrey. Ruhan was doing her a mercy—and their relationship a vast favor—that shouldn't have needed to be.

She looked at him, and he nodded slowly, almost imperceptibly. Alexander didn't seem to have noticed the exchange. A guard came up the stairs with a note, and Alexander went to receive it.

"There's an ongoing argument at play here," she said, nodding briefly toward Alexander. "Something about archaic traditions."

"I know," Ruhan acknowledged.

"Are you listening?"

"I am. And where I can, I'm making changes. You'll have to trust me."

"No, I don't think I will," she countered. "I think I'll hold you to it, if you're that keen on keeping me around."

He smiled. "Very good."

"Ru," Alexander said, holding up the note. "Lomor has need of us. Something about the honeymoon."

"Let me handle this one, friend," he said. "Gods know you've been running all over creation this morning. Talk it over. Let me know the terms."

He descended the stairs, taking a good few of the guards with him. Alexander rounded the sofa and slung himself down next to Cass with a bit of an exhausted sigh, then took up her hand. "Are you all right?"

"Me?" she asked, surprised.

"Heartbeat," he reminded her simply.

Right. She pushed out a breath. "I suppose," she said carefully, "I haven't really given much thought to how work things will be when this is all over."

"How so?"

She looked down at his hand around hers. "Well. I knew this was the kind of job that would change everything. I had just…rather expected more of the same afterward, if not better of the same. Now, I guess, there are other options. Potentially better options."

Alexander's brow furrowed slightly. "Wait—you think you'll be expected to give up your work?"

"No," she said with a bit of a smile. "I know you wouldn't ask."

"This knighthood thing—it can be completely symbolic, if you want it to be. If you want to keep at events, you will have no shortage of clamoring clients-to-be."

"I don't know," she realized aloud with a laugh. "I don't know what things will be like. That's what nobody's said. Where do you go from…?" She failed to find words to sum up the complexity of this job. "Well, we have to succeed, first, and then I have to talk to my company and see what *they* want. But I was considering taking on different sorts of work, and this would be the way to do it. I can't do it without them."

"You wouldn't have to."

This sounded much more agreeable all of a sudden, but Mum always told her never to rush into anything. "I…hmm. I'm starting to want to say yes."

He smiled. "So say yes."

"Yes."

"And the terms?"

"See, that's where I get hung up. I am not quite ready to say goodbye completely."

"So don't."

"I….won't. All that to say I couldn't possibly begin to know the terms now, so it's a dangling title and I'm borrowing honor based on a half-finished deed."

Alexander turned to her and looked at her with a little sympathetic smile and his slightly wincing eyes full of both recognition and adoration at the same time. The rarest of moments—complete and total understanding, even despite how fumbled her unburdening felt. Somehow, those moments came often with him. He held her hand fast and spoke directly to that anxious place at the center of her. "There will always be more to do," he said. "That particular honor wasn't a loan—well and truly earned. But the terms can and will wait until the next deed is done."

Cass pressed out a breath and watched the boats for a moment more. "Nothing left to do but do it, then," she murmured.

33
Nothing Left to Do but I Do

It wasn't the worst dress she'd worn. Plenty of range of motion, no irritating petticoats, and actually rather pretty. After the Joran fashion in Amaranthine lilac, it was mostly drapes and soft structure apart from a pauldron—useful—and her weapons worn auspiciously. Cass wasn't used to that. Ordinarily they'd be tucked under the skirt for sensibility's sake.

Ifalna, on the other hand, was bereft. She paced the small chamber, fidgeting with her hands. Thalia's eyes followed her movements as though she was tracking a falcon. At length, she looked at Cass and frowned.

Cass cleared her throat. "Your Highness," she said, "given the circumstances, if you wished to carry a weapon, I don't think there'd be a soul in Amaranth who'd blame you."

Ifalna stopped, her trailing train and single-shouldered cape drifting to an ethereal halt behind her. "Do you think…? No. I shouldn't."

Thalia's sense of propriety cracked. She alit on the vanity and swung her legs in irritation. "Who gives a flying fig about what anybody else thinks? You're about to be Queen."

"Assuming my father doesn't drag me back to Joranhelm for making a mess of things."

Thalia's fingers curled around the edge of the vanity, her nose twitching. "Let him try."

Cass folded her arms. "Thalia. We don't threaten regicide."

"But—"

"We must assume Princess Ifalna wishes her father to return home safely."

Despite everything, a little of the floury nervous pallor taking over Ifalna's face cracked. "He can be a bit of a boar, but no, I do not wish him dead. I admire your fire."

"Okay, but he can't literally stop a wedding that's in the middle of happening, can he?" Thalia asked, peeved.

"By law?" Cass said, cringing. "Yeah. Anyone can object up until the end."

Thalia threw her head back and groaned, "Newt nipples! Traditions are the worst."

Ifalna resumed her pacing, setting her jaw. "*Felche,* but I feel so useless, standing by while others prepare for battle on my behalf."

Cass knew. She even felt it a bit now. Gideon had caught her in the hallway, cautioned her. Not too much, he'd reminded her. Still recovering. As though her body would let her forget the misery that just training had wreaked on it.

She picked her head up. "Hey. That folding spear you used on me. You carry that thing often?"

Ifalna reached past Thalia and picked up the golden cylinder from the top of the vanity. "Every day but today," she answered. "There's nowhere to hide it."

She was right. There were plenty of layers, sleeves, but lots of nearly diaphanous white fabric clinging to her. Cass held out her hand. "May I?"

Curiously, the princess tilted her head and handed it over. Cass took up the small bouquet she'd be carrying and carefully parted the flowers. A bit at a time, she eased the cylinder down into the bundle of stems. "There we go. If you want it, you can tell me and I'll get it to you."

"Brilliant," Ifalna declared. "That will do nicely."

"Not that you should need it," Thalia prompted pointedly, looking to Cass with her eyebrows raised. "Things are under control."

"Oh—of course," Ifalna said quickly. "It's more of a…how would you say…well, I feel rather naked without it."

Most people checked their pockets for their keys before leaving the house. Ifalna didn't leave without light arms. Possibly not a terrible idea, if this much excitement tended to follow her around. Cass got it. Her leg felt wrong without at least two knives strapped to it these days.

A knock at the door interrupted. Ifalna moved to open it, but Cass stopped her and went to answer it instead. An impeccably dressed Alexander stood on the other side, practically vibrating with nervous energy. "Hi," she said with a smile.

"Hello," he managed. "I, er…I had come here for some—actual intended purpose, but it seems to have vanished. You look…glorious."

"Thank you. As do you." She looked him over a little more appraisingly. "Is everything all right?"

"Yes, yes, it's…I've been ejected from the groom's chambers while he practices his vows. Something about being nervous. He's told me to check in with you."

Cass glanced back over her shoulder. Jules napped heavily on the sofa after a long night of last minute preparations, Thalia practiced a series of runes in the air without pushing magic through them, and Ifalna seemed relieved to have something else to focus on other than what was going on in her mind.

"Blessedly average, so far," Cass reported.

"Good," he said, a little relief blossoming in his features. "Good. I wondered if, while we're waiting, you might take a little walk with me."

Cass looked back into the room. "Oh—I think—"

Ifalna stepped forward and tucked her arm through Cass'. "A lovely idea. Please, go on."

"Are you sure? We're not terribly far from the first arrivals—"

"Go," she urged with a smile, relieving her of the bouquet. "We'll be fine here."

"Okay," Cass said, a little bewildered, as Ifalna passed her arm off to Alexander. "Just—"

"Listen for Gideon," Thalia acknowledged, bored.

"You'd think it wasn't the most important wedding we'd ever worked," Cass muttered to Alexander.

"Nobody likes waiting," he said, patting her hand.

Him least of all. She could feel his nervousness in his tight muscles. She let him walk on in quiet for a while, leading her through the castle to a garden off the edge of the training grounds that faced that breathtaking view of the harbor she loved so well. This one was all vast round white marble pots spilling over with wisteria blooms and draping greens. They walked along the stone railing on the edge, where he paused to take a breath. She slipped her arm about his waist.

"Is it the wedding?" she asked. "Or the danger? Maybe worrying about being caught out, or the prospect of giving a speech…?"

"A little of all of it," he said, "thank you for the highly calming list."

"Sorry."

"I suppose I should say it's mostly the demon threatening to drag us into limbo, shouldn't I."

"What is it mostly?"

Alexander rested his chin atop her head for a moment, looking out on the water below. "Do you remember the promise you made me?" he asked quietly. "In your apartment."

Cass laughed quietly. "You brought me here to remind me of it?" When he didn't answer, she said, "Yes, of course. Not everything. Not this time. We'll be leaving together, tonight, from this plane. Deal?"

He pressed out a breath slowly, a little of the tension leaving his muscles. "Thank you. I just…needed to hear it."

She ran her hand along his arm comfortingly. "Then I will say it."

Never mind that she had a hard time thinking past this afternoon, that it felt foolhardy to imagine anything beyond the fight that was coming. Even discussions of the reception felt premature. He knew what she wasn't saying, and it had apparently been weighing.

Alexander cleared his throat slightly. "I've, er…never been to one of these. I've had thorough instruction, of course, but until now it's been hypothetical."

Cass tried not to appear too surprised. Even knowing how cooped up he'd been, it still seemed hard to completely escape some distant stranger's wedding in childhood.

"Well, you just stick with me, then. I'll have you covered."

"That is very much the plan. Today and from now on, if that's agreeable."

She couldn't quite manage to temper a grin. "Are we renegotiating a contract?"

He broke into a laugh. "Forgive me. You know by now that I have three modes of communication: feral, overly familiar, and overly formal, and I daren't avail myself of the first two right now for fear they might stick." He turned, ran his thumb along the side of her face contemplatively. "It was just supposed to be a contract, wasn't it?"

Her hand closed around his. "If I'd managed to stay professional, this conversation would be very different."

"I am…beyond grateful it isn't." Alexander tried hard to capture a breath that seemed to keep sliding around his chest, and after a moment of failing, decided to go for it anyway. "Cassandra, you are…the most—"

His eyes flicked up and he cut himself off even before he was interrupted. Armored shapes moving from the direction of the Rest. "Ser Cassandra," one of them called.

Cass looked to Alexander, a fawn caught on the green. "Should I…?"

He closed his eyes and laughed slightly. "No, it's all right."

"I can get rid of them. This is important. I'll get rid of them."

Alexander caught her hand and took up her face in his other. "Cassie, I know this is important. It's your job. Go on."

She looked back, wide-eyed, a little fretful. He smiled, and she relaxed, stood on her toes, and kissed him in the sort of way usually kept out of the public eye. He leaned in and held fast for as long as he could. "I'll see you in there," she said as she slipped away. "I love you."

"I love you," he said. "Be…so careful."

Under her breath, she said, "Take me home tonight and you've got a deal."

He stood and watched her go for a while, then smiled at her once more, slipped his hands into his pockets, and headed back into the Rest by the side door. She brushed her hair away from her eye and the wreath of flowers atop her head and approached the knights, who knew better than to say a damned word.

"Yes?" she asked, trying not to sound too terse about it.

"It's the undercroft," the second one said. "Your man sent for you."

Her innards clenched. She'd expected this, she tried to remind herself. Listen for Gideon. "I'll be along. See to the princess' chamber, please."

They nodded curtly in lieu of a salute—technically, she only outranked them for today. She was sure it bristled. Cass hiked her skirt a little and hurried through the halls. Today, everyone pressed themselves practically to the walls to clear the way. Bad news comes when a bridesmaid runs.

The undercroft was still and silent, even with the guards. She knew the look they wore. Grim preparedness. Lomor had insisted on telling them what may be coming through. Only fair, she supposed, even if the tension choked the air the rest of the way from the basement. By the time she made it to Gideon standing before the cornerstone, the unease permeated her, too, as she looked around. "What? What is it?"

She expected to see some distortion, warping, a rift growing in space. Instead, she saw…nothing out of the ordinary. Her eyebrows pulled down. "What am I looking at?"

"Absolutely nothing," he said, tapping his fist to his chin in bafflement. "That's…wrong, isn't it. Were we wrong?"

"You called me down here to look at nothing."

He dropped his hand, started to pace, still observing the cornerstone. "We weren't able to finish buffing this to where I'd like it to be. It's still considerably weakened. There should be some sign of him here."

"Maybe he's sleeping in."

Gideon shook his head, folding his arms and working his fingers in and out of the lavender silk of his tunic sleeve. "A massive shift like he's planning? He'd have started working up the energy long ago."

Now the unease started creeping back in. "Time does work strangely there."

"Maybe that's it," he answered, sounding entirely unconvinced.

"You checked in with Hubert yesterday, didn't you?"

"Yes. The bells were consistent. But there was still time for him to change his mind." His brow furrowed. "He knows we're here. He knows we're waiting. What if…?"

Cass went through shades of reactions, like Alexander's shifting night skies inside his mother's brass cylinder. If he didn't show—well, that would be good, wouldn't it? But he would still be out there, festering inside limbo, waiting and conspiring for another opportunity. Would that still be their problem? Could anyone do anything about him?

"That's…but when else will he have this kind of opportunity?"

"I don't know," he said, rubbing at the back of his neck. "But we've laid him pretty low. He may choose to regroup instead."

She looked at the perfectly undisturbed cornerstone. "That would be…I mean, our contract is for this wedding."

"Yeah," he said numbly.

"Gideon," she prompted quietly.

"I can't let him slip away from me again," he said, his clenched hand shaking.

"I know. You'll get him."

"And if I don't?" he blurted, his face creasing. "If he bides his time until my mortal existence expires? What then?"

She reached out and disentangled his fingers from his arms. "We don't know he's not coming," she told him. "And if he doesn't show…we'll hunt him. You have my word."

He took a shuddering sort of breath, then smiled weakly at her. "Thought we weren't heroes."

"I can make an exception." The layers of stone muffled the sound, but she could feel the bells' resonance from here. "Half an hour till ushering begins. We should get to our bride and groom."

Gideon cast one more look back at the unbothered cornerstone, then grimaced down at himself as he started toward the undercroft. "I wish you'd talked them out of the purple."

"Why? It looks nice."

"You think? It clashes a bit with the red eyes."

"It's better than the pea soup green velvet suit couple."

"Ugh. Don't remind me. I looked like a shoemaker elf. And then with the blood all over it…." He shuddered. "Horrendous."

She nodded as they made their way up the last of the steps. "Do me a favor?" she asked, keeping her voice low.

"As long as I get to hold it over you for the next few months, sure," he chuckled.

"Just…look out for Alexander, please."

"Why, Cassie, I was planning to trip him and leave him as an offering to the Demon Lord."

She glared. "I meant before the wedding, but since apparently you need a refresher on how to take care of clients during, maybe I'm slightly more nervous about letting you take on coordination."

He held up his hands. "All right, all right. I take it he's nervous."

"Extremely."

"I'll turn on the charm." He paused. "He's…going to be all right if things come to blows, yes?"

Cass' eyes darted around the hallway. Thankfully, everyone seemed mostly caught up in their own tasks. "He and I have made an arrangement," she said.

"And that is…?"

"I've promised not to die."

Gideon set his hands to his waist. "Well, given that the last time we rather botched that, we'll make you not dying a priority this time."

"Then as long as you get him to his appropriately warded area when the blows start, he will be just fine."

That was the deal. It helped that within the warded area, he wouldn't be able to see or hear until the dust settled one way or the other. As long as he kept breathing….

They'd made a deal, she reminded herself. "It'll be fine," she told herself and Gideon and the portent bells and the unbowed undercroft and anything that might be listening.

There were very few clauses for *it's not fine.*

*   *   *

It was a newer-fangled thing, having the bridesmaids walk in on the arms of the groomsmen. Not every wedding contract asked for that, and Cass had not been terribly surprised when this one kept to the traditional menfolk-march-in-the-groom-in-case-he-runs-off, maidens-attend-to-the-train-in-case-she-runs-off format. She hadn't anticipated how much it bothered her not to be able to give Alexander any smidgeon of comfort before they went to stand before much of their kingdom and a good chunk of Ifalna's.

Even quiet, she was now so much more aware of how *not* quiet the audience was. That had always been her job to begin with—cataloging the strange fidgets, the out of place sounds amongst the sniffling or shuffling in the chairs. Now that Alexander had told her just how noisy people were, she was acutely aware of ruffling fabric and coughing and breathing, and gods, how could he stand it?

For his part, he bore it as he always did: under a mask of near-unshakeable placidity, his hands folded in front of him. He did seem to be listening to what the Hierophant was saying, which probably made the difference. Cass and her team never listened to the actual wedding proceedings. Not really. They usually didn't mean much, and even today, when it did—Ruhan and Ifalna had really grown on her—there was something much more pressing to be wary of.

Even if it had yet to materialize. Cass' grip clenched harder around the stiffer-than-usual bouquet stem. Every passing moment felt like a deepening of that question from down below.

She particularly watched the long purple carpet. Demons often made use of the aisle. Something about liminal spaces—the betweens made humans vulnerable. She supposed that's why he liked limbo. Nothing except the expertly scattered flower petals occasionally drifting in the draft, though those made for plenty of heart-in-throat moments. Why did they always have these things in drafty old places?

The drafty old Hierophant swept his brocade-clad arm for the small kid who carried the rings in a glass case, and Gideon made eye contact from his place across the way. Cass gritted her teeth imperceptibly. She knew, she knew. If he was going to make an appearance, the bonding of the couple was the most likely time.

The rings slipped on with a murmured call, response, one, two. Gideon leaned forward on his hooves. Cass held her breath. The Hierophant smiled, and the wedding went on.

The rings were done; next came the crownings. Cass almost nodded to herself. That made more sense. Why would he show up for a simple church-scripted declaration of true love when there was a joining of nations to be done? The King of Joranhelm came to stand beside his daughter, and Alexander stood to symbolize the late King and Queen's blessing as the bride and groom knelt.

Cass rearranged Ifalna's skirts for an excuse to be close at hand, her helpfulness absolutely transparent to anyone who'd ever been to an important wedding. Too many noble eyes traced her movement curiously, wondering what she prepared for. She returned to stillness, the bouquet loose in her hand in case she needed to drop it to Ifalna.

A band of singers who seemed to travel with the King picked up a song, wordless, soaring, reaching to the rafters in the same way the portent bells seemed to fill every hollow space—but gentle. The anxiety in Cass' chest almost ebbed a little. The King spoke—Joran. As usual, his voice rang in authoritative tones that sort of felt like someone was being tested. Any attention Cass held was gone now as the nobles squinted and strained in their chairs to get a look at the warrior King, as though seeing him might somehow help them understand him. He strode in front of the Hierophant, his long furred cape dragging behind him, then stopped in front of Ruhan and observed him. His tone softened, and he spoke something that sounded like a question. Ruhan bowed his head and answered in Joran.

A moment, two, the King stared him down. Was this performance, or was something the matter? Ruhan held steady, his eyes to the floor. Alexander looked perfect, as usual, but when Cass made eye contact, he showed her just a hint of doubt, anxiety. Ifalna, too, stared ahead with a little more intensity than a perfectly assured person might.

At length, the King pivoted sharply. When he turned around again, he held a golden crown with many branching points that reminded Cass a bit of Thalia's antlers. He raised it high, then lowered it to Ruhan's head. "Be welcomed, Prince of Joranhelm."

He reached out and clasped Ruhan's arm, making direct and deliberate eye contact as he hauled him to his feet. Ifalna melted into a relieved smile. Cass wasn't quite there yet. At that moment of contact, she scoured the betweens again, the spaces the eye usually glanced over. And again, no movement.

Alexander stepped forward, his knees a little wobbly. He kept his eyes on Ifalna, his lordly demeanor broken into a shy sort of fondness. "Princess, will you promise to cherish and keep this nation as well as you do this man?"

She looked up at him, resolute. "With everything that I have."

He took up a golden band with the traditional Amaranthine wyvern adorning the front and set it atop her head. "I am honored to welcome the Queen of Amaranth."

Alexander took up her hands and placed them into Ruhan's, breaking into a genuine smile as he clasped them both together for a moment before stepping back for the Hierophant. Cass' mouth went dry as the old man looked up to the light streaming in from the high stained glass windows above.

This was it. The final official oath. "In the name of the most sacred, I call upon the workings of the heavens and earth to witness the joining of Ruhan, King of Amaranth, Prince of Joranhelm, and Ifalna, Queen of Amaranth, Princess of Joranhelm. Let our lands and peoples unite as you do now."

Ruhan and Ifalna turned to face the rows of guests, faces flushed with joy—as it should be. They were completely unaware of the auspice of the moment for any reason other than what it meant for them. Again, Cass couldn't begrudge them, but her pulse thrashed as she checked up and down that aisle, in the shadows, the corners, the spaces in between the applause as their lips met.

Motion out of the corner of her eye. She turned. Just the hem of the Hierophant's sleeve. Odd creaking. A nobleman's child on a chair trying for a better vantage point as his mother tried to pull him down. Cass' heart rate slowed, and she looked back at Gideon, who stood sallow and stunned.

He really wasn't coming.

The King bellowed out in Joran for the archers to find their marks, and Cass nodded both herself and Gideon out of their stupor. There was still the recessional through the streets to see to. Minor fey made trouble sometimes on the way out; they would have to put the shock aside and deal with that if it came up.

The arrows released on the call to fire and arced gracefully through the air, the royal mages standing ready to deflect them into the pools along the side of the room once they sailed over the bride and groom. The crowd gasped in awe.

Even Cass had to admit it was a hell of a thing. The arrows effortlessly crested, trailing strands of curling golden and silver threads. Ifalna and Ruhan clasped hands and reached up their free ones, ready to try to catch as many arrows as they passed overhead as they could. For luck, Ifalna had explained.

Instead, however, the arrows froze in midair. The mages started, looked at each other as though to ask *did you…?*

Cass didn't wait. She made eye contact with Ifalna and hurled the bouquet to her and called to Gideon, "Barrier. Now."

The blue rift appeared right next to Cass an instant later.

34

Forever Hold Your Peace

Relief was absolutely the wrong word for staring into the even more monstrous than usual visage of Azorael, Lord of Demons, but it was nice to know where he was. He made good and sure Cass saw him, fanged now, his red cut through with silver, those terrible eyes of his sunken in an awfully familiar way.

"Terribly sorry to be late," he said.

The room around them lit up almost white hot, thrumming with the electric energy of Gideon's barriers come to fruition. The guests were safe, cut off from all of this as though in an entirely different space.

Cass chanced a smile. "Practiced that one ahead of time, did you?"

Bjorn charged, his axe raised. Cass vanished and resolidified a few feet back to take up her blades. Her back butted up against the dome of force encapsulating the Hierophant, Ifalna, Ruhan, the King, and Alexander. Like running into a taut sheet, as it should be.

She looked to Thalia, already amassing energy between her hands. "Go wild," she said.

"I love it when you say that," Thalia answered, releasing her magic.

The actual heralds were protected within the barriers, but whatever Thalia did produced a cacophony as though they'd all decided to practice different songs at the same time. The horns were strident enough to bother Cass' ears. Irividius snarled, coiling up low to the ground and shuffling away from Bjorn like a skink. Jules grabbed hold of the nearest piece of furniture—a small stone fountain, by the looks of it—and charged in to help.

The demon faded from sight. Gideon whirled, panic forming in his features. "Where'd he…?"

Cass held up a hand around the hilt of one of the blades. The air near her left elbow felt unsettled, somehow. She turned sharply just as he reappeared and drove the new dagger down toward an eye socket. He parried ably with a claw, and she threw a brief look back toward Gideon. He nodded and began tracing runes.

Irividius' tongue flicked out, and his eyes narrowed as he bore down against the edges of Cass' knives with his staff. "We have unfinished business."

"Do we?" she pushed back hard, then vanished.

This time, she returned just behind him, ready to jam a knife into the scaly plates along his back. He whirled quickly and backed away as though bowing out. "You took something from me without fulfilling your end of the bargain."

She glanced down at her semi-translucent blue arm and the silver freckles standing out among the stained glass refractions. "That's what you'd like me to believe, yes. The bells say differently."

Gideon let his spell go, and the ground, the air, the building itself thrummed with vibrations. Cass couldn't hear anything new, but in the same way she had felt the song in that brass dome, she knew Gideon had taken the wrath fomenting in his soul and channeled it all into sound.

Irividius whipped around as all five approached, his eyes wide, his teeth bared, thin veiny ears flattened. His eyes seemed unfocused. Cass firmed her grip on her blades, and she lunged forward at the same time Thalia let go of a cage of brambles, expanding from a single briar into the sort of thing that could well lock a creature of Irividius' size in place.

He opened his mouth and drew in what could be mistaken for a breath. The brambles began to crumple, locked in midair. The thorns dropped to the floor then whipped up into a spiraling lash outward. Jules cursed and pivoted and cut aside to avoid. Bjorn barreled straight through, swinging his axe out wide. Irividius' eyes seemed to widen, but he reached out with a single obsidian claw and touched the very edge of the axe blade before disappearing in a smear of dark blue against the air again.

Bjorn wheeled back around, his eyes dark and pupiless in an upsettingly familiar way.

"Possession!" Cass yelled. Jules skidded to a stop.

The axe came down toward Jules, but she pulled back and out of the way. "Ah, shit," she grumbled, fists up in front of her. "This is *not* the way I like to spar with you."

Bjorn didn't answer. He brought the axe back around. Cass grabbed Thalia's shoulder. "Do…do something with him. If you can't, it's nap time. Gideon—"

"He's still here." He looked around the room uneasily.

Cass nodded and adjusted her grip on her hilts. "Get ready," she said. "You and me. He pops back up, we're pinning him down. Thalia, keep an ear out. We'll need you to put him away."

"Okay," she said, puffing out a breath and stretching out her shoulders. "Come on, Bjorn, let's settle down now."

Cass gestured for Gideon to edge down the aisle in the path still left clear by the two barriers. She moved forward toward the altar, checking for the slightest hint of spatial displacement. Usually the carpet was a good place to start—it tended to waver under the strain of the magic.

After a few moments of laborious searching, she picked up her head. She was going about this the hard way for no reason at all. No one *else* could see.

She let herself slip between the planes and blinked at the distorted version of the great hall. It was odd—here, she could see but not walk past the barriers to the the gathered nobles chatting worriedly to each other. It was strangely banal. Weddings did get attacked often enough—that she had a job was proof of that—but the orderly yet anxious calm seemed so otherworldly to her in the same way the captured souls in the city beyond had.

Against her own better judgment, she looked toward Alexander in the wedding party's barrier. He kept his arms folded, his breathing mechanically regular, but his eyes kept moving over the wall of magical force separating them as though he might at any moment be able to see through it.

And a few feet away, struggling hastily with a surge of energy pooling from the darkness itself, was the shadowy, not-quite corporeal form of Irividius. Cass gripped her daggers—strange, here. Not blue and vague like her, but neither were they quite solid. "Found you."

His head snapped up. "You. Gnat."

She glanced around surreptitiously again. She saw Gideon strafing in their direction, clearly detecting the disturbance, but he couldn't break through. She needed to get him back to the wedding. "Not working the way you hoped, is it."

He gritted his teeth, pulling his hands free of the magical energy. "Your paltry attempts at bolstering the cornerstone are but irritations. As is your presence. We cannot hurt each other here."

Cass held up a knife. She didn't doubt he was right, but there was something to the strangely flickering physical object. She'd brought it through with her. Perhaps it worked the other way. "Do you want to test that?"

"I have no need."

"Yeah, well, I do."

She ran for him, raising the knife high. He watched her come, bemused, not bothering to move. With the other hand, she reached out, balanced the hilt between the thumb and the heel of her hand, and grasped at him.

The second her fingers made contact, she willed herself back to the material. It felt very much like dragging him along, but the moment she felt herself solidify again, she did so still in mid-lunge, bowling him backwards. The dagger he'd scoffed at before still swung downward. His massive shoulders hit the stone floor, and the alloyed blade drove between the scales.

Irividius screamed. Quickly it turned into a snarl, and he threw Cass away from himself. She rolled with it, caught herself before she fell too far, but not before the pain in her side reminded her why she needed to keep him at arm's length.

"What—did you—just *do*?" he roared.

"You wanted the insurance," she spat around a fattening lip. "You get everything else that comes with it."

He lurched to all fours, his back arching in a bizarrely familiar way, despite the massive tail thrashing across the ground. He wasn't containing the wolf well. Irividius' eyes darted as Gideon helped Cass up.

"Was that enough?" he said.

She shook her head, firming her grip again. "Poison's too slow. Get after him."

He let her go and started forming circles in the air. She darted forward again. Between convulsions, Irividius swung backward, reached out with a claw, and slashed at the barrier.

The energy flickered, faded, and dissipated with no fanfare. They were back in a room full of exposed guests. The ordered but nervous calm quickly turned to panic as the arrows began falling again.

"Gideon!" Cass shouted.

He abruptly left off the spell, straining to reignite the barriers. They were thin, flimsy, but at the very, very least, he managed to get the dome top back in time to deflect the barrage. As the arrows fell like jagged hail, Cass had no choice but to vanish once again.

35
Succumb

Torturous minutes of blank nothing, safe behind these magical curtains. Alexander waited, his arms pressed to himself. Ifalna's sharp anxiety nearly rivaled his, her jaw set as though waiting for something to burst through. Her father behind her seemed to ripple with the same tension.

Ruhan kept looking over at him in between exchanging comforting words with his bride. Alexander knew why, but it didn't make staying calm any easier. At last, he said under his breath, "I'm keeping a lid on it."

"I know you can," Ruhan answered lightly. "I'm just…."

Checking to make sure they wouldn't wind up magically locked in with an anxious ravenous beast. Sure. "It's somewhat easier if I'm not being stared at."

"Right. Right."

The king glanced their direction with an arched eyebrow. Ifalna threw up her hands. "I can barely stand this. They're out there fighting my fight while I cower."

"It's not cowering, darling," Ruhan said gently.

"Tell me you don't want to be out there."

He hesitated. "It…would not be seemly."

The king rumbled, "Ifalna. Respect the traditions of your adopted land as you respect ours."

She puffed out a breath, her cheeks flushed. "Has it occurred to either of you that perhaps it is not about traditions at all, but about who *I* am? You ask me to hide for the sake of others. I am done hiding."

Alexander almost missed a breath.

Ifalna glowered over at him. "And what say you, Lord Protector? Have you words to make me complacent?"

Oh, dear gods, this was the worst possible time for this. He managed to keep a breath held for a moment, then turned to answer.

He didn't get the chance. A set of claws appeared and ripped through the veil closing them off from the room. It flashed brightly once, then dropped. Without even thinking, Alexander grabbed Ifalna and Ruhan each by an elbow and yanked them back.

His heart jammed itself in his throat. The demon at the other end of those claws was even more hideous than his hazy memory permitted, and worse, he was changing. Whistles sounded in the air, and Alexander jerked his head up. The arrows.

The guests shrieked, screamed, threw their arms above their heads. He heard Cass shout, and the magical barrier reinstated itself, at least briefly. The arrows clattered off their shield harmlessly, but—

Cass was in the way. She swallowed hard, then went blue and disappeared.

Alexander's blood rushed in his own ears. Was it better or worse to have a view to this? The barrier reformed a bit, but not enough to block the scene. Gideon snapped something under his breath and left off, hurrying to begin a new spell.

Ifalna looked at Ruhan. "I am sorry," she said. "I love you, but I cannot pretend, even for you. It is not me."

She shook a metal cylinder free of the bouquet and tossed the flowers aside. Ruhan called out her name, reached for her wrist. Even between his own tremors, Alexander caught his shoulder. "Let her go," he advised, his voice a little too ragged for his own liking. "The mask isn't worth it."

Ruhan turned back anxiously to the window the demon had created. Ifalna extended the cylinder into a spear as she ran into the open. "Come on, then, beast!" she yelled. "I'll show you what a woman of Joranhelm does to spirits who attack her wedding!"

The king chuckled, muttering in Joran under his breath. *My girl,* he said.

A flash of blue, and Cass came back. "Your Highness," she acknowledged, darting forward.

Alexander's shaking hands clenched. He knew what she was rushing to do, to try to get to the Demon Lord before whatever transformation his tortured form would produce could complete. It wouldn't keep her safe. He'd still lash out—

He had to look away. A wave of nausea overtook him, and he tried again to get his breathing back in a rhythm. He felt Ruhan's hand on his shoulder, heard him say something, but he couldn't process the sound or he'd hear the rest of the room, too. There was already blood in the air— her blood and others'—why did he think he could handle this?

Because he had to. Ruhan was his brother. What other choice was there but to be here? To be anywhere else was unthinkable.

His breaths began to steady, and he turned to his first friend, who smiled encouragingly despite...well, everything else going on around them. Alexander nodded, forced his shoulders down. "I'm—sorry."

"Doing wonderfully." He glanced back. "So are both our ladies. I think. Don't look."

Alexander caught himself. "You think."

"Is...it normal for...this sort of monster to have so many things sticking out of him and still live?"

"Unfortunately, yes."

The king frowned deeply. "You are too afraid to look?"

Alexander felt his hackles rise, but Ruhan kept his hand firmly clamped on his shoulder. "Lord Fremont has a...rare condition that—"

Somewhere behind them, Thalia shrieked. Cass shouted, "Jules!"

He couldn't help it. He turned. Bjorn stood over Jules with his axe raised, his face not quite right. Jules skidded across the floor, flailing for purchase.

The Demon Lord leapt up in a second and jumped nearly across the whole dais. There was no fur, no wolfish tail, but the rest of his body had finished mangling itself. Arrows stuck into him, he bled profusely from several gashes, and there were several spots of silver-discoloration, but he wasn't even slowed. Alexander knew the look of him. The hunger. And Jules was bleeding.

Cass disappeared and reappeared directly between them. Alexander's stomach lurched. She can handle it, he reminded himself quietly. She'd handled him, she'd handled far worse. She checked behind her wildly.

"Gideon," she called desperately. "Put him down."

Gideon grabbed Bjorn by one enormous arm, his hooves sliding uselessly across the floor as he attempted to slow him from approaching Jules again. Then he gritted his teeth and hissed something in a language that almost hurt to hear.

Bjorn started to wobble, sway. Thalia recovered herself from behind a row of discarded chairs and flew straight for Jules. In her false shape, it looked bizarre, like she was gliding on air, and some of the assembled gasped.

Their awe didn't last long. Cass and the Demon Lord were fighting.

It seemed to pass in a blur. She ducked his massive claws, struck out at him with elbows, knees, knives, whatever it took. His eyes kept training on Jules, and Cass kept making herself a nuisance as best she could. Ifalna came to help, striking at his flanks, shouting for his attention. Behind Alexander, the king called out as though he were watching some sort of sport. Alexander worried the edge of Kaye's sachet in his pocket and tried desperately to keep from lunging.

Thalia took Jules under the arms and started to pull her away. The Demon Lord broke his attention away from Cass and bounded forward again.

Cass flung a dagger as hard as she could. It stuck into the hunch of his back and stayed there, but this time, he didn't turn back. She cast desperately about her blue form, and then all at once, dropped it.

Alexander's stomach dropped to his knees. "No, no, no," he murmured fervently.

Ruhan looked his way. "Xander?"

She glanced up and made eye contact with Alexander, apologetic. The Demon Lord turned, and she nodded once at him, breathing hard.

"That's right," she said. "Come get me."

Of course she would. There was no other choice for her. Jules was her sister, she would always take it for her. That did not mean he could watch helpless as the Demon Lord chased after her. Ruhan kept his hand on his arm. "Xander—"

"I have to," he said, his voice shaking.

"You've worked so hard. Don't give in."

He heard Cass' breath get knocked out of her, looked out at the people gathered. Every person he'd ever feared, and somehow, none of it mattered. "I'm not," he answered, and he let go.

They screamed when they saw him, just as he'd feared. His clothes fell away from him in shreds like he'd always worried about. He dashed through the weak barrier and landed on all fours, heading straight for the overwhelming scent of her blood, just as he'd always desperately dreaded. But when he got there, it was amazingly clear. He let himself do what needed to be done.

Alexander sank his teeth deep into the Demon Lord's neck and flung him aside. He recovered his feet fast, but Alexander didn't even give him a second to react. He snarled, lunged straight for him, barreling him backwards. They traded blows, but the ground was lost. Alexander did what he needed to. Somewhere in the place he'd abandoned, the king shouted, "*YES!*"

Ifalna caught up, surprise in every feature. She took a swipe down at the Demon Lord, then looked back at Cass, still struggling to recover herself on the ground. "I'll harry him," she said. "See to her."

Alexander gave her a brief glance, his own blood and the Demon Lord's both slipping off him. The thrumming of his blood said stay, rip into him, see how well he does without a neck, but his pulse hammered her name.

In the end, he turned and loped away.

36
Reign

Cass lay on the floor, feeling the warmth saturating her side again, but not much else. That dull ache obscured everything, threatened her vision. Not now, she said to herself, irritated. There was still work to do.

Gideon and Thalia were still unhurt. That was the most important thing. She let her eyes sink shut for a moment as she gathered her breath. If Thalia could pin him down, Gideon could banish him.

But they needed a mortal wound still. Maybe Jules was up to it. Bjorn's axe was somewhere nearby.

Her eyes opened. No, she couldn't count on that. She needed to get herself up. She struggled, pushed up on her elbow.

But oh, *gods*, her side ached. She fell back again, breathing hard. The edge of consciousness came toward her fast.

Something hit her head gently, pushing, nudging. Her eyelids fluttered again. Silver. Oh—oh gods.

She forced her eyes open and recognized the massive wolf standing above her, his tail low to the ground, whimpering. "Alexander," she got out. "What—?"

He whined again, pushing at her shoulder with his muzzle. His eyes were terrified, but very much his. Cass reached up and touched his face. "I'm okay," she promised. "I'm okay."

His eyes closed, and she pulled his forehead to hers. "I'm sorry," she said. "I still have…a job to…do. Can you help me up?"

Another whine, and he cast a look back. "Hey," she said. "I made you a promise and I'm still going to keep it, okay? I just—I need your help doing that."

Alexander hesitated a moment longer, then bowed his forelegs. She wrapped her arms around his shoulders, and he pulled upward. She gritted her teeth through the searing on the way up, then sat there for a moment to breathe. Of course the bastard had got her right in the old wound. Irividius was looking for blood, but he was aware enough to remember revenge.

She sat up, then looked to Alexander, who still managed to look worried despite being an enormous hulking wolf creature. "I'll be right back. Keep him busy for me?"

He tilted his head, and she kissed it briefly, then vanished all the way into limbo.

The dark and the quiet was unnerving after all of that, but she steeled herself. The pain was gone, and she needed to hurry.

It was easier this time, like she knew how to find her way. The city came into view almost immediately, and she crossed the gate into the dusk streets.

The other shadowy figures were there, still working, still hissing at each other. They took note of her running, curious. "Come with me," she screamed, flying through the paved pathways. "I can get you out of here! I can get you free."

The working stopped. A bit at a time, the shades started to follow after her. Good, she thought, heart pounding. She ran all the way to the square with the ziggurat and stood in front of it, waving her arms. "Listen!" she shouted. "I'm like you. Azorael tried to keep me here, but I escaped, and now he's in my world. *Our* world."

The blue figures started to collect around her, some lingering at the edges. "I know. I know they killed you and then they took you here. He tried to do the same to me. But someone helped me out. If you come with me—we can take him down, and once he's gone, you'll be free. Look."

She set her hand to the ziggurat and focused hard. He had bound her to this place, to himself. He had used this thing to shift the world he'd crafted around—she might be able to do the same.

She loosened the bounds between limbo and the material. She heard the fighting first—growling, snapping, shouting. Cass opened her eyes and looked. Jules was standing—not well, but standing, helping Thalia barricade herself behind the chairs. Ruhan had joined, borrowed a pike from some guard, cast aside his long cape and took up his bride's side. Gideon threw spell after spell in Irividius' way, slowing him down.

Cass gestured behind her. "If you help me—he can't hurt you there. You can hold him down, and my friends and I—we'll finish him. I can't promise what will happen next, but you won't be bound to this place any longer. What do you say?"

The figures looked between one another, a cacophony of hisses filling the air. Cass waited, her heart pounding against her chest. At length, a figure approached her, their hand outstretched. A few more. Others shifted. She nodded. "Grab hands," she said. "We leave now."

Alexander panted, his breaths burning in his lungs. It was getting harder to think. Every new hit he took, his body screamed at him. He wasn't immortal. Eventually, this would get to him, too.

The next time he bit down, the fury overtook him. This monster had nearly destroyed his other half, and he challenged him. He held tight, jerked the thing's body in midair a few times, slammed it back into the ground.

Someone approached from behind. "Your Lordship—"

Alexander whirled, his teeth bared. The devil…Gideon. Gideon was there, and he held his hands up. "I think it's time to stop," he said simply.

Alexander huffed, his sides slick with blood. He was right. He was on an edge that he didn't want to be standing on with any number of feet. But he'd promised his…he'd promised Cassandra….

A blue flash from the side. Alexander whipped about again, but the figure that appeared wasn't hers. Nor was the next one. Or the next, or any that followed. Gideon laughed in disbelief.

"I'll be damned," he said softly. "Thal, get ready."

The blue figures swarmed into the room toward the demon. Ruhan and Ifalna backed away, uncertain what to make of this as one after another the silhouettes piled on top of the Demon Lord, hissing, clawing to get a hold of him. His head appeared above the swarm, jaws snapping uselessly, his eyes wide.

At long last, Cass appeared, the last of them. Relief flooded Alexander, and the wolf calmed. His job was done.

Cass ran straight for the seething mass of souls. She'd get one shot at this, so she wanted to get it right. "Company, prepare banish," she called.

"Ready," Thalia answered.

"Extremely," Gideon returned.

"Okay, here we go," she said, and blinked one last time.

Aside from the stairs of the church, she'd never tried to go vertically before. Certainly not without a floor. There had to be a first time for everything.

She reappeared in the air directly above Irividius and dropped about a foot, landing on the bit of hunch protruding from the huddle of souls holding him down. Cass took one last unhampered breath and let the dusk form fall away so that she could grasp the silvered knife from the sheath.

He twisted, jerked, tried to shove her off, but it was no good. She took her blade and brought it down directly into his eye. He screeched, an ungodly noise, gave one last wrench. Cass let go and was thrown back to the stone floor.

Around her, the wind picked up, and Thalia's petite form rose from behind the barricade of chairs along with it.

"In the name of the wood—three times speak I, three times heed me. I lend the strength of the wood to the devil Gideon to complete his work. I lend it. I lend it. Begone, Dmitri Irividius, and good bloody riddance, you great creep."

Gideon stepped up to the dais, his hands at his sides. Cass straggled upward, first to her knees, then her feet, forcing the dizziness aside. He stared at the seething demon, or what remained, his face wet.

She took his hand. "Finish it," she told him gently.

He nodded, wiped at his eyes, then observed the tear streak in the palm of his hand and held it out. "Dmitri Irividius, I cast you from this place. In the name of the sacred balance, the safety of this world, and the many you have wronged, *I rebuke you.*"

The wind churned from a stiff breeze to a gale that ruffled Alexander's fur, furled Cass' skirt and Gideon's tunic, and picked up in a swirl around him. She had to let go and step back, shielding her face from her hair getting swiped into it. It coiled around his arm, and as it passed his fingers, picked up the hints of shadow and carried them toward the mound. A bit at a time, the blue figures began to dissipate and joined the air and the shadow as motes of blue, drifting upward, higher, toward the ceiling, leaving Irividius bare.

Once the last of the souls was gone, he started to charge forward, despite the magma dripping from his eye socket. Gideon closed his fingers, and flame erupted from the ground. Irividius cried out once, and as the hellfire roared up to engulf him, the dagger clattered red-hot to the ground.

In an instant, the fire died back, leaving nothing but a scorch mark to suggest he'd been there at all. Gideon sagged, and Cass came back to him and put her arm around his back. "Well done," she said.

He shut his eyes and let a breath fully come and go before tugging her close. "My hero," he answered.

Behind them came a groan, and Bjorn pulled himself up. "All right, where is demon?" he said blearily. "I am ready to decapitate."

"You damn near decapitated me," Jules told him.

He gasped. "A thousand and one apologies borne by the ravens, Jules! That is hefty wound."

"Congratulate yourself later," Thalia said, fluttering closer. Cass started. Short hair, delicate antlers, wings. She caught her looking and wrinkled her nose. "The source giveth, the source taketh away."

Gideon cringed, glancing around at the room full of nobles now very much staring at the assembled. Cass took the meaning a little too acutely.

Alexander stood very close to her side. "Well, it's got to happen at some point," Gideon said under his breath. "Should I turn them loose?"

Cass swallowed, her hand on Alexander's ruff. "Okay."

He let down the barriers. The one at the head of the church had been by far the weakest. With the sides free, that meant the guards could approach, and approach they did, spears pointed directly at Alexander.

He growled, and Cass held out her hand to the guards. "I wouldn't."

A knight took the fore, staring her directly in the face. "That thing must be disposed of."

As calmly as she could, she answered, "Touch him and you can join the Lord of Demons."

"Enough," Ruhan thundered, his voice carrying across the room as he made his way past the scorch mark. "Guards, you will stand down."

The knight and Cass both turned to him in equal measures of surprise. The knight protested, "Your Majesty—it's a danger—"

"I said *enough*."

The room fell silent. Ruhan stared at the floor, his face stricken. Cass swallowed on a dry throat. "Your Majesty, please—"

"You and I are both aware of the law, Ser Cassandra," he said, his eyes closing. "Something has to be done. It is not…ordinarily my custom to flout it, but I must in this case make an exception." He looked to the room at large. "Alexander Fremont has proven in every way that a curse is not a comment on his character. Nor do I believe that a curse should be a comment on anyone's character." He looked to Ifalna, a few steps up the dais. "There is enough judgment in the world. Enough intolerance for difference. I cannot…I will not let my reign stand as part of that legacy."

Cass' fingers worked in and out of Alexander's fur. He stood stock still, and she didn't dare bend down to check on him. He didn't seem prepared to spring, and Thalia, around his front, didn't seem nervous. Ruhan came closer, and Alexander didn't move. Cass put herself between them, and Ruhan stopped and regarded her.

"Ser Cassandra, thank you for your service here today. The court is forever grateful to you and your company for stopping the demon Azorael from pulling this world into his realm. As should the world be. And I am grateful to Lord Fremont for putting his comfort and safety absolutely last…yet again…in service of the people he loves. I would like to thank him."

She looked back at him warily. "Honestly?"

"It's high time it was done publicly." He glanced back to the room at large. "Lord Fremont's curse should have been mine—would have been mine, had he not put himself between me and an attacking creature. And this was his terrible reward." He looked to Cass again. "I will not allow anyone to reward him with anything terrible again. You have my word. Please."

Cass felt Alexander slacken beneath her fingers. She looked back at him and found his eyes. They were soft, his, nervous, but not unfocused. When he looked at her, she ran her hand over his shoulder one more time and stepped a little aside.

Ruhan stopped near her. "Can he hear me?" he asked softly.

She nodded, trying to refrain from biting her lip. Ruhan passed her and stopped in front of Alexander, who shied a little. Ruhan knelt, and this time when he talked, it wasn't to the room, too.

"My brother," he said, making eye contact. "I should always listen. You're usually right. And whether they know it or not, everyone here owes you nearly as great a debt as mine. I'd have no one else standing beside me today."

He put his arms around Alexander's body. The room went up in gasps. Cass tensed whether she meant to or not—he was remarkably lucid today, but there was a large bloodstain on Ruhan's leg and plenty of wounds underneath the fur. She stepped forward again and said in his ear, "Very lovely, but you may still want to step back and get him somewhere with fewer people."

Ruhan stood and cleared his throat. "Right. Good. Yes. Thank you for looking after him."

"Always."

He stepped away and took up Ifalna's hand. "I am making an edict.

The ban on cursed individuals in Amaranth is lifted. The fact of the matter is that they have been here. They have been contributing to our society. They have just had to hide." Ruhan held Ifalna's hand more tightly. "I won't have people hiding their gifts and their hardships when we can celebrate and help. And celebrate we shall. My friends, come. Let us prepare for the reception."

He held out his hand, beckoning toward the door behind the dais. Confusedly, the audience clapped, and Cass ushered Alexander on ahead. Jules fell in behind him. Gideon flanked to the side. Thalia looked the knight in the eye and muttered, "Don't come after my boss again."

"Thalia, don't scare the knights," Cass said.

"What?"

Gideon poked a wing with his tail. "They're going to think you're cursing them."

"Lucky them. It's not banned anymore."

Bjorn chuckled. "Tiny witch fairy is protective. Should get her axe."

Thalia nearly fluttered off the ground in excitement.

Jules snorted. "To do what?"

"It could be decorative," Thalia protested.

The door closed behind them, and Ruhan turned around. "Holy *shit,*" he managed.

Cass touched Alexander's head. She hoped he remembered that. "Do you happen to have a spare room we can borrow?" she asked.

"Of course. Any door. Anything you need."

She hesitated. "Actually, hold on." Cass stepped to a door a few feet away, glanced inside, found it to be an empty bedroom, and ushered Alexander in. He turned to watch for her, but she closed the door instead and stepped back down the hallway. "In his pocket, there would have been a little red…pillowy…thing. Could you…?"

Ruhan nodded. "Of course. I'll go. You…should probably get some bandages."

Cass glanced down. The red spot on the side of her dress had grown considerably larger. "Not a bad idea," she said, leaning into the wall.

"Yep, you're wilting," Thalia said. "Come on. I've got a really nice spider for you."

Cass fell into the bed next to Alexander and into a heavy nap, with the sachet between them and her face buried in his fur, her hand running over his head. Occasionally he twitched in his sleep. It was probably still dangerous, but she could not bring herself to care.

She woke a while later with fading orangish light coming in through the lacy curtains. She blinked, tried to clear her eyes, found that her cheek was pressed to his bare skin. Cass pulled back, found him blinking back blearily. "Hi," he managed hoarsely.

"Hi yourself," she answered, reaching out to smooth his hair from his face. "Are you all right?"

"Am *I*—?" He laughed in disbelief. "You...."

"It was just his claws," she promised. "I've had a spider look at it and everything."

He shut his eyes, relief settling into his features. "I didn't...I couldn't tell...."

"It's all right. I'm all right." She kissed his forehead, careful to avoid a burgeoning bruise. Gods, he must have been hit hard. He opened his eyes again and watched her watching him. "Gods, I'm sorry," she said at last.

"I'm not," Alexander answered, a weary smile taking over. "You're here."

He reached out an unsteady hand to her. She took it and kissed the knuckles—some of which were battered—and held it close to her chest. "Thank you," she said.

"And again, you're thanking *me*."

"Yes," she said. "I know...I know what that took."

"Nothing at all. It was hardly even a choice."

"How much do you remember?"

"Everything." Alexander laughed in wonderment. "I never want to do it again, but it was rather...incredible, actually. You were incredible. *Are*."

She smiled a bit. "Job's done. You don't have to flatter me anymore,

Lord Fremont."

"And if I want to?"

"Well, then I suppose I'd better let you."

"I'm not your employer anymore. You don't have to let me."

"Hmm. Well. Perhaps I'll see you at home, then."

"Home," he sighed.

"Do you want to go?" she asked, moving her fingers over the hair behind his ear. "Ruhan said he'd understand."

He winced. "Mm. Ballroom full of the people I just exposed myself to. But I did agree to be the best man."

"The groom said not to worry about that."

"You'll need to stay?"

"I have the end of the contract to see to."

"Then here is where I'll be. Besides. I'm…not looking forward to facing down Humphrey. I'm sure he'll have heard."

Cass laughed. "I'll take the blame for it."

"No. There's no blame to take." He closed his eyes and breathed. "Truthfully, it's a relief. It will be awkward, yes. Perhaps still dangerous in some ways. But I can't…quite bring myself to mind any of that at all."

"No?" she asked quietly.

"No. The secret is dead and you're alive and the demon is gone. What is there to mind?"

Cass smiled and leaned her forehead against his shoulder.

The ballroom at the Wyvern's Rest was the only ballroom Cass had ever been in that wasn't unreasonably, unbearably stuffy. The grand windows opened outward as doors, and people came and went off the balcony. The glass roof raised up like petals to let the night air in and the plants dangling from trellises swung in the air, seemingly in time to the music. She didn't mind sitting back and watching the aftermath of this wedding as much as she normally did.

For one thing, the Jorans made companionable drunks. She couldn't help but smile a little as Bjorn reconnected with some of the King's retinue. They sang loudly in a corner, which flapped some of the Amaranthine nobles. Others remembered him from their ill-fated party and came to join in, amusingly enough.

Thalia stayed out of the way. Cass spotted her feet dangling along with some vines here and there and other times at the dessert table. Before today, she'd only seen the real Thalia for a few moments. Now she couldn't help the curving diadem of antlers and gossamer wings, and it seemed she was eager to blend those into the shadows as much as possible.

Cass tried to catch her near the wine, but she smiled and shook her head.

"You're going to have a reputation to uphold," Thalia reminded her, raising her glass. "Hanging around with the half-fey witch kid isn't going to help."

"I think we pretty much blew that to hell and back today," Cass said. Danae Lomor refused to make eye contact. She wasn't sure if that was a good thing or not.

"All the more reason not to make it worse."

"I don't like that," she insisted. "You're my friend."

"And I will be later, too. Besides. Somebody should watch Gideon. I hear his alcohol tolerance isn't what it used to be."

Cass glanced around the crowded room. "Where is he?"

"Looking at the view. He needs some time. I'm good at being together alone with people, so that'll be my job tonight."

"Is he…?"

"He's gonna be okay. In a while. As long as he doesn't give himself alcohol poisoning." She smiled a little. "Go on and mingle with the humans. Let me know if you hear anything fun."

Cass wanted to protest that she herself wasn't entirely sure that she qualified, but someone hooked her arm from behind.

"You," Lissa gushed, "are the woman of the hour."

Jules caught up, favoring one side. "Don't grab people who just fought demons," she told Lissa.

"It's true," Cass said. "You never know what residue is left over."

Lissa dropped her hands and immediately wiped them on her skirt. "I have to say, no one here has ever actually *seen* what happens if a wedding gets attacked. It always happens so very neatly behind those magical drapes you put up. It was terribly exciting."

"Glad to be of help," Cass said dryly.

"Is it true you saved the entire world today?"

Jules cut in. "I'm just going to go ahead and say yes, because she's going to give you a nonsense answer."

"And just how long ago, exactly, did you know the entire world was in danger?" she asked indignantly. "And you never thought to mention?"

"It never came up," Jules said with a shrug.

"You could *make* it come up."

A throat cleared in front of them. Lord Evards stood there, holding a glass of champagne, conspicuously alone. "Good evening," he said. He regarded Lissa. "Lady Ironwelt. I— er, well done, Julia."

She stared as though she wasn't positive this was happening. "Thanks, Dad." He nodded gruffly to her and then again to himself and walked away.

Jules continued to stare in disbelief at the space he'd just occupied. "Well, that was fucking weird," she muttered.

"Are you good?" Cass asked quietly.

"I mean, yeah, kind of, though I don't know if he was watching the same fight. I did shit all."

Cass shook her head. "You held your own against Bjorn for a pretty long time."

"Yeah, well, it was stupid to begin with." She nudged Cass. "Thanks for coming to get me."

"I've always got you."

Jules beamed, then looked up across the crowd. "Oh, look who."

Cass glanced up a little less obviously. Alexander in a borrowed suit made his way into the room, his shoulders a little tense around his ears and his eyes definitely a bit sunken, but much heartier than when she'd had to leave him. He caught her eye and smiled, and she smiled back. He started toward her but was quickly waylaid by Ruhan, who pressed some-thing into his hand. Jules nudged Cass. "I think he liiiiikes you."

"Oh, shut it."

Lissa leaned forward, a dozen questions clearly fomenting behind her sparkly blue eyes. Cass wasn't sure whether this was going to be about her love life or something to do with Alexander's curse, but either way she didn't want anything to do with it. She pretended to be very interested in something else as Lissa directed her gush of words to Jules.

People in the room were definitely watching him. They'd been watch-ing *her* all night. Very few had actually spoken to her, which was more or less fine. Trying to figure out what they made of all of it, she guessed. They were both very much in the King and Queen's favor—she was even wearing one of Ifalna's dresses. Would that cancel out what they'd seen today?

Either way, she didn't want to leave Alexander to grapple with that alone. She looked across again, and Ruhan clapped him on the shoulder. Alexander went very red.

"This looks like something I should interrupt," she said. "Excuse me."

Jules laughed. "Good luck!"

Cass inched her way across the outer edge of the ballroom, excusing herself to various people who seemed somewhat startled to see her. Along the way, Ifalna darted out—a perfectly executed ambush. "Cassandra, you must come," she said.

"Must I?" she asked, alarmed.

"Nothing is wrong," she said with a bit of a giggle. "I wish to thank you."

"Oh," Cass said. "It's really not necessary."

"But it is!" Her light eyes glinted. "I am married to my love, I had a wonderful wedding, and I have my first friend in Amaranth. All because of you!"

"It's really my job—"

"You are always so modest. Amaranth must learn how to boast!" She pulled her along by the hands. "I'll teach you the Joran way. Later. Perhaps when next we spar. For now…." She tugged her toward the dance floor.

"Oh—oh, no. No."

"But yes. Come. Your Queen commands it!"

"Oh, dear."

Ruhan steered Alexander toward Cass. "—and if you'd let me give you some advice for once—"

"I readily admit you have the advantage of me in this particular subject," Alexander said.

"It's my wedding day, Xander."

"Precisely, which is why—" He cut off when Ifalna reached out and plopped both of Cass' hands into his. "Hello," he said, flustered.

"Hi," she answered, equally bewildered.

Ifalna grasped Cass' shoulders and gently pushed them in the direction of the floor. Ruhan laughed and mimed leading, and Alexander hurriedly shuffled his hands around and followed suit.

"It appears we're dancing," he remarked.

"So it would seem." She made a face over his shoulder at Ifalna, who grasped hold of Ruhan's arm, beaming, as they made their way around.

"I would like to make it perfectly clear that I did not ask," he told her.

"So it would seem," she replied with a laugh. "I suppose I can enjoy myself a little on the technicality."

People started to gather on the edges. There were a few other dancers here and there, but Cass was very much aware that most of the observers were watching them. Alexander glanced over nervously. "This is the only time I've ever done this in public," he admitted.

"Really?"

"Mmhmm. I suppose now that I've faced one fear I'm to get over all the others all at once?"

"That is not how that works." She paused. "Does that mean I'm your only dance partner?"

"Outside of lessons? Yes."

"Huh." She smiled slightly. "Well. If it helps, this is the only wedding

I've ever danced at."

He nodded over at a cluster of people toward the side. "I can tell."

Alexander brought Cass around, and she frowned deeply at her company. Thalia and Gideon came out of reclusion specifically to gape, and Jules covered her mouth as though either horrified or trying to cover up a squeal. Bjorn chuckled.

"It's a good thing I'm going to be semi-retired soon," she muttered. "I'm beginning to think they might not respect me."

"I think it's the contrary, my dear."

"I know," she fumed. Alexander smiled, and she broke and laughed a little. "So what was all that about?" she asked. "With His Majesty."

"Ah. Yes. He, er…returned something I had left in the remains of my pockets. And reminded me to stop tripping over myself."

"Granted, I know very little about the subject, but you seem to be a plenty fine dancer."

"You're doing very well yourself."

"I suppose it must be all the knife training."

He grinned. "Impertinent as ever, Miss Friend."

"And that's never bothered you before, Lord Fremont."

"On the contrary." He brought her closer. "I've always found it delightful."

"Then I suppose it's only fair that I tell you that per the actual wording of the contract, unfortunately, the dancing is in fact, a breach, regardless of who does the asking."

"I wondered," he said carefully, "if you might be amenable to a new contract."

Cass looked at him a little sideways. He slipped his hand from her waist and into his pocket, and tucked something small and round into her hand. She looked up at him, and he smiled back, nervous, questioning.

She slid the ring onto her finger and tucked in close so that she could hear his heartbeat for once. "I think we can work something out."

Acknowledgements

Jason must at some point grow tired of coming first in the acknowledgments, but in this case, he deserves the lion's share, not only for his usual contributions, but for generously lending a few story elements. Alexander in a minor way, Jules in a larger way, and the system of nobility originated in a TTRPG that he ran that unfortunately fizzled a while ago, and when I mentioned that I loved, missed, and wanted to preserve some of these facets, he didn't bat an eye. Thank you for letting me put my own probably irritatingly different spin on these beloved characters and really interesting political idea.

Emmy is not the cheerleading type—that's not really our family's style. But every time I mention something happening in my writing life, she exclaims, "That's cool!" I know how much it takes to learn that. I love you for it.

Scoot (I tried to write it correctly and autocorrect kicked in because I write it wrong so often, so Scott, there you are) and Alayna, you two are the keepers of my ability to laugh, at myself and at life. Thank you for always being there. Thank you for letting me revive Fate, who's meant so much to me, and giving her such wonderful friends.

Steph, twelve years of support for each other's work and counting. I couldn't ask for a better partner in crimes against the English language.

To the EDI Allies team, thank you. This year has been incredibly isolating, and you have always lifted each other and me up even when the entire establishment was short-circuiting. Emily, Phil,

Mary, Miranda, Michael, Jenny, Kendra, Kaley, Inseon, Christal, Megan, Amy- you are all amazing. Kate, an amazing partner in advocacy and support when it feels like the whole world is not built for you. MUK, as always, you are a great group of people, and we leaned on each other hard this year. I am glad to have been there with you.

Disability Twitter literally saved my life this year. The pandemic was not good, and I would not have known what to ask for for myself if not for you. Thank you.

Free Novella

For the exclusive inter-dimensional gender-bending fantasy novella
The Scattered Writings of the Family Fartherall
go to elyssiabooks.com/fartherall
Not available anywhere else.

You'll also find a link to a monthly opportunity for updates on writing, upcoming appearances, and pet photos. The pets are very cute.

Contact the Author

Email: annaholmeswritesbooks@gmail.com
Website: AnnaHolmesWritesBooks.com
Facebook: facebook.com/EmberofElyssia
Twitter: @annabookwriter
Instagram:@annawritesbooks
Pinterest: @annaholmeswritesbooks